ESCAPE

FROM METRO CITY

RICHARD MANDEL

SEVERED PRESS
HOBART TASMANIA

ESCAPE FROM METRO CITY

ISBN: 978-1-922323-73-6

PROLOGUE

It was late in the evening of the 24 of July, 1983. It was also the third day of what eventually became known as the Metro City Outbreak -- that terrible event in which almost everyone both in town and the surrounding countryside were transformed into bloodthirsty zombies. There was a longer and more official sounding name for what happened, of course, having far more syllables but saying far less. To the general public, and to the pitiful handful of area residents who somehow survived that terrible event and lived to tell their tales, they referred to it simply as the Outbreak. For them that was name enough.

The history of Metro City prior to the Outbreak can be summed up in brief. It was at one time a small city of just over seventy-six thousand residents, per the last official census, located in that part of the United States where the American Midwest and Southwest areas came together. That figure did not count another several thousand or so illegal immigrants, mostly Mexican but with a fair smattering of other nationalities and ethnic types, who also lived both in the city proper and just outside its official limits. It had been founded on and later expanded to both sides of a bend to the south of the Catachee River. The shape of both the bend and its banks had proven to be an natural anchorage for flat bottom boats and barges in pioneer days, and later steamboat docks and piers in Western times. The surrounding area was fertile thanks to periodic river flooding, which encouraged the settlement of many flatland farms with crops suitable to such conditions, such as rice, soybeans, and so on. As the years passed, it had both grown and become important enough during those early decades for a branch line of the local railroad to be built through it, which in turn reinforced its status as one of the major transportation hubs of its region.

Metro City's size had stabilized and declined somewhat with the arrival of the twentieth century Gregorian calendar, as its younger generations moved away to the bigger cities in the Midwest and Southwest and left the heartland behind. Even so, the arrival of the Pandora Corporation immediately after World War II had done much to revive Metro City in the years that followed. Better known as PandoraCorp or just Pandora for short, it had built a large industrial complex just outside of town, to the northeast of Metro City's own industrial district on the northern bank of the Catachee. Both it and the city had grown considerably during the postwar economic boom and subsequent Cold War decades. It should also

1

be noted that nobody knew exactly what went on inside the Pandora properties, although there was much talk of private government contracts and secret military projects and such. They employed plenty of locals on non-sensitive matters, such as custodial and catering duties and frequent on-site construction, so no one really complained. Business was good and steady, and Pandora was thought of well by practically everyone save the nutcases and environmentalist wacko jobs. They would come and spin their spiel and then leave, and then life as its citizens knew it would resume exactly as before. That is, until the Outbreak went down in Metro City.

The fact that the Outbreak took place in Metro City didn't really matter. The same thing could have happened anywhere in that region, or in any part of the United States were circumstances were similar. As for the particulars, everyone knew the Outbreak had definitely originated within the Pandora industrial complex, but nobody seemed to know what it was or how to stop it. All they knew was that it spread like wildfire, and within a day over 90% of the population both within the city and a roughly five-mile radius outside of it were showing definite signs of infection. By the evening of the first day almost all of what few humans were left were also showing the signs, the federal government was on the scene in force, and the U.S. Army had sealed off the entire area under biological quarantine. By late morning of the second day, almost everyone who was infected had turned into zombies or were showing the advanced signs of infection prior to turning. That was when the killing began, spontaneously initiated by the tens of thousands of zombies now populating Metro City and everywhere else within the quarantine zone. It continued non-stop for the rest of that terrible second day and well into the third. The zombies were doing most of the killing, but the U.S. Army was shooting anyone and anything that tried to breach the quarantine barricades from Metro City ... no matter if it were still human or not.

CHAPTER 1
ENCOUNTERS

Cy was running. It was the only thing he could do. He didn't have enough ammo left to stand and fight. He had one partial clip in his M-16A1 assault rifle and one full one left in his bandolier. The rest were empty, as were his ammo pouches. Forget about discretion and valor and all of that. This was survival, pure and simple, doing his best to stay alive for as long as possible, and with a rampaging herd of bloodthirsty zombies hot on his heels. He could still hear the dying screams of the other three convoy survivors in his group who had fled that debacle, as the zombie horde first caught up to and then promptly overwhelmed them. He was the only one left, and there wasn't any choice in the matter. Cy ran, as a large flock of crows led by a big black raven swooped over him, apparently following the street to their next feeding ground. There were plenty of bodies in Metro City for them to feast upon. As far as they were concerned, the little green Army man running below could hold for now. His turn would come soon enough.

There was an intersection coming up and it appeared to be clear. Three possible choices: straight ahead, go left, or go right. Going left was the closest option, given that he was running down the left side of Matheson Avenue, so he took it. He made the turn onto Derleth Drive at full tilt, with the zombie horde also making the turn a few seconds later. Slowly but surely Cy was pulling ahead of his undead pursuers, largely due to his being in better physical shape than them. If only he could keep running long enough, then maybe he could come across some means of shaking them loose for good. Once that was done, maybe he could find some new means to defend himself, maybe even find a vehicle that had the keys in it and still worked, and then he could high-tail it out of town back to the Army quarantine line. He could almost imagine the reaction of General Ryan, the officer in charge of enforcing the federal quarantine on Metro City. *Where's the rest of your unit, soldier?* He knew what his answer would be too. "We got mobbed, sir, and our weapons weren't enough to stop them. There must have been thousands of them. We didn't stand a chance, and I'm just lucky to be alive, sir." Cy now laughed to himself as he ran. The Army had been foolish to even send in the rescue convoy, knowing the threat that it faced inside the infected city. Even so, there were some things you did because you had to, because it was the right thing to do, because that way you wouldn't look bad in the history books and never mind the cost in lives. This had been one of those things. Now it was done, and everybody except him had died, and now he was running for his life. He had been incredibly lucky so far. If only his luck would hold.

Cy heard it long before he saw it coming. It was the deep-throated roar of a muscle car motor, and not long after he first heard it the car itself popped into view, swinging around the turn from a side street onto his at high speed. It was green with black highlights and a black breather sticking out of its hood, and it was heading straight for him. The car's driver must have seen him about the same time that he saw the car, because it promptly decelerated and came to a stop. The driver cut the wheel hard left at the end and slung it around as it did, so that it came to rest broadside to the street. The left side door opened, and a female figure dressed in a black racing suit with red and white trim popped out. The visored racing helmet that she was wearing hid her face, but not the long black hair coming out from under its back. She had an AK-47 assault rifle in her hands, and she immediately went into a firing crouch behind the front of the car. "RUN!!!" she called to Cy. "I'll cover you!!!"

Somewhere within him Cy found an extra reserve of strength previously untapped. He sprinted for the muscle car, trying to keep as low as he could. He heard the distinctive loud and heavy chatter of an AK-47 on full auto blasting away as he ran. He heard zombies scream and wail behind him, and a number of bodies falling to the pavement, but he never looked back. He kept his eyes front and focused on his improbable savior as he ran. The firing briefly stopped as the woman changed clips and then it picked up again, but by that time Cy was almost there. He crossed the last dozen yards or so in record time and almost fell against the passenger side of the muscle car. "Get in!" the young woman driver yelled, as she came up out of her firing crouch and tossed her assault rifle in the back of the car. By that time Cy already had the door on his side open and had lurched into the passenger seat. She was already in her seat on the driver's side and had slammed her door shut about the same time as he got his closed. One of her hands went to the stick shift while her right foot found the accelerator. The muscle car's motor, which had been idling until now, suddenly roared to full life. The rear tires squealed as the muscle car took off, its driver forcing it to swerve around again and go back the way it came. The survivors of the zombie horde were left far behind as the muscle car thundered back down to the intersection, took the other cross street turn, and was gone.

Cy caught his breath as he sat inside the muscle car. He didn't argue and he didn't ask questions. He was just glad she had been there, and that he was alive. As his panting slowed into normal breathing, his eyes focused on a four letter word that was part of the dashboard before him. 'CUDA. He suddenly looked at his savior. "Barracuda?" he asked.

"HemiCuda," a husky female voice corrected. "1971 Plymouth HemiCuda. Last of the old style muscle cars, and not many of these was made. I paid a lot to get it, but I'm glad I did." The female driver turned and gave Cy a quick look. He had just enough time to see a pair of intelligent brown eyes regard him behind the helmet's visor, then they just as quickly turned back to the road. "Name's Lisa Stanridge," the young woman said. "What's your name?"

"Cy," Cy responded immediately. After a beat, he added, "Corporal Cyrus Rappalo, U.S. Army." He paused, almost did a double take, and then added. "Not *THE* Lisa Stanridge? As in the stock car racer who beat Pandora's team for the Bellville Cup last year?"

"The same," Lisa replied. "Pleased to meet you, Cy." She stopped talking for a moment to thread the rapidly moving 'Cuda through a series of abandoned and wrecked cars on their side of the street, then spoke again. "You were with that Army convoy that rolled into town not long ago."

"Yeah," Cy admitted, looking down. "I was."

"I was coming to meet you," Lisa said. "Heard about you on the radio. Got delayed by a pack of overeager zombies who didn't want to let me out of where I holed up last night. I was hoping you guys would be my ticket out of town. Now I'm glad I was late."

"So am I," Cy said, "both for me and you. We got wiped out. Too many zombies and not enough of us, even with our heavy machine guns and grenade launchers and all."

"So I gathered," Lisa said. "You the only survivor?"

"As far as I know," Cy said.

"Damn," Lisa said, shaking her head as she did. "Still, I give you guys points for trying to save what few of us are left, if any." She gave a sigh. "I haven't seen anyone else still human like me since yesterday."

"Yeah," Cy said with a little laugh, then fell silent. They drove on like this for about another minute or so, then he spoke again. "So where are we going?"

"National Guard Armory," Lisa responded. "We're about five minutes out. I'm guessing you need to ammo up, and I'm eventually going to need a gun like yours with the ammo to go with it. They'll also have a radio transmitter that you can use to call out, and I'm guessing you need to do that too." She then gave her own laugh. "Unless you want me to take you back to your convoy and we try our luck there."

"Lord, no," Cy said with a shudder.

"Then that's settled," Lisa said.

Cy now gave Lisa a curious look. "May I ask a question, ma'am?"

"Lisa," Lisa corrected. "Save the manners for later. Ask away."

"Okay, Lisa," Cy said, "and you can call me Cy. Why haven't you turned?"

"Beats the hell out of me," Lisa said. "Everyone around me last night was already a zombie. Everyone I was with yesterday turned. I was at the racetrack outside of town when it happened, and I was the only person there who either didn't turn or got killed. The only way I could get out was to drive off the track, dodging wrecked cars all the way, and plowing straight through a crowd of zombies to get to my regular car outside." She now chuckled. "This one."

"Why didn't you just keep going in your stock car?"

"Because stock cars get lousy gas mileage, and my AK was in the trunk of my 'Cuda along with my ammo," Lisa said with a grin. "Call me a gun nut if you want. I grew up with guns, and me and a bunch of the other drivers, we were planning on going shooting together on the local gun club range after the race. Good thing I was armed when all of this started."

"Yeah," Cy agreed. He thought for a moment, then asked another question. "So why did they go ahead and hold the race, given the Outbreak?"

Lisa shrugged her shoulders. "Because they thought it would be good for everyone's morale, or something like that. We weren't going anywhere given the quarantine, so why not? Live life as usual as much as you can, you know?" She gave a little laugh. "You know how crazy people get in situations like this. Hurricane fever, and all that. The only thing they didn't count on was everyone turning zombie."

"Yeah," Cy said.

Lisa shot him another quick look, then put her eyes back to the road. "There's more to tell, Cy, but the Armory's coming up. I'll save it for later."

Cy raised his assault rifle, cradling it before him in a ready position. "Just so you know," he said, "I've got only two clips left: a partial in my gun and one full one in my bandolier."

"Not so good on ammo myself," Lisa said. "Shot that batch off rescuing you, and the rest getting out this morning and ... well ... I'll tell you once we're ammoed up." She swung the car around a sharp turn. "Here's our first stop. Get ready."

"Ready when you are," Cy said, as Lisa guided the 'Cuda into the Armory's main drive.

Metro City's National Guard Armory looked like it had been the site of a major battle, and the National Guard had lost. The front gates had been knocked from their hinges, and twisted sections of the surrounding mesh fence were likewise torn out and lying on the ground along with their former support poles. Bodies were everywhere: lying on the pavement, tangled up in the barbed wire barricades, sprawled over sandbag emplacements, splayed on or hanging out of various vehicles (some of which were wrecked), and so on. Spent shell casings were also everywhere. It was quite obvious that the local National Guard contingent had put up one hell of a fight against the zombies before they too were overcome by the sheer number of their undead foes.

Lisa popped the door on her side of the parked 'Cuda. She took a moment to take off her racing helmet, revealing a head full of luxuriant long black hair, then in a flash she had her AK-47 assault rifle out of the back seat and in her hands. Cy also popped out of his side of the car, his own M-16A1 in hand. He noticed that she was wearing something very much like a military style pouch slung around her waist, and he guessed that it held spare preloaded ammo clips. She glanced around quickly, then turned to him and spoke. "Start scavenging. I'll cover you."

Cy quickly went to the closest body clad in woodland camo and bearing military gear, and gave it a quick once-over. He looked back at Lisa, shook his head, then jinked to the next one. It wasn't until the fourth body that he hit paydirt, but by then the zombies had started to appear. Two clad in the remains of civilian clothes came out from around one side of a wrecked M35 transport truck, while three in bloody woodland camo rose up from behind one of the sandbagged emplacements. Two long bursts from Lisa's AK put both groups down. She was changing clips when Cy dashed back to her, carrying a bandolier in hand out of which stuck a number of 30-round spare M-16 ammo clips. "Almost full," he said. "Got lucky there. I'm good on ammo now."

"My turn," Lisa said.

"Got your back," Cy said, as he began to swing around and sweep the area.

It took Lisa a little longer. Getting a new assault rifle was easy enough, as there were two lying within sight near the half-eaten bodies of their former owners. Getting a sufficient amount of ammo was something else, and Cy ended up using two full clips of his own keeping the zombies away from Lisa until she too returned with her own scavenged bandolier. It had already been three-fifths full, but Lisa had filled both it and her side pouch with extra 30-round clips she had picked up whenever and wherever she had come across them. Lisa was also now wielding her new weapon, an

M-16A1 military assault rifle identical to Cy's, with her own AK-47 slung over one shoulder and behind her. She promptly pulled out one of the spare M-16 clips from her new bandolier and handed it to Cy, who took it. "Thanks," he said.

"You're welcome," Lisa replied. She again hefted her new assault rifle. "Now let's go find that transmitter."

"Right with you," Cy said, as he swung around beside her, his own assault rifle at the ready.

The two of them ran for the Armory front doors. One was closed but it was neither locked nor pegged. The other lay on the ground nearby. It was covered in blood and its window glass was broken out. Some distance behind the door that remained up was a lone Guardsman zombie staggering about in the lobby beyond. It turned towards the two with a moan, reaching up and towards them with its arms and letting out a pitiful wail, just in time for Cy to blast it with a burst from his assault rifle. It spun around, gurgling and spitting blood, and then fell to the floor. It did not move again. After that Cy and Lisa were through the lobby and into the long hallway beyond.

"Do you know the layout of this place?" Lisa said as they walked together, both of their weapons at the ready and always looking around for any possible foe.

"No," Cy admitted.

"Me neither."

Cy laughed softly. "Well, if it's like most such places I've been in, the local weapons and ammo store will be in the back somewhere, away from street side, or even down in the basement if this place has one. We'll probably find the radio room on the way."

"Hey," Lisa said, pointing down the hall. There was a large sign to one side with a large map of the place on its top half, a lengthy legend below it on the bottom half, and the word DIRECTORY in big bold letters at its top. She chuckled. "How 'bout that? Cover me."

Cy did as she asked. He kept between her and the rest of the hall, looking in both directions and sweeping it with his aimed weapon, while she read the room lists on the sign. After a quarter-minute or so, she spoke. "No basement. Everything's on one floor. Oh! Found the Radio Room. It's Room 105, three doors down and at the end of the hall ahead. No listing for the weapons store, but I did find one for the Firing Range. That's Room 112, in the back like you said. There's an fair-sized room next to it which only says Storage. That's Room 113, and I'm guessing that's the weapons store."

Cy grinned. "I'd say your guess is right. We got lucky again."

"Yeah," Lisa said, looking at him and grinning also. "Let's hope our luck holds."

It didn't. They were about halfway down the hall, heading for the Radio Room, when five zombies popped out into the hallway at the far end. Three of them came from the last door to the right, while two came from the last door to the left. Within a split second two more came out of another side door to the left closer to them, while a lone zombie came through the hallway's only other door on the right. Every one of them turned down the hall and began running towards the humans as fast as their various obvious injuries and virus-numbed minds and bodies would let them. Cy and Lisa immediately raised their weapons and began firing. They didn't stop shooting until the last of the zombies fell only a dozen or so feet away from them.

Lisa took a long breath, let it out again, and then looked at Cy. "That far door down there on the left," she said. "That was the Radio Room." Her words came out flat and dull, as she stated an obvious and unavoidable fact.

"Yeah," Cy said grimly. "Let's go see anyway."

It was useless and they knew it, but they did it all the same. The pair carefully picked their way through the bodies lining the hall, watching just in case any of them were only playing possum, until they made it to the open door of the Radio Room. One look inside was all they needed. It was in shambles. Everything that could be broken had been, every cable that could be ripped out or torn in two was, and the smashed microphone for the transmitter was halfway sticking out one of the room's ruined speakers. Lisa looked at Cy and he back, and then snorted. "Hope the weapons store is in better shape."

"Me too," Cy answered.

The door across from the Radio Room opened into another long hallway, which ran a ways and turned again to the left before it dead-ended at the Armory's double back doors. The pair of rooms they sought, the Firing Range with its accompanying Storage Room (presumably the weapons store) were at the end of the hallway to the left and around the turn. This time, there were zombies already moving down the hall in their direction. They could see at least four fatigue-clad ones and two in the remains of civilian garb, and there were the sounds of more around the turn. It was the same as before. Cy and Lisa immediately opened fire, gunning down zombies until there were no more left to gun down. Only when the last one was dropped did they stop shooting and begin to pick their way down the hall.

"Damn," Cy muttered as he walked beside Lisa. "We're gonna use up all of our ammo getting back out again, if we don't get more."

"I know," Lisa said evenly, keeping pace with him as her eyes darted everywhere, looking for any possible threat. "Maybe this time we'll get lucky."

They did. The label on the door looked unobtrusive enough: ROOM 113 / STORAGE. Fortunately it was unlocked. Opening the door revealed weapons storage cabinets and shelves stocked with ammo crates. It was fairly obvious that a lot of what had been in there had been removed, presumably to deal with the Outbreak, and that probably also explained why the door was unlocked when it should have been locked. All the same, there was still plenty left of almost everything for Cy and Lisa to replenish their supplies.

"Good God Almighty!" Cy exclaimed. He let Lisa go in first and he followed, closing the door and turning its deadbolt behind them. "Looks like we've got everything we need!"

"It's about time things started going our way," Lisa agreed, as she moved to one of the ammo storage shelves and immediately began pulling boxes of 5.56mm NATO standard assault rifle rounds. "I'll reload our M-16 clips. You see if they've got anything else in here we can use."

Cy left his own empty clips with her and then began to thoroughly search the room. "Yeah," he said as he did so. "I hope we take more out than we used getting in."

"If we do, then I hope we get something bigger in which to carry it," Lisa observed, her fingers working nimbly as she reloaded one 30-round M-16 ammo clip after another.

"Got you covered there," Cy said, as he scooped up a couple of somethings from one of the shelves and held them towards her. "Here, catch," he called.

Lisa put down the clip she was reloading, then caught what Cy tossed to her. It was an Army rucksack, the kind that is worn around the waist and behind and under a field pack. She grinned back at him. "Good find!" she said, setting it down and resuming her reloading again.

"You got that right," Cy said, as he quickly donned the second one, then resumed his search of the room. A half-minute or so later, he turned and spoke. "Hey, can your AK take these?" he asked, holding up an oversized rifle round.

"What is it?" Lisa asked.

"M-14 round," Cy answered. "I know they're the same caliber, 7.62mm."

Lisa shook her head. "Too long. Won't fit my clips. An AK round is shorter."

"Oh," Cy said with disappointment, as he put the shell back in the box where he had found it. "Sorry." He looked around again. "I don't see any M-14s in here."

"I wouldn't take it if you did," Lisa said. "Uncle Ray once told me that it was a battle rifle, not an assault rifle, and you should never use an M-14 like an assault rifle because it wasn't designed for that, but both the M-16 and AK-47 were."

"Uncle Ray?"

"My mom's older brother, better known as my gun nut uncle. Gave me all of my weapons training, and with my dad's permission and blessing. He and dad were good friends. Anyway, Uncle Ray was a sergeant in the Marines and he fought in Vietnam. He said the M-16 was too light and didn't pack enough of a punch, but he took it because that's what they issued him and it was easier to handle." She gave him a grin. "Anyway, thanks for looking."

"No problem," Cy grinned back.

Lisa nodded, and then she began reloading ammo clips again, talking as she did. "Now that I've got an M-16 like yours, I can save the AK, what ammo I've got left, and its bigger bite for when we really need it."

"How'd you end up with an AK anyway?" Cy asked, as he opened another box full of loose M-16 rounds and began to pour them into his new rucksack.

"It was originally Uncle Ray's," Lisa said, still reloading. "He said he picked it up from a dead gook in Vietnam, because he was tired of messing with his M-16 and it jamming on him half the time. That's the story he told, anyway. He saw how fascinated I was with it once he got back and it arrived, and promised it to me once I was old enough and knew how to use it responsibly. That's why I have it now. Don't ask me how he managed to keep it, Cy, or how he got it over here once his tour of duty was over. Frankly I don't want to know."

"I know what you mean," Cy chuckled. "My grandpa's got an SKS rifle he brought home from Korea the same way." His eyes now lit up as he spotted the stenciling on a crate in one of the far corners. "Hullo, what do we have here?" he said aloud as he rushed over to take a look.

"What'd'ya find?" Lisa said with interest.

"These," Cy said, as he opened the topmost crate, then pulled out two cylindrical objects with handles that had pins stuck through them. He held them up for her to see.

"Grenades!" Lisa exclaimed. "Good find, Cy! How many, and what kind?"

"One full crate," Cy said. He looked around a bit. "Don't see any more." He now looked at the crate stenciling. "Frag-apples, looks like."

"Best kind, for what we need," Lisa grinned.

Cy nodded. "One crate, twelve frag-apples, six apiece. I can hang 'em off of my gear harness, but what about you?"

"I can do the same off of my firesuit, if I need to," Lisa said, as she resumed her reloading again. "All the same, see if there's another harness in here for me."

"Will do," Cy said, as he put the two grenades back into their crate, and then picked up a long cylindrical object with a stock that somewhat resembled a clip-fed shotgun with a barrel three times its normal diameter. "Holy hell," Cy said, as he looked his find over. "I haven't seen one of these except in training manuals."

"What's that?" Lisa said, looking up again. She spotted what Cy was holding. "Is that the launcher for those grenades?"

"Yeah, except it's not a regular M79," Cy said. He gave Lisa a look. "It's a China Lake lever-action grenade launcher. They're called China Lakes after where they were first developed. They never became standard, as the Army preferred to stick with the simpler single-shot M79, so they never got issued. I wonder how these guys wound up with one."

"No way to tell," Lisa replied, "but I wouldn't question it. I'd take it along with the grenades." She set down the newly refilled clip she was holding, the last of the ones she had been reloading, and then began to rake as many loaded ones as she could into her new rucksack. "All done. Give me a minute and then I'll come help you."

"Right," Cy said, as he slung the China Lake around and over the shoulder opposite of his M-16, and resumed his search again.

They talked as they worked their way through the various crates, boxes, and supply lockers. "I've got another question for you, Lisa, if you don't mind."

"Shoot," Lisa said, and then grinned. "But not with your gun."

Cy grinned as well before he spoke. "Okay. If you were at the racetrack when the Outbreak went down, that means you were outside of town. You had to come back in to be with me now. Why did you come back, knowing what was happening here?"

Lisa stopped her searching. She looked down, and Cy saw a wave of sorrow wash over her face. She quickly composed herself again before speaking. When she did her voice was flat and dull, devoid of all emotion, and her face was a mask of stern formality, as if she were a newscaster reading a report. "That's the other half of my story, Cy. I came back for my little brother. He was staying with my Uncle Phil and Aunt Jocinelle in town so he could spend some time with his cousin Buddy, who was their son. They were really good friends. I came back because I hoped there was a chance I could save him, me being armed and all. It was foolish and it was stupid, but ..." and with this she looked up at Cy, "... I had to try. You know, like you guys with that convoy?"

"Yeah. I know," Cy responded quietly.

"Only when I got there," and here Lisa almost choked on her words, "I was too late. My aunt and uncle had already turned by the time I got there. They killed Buddy and they killed my brother, and they almost killed me before I killed them."

Cy's eyes opened wide with the horror of Lisa's news, and then he looked away. "I'm sorry," he said in a rather small voice.

"Thanks." Lisa took in a deep breath and then let it out again. "Don't worry. I cried myself out last night. I'm not going to cry again. It's over and done with. Time to move on." She then pointed to a nearby locker that was marked SMALL ARMS. "Maybe we ought to get some pistols while we're here too."

"We don't want to get too loaded down," Cy pointed out, as he followed Lisa to the small arms locker.

"I think I've got enough room left for a pistol with some ammo," Lisa said, as she opened the locker. Her eyes lit back up as she turned to Cy. "Well, well! There's still some in here, and with the ammo to boot." She pulled out two well-worn but well serviced Colt M1911 .45 automatic pistols and then handed one to Cy. "See if there's any holsters, Cy."

"Will do," Cy said. He was back half a minute later with both holsters and ammo belts, as well as an extra gear harness. "For you, Lisa," he said, as he presented it to her with a flourish.

"Thanks," Lisa said, smiling for the first time since her sad revelation. She had already pulled out four boxes of .45 ACP ammo for filling the pouches on their belts. "Any truth to the rumor that the Army's going to ditch these for modern nine millimeters?"

"That's the story," Cy said.

"Bad idea," Lisa said, shaking her head. "The Colt .45 automatic is one of the best handguns in the world. You hit a guy with a round from one of these, and he not only goes down but stays down. You've got to hit 'em two or three times with a nine millimeter."

"Yeah, but nine millimeter is NATO standard," Cy replied. "Also don't forget that most of the forty-fives that the Army has are decades old and wearing out fast. They need a new gun and soon, and they want it to work with the same ammo that our NATO allies have. I also hear they're working on some new rounds that will make a nine millimeter work almost as good as a forty-five."

"That I'd have to see for myself," Lisa said doubtfully. She finished adjusting her new gun belt, and then looked around. "Say, you didn't happen to see any more body armor in here like what you've got on, did you?"

"No, but I wouldn't recommend what I'm wearing," Cy said, as he finished fitting his own pistol and began to fill his new belt pouches with pistol ammo. "This is a leftover from the early years in Vietnam. It works, but it's made out of ceramic sheets. It's not very flexible, and you ... well ...." He smiled, and Lisa smiled back in understanding. "The only other thing the Army's got that would work with you ladies is made from layered nylon, but it isn't that much better than a flak jacket and those only protect you against loose shrapnel. I would have got one of those, but Supply had run out of them by the time they got down to the 'Rs" in our detachment. That's how I wound up with this thing instead. Anyway, what you want is Kevlar body armor, like the police use. It's lighter, more flexible for what you need, and does almost as good of a job as this old stuff I'm wearing."

"Point taken," Lisa said, as she finished fitting her new gear harness and began to hang grenades and other gear from it. She then picked up her AK-47 and slung it over one shoulder. She did the same on the other with her new M-16A1, moved it around so she could hold it in a walking carry, and then looked at Cy. "So what now?" she asked.

"We go back out and see if we can get one of the radios in the vehicles outside to work," Cy said. He slung the China Lake behind him and hefted his own M-16A1. "That's the only way we're going to be able to call out from here."

Just then there came a slow banging noise from the door. Both Cy and Lisa whipped about, weapons raised and at the ready. The door held, but the banging continued. The two gave each other a look, then slung their weapons to one side and finished filling their rucksacks as fast as they could. It took them only a minute or so, but the banging continued nonstop the entire time.

"Sounds like our undead friends are back," Lisa said evenly, as she closed her own rucksack, quickly put it on, and then slung her M-16 back around to the ready.

"Yeah, and we're pinned in here," Cy responded.

"Not as long as you got that thing," Lisa said, pointing to his China Lake.

Cy nodded and swapped weapons. "Let's get to the far end of the room," he said, "so we won't get caught in the blast."

"Right with you," Lisa said, falling in beside him.

Seconds later there was a muffled roar as the door to the weapons storeroom was blown away from the inside. Both its remains and multiple zombie body parts littered the hallway beyond. Smoke billowed from the room, and right behind it came Cy and Lisa. They rushed through and down the hall, heading back out of the building the way they had come in, but they were forced to stop once they had passed the door back into the main hallway. It had filled with new zombies eager for prey, and they began to move towards the two humans who had appeared in front of them. Cy and Lisa resumed firing with their M-16s, slowly but surely working their way though an ever-growing pile of zombie bodies beside and behind them.

"Where the hell did they come from?!" Lisa exclaimed, as she pulled an empty ammo clip from her weapon, slapped in a fresh one, and began firing again.

"These look like some of the ones that chased me through downtown," Cy said loudly above the chatter of his own weapon. He kept up a steady stream of fire while Lisa reloaded, and then it was his turn. "There's been enough time for them to get here since we arrived, and I'm guessing the main horde is not far behind them."

"Aw, hell!" Lisa half-shouted back, so she could be heard above both the zombies and the assault rifles. "New plan! Forget the vehicle radios! There's too many of them! Let's just get to my 'Cuda and get outta here!"

"Right!" Cy called back.

They had almost made it to the front doors when a group of four fatigue-clad zombies appeared outside from both sides, as if to block their way. Cy quickly switched weapons, swapping assault rifle for China Lake, and hit them with a grenade. The explosion not only took care of the four zombies, but blew the remaining door off of its hinges and opened a wide swath through the hundred or so zombies half-shuffling and half-trotting towards the Armory. Cy and Lisa raced through and into the opening, coughing at the smoke and opening it up even more with their continued assault rifle fire. They cleared a path to Lisa's car, Lisa jumped in first and got the car started while Cy covered her. As soon as it was running Cy dived in, Lisa gunned the engine, and then they took off. She hit at least three zombies on the way back out of the now gateless front entrance, leaving long splatters of blood on the hood, front grille, and fenders of her 'Cuda, but that was all. The 'Cuda's tires squealed as Lisa swung around and away from the zombies, then peeled down the opposite end of the street at full throttle, the 'Cuda's Hemi roaring as it raced away.

Undead heads swiveled as the 'Cuda thundered by, and then it was gone. The zombies stood there as if befuddled, having lost their prey, and then watched in apparent amazement as a large flock of crows descended and began to feed on the bodies scattered in front of the Armory. With them came the large black raven that had led them, and it was the same that Cy had seen on his dash for survival earlier. It alighted on the nearest body and the surrounding zombies immediately backed away, as if sensing that this one lone arrogant raven packed more evil in its tiny little body than did they and all of their undead comrades combined. The raven cocked its head at them, and then gave a mournful cry so loud and intense that all of the zombies cringed. After that they began to shuffle away. Soon enough all of the zombies were moving away from the Armory and heading back the way they came. That was how both the crows and their fearless leader were allowed to feed in peace, and they fed heartily on the feast of meat that was laid out before them.

"Where to now?" Cy asked, as Lisa gunned the 'Cuda and sent it flying down the city street.

"Hospital," Lisa promptly replied. "It's the closest place that'll have a radio transmitter. It's about ten minutes away normally, but it'll probably take us twenty or more given all the wrecks on the main beltway. There's also a Metro City police substation on the other side of the block where it's at. We might be able to get Kevlar body armor there. If they don't have any, Southwest Sporting Goods might have some, and I'm going there even if they don't."

"What for?"

"Ammo for my AK," Lisa said. "It's the only place close to us where I can get some. Both they and the hospital might also have other supplies we need to get out of town, like food and medical stuff."

Cy thought for a moment, and then nodded. "Makes sense." He gave her a friendly look. "You're a very sensible girl, Lisa."

"Thanks," Lisa said, and then added quickly, "Here comes our exit. Hang on!"

Lisa took the exit to the Metro City beltway on two wheels, having to dodge around a wrecked city bus at almost the last minute. A pack of zombies trapped inside the wreck howled at the 'Cuda as it swung past at a crazy slant. There was a loud *WHUMP!* as the car came back down on all four wheels, and then it was up the ramp and on the beltway seconds later. Thankfully the section they had just entered was fairly straight and had only a few stalled or wrecked vehicles, so Lisa was able to open up the Hemi and let it go full. The 'Cuda took off like a rocket down the beltway, heading towards its next destination and whatever new unseen foes and dangers lay ahead.

"Hey, Cy?"

Cy turned to look at Lisa. She still had her eyes on the road. "Yeah?"

"When we get to the hospital, I want some of your blood."

This time Cy did a full double-take. "What? Why?"

Lisa gave a stern smile. "I'm guessing the Army or the government gave you and everyone in that stupid convoy some shots or something to protect you from the virus. I don't know what the deal is with me, but I'm not counting on my luck holding. You know? That's why I want some of your blood."

Cy nodded. "Yeah, I know. Yes they did, and I'll gladly give you some, only I don't know how to do a transfusion."

"Neither do I," Lisa said. She grinned this time, and he could see her eyes twinkle even though she kept them on the road. "I know they've got the equipment there. Maybe they'll have an instruction manual or something. If nothing else, they'll have needles."

"That's dangerous," Cy noted.

"You got a better idea?"

Cy thought a moment, then shook his head. "No. I guess we'll cross that bridge when we get to it."

"We'll have to," Lisa said. She paused a beat, and then added, "Thanks, Cy."

"You're welcome, Lisa."

The inside of the 'Cuda became silent again, save for the steady rumble coming from the Hemi in front. While Lisa remained focused on her driving, Cy turned away and looked out his window. Behind them, downtown Metro City was beginning to recede in the distance. He could see the tall columns of smoke from the fires that were burning in there, and knew that some of them were coming from the remains of his convoy. He could do nothing for his friends and fellow soldiers back there. All of them were dead, and he had been very lucky to escape the carnage surrounding that debacle. There had never been any hope that the convoy would succeed in its mission to begin with, but it had gone in because it was something that had to be done, and it had its orders. Even so, despite the longest odds Cy had ever known, somehow, incredibly, miraculously, he was still alive. For that he had to thank a female stock car racer by the name of Lisa Stanridge whom he hadn't known personally before today, but whom he was beginning to appreciate more and more the longer he stayed with her.

Cy's gaze remained on the view behind and beside the fast-moving HemiCuda, a view that was straight out of a Hieronymus Bosch painting, but he found himself thinking instead about Lisa. She was something else. He liked that something else too. He liked it a lot. He could only hope that he was impressing her as much as she had certainly impressed him. Cy found himself smiling at the thought. What a thought to have in the middle of a zombie outbreak! Nonetheless it was there, and he was glad it was. It gave him hope. *Hope.* He had hope again, thanks to Lisa, and that was something. In the middle of all of the death and destruction within Metro City, he had hope again ... and he had his unexpected savior to thank for that.

Cy gave a sigh, and then turned back around to face the road ahead while the HemiCuda roared down the beltway. It deftly zig-zagged around the occasional obstacle, Lisa giving it all the speed that road conditions would allow as they sped to their next destination.

CHAPTER 2
ROAD TRIP

Lisa had been right about the beltway. Once they got around the first big turn, they began to encounter multiple abandoned and wrecked vehicles. In fact it got so bad in places that Lisa was forced to slow down to almost a crawl and take to either the median or shoulder as needed, or even cross over and drive on the opposite lanes until they could get clear of the worst of the jams. A 1971 Plymouth HemiCuda is not a car designed to crawl along at what for it would be a snail's place. To Cy it often seemed the car was complaining, its 425 Hemi motor grumpily growling away through the 'Cuda's Shaker hood as Lisa zigzagged her way around these metal derelicts at a speed well below what it could really do in search of the next open path. It was never boring, for any time they were in sufficient number, then the zombies of their former owners or occupants were often there to greet the pair. It was on occasions like this that their newly acquired Colt .45 pistols came in very handy, in the few instances when they had to fight their way clear. Both Lisa and Cy were crack shots, and the large and heavy .45 ACP rounds they were firing meant that usually it only took one or two shots from either of them to make any given zombie threat eat pavement, instead of the human flesh it desired. Still, it was slow going. A drive that should have normally taken only ten minutes or so, and that Lisa had estimated would take at least twenty, wound up being almost a good half-hour instead.

The two talked during their slow journey to the hospital. It was as good a way as any to pass the time, save for the occasional zombie encounter and put-down. The local radio station was off the air for obvious reasons, and all of the others were carrying 24 non-stop hour news coverage about the Metro City Outbreak. Neither Lisa nor Cy needed to hear the news. They didn't have to be told what was happening. They were living that experience. They talked as Lisa's HemiCuda moved along, weaving its way around the many obstacles on the beltway and towards their far-distant target: the Metro City Medical Center's off-ramp and exit.

"I knew it would be bad, but I didn't know it would be this bad," Lisa was saying, as she scanned the road ahead. "I've been sticking mostly to the side streets and alleys until I rescued you." She thought for a minute, and then added. "You know, maybe we could stop by one of these big rigs, deal with any zombies nearby, and use its CB radio to call out."

"Wouldn't matter," Cy said from his seat beside her, working to reload the rest of their empty ammo clips. "The Army's not listening to any civilian racket. It's as bad on the CB bands as it is on the regular radio, or so I was told from our convoy's radio operator before he got killed. Everybody yakkin' about the Outbreak and all. Oh, I'm sure some people tried to call out from here before they turned, but only other civvies would have heard them. The Army's only listening on official military or emergency bands. That's what we gotta use to call out if we're gonna be heard."

"What about using a police car or ambulance radio?"

Cy gave her a look, although he made sure to smile when he did. "Have you seen a police car yet that isn't wrecked? Same goes for the two ambulances and one fire truck we've seen so far."

Lisa bit her lip, and then nodded. "Okay. Point taken." She gave a sigh. "I wish there had been time to use one of those vehicle radios back at the Armory."

"You did the right thing in getting us out of there when you did, Lisa," Cy said. "We didn't have the ammo to hold out, what with that entire downtown horde about to drop down on us and all." He too now sighed. "We'll just have to hope that the hospital's main transmitter is in better shape."

Lisa now gave a chuckle. "You'd think they would have issued you guys personal radios. I know they have them."

"They probably didn't think we'd need them, given that we were all together in one big convoy," Cy said. "I'll concede the point, though. That would have been a good idea."

"Yeah."

Cy now put the ammo clip he had just reloaded into his bandolier. "There," he announced. "All done, both you and me. We're about as ready as we're going to be."

"Thanks."

"You're welcome."

Lisa gave a chuckle. "I'm glad I met you Cy. It's making this easier, you know? Going through it with someone, instead of being alone?"

Cy nodded. "Yeah. I know what you mean." He too gave a low laugh. "I thought I was stuck on my own there for a bit, and then you came along to the rescue. Boy was I glad! Hey, just think of how the news will handle this once they hear of it. *Stock car driver and Army corporal survive zombie plague*." He laughed again. "God, but I hope we live long enough to actually make that headline somewhere."

"Me too," Lisa agreed, and she chuckled again. "Me too."

Cy took in a deep breath, let it out again, and then looked at Lisa. "May I ask a question?"

"Go ahead," Lisa answered. "Looks like we've got plenty of time."

"How did a good-looking girl like you wind up being a stock car driver?"

Lisa smiled. "Oh, that! Well, racing's in my blood. I got it from my dad. He's a full blood Cherokee from Oklahoma, and he used to race horses. He was unusually small and light, which would have worked against him in the old days, but it was just right for being a horse jockey today. He loved horses, and horses loved him. That was his ticket to bigger and better things when he was young. He wound up becoming a professional horse jockey, racing with various farms and outfits up and down the East Coast, and that was how he met my mom. They met at a race track in Virginia, I think it was, and they got married at another one in Kentucky the next year as part of a big festival they were having there. I was born the year after that, so that kept Mom busy for a while. Dad still raced, but he spent as much time with us as he could.

"We moved around a lot when I was little, but Dad eventually retired and took a job as a horse manager and trainer at one of the breeding farms near here, because it was within easy reach of the Cherokee Nation. Dad wanted to make sure I was thoroughly grounded in the ways of our people, you see. Mom supported him on that, although she made it clear she didn't want to live in Oklahoma, so Uncle Ray came to the rescue. Remember, Mom's brother and the gun nut of the family? He and Dad had hit it off immediately because Uncle Ray had served with some Indians from another tribe in 'Nam and had become good friends with them. Anyway, he found Mom and Dad a place in the country just outside of town and within easy driving distance of the Nation, so they could have it both ways."

Lisa gave a short laugh, and then continued. "As I was growing up, Mom let Dad school me in the old ways of the Cherokee as much as he could, and he took me to the Nation a lot on visits with his relatives there. I developed a great respect for them, and both their ways and what they know about the world that I wouldn't have had otherwise. They in turn eventually accepted me as part of the Nation even though I'm a half-breed and don't actually live in it. On the side, Dad and Uncle Ray also made sure I knew weapons and was trained in survival techniques, even though I was a girl. I remember one week in the summer, right before my senior year in high school, when they had me try out my survival skills in one of the more desolate areas of the Nation with nothing except the clothes on my back and a hunting knife. What an experience that turned out to be, but you know what? I did it, and knowing I did it made quite an impression on the tribal elders. 'Too bad you're not male,' I remember one of them telling me. 'You might have made a good brave back in the day.'" She laughed again. "I thought learning all of that was pretty cool, and maybe I might use it someday if I ever went on an adventure far away or anything, but I honestly never thought I'd have to use any of it until now." She paused, shaking her head as she did, then resumed. "Anyhow, back to your question. Dad's thing was horses and mine turned out to be cars. Once he figured out that was my talent, both he and Mom supported me in every way they could."

Cy nodded. "I'll bet you met a lot of prejudice along the way."

Lisa nodded back, although she kept her eyes on the road. "Yes, I did. I got it both ways, you know. Both for being a girl and for being an Indian. It wasn't so bad for my dad, since horses and Indians kind of go together, but it was bad with me when I was trying to get started. I got prejudiced against because of my Indian blood, but the worst of all was the harassment. People kept telling me that I was a girl and I needed to be a secretary or even a model, not a stock car driver. There were also the hints too, both veiled and not-so-veiled, about how certain people would help me get what I wanted if I'd sleep with them. I turned those down flat, because I knew they were lying. They weren't going to help me. They just wanted to take advantage of me. I already knew what I wanted was possible without them, so I refused them each and every time."

"Good for you," Cy commented.

"Yeah," Lisa agreed. "You know, maybe I did miss some opportunities early on because of my bullheadedness, but I eventually found some decent people - Rob and Cathy Vesper - who were willing to give me a chance, and it all clicked from there. I also had some good examples to inspire me along the way. Jim Thorpe, for one, the Indian who wound up winning at the Olympics. There's also Shirley Muldowney in the NHRA and Janet Guthrie in NASCAR. If they can do it, then so can I. I just kept them in mind every time somebody told me that an Indian couldn't compete against whites, or that a girl shouldn't be a race car driver, and all that. I found somebody who would sponsor me, I did better than everyone expected, and that's how I eventually wound up being a Sportsman division driver and winning the Bellville Cup last year, even though I'm still in my twenties." Lisa laughed "Hopefully I'll earn the right to race NASCAR someday too." She smiled and gave a chuckle when she finished, then spoke again. "So what's your story, Cy?"

"Eh?"

"How'd you end up in Metro City? I mean, I know you came in with that convoy, but how'd you end up in this area in the first place?"

Cy was about to respond when a concerned look crossed Lisa's face. He felt the 'Cuda slow. "What is it?" he asked.

"Look ahead," Lisa said calmly.

Cy looked. There was a large multi-car pileup at the next off-ramp exit, and there were at least a dozen zombies roaming freely in and around it. He gave a disgusted grunt, and then pulled his pistol. "Zombie clearing time again."

"Better get your rifle ready too," Lisa said, "and see if you can reach my AK. You may need its bigger bite before we're done. Save the 'nades for later, for when we really need them."

"Right with you," Cy said, even as he reached behind Lisa's seat so he could get to her AK-47.

It took all of five minutes to clear the zombies at the multi-car pileup, and fortunately Cy's pistol was sufficient to do the job. It took another five minutes for them to figure out a way around it, because all of the lanes and the off-ramp were completely blocked. Lisa eventually had to back up enough to get to the last emergency crossover they had passed, get into the opposite lanes, drive on the other side until she could get past the pileup, and then get back over when she could. Fortunately the Outbreak ensured that there was no oncoming traffic, so she made the next crossover with no difficulty. After that, it was back to the proper beltway lanes and on their way again.

"Man, oh man," Cy said, as he rested in the 'Cuda's front passenger seat again. "I hope it's not like this all the way to the hospital."

"Me too," Lisa said. "We've still got three more off-ramps to go before we reach ours."

"We do?" Cy said, cocking an eyebrow at her.

"'Fraid so," Lisa said. "Tell you what. Let's pick up where we left off. How'd a nice guy like you end up in Metro City?"

Cy grinned. "You really think I'm nice?"

"Yes," Lisa said pleasantly, "but please answer the question."

"Thank you," Cy answered, and then he began. "I'm not from around here. I was born and grew up in Belknap, Tennessee. Don't worry if you've never heard of it. It's a little farming town out in the middle of nowhere on the eastern side of the state, total population just under two thousand, and about as segregated as towns in the South these days can get. It had two railroad lines coming through it, one north-south and one east-west, and it split the town into four quarters. That's also how everyone grouped themselves who lived there. All the rich whites lived in the northeast quarter, all the middle-class whites in the southeast quarter, all the poor whites and white trash in the southwest quarter, and all of us blacks and other types in the northwest. We even had our own separate schools at one time too, until the feds came in and made 'em mix everything up, but that town is still split up that way even today and most folks there think it's the right way to live."

"I don't know if I'd want to live there," Lisa commented, still keeping her eyes on the road. "Sounds too stratified."

"It was," Cy replied, "Most of us blacks were poor, all the whites had almost all of the good jobs and made sure they kept them, and there just weren't that many local opportunities for a young black man like me to get ahead in life. If I'd stayed, I'd have been stuck with a menial job, like being a laborer or worse, and I wanted more. I also didn't have the grades for a college scholarship, and I couldn't play basketball, and I wasn't big or fast enough for football, so I went into the Army. That was my ticket out of town, and I've been with them ever since. My last posting was at Fort Carnacki north of here, so I was in the area and available when the Outbreak went down. That's how I got here."

"Speaking of fast, you seemed pretty fast to me earlier today," Lisa said, "when I first saw you running ahead of that pack of zombies."

Cy laughed softly. "That's Army basic training for you. They stripped me down to the essentials and then remade me as a good fighting man. That meant they made sure I was in good shape too. Lots of PT and all that. Honestly, though, I've never run so fast in my life as I was doing when you first saw me. Hope I never have to again."

"I hope neither of us do," Lisa said.

Cy nodded, and then fell silent. After a while, he spoke softy. "You know what, Lisa?"

"What?"

"I wasn't running just to run away."

"I never thought you were, Cy."

"I know. It's just ...." Cy paused, trying to find the right words. Lisa said nothing, letting him do so. After a while he spoke again. "I can still see Lt. Stevens turning to the rest of us and yelling *Get out of here!* right before a half-a-dozen zombies took him out. Our unit was at the rear of the convoy, and the zombies attacked mostly from both sides and the front. That's how we were able to fight our way out, but there were plenty of them back there too. Only four of us managed to break into the clear. Only four. The zombies caught up with the other three right before you found me. That's how I'm the only survivor." Cy paused, and then added quietly, "That's my story, Lisa." With that Cy looked down and fell silent again.

Lisa waited until she was sure Cy was finished, and then she spoke. She spoke softly but gently, with no hint of reproof. "Cy, I don't think anybody would blame you for running like that. As you said, both you and everybody else knew the convoy was lost, and you were following the last order you were given: to run and save yourself. It's not like you cut and ran because you were a coward, because you're not. You've already proven that to me back at the Armory." Cy looked up at Lisa at that last statement, and saw compassion and understanding in her eyes even as she kept them to the road and continued to speak. "Also, let's be honest. Having to deal with a zombie apocalypse is something nobody expects, and I'm willing to bet that wasn't included in your Army basic training."

Cy cracked a smile. "No it wasn't, Lisa," he said.

"Well, there you go," Lisa replied. "Think nothing of it, because I don't. You're a survivor and I'm a survivor, and we're very lucky to have found each other in all this mess. That's all that matters to me, so hang the rest. Let's just worry about surviving, okay?"

"Okay," Cy said, nodding his head.

Lisa was about to say something else when she suddenly swore. "Damn. This next exit's almost as bad as the last one. Hold on."

Lisa cut the 'Cuda hard to the left. They were right beside an emergency crossover, and Lisa just barely made it. She was now driving in the opposite lanes. She slowed a bit but never stopped, so that this time they drove past the off-ramp pileup instead of running up against it. The batch of zombies ambling or shuffling about at this one stopped in their tracks and turned almost as one to look at them, but that was all. They watched as the 'Cuda quickly made its way past them in the opposite lanes, their hungry eyes never leaving it from the moment it came into sight until the second it disappeared around the far turn. After that, they went back to ambling and shuffling again.

"Well, I'm glad I saw that in time," Lisa said with forced cheerfulness. "Here comes another crossover. Hang on."

Lisa whipped the 'Cuda back into the proper lanes as ably as she had whipped out of them at the previous crossover. Cy quit gripping the dashboard and shook his head, laughing as he did. "Are we going to have to do this every time?" he asked.

"I hope not," Lisa said. "We've only got two more exits to go, but we'll be able to see ours from the one before it. If it looks as bad as the others, I'm going to take the next one and get to the hospital from the side streets. I know the way and I can do it once we're down there."

"I trust you, Lisa," Cy said.

"Thanks," Lisa replied. She shot him a quick smile before she put her eyes back on the road. "I trust you too."

"Thanks," Cy said, and this time he was the one who was smiling. "I appreciate it."

"Not a problem," Lisa replied.

The two said nothing more for a while as the 'Cuda continued to move down the beltway, Lisa still going as fast as road conditions and the occasional obstructions to dodge along the way would allow. Both continued to smile as the 'Cuda rolled on. Whatever thoughts each was thinking they kept to themselves.

Lisa's fears proved to be well founded. Even as they made the final turn before the next-to-last off-ramp and exit before the one they needed to take, all the signs of a major pileup quickly began to appear. This time Lisa didn't say anything. She looked for and spotted the crossover, whipped the 'Cuda over into the inside lane, and took it as soon as she came to it. She then used the mostly clear off-ramp in the opposite lane to get off the beltway, worming her way around stalled or wrecked vehicles on either road shoulder as needed. The 'Cuda made it down to street level without incident, Lisa took a hard right at the four-way at the off-ramp's end, and then took off down a mostly clear four-lane street at high speed. Cy tightly gripped the dashboard in front of him through the entire turn, wishing all the while that his seatbelt had enough reach to go around both him and the gear he was wearing. He came very close to losing the contents of his stomach given how hard and fast Lisa took that turn, but he gritted his teeth and somehow managed to swallow just in time. As his stomach settled back down and the 'Cuda went into straight ahead mode again. it sounded to him as if it was happy for the first time in the past half-hour or so. It seemed to enjoy Lisa loosening up its leash and allowing it to zip along at a pace far faster than the obstacle and pileup littered beltway had permitted.

"This is Bloch Parkway," Lisa explained as she drove. "We've got to take the next right two blocks up onto King Avenue, head down it for half-a-mile, then right again onto Munro Street. Metro City Medical Center is at the corner of Munro and Carpenter Avenue, which would have been our exit from the beltway had it not been blocked. We'll be coming in from its right side, if you at the front doors looking out. It's shaped like a big letter 'L,' with one wing sticking out towards Munro Street and the other towards Carpenter Avenue, with the main building and entrance in the middle and a double-lane drive thru right up to the front doors. They'll probably have them sealed and the drive blocked due to the Outbreak, but there's plenty of open spaces and parking around. Let's hope some of the ones close are still open."

"Agreed," Cy said. "I hope we don't have to park too far away. We may have to get back to your car in a hurry if we can't get in."

"You've got that right," Lisa said. "Hang on. Here's our first right turn."

Lisa didn't even bother to slow down. She almost put the 'Cuda on two wheels again, given how fast and how sharp she made that right turn at the intersection, but this time she got the sound of a lot of rubber squealing instead of going partially airborne. The 'Cuda skewed and slid through the turn, Lisa straightening it back up in a jiffy as only an experienced or professional driver can, and then they were off again at high speed down a mostly empty King Avenue. Cy again had to swallow and grip the dashboard tightly before him as they made the turn. He thought he saw Lisa grin at him from out of the corner of his left eye, but when he turned to look her face was a mask of innocence and her eyes were on the road again.

"How big is it?" Cy asked, once the 'Cuda had settled down in its new course and he judged Lisa free enough to talk again. "The hospital, I mean?"

"Fairly big," Lisa said, still keeping her eyes on the road. "Five stories, and that includes both the main building and both wings. Where we want to go is outpatient surgery, and that's on the third floor." When Cy raised an eyebrow, Lisa explained. "I had a friend of mine at the track who got messed up in a race collision a couple of years ago. We were close, so I spent a lot of time visiting him at the hospital. That's how I know my way around in there."

"Oh." Cy thought a moment, and then looked at Lisa. "How close, may I ask?"

This time it was Lisa's turn to raise an eyebrow. Her lips formed into a mischievous grin. "Close enough." She then frowned. "He never raced again after that, of course, and we eventually broke up once my star began to rise. He was too messed up, and he began to resent the fact that I could still race and he couldn't, and I was getting famous and he wasn't. Every time I'd visit him it would turn into an all-out pity party. I eventually got tired of it and stopped seeing him. Last I heard, he had found himself a new girlfriend and was doing her the same way." She sighed, and then added sadly. "Price of fame, I guess, or not having gotten it. For all I know he's probably a zombie now."

"I'm sorry to hear that," Cy said.

"Yeah," Lisa said. "He was a good guy once, before the accident and his going into professional victim mode not long after. I would have liked to have stayed with him, but ... well ... you know how it goes. I had places to go and things to do, and he couldn't be part of that picture being like that. He was too jealous." She sighed. "I don't know. Anyway, if I'd stayed with him and given up racing, like I know he wanted me to, I'd probably be a zombie now too." Lisa let out a low laugh, and then furrowed her brow. "Next turn's coming up."

"I'm ready," Cy said, tightly gripping the dashboard in front of him.

Lisa took the turn onto Munro Street at high speed as before, the tires of the 'Cuda squealing as she swerved around and then straightened back out in a snap once they were heading in the right direction. Cy took it better this time, although he still felt his stomach heave at the way Lisa took the turn. He had to remind himself that she was a professional racer and he wasn't, and she knew how to do this kind of thing. He couldn't have done it, he admitted to himself. Well, not at that speed, anyway. Again he thought he saw Lisa grin at him, and again he saw nothing but eyes to the road once he turned his head for a better look.

"Last turn," Lisa announced. "Next stop, Metro City Medical Center. Please be prepared to unstow all gear once we're down and return all tray tables to their upright position."

Cy gave her a look, furrowing his brow as he did. "You're a funny girl, Lisa."

"Yes I am," she responded playfully, her eyes never leaving the road but letting the impish grin that had formed on her face speak for her.

Lisa slowed once they got within sight of the hospital. The approaching rumble of her 'Cuda's Hemi motor startled a flock of crows feeding on the bodies scattered in front of and around both the main entrance and the building's two wings. There must have been a couple of hundred of bodies, maybe more. The crows rose into the air in confusion and then quickly flew away in search of a more peaceful feeding ground. One bird remained behind, however, perched on the arm of one of the nearby telephone poles. It was not a crow, but a big black raven .It cocked its head sideways at them as it watched the approach of the new arrivals, but otherwise did nothing else.

The hospital's main drive was blocked as Lisa had predicted. Two parked police cars on each end sealed it so effectively that the only room left to get by was for pedestrians, had there been any left alive to do so. Fortunately, as she had hoped, there were still empty parking spaces close to the building. Lisa deliberately picked one in the staff parking lot, which was the closest, and slid her 'Cuda into it. She put the car into parking gear, turned off the motor, and then looked at Cy. "Let's take all of our gear with us, Cy. We don't know what it's going to be like in there."

"My thoughts exactly," Cy said, as he looked back at her. "You beat me to it."

Lisa looked at him for a moment, then offered him her hand. "For luck," she said.

Cy took it and gripped it firmly. "For luck," he said back.

That grip only lasted a few seconds. For Cy's part, he wished it would have lasted far longer. He could have sworn he felt a surge of energy rush into him from her as soon as their hands clasped. He felt as if he were tingling all over when they let go. Judging from her reaction, it appeared she had experienced something similar. Then the moment was gone and the two were getting out of the 'Cuda, getting the rest of their gear and weapons out of the back, and making sure everything was arranged on their persons. As Cy finished and brought up his assault rifle into a walking carry position, he heard a click from the lock on the Cuda's closed passenger door beside him. He looked across the top in time to see Lisa on the other side putting her car keys in one of her front pockets, and then putting her firing hand on her weapon. She noticed he was looking at her, gave him a curious look for a moment, then realized why and smiled. "Well?" she said. "I don't want any zombies getting in here before we get back."

"I didn't think zombies could open doors," Cy said with a grin, as he came around the front of the car to join her. Her side was closer to the hospital than his.

"In *Night of the Living Dead* they could throw stones and beat people with sticks, and that little girl who turned zombie stabbed her own mother to death with a gardener's spade," Lisa shot back. "Most folks don't remember those parts of the movie."

"True," Cy said, holding his assault rifle at the ready as he scanned the area around them. It was quiet and it was clear save for the raven on its perch over at Carpenter Street. Too quiet. "Is it me, or are we all alone here?" he asked.

"Yeah," Lisa said. She too had her own assault rifle up and ready and was doing her own visual sweeps. "This isn't right. This is too creepy."

"Well, let's get to those doors and get inside, before anything happens," Cy replied, nodding with his head towards the front of the building.

The pair quickly raced across the staff parking lot and front drive, sidestepping bodies and other obstacles along the way. Off to her left and almost immediately behind the two parked MCPD patrol cars there, Lisa saw and noted the presence of a set of deployed police road spikes. They had been hidden from view during their arrival by the parked patrol cars obstructing the hospital's main drive on that end. Lisa guessed they had probably been put there to keep vehicles with either desperate infected drivers or ones who had already turned far enough away from the hospital to do it damage. Inwardly Lisa breathed a sigh of relief at having avoided this potentially fatal obstacle to her 'Cuda without knowing it. She was still thinking about those road spikes as they ran under the roof of the hospital's main entrance and up to its front doors, where they were forced to stop. The doors were closed and locked, but plenty of spiderburst cracks in the two inch thick safety glass with accompanying blood splatters and smears, not to mention a fair number of apparently dead bodies both official and unofficial scattered about, testified as to what might have happened here earlier that day.

"Cover me," Cy said. Lisa nodded and put herself between Cy and the street side of the building, while he let go of his assault rifle and tried to force the doors by hand. They never budged.

"I could have told you that wouldn't have worked," Lisa quipped.

"Never hurts to try," Cy said, flexing his fingers for a bit before returning his hands to his weapon. "You never know."

"True," Lisa said. "Hey, you see that big black raven on the arm of that telephone pole way off there? It makes me think of the one that was leading that flock of crows that flew over and past us while we were getting here."

"Yeah," Cy said as he walked up and down both the front entrance and the area its damaged safety glass panels on each side enclosed. "I saw one of those things as I was escaping the convoy attack. Big ugly mother, and looked evil as all out. So did the crows that were flying with it, just like those ones that flew away when we got here."

"They're probably all infected from feeding on the dead," Lisa observed. "No telling what the virus is doing to them."

"Well I don't want to find out," Cy said. "I want to get inside, where it's safe."

Lisa chuckled. "Strange definition of safe, what with there probably being zombies inside too."

"Yeah," Cy said, continuing to search for any means of breaching the way inside.

Lisa now looked thoughtful. "You know, the Cherokee have legends about ravens, especially were death is concerned. They say if you're unlucky enough to hear the call of the Raven Mocker instead of a real raven, then you're going to die."

"What's that?"

"A vampire that feeds on the souls of the living. They take the form of giant fiery ravens whenever they visit our world in search of new victims, or so the legends say."

Cy shook his head. "Oh, God. What, are all Indian legends creepy?"

Lisa smiled. "No. Just some of them."

"Anyway, don't encourage that one over there to start cawing," Cy grumbled. "Just in case, okay?"

"Ravens don't caw," Lisa shot back. "Crows do. A raven cry is more like an *awk, awk--*"

"Lisa ... !"

"Easy there, Cy," Lisa said. "Sorry. Didn't mean to make you mad."

Cy gave her a look, calmed himself, and then forced a smile. "I'm sorry too, Lisa. I shouldn't have snapped at you like that." He stepped back and let out a big sigh. "It's just this whole setup, you know? It's creeping me out, and that business with the story of the Raven Mocker isn't helping."

Lisa nodded. "Yeah, I guess I was laying it on a bit thick there."

Cy nodded. "Apology accepted. Anyway, it looks like there's nothing for it. We're going to have to blow out one of these panels to get in."

Awk! Awk! Awk!

Both Cy and Lisa whipped around, their assault rifles up and aimed at the raven perched on the telephone pole. A split second later another noise rippled through the area. It was not unlike the stirring of larges piles of leaves in the autumn wind, save it wasn't leaves that were stirring. It was bodies. Almost every body in the area in front of and around the pair was staring to stir. The ones that were intact or mostly so, the ones that were not so intact, and even isolated partial bodies which still had a head on them. In fact, the only thing organic that wasn't moving were isolated limbs, but what if the virus had the power to re-animate them too? It was very slow at first, both the noise and the motion, but it began to pick up speed as the formerly dead denizens in this place began to re-animate and rise back to their feet, resurrected by the virus as bloodthirsty zombies.

"Oh, shit!" Lisa gasped, bringing her weapon to bear.

Cy hadn't bothered with exclamations. He had instead quickly traded his assault rifle for his China Lake. "Stand back!" he commanded, as he quickly back-pedaled and brought it to bear on one of the damaged glass panels by the locked front doors. Lisa followed a half-beat later, dodging to one side and getting clear as he stopped and let loose with the China Lake. The glass panel at which he had been aiming instantly disappeared inside an explosion which then sprayed millions of tiny glass shards in all directions. So did the glass in the locked door on one side of his target and the panel next to it on the other. It was accompanied by a mini-shock wave and a very loud explosive roar that both swept by the pair and startled every newly revived zombie within reach. The raven immediately took off from its perch, silently sailing away into the darkened sky.

By this time every newly revived zombie in the area had recovered from the shock of the explosion. They turned as one and focused on the two humans in front of the hospital front doors. Cy and Lisa didn't wait for them to attack. They immediately ran through the opening and into the front lobby of the Metro City Medical Center as fast as they could. They were inside their goal at last, but how were they going to stop the zombies from following them in? More importantly, how were they going to get back out again and escape the Outbreak for good?

CHAPTER 3
ANOTHER SURVIVOR

Lisa and Cy ran into the front lobby of the Metro City Medical Center to find the same mess inside that there had been outside, save that there were neither bodies nor zombies. There was still plenty of evidence that they had been there, judging from the overturned furniture and various objects liberally scattered around, as well as a fairly copious amount of bloodstains large and small. Some of the furniture was bunched around the inner doors, as if to suggest that there had been a barricade of sorts there at one time, but it was in ruins now if that was what it had been. Aside from those forms of Outbreak-caused chaos, it was fairly typical for the front lobby of any large hospital. There was a central information desk, waiting areas to both sides, and one set of check-in counters running the length of the back and on either side of the double doors to the hospital's main hallway. These also doubled as fire doors per safety codes and were made of solid steel. The pair ran to these at once and tried them. Both were locked and pinned in place.

Cy turned to Lisa. "You find a way in," he said hurriedly. "I'll hold them at the front as long as I can."

"Gotcha," Lisa replied. They shared the briefest of looks and then Cy was gone, turning on his heel and scurrying back toward the opening they had blown to get in. His tough Army boots crackled on a liberal spread of broken glass as he ran up to and positioned himself directly in front of the broken glass panels on the side of the front entrance. Almost at once he began to fire, his M-16A1 barking away, and almost at once there were the sounds of zombie wails and blood-gurgling moans.

There were two side doors on the left side of the hospital lobby. Lisa didn't bother with these, since they were clearly marked as being restrooms. There was a service entrance to the right, presumably for hospital staff only, but it was as solidly sealed as the main hallway fire doors. That left the area behind the check-in counters. Since she was already on the right side of the lobby (as she had come in), Lisa promptly slung her assault rifle back over her shoulder, ran up to the counter, and did a two-handed cowboy's fence vault to get to the staff area. She landed firmly on her feet and had her weapon back around and at the ready in a flash. It was the same as out on the lobby proper. Plenty of scattered debris and overturned furniture, but no bodies or zombies. The staff entrance was to her right, and three quick steps later she had her hand on the door handle. The lock was on her side and she unlocked it, but opening the door revealed the back side of a soda machine. It had apparently been pushed in place to block the doorway. It was both too big and heavy for her to move by herself without considerable effort, and there wasn't enough time for that.

Lisa cursed even as the chatter from Cy's assault rifle continued. "Hurry up, Lisa!" she heard him call. "There's more of them coming in from every which way!"

With only one option left to try, Lisa re-slung her weapon and vaulted back over the counter. She ran across the lobby to its left side check-in area, vaulted the counter, and tried its staff door. She threw it open and brandished her weapon, half-expecting to find it blocked as had been the other, but she was instead greeted by a empty hallway and total silence. "I found a way in!" she promptly cried out.

"Be right there!" Cy called. He let off a few more bursts from his assault rifle, then turned tail and ran back into the lobby. He saw Lisa standing behind the check-in counter on the left holding open the door back there. He crossed the lobby at full speed, quickly scrambled over the counter, and was through the door with Lisa while the first of the zombies began to pour in through the lobby opening. Lisa slammed the door shut behind him, then looked about quickly. She saw what she was seeking and pointed it out to Cy. "That soda machine!" she cried. "The staff used one to block the other door! Let's use it to block this one!"

It took both of them to push the heavy soda machine in front of the door. By that time they could hear plenty of zombies beyond in the lobby, and at least two had made it over the counter. Less than a half-minute after they had pushed it into place, the door opened from the lobby side. There was a frustrated screech, followed by the sound of fists pounding on the back of the soda machine. It rocked slightly but stayed in place.

Lisa looked at Cy. "That's not going to hold if more of them get back there," she stated. She then waved down the hallway "Down the hall and pin the fire doors behind us."

"Sounds like a plan to me," Cy replied.

Together the two of them ran down the hospital side hallway. As soon as they got to the fire doors, they dashed by and then turned and shut them. They set the pins and turned the locks, and that was that. They were safe ... for now.

Once they had the fire doors secured, Lisa and Cy took a few minutes to catch their breath. The sounds of the lobby zombies remained distant, and there was no crashing sound to let them know that they had successfully topped the soda machine blocking their way.

Cy drew in a deep breath, let it back out slowly, and then resumed normal breathing again. He looked over at Lisa. "Well, we made it," he stated.

Lisa looked back at him, and then her face broke into a broad grin. "Yeah. We did, didn't we?" She began to laugh.

"We sure did," Cy said, returning her grin with one of his own. He too began to laugh.

They laughed for almost a full minute or so. After it was over, Lisa's face resumed a sober expression. "The real problem's going to be getting back out again," she observed.

"We got in, we can get back out," Cy said confidently.

Lisa looked at him, and then nodded. "Yeah. So we did, and so we will."

They did nothing but look at each other for a few beats, and then Cy brought up his weapon. "Let's get going. The sooner we get our business done in here, get out, and get back on our way out of town again, the better." He then looked down one end of the hallway and then the other. "Which way?" he asked.

"That way," Lisa said pointing to their left. "The main hallway junction is down there. We want to go left once we get there. Going right will take us straight to the lobby fire doors."

"No thanks," Cy said. "To the left it is, then."

The intersection of which Lisa spoke came up fairly quickly. They turned left, and soon enough were approaching the next intersection. It was for another main hallway, judging by the fact that it was as large as the one they were now in and ran crossways to theirs. Cy guessed it was the one used as the main access for both wings on this floor. There was a large nurse's station tucked into one of the hallway corners, a small waiting area in another, and a nice assortment of wall signs pointing visitors to the various sections of each part of the hospital on this level. There were also the bodies, or rather what was left of them. These were the first that Lisa and Cy had seen upon entering the hospital, and the way they had been savaged was enough to turn the stomach of most normal people. There were the mutilated remains of two women and one man in the bloody tatters of hospital staff garb in and around the nurse's station, and there was a group of four up against the walls in the waiting area. They had probably been a family, and two of them had been children. If that horrible sight wasn't bad enough, the odor was incredible. That hallway intersection smelled like an open-air butcher's shop on a very hot summer day. Lisa sucked in her breath while Cy tightly gripped his assault rifle, swallowing hard in an effort not to gag. "Oh God," Lisa half-whispered. "I didn't need to see this. It's just like what I saw when I found my brother. Oh God ...." She fought hard to keep her face an emotionless mask.

Lisa felt a hand touch her arm. She turned to see Cy's hand, the one that had been gripping his rifle's stock as tightly as she had her own weapon's. "Hey, you gonna be all right?" he asked.

Lisa nodded. "Yeah. Thanks, Cy." He watched as she set herself, and her features hardened back into the resolute and determined young woman who had rescued him earlier that day. After a beat, she spoke. "I just hope they don't revive."

"Where is everybody, anyway?" Cy wondered aloud. He looked down the closest hallway to theirs. "I mean, you'd think there would be a lot of people in here, or zombies, or whatever now."

Lisa too was looking around again, trying to avoid any further looks at the cannibalized corpses in the waiting area. "Yeah. It's kind of like outside, you know?"

"Well if it is, then our coming in might be the trigger to bring everyone back from wherever they are," Cy said uneasily. He flexed his fingers on his assault rifle. "Keep on your guard."

Both Lisa and Cy almost jumped out of their skins when one of the phones at the nurse's station began to ring. They did a classic double take. They looked at each other, then at the phone, then at each other again. The phone kept ringing. Lisa gave it a sideways look, then returned her gaze to Cy. He shrugged his shoulders. Lisa nodded, and then walked over to the nurse's station. She let go of her assault rifle's stock, picked up the phone left-handed, and held it up to her left ear. "Hello?" she said into the mouthpiece.

"*You ARE real!*" a female voice exclaimed loudly. "*I thought I was dreaming! Please come rescue me! I'm trapped up here!*"

"Whoa, whoa, wait a minute," Lisa said. She motioned for Cy to come over so he could hear the call. Cy obliged, looked over the phone for a moment, and then found and hit its speaker button. Lisa then set down the receiver on the desk instead of cradling it, since doing that might have ended the call. "Okay, we've got you on speaker and we're listening. Who are you?"

"*Mercy Parks!*" The woman's voice was quite loud and rather agitated. "*I'm one of the senior nurses here. The zombies are everywhere, and I can't get back out again! I'm the only one left! You've got to get me out of here!*"

"Where are you?" Cy asked.

"I'm barricaded inside the security office on the center section of the fifth floor. They can't get in, but I can't get out either because there's too many of them!"

"Now we know where all the zombies are," Lisa noted quietly. She then spoke to the phone. "How'd you know we were here?"

"I heard your car and I saw you come in. I've been following you on the security cameras ever since you made it inside. Look up and to your left." They did, and both of them saw a CCTV camera mounted high on one hallway wall near the ceiling pointing at them. They saw its lens zoom out and back in, and then the voice sounded again. *"Did you see that?"*

"Yes we did," Cy said. "Ms. Parks, how many zombies are up there with you?"

"A whole bunch! I don't know! I just know there's too many of them to open the door again! I know they'll kill me, just like they killed John! They got John! I heard him die, and they'll kill me next if I open the door!! Ohhhh, Jooohhhhhnnnnn ... !!!"

"Sounds pretty upset," Lisa said.

"Can you blame her?" Cy responded.

Lisa shook her head. "No, not after what I've been through." She then looked up at Cy and forced a smile. "Correction. What *we've* been through."

"Maybe she can help us with that transfusion you want," Cy suggested.

"Transfusion?" came the voice over the speaker. The use of the medical term seemed to provide a lifeline of sanity for the woman on the other end, because the sound of her crying stopped almost at once. *"Who needs a transfusion, and why?"* she asked, and in a more clear and stable tone than before.

"Lisa does," Cy answered. "I was immunized against the virus before the Army sent me in, and she needs some of my blood to keep from turning."

"Is she infected?"

"No, and I don't know why," Lisa responded, "but if I don't get that transfusion, I could still be."

"All right," came the voice over the speaker again. *"I'll help you if you promise to get me out of here."*

"Be there as soon as we can," Cy said. "How do we get to the security office from where we are now, and in a way that avoids as many zombies as possible?"

"Go to the intersection and turn right as if you're going to the east wing. As soon as you get to the elevators - they'll be on your left, but they're not working - take the stairwell and go all the way up to the fifth floor. You'll have to start shooting as soon as you come out because the

hallways up here are full of zombies, but once you get clear take the first hallway to your left, towards the east wing again. The security office door is at the end of the hall. You can't miss it. I'll let you in as soon as you get here, and if you can keep it clear of zombies."

Both Lisa and Cy nodded. "Got it," Cy said, as he picked up the receiver from the desk. "We're going to let you go now, Ms. Parks, but we're on our way."

"Thank you!"

Cy hung up the phone. He looked at Lisa with a wry smile. "Well, here we go," he said, as he hefted his assault rifle.

"Let's rock," Lisa responded with a grin, as she hefted her own. With that the pair were on the move. They left the nurse's station, took the hallway to the right, and made their way towards the stairwell door at a quick trot, weapons in walking carries all the way.

It proved quite the fight for Lisa and Cy in getting to the nurse trapped in the security office on the hospital's fifth floor. They didn't have any problem getting into the stairwell, nor going up it, but as soon as they popped open the fifth floor stairwell door they found a hallway full of zombies. The nurse's warning about them proved fortunate, because the pair came out of the stairwells with weapons up and ready to fire. They started firing as soon as the zombies turned in their direction, and they continued until they made it to the security office door. It was slow going, though. New zombies would appear from side rooms or intersecting hallways, and a whole pack of them tried to ambush the pair of humans from behind as they came up the other end of the main hallway. Lisa and Cy didn't have any more trouble dealing with them than they had the rest; however, the sheer number of zombies they had to kill made a rather serious dent in their individual ammo supplies.

What made things more difficult this time around was the fact that some of the zombies were former hospital security guards, and they were wearing body armor. They weren't any more or less fearsome than the others, but that body armor made them harder to kill. The pair had to resort to either head shots or capping them at the knees and then doing a head shot as they fell. "Hey," Lisa called as she was downing her share of the hospital zombies, "maybe we should snag some of this body armor, eh?"

"Contaminated," Cy called back, taking out out his own share of their undead foes. "I'd rather have a nice clean set."

"Oh, yeah," Lisa replied with a grin, and then turned back to more zombie killing.

It was the same as it had been back at the National Guard Armory, save for the numbers. That was the biggest threat the zombies posed, as both Lisa and Cy realized. They weren't very fast and they were fairly easy to kill. All it took was one to three well-placed shots, depending on where you shot them. It was their sheer numbers that proved daunting, and which frequently limited the ability to place their shots well. Both Lisa and Cy used far more ammo than they would have liked because of the mass of their foes. They eventually had to resort to their pistols in order to conserve assault rifle ammo, but by then the ranks of their foes had thinned considerably. Another ten to fifteen minutes worth of dodging and firing later, and it was over. The last zombie went down and stayed down, and after that the way to the security office was clear.

Cy found himself holding his breath as he stood braced in a two-handed pistol firing stance behind an overturned gurney, with Lisa beside him in a similar pose. He let his breath out and looked at her, and she looked back. "Good God," he uttered aloud, in a low tone of frustrated relief.

"Amen to that," Lisa echoed. She then chuckled. "Man, oh man. This is an experience I definitely don't want to repeat any time soon."

It was then that the lock on the security office door behind them clicked from being unlocked. Both turned in time to see the door open. Framed in the open doorway was an adult woman with Asian features in early middle age wearing a rumpled blouse and slacks with matching flats, and with a bloodstained short white lab coat over her blouse. She had disheveled black hair pulled back into a bun, and her blue eyes were full of fear. Nevertheless there was open relief on her face as she greeted them. "I'm Mercy Parks. Thank God you made it! Hurry, before more come!"

Lisa and Cy didn't argue. They quickly followed Mercy through the doorway and into the security office beyond, sidestepping a bloody pile of bones and other human remains just outside the door as they did. Behind them, they heard the sound of the door being slammed shut and locked again behind them. They were safe once more ... for now.

The hospital's security office was fairly typical for the type. Lisa and Cy saw several workstations to their left running the length of the wall, on which were mounted multiple CCTV video monitors and with camera control boards beneath them. In the left corner was an open storage shelving unit which housed chargers for two-way radios on its upper shelves and various boxes and binders on its lower ones. All of the radios were missing, presumably still being carried or dropped somewhere else in the hospital by their now undead users. Along the back wall were two large metal storage cabinets, one of which had a padlock on it, along with several smaller unlocked ones and a couple of medium-height three-drawer filing cabinets. Above the filing cabinets was a large wall-mounted first aid cabinet, and sitting on one of the file cabinets below and to one side of it were a bottle of rubbing alcohol and bottle of hydrogen peroxide, along with a sealed box of large gauze pads. Along the wall to their right were a bookcase full of books and more binders, and two desks with office chairs, with various official and personal effects on top of the desks. Some of the desk drawers were opened in such a way to suggest they had been recently rifled, and the haphazard arrangement of the items on their top suggested that they had been hurriedly searched as well.

Cy went at once to the locked storage cabinet. He pulled on the padlock, and as expected nothing happened. "I've already tried that," Mercy said. "I also tried to find the key, but couldn't."

"Weapons store?" Lisa asked.

"Probably," Cy said, "and we aren't going to get this lock off without the key. This is a Yale® lock, one of the best made."

"Hang on," Lisa said. She went over to one of the desks, fished around in its middle drawer for a bit, then pulled out a large paperclip. She came back, unbending it as she walked. "Maybe I can pick it," she said.

Cy raised an eyebrow. "I didn't know you could pick locks."

"You didn't ask," Lisa said with a smile, as she knelt down in front of the cabinet and began to work the lock with the unbent paperclip. "This may take a bit. One of my Cherokee uncles living in the Nation had an old tool shed with a lock that he had to pick half the time because the key was so old and worn out, and he wouldn't get a new one. He taught me how to pick it during the time I spent with him, and ... well ..." and with that she gave a little laugh, "... I further developed the skill on my own."

Cy laughed softly and shook his head. "You're incredible, Lisa."

"Thanks," Lisa said with a grin, as she continued to work the lock.

Cy turned away from Lisa to face Mercy. "While she's doing that, Ms. Parks, let me introduce us. I'm Corporal Cyrus Rappalo, U.S. Army, but you can call me Cy."

Cy was about to continue when Mercy cut him off. "And she's Lisa Stanridge," she said, finishing for him. "I recognize her."

"You do?" Cy said, looking surprised.

Mercy nodded. A sad expression flashed over her face when she spoke. "John, my late fiancé, was a NASCAR fan. He used to watch all kinds of car races, and went to some of the local ones as his work permitted. He even took me a few times, although I'm not a big a fan as he was. I was there at the track with him when Ms. Stanridge won the Bellville Cup. I remember seeing her at the awards ceremony." She then turned to Lisa and addressed her. "Nice to meet you, Ms. Stanridge. You're good."

"Thank you," Lisa said in reply, although she remained focused on picking the padlock, "and you can call me Lisa."

"You're welcome," Mercy said. There were tears in her eyes as she spoke. She quickly walked over to one of the desks, pulled a tissue from a box on it, and used it to dab at her eyes. "Forgive me," she said. "I've probably shouldn't have mentioned John."

"You said he was dead?" Cy asked.

Mercy nodded, still dabbing at her eyes. "We were both on the staff here, and we were the last two left alive. At the end, he shoved me in here and shut the door behind me. It opens out, as you noticed, and the zombies couldn't get in with him in front of it. That gave me just enough time to lock it, and ... and ...." She then choked out a sob. "I ... I heard him die. Th-the zombies ... they .... John ... he gave .. .he gave his life ... to save mine ..." With that she couldn't say any more. She began to go for the tissue box again, but by this time Cy had already snagged it and held it up before her. She gave him a look of gratitude as her tears flowed freely. "Thanks," she managed to get out, as she pulled another tissue and used it on her eyes..

"Not a problem," Cy said softly. He remembered the human remains just outside the security door, and then realized that was probably what was left of John. He shook his head sadly, but otherwise remained silent.

Just then there was a loud *klik!* from the cabinet in front of Lisa. "Got it," she said triumphantly, as she removed the open padlock from the door.

Mercy handed the box of tissues back to Cy, who took them and set them back down, and then he walked over to Lisa. "That's amazing," he said to her with admiration.

"It's nothing," Lisa said. She opened the cabinet. "Sweet Jesus," she exclaimed, looking at the various weapons and boxes of ammo inside. "Looks like we hit the jackpot."

"Yeah," Cy said, reaching for and picking up the weapon in the cabinet's lone center long gun storage slot. He eyed it appreciatively. "Police riot shotgun," he noted. "Probably something they had for emergencies."

"Ithaca M37," Lisa commented. She pointed to the lowest shelf in the cabinet, where several large and long metal shell boxes were arranged. "And there's the ammo for it."

"How do you know it's an Ithaca?" Cy asked. "I thought it was a Remington or Mossberg."

"Ambidextrous grip and its slam-fire underside shell feed," Lisa promptly responded. "Ithacas are made so they can be fired with either hand. Most shotgun makers don't do that, including Remington and Mossberg. You have to order theirs custom most of the time if you want a left-handed shotgun."

"The lady knows her weapons," Cy said with a smile. "I guess that comes from that gun nut Uncle Ray of yours."

"Uh-huh," Lisa said, while she removed an oversized weapons case from under two smaller ones inside the cabinet. She propped it up on one edge of the middle cabinet shelf and opened it. Her eyebrows went up and Cy whistled at what they saw inside. "Now that one I know," Cy said. "Ingram MAC autopistol."

"MAC-11, to be specific," Lisa said. "The .380 ACP version, not the original MAC-10 .45 ACP one. Still, it's got both the suppressor kit and plenty of .380 ACP ammo to go with it, and that's not a bad thing given our current fix." She closed the case and set it on the floor, then pulled out one of the smaller pistol cases, opened it, and examined its contents. She then turned the case so Cy could see as well. Inside was a compact automatic pistol and spare clip. "Walther PPK," Lisa explained. "American-made version by Ranger, rechambered for .380 ACP rounds instead of .32 ACP like regular Walthers."

"That's good," Cy said. "We're running low on .45 ACP ammo anyway."

"And both it and the MAC fire the same size and kind of round," Lisa said. ".380 ACP. Plenty of it here."

"Hey," Mercy said from behind them. Both turned to see her pull a compact revolver from one of her lab coat pockets and presented it to them. "Will that stuff work with this gun?"

"Where'd you get this?" Cy asked as he took the gun, looked it over, and then showed it to Lisa. She looked over, then back at him with a bemused smile.

"From John," Mercy answered, and a note of sadness again crept into her voice. "It was his personal gun. He gave it to me when things started getting bad. It helped get me in here, but I've only got half-a-box of shells left for it."

Lisa maintained her bemused smile as she spoke to Mercy. "I'm afraid not. That's a Smith and Wesson Model 36, better known as a Chief's Special. It's chambered for .38 Special rounds, not .380 ACP. Those have a flared rim on the end, and .380 ACP doesn't. Chances are these bullets would just fall out of the gun, since they're rimless."

"Oh," Mercy said, as Cy handed the pistol back to her and she returned it to her pocket.

"I'd hang onto it all the same, as long as you have ammo for it," Lisa said encouragingly. "You never know in situations like this."

"Now might be a good time to divvy all of this up, and maybe redistribute our weapons as well," Cy said, "since we've got such a mix now. It's not a good idea for any one of us to get too loaded down, you know."

Lisa set the pistol case down by the MAC-11 case on the floor, stood up, and turned so that she was facing both Cy and Mercy. "Before we do that," she said, "what about my transfusion?"

"Then you still want it?" Mercy said.

"Yes," Lisa answered. "I've been in constant exposure to infected people since this whole thing started. I don't know why I haven't turned yet and I'm glad I haven't, but like I said earlier I may already be infected and the virus is just taking its sweet time with me. Cy here got immunized by the government before he came in with that convoy," she said, thumbing in his direction. "That's why I want that transfusion. I know he's immune."

"Speaking of which," Cy said, "why aren't you infected, Mercy?"

The nurse smiled faintly. "It's because I've been immunized too."

"Whoa," Lisa said, lifting a hand up to one of the weapon cabinet's open doors and gripping it. "You mean to say that the hospital's had the antidote *all this time?!*" Anger now began to lace her words. "And you didn't *use it?!*"

"We didn't have enough," Mercy said weakly. "As soon as we realized what was happening, everyone on the lab staff with whom I worked promptly immunized ourselves, so we wouldn't turn and could still help others. We started using what little we had left, but we ran out fast. After that we then tried to get more from Pandora, but they refused every request for more." Her own voice became agitated. "We were begging and pleading with them by the end, because we knew what was going to happen, but they wouldn't answer." She now looked sick. "After that, what happened was inevitable." She cast her eyes to the floor. "A lot of good it did them. They're all dead now, including John, and I'm the only one left."

Now Lisa looked really angry. "Pandora. I should have known," she muttered. She looked at Cy and spoke more clearly. "Word on the street had it that the infection originated at the Pandora complex north of town."

"That's what the Army was told too," Cy replied. He then looked sternly at Mercy. "We'll deal with that issue later. Right now we need to deal with the matter of Lisa's transfusion."

Mercy looked back and forth between her two new companions, both of whom were visibly angry. She gulped and nodded. "I'm still willing to do it," she said. "I couldn't save those other people, but I can certainly save you."

"I'm properly grateful," Lisa growled. "As I understand it, we need to go to the third floor for the transfusion gear."

"No we won't," Mercy interjected. "There's transfusion equipment on this floor in the lab where I worked. We can get it there and bring it back here where it's safe, provided we can get there. Also Lisa, if you don't mind, I'd like to take some samples and test your blood first."

"Why?" Lisa asked.

"Because I want to know why you haven't yet turned," Mercy replied. "Like you said, you've remained clear all this time despite all of the infected around you. That's not only remarkable but incredible, given how contagious the virus is. I'd like to know why."

"As long as I get that transfusion," Lisa said evenly.

"Agreed," Mercy said. She then spoke to Cy again. "Corporal, the lab where I worked is on the far end of the east wing on this floor. The equipment I need is portable, so like I said all we have to do is go get it and bring it back here. After that, I can work in safety while you do whatever else you need to do in here with that weapons locker."

Cy looked at Lisa, who gruffly nodded, then back at Mercy. "Okay. We'll help you go get it. However, after that and while you're helping Lisa, you need to level with us. You obviously know more about what's going on with this Outbreak than we do."

Mercy nodded. "Agreed. You saved my life, so it's a deal." She pulled her pistol and brandished it. "I'm not very good with this thing, but I'll do what I can. I owe you that much."

Lisa and Cy looked at each other, and then back again at Mercy. "It's a deal," Lisa said.

Getting to Mercy's lab and back to the security office again with both the equipment and supplies she needed proved surprisingly easy, given the fierce firefight Lisa and Cy had to go through to get to her. There were still a dozen or so zombies roaming the halls on the way, but there were never more than two at a time and these were easily dispatched with pistol shots. Once there, Cy grabbed a convenient gurney and the three of them put everything Mercy needed on it, then he and Lisa provided cover while Mercy wheeled it back with them. Once all three were back in the relative safety of the security office again, Lisa removed her gear and weapons and left them with Cy before going over to one of the nearby desks with Mercy, so the nurse could begin her blood work. Cy remained at the weapons locker with all of their gear old and new, as he began the job of sorting everything out and dividing it up among them as evenly as he could. At the same time Mercy drew three samples of Lisa's blood, then started testing the first one as soon as she was done. "This won't take long," she explained. "I know what I'm trying to find."

"That's good," Lisa said. "I wouldn't know where to begin."

Mercy gave a soft laugh as she adjusted the settings on the blood analyzer. "The virus has a very specific chemical and genetic signature. It's very easy to spot, if you know what you're ...." Her words trailed off as a chime sounded and she looked at the readout display, and then a look of amazement began to fill her face.

"What is it?" Lisa asked. Cy too looked up from what he was doing, having taken note of Mercy's unexpected reaction.

"Just a minute," Mercy said. She pulled out the blood sample that was currently in the machine, reset it, and then took another one of the samples she had taken from Lisa and inserted it. She set the machine and waited for it to return its results. When it did, her look of amazement grew. "This is impossible," she said in wonder. She then pulled the second sample, replaced it with her third and final one, and tested it too. She got the same results as with the first two. "Incredible," she said, and this time her voice was filled with awe. "Absolutely incredible."

"What's going on?" Cy asked from his spot at the weapons locker.

"Yeah," Lisa said. "What does it read? Am I infected or what?"

"No," Mercy said, and now a tone of reverence touched her voice. "You're clear, Lisa. Absolutely clear. Furthermore, you're going to stay clear. You don't need a transfusion and never will."

"Why?" Lisa asked.

"You're naturally immune to the *untotenvirus*."

"What?" Lisa said in surprise. "I am?"

"Yes," Mercy said. "You are."

"*Untotenvirus*." Cy said, loud enough to draw their attention and causing both of the women to turn towards him. "That sounds German."

"It is," Mercy said. She gave both him and Lisa a look. "Lisa, you might want to take a seat. You also might want to get more comfortable over there, Corporal. How the virus got that name is a long story. It's going to take me a while to tell what parts of it you need to know, and how it ultimately connects to the Outbreak in Metro City in the here and now."

CHAPTER 4
REGENSCHIRM'S LEGACY

Lisa had moved away from the desks and was currently sitting in the swivel chair in front of the closest security monitor workstation. That way she could be close to Cy if he needed her help with their gear, but also to give Mercy plenty of room to clean up her gear as she told her tale. Cy continued to work but listened intently, for the story Mercy was telling was as fascinating to him as it obviously was to Lisa. Mercy's revelation that whatever had happened with the Outbreak in Metro City in modern times had something to do with the Nazis back in World War II was both shocking and troubling. Cy had long been an avid fan of World War II inspired media and had several older relatives who had fought with various black units in the war. It had been over for forty years, and yet its aftershocks still sent out ripples that could be felt in modern times. This was apparently one of the most severe yet.

"All of this started with Himmler and his goofy SS science teams before the war," Mercy was saying as she stowed her medical gear. "They were into some really weird stuff. Most of it was nonsense, of course, tied into supporting the Nazi's wacky theories on race and eugenics and all that. They sent science teams on expeditions all over the world before the war in search of anything that would support their cause. You know, like those stories about secret Nazi bases in Antarctica and those *Raiders of the Lost Ark* movies about the Ark of the Covenant and the Holy Grail and all that? Those stories themselves aren't true, but they're based on things the Nazis did that actually happened before and during the war. They actually *did* send out official expeditions in search of holy relics, and ancient artifacts, and forbidden knowledge and all that."

"I know," Cy said. "I read about some of this stuff myself."

"And it was during one of those that they came up with this undergoat virus or whatever?" Lisa asked.

"*Untotenvirus*," Mercy corrected, as she stowed the last of her gear in her bag. She picked it up, walked over to the workstation next to Lisa, set the bag down by it, and took its swivel seat next to Lisa's, talking as she moved across the room. "You can call it the U-virus for short. That's what both the Nazis and later the Allies called it in almost all of the official reports." She let out a soft laugh. "Even today, we don't know exactly how they came up with it, when they did, or where. Those records were destroyed before the Allies could get their hands on them. All we know is that the U-virus was developed shortly before the war, because by the time the Allies heard about it Project Regenschirm was already well underway."

"What's that?" Cy asked.

"It was the name for a series of various related efforts connected with developing the U-virus as a biological weapon for multiple applications in the coming war. *Regenschirm* is the German word for umbrella, so that's why they used it. A lot of different stuff but all under the aegis or umbrella of the Nazi's weaponizing the U-virus for use against their foes."

"That's incredible," Lisa said. "Why isn't any of this in the history books?"

"Well, look around you," Mercy said with a sad smile, "and imagine all of this happening back during the war, or coming very close to it. Can you imagine how different the world would be today had the Nazis succeeded? That's why it isn't in the history books. The Allies suppressed knowledge about both the U-virus and Regenschirm, along with where it was being developed, for the common good."

"Where was that?" Cy asked.

Mercy gave a little laugh. "At a place the history books will tell you never existed. At an installation that the official Allied war record says was never built, and was nothing but a big propaganda bluff instituted by Goebbels at the end of the war to fool Allied intelligence. It was real, though, and its name was the Alpenfestung. The English term is National Redoubt, by the way."

"The National Redoubt?!" Cy said incredulously. "Oh, come on. You're yanking my chain."

"No I'm not," Mercy said. "I've talked to people who went to the ruins after the war was over, and I've read the official post-war Allied reports of the investigators they sent there. The ruins are buried so deep in the Bavarian Alps in southern Germany that you won't know they're there unless you know where to look. The Allies made sure of that after the war. All you'll see these days are a series of rock falls, but it's there. It was real, and it really existed, and if you could get away with getting there and digging down deep enough, eventually you'd find what's left of the Alpenfestung and Project Regenschirm."

Lisa snorted. "I don't know if I can buy all that. I mean, it's a pretty tall story, and we have only your word for it."

"And the U-virus," Mercy added. "Don't forget the U-virus."

"How can I?" Lisa shot back fiercely. "My brother's dead because of people who got infected by it."

"And so is Mercy's fiancé, and everybody in my convoy save me," Cy said hurriedly, "not to mention the whole town and almost everyone in the surrounding countryside." He had noted the anger in Lisa's voice. "Settle down, okay?"

Lisa gave him a look and then continued. "May I ask a pertinent question?"

"Sure," Mercy said. "What is it?"

"How do you know all of this? That's pretty offbeat stuff for a nurse at a hospital to know. And assuming your story is true, which I'm still not sure of, a lot of that stuff would have been classified. How come you know about it?"

There was a pause as Lisa locked eyes with Mercy. Both Lisa's anger and skepticism were plain to see on her face. For her part, Mercy smiled faintly, cleared her throat, and then spoke again. "I may as well tell you now, because it would have come out sooner or later anyway. I'm not a real nurse, although I know how to do the job. The fact that I could do my own blood tests should have tipped you off. Real nurses don't do that. They hand that work off to lab technicians." She again paused, noting Lisa's suddenly furrowed brow and Cy's intent look, and then continued. "My nurse's job was merely a cover for my real work. I'm a senior biogenetic research specialist with Pandora Corporation on loan to Metro City--"

Mercy never finished her sentence. In a flash Lisa leapt out of her seat, grabbed the older woman by the throat, knocked her out of her chair, and bore her down to the floor with both hands locked tightly around Mercy's windpipe. *"PANDORA?!?I"* Lisa screeched. *"YOU'RE WITH PANDORA, BITCH?! THEY KILLED MY BROTHER!!! YOU KILLED MY BROTHER!!! YOU AND ALL OF THOSE SONS OF BITCHES KILLED MY BROTHER!!!"* She would have screamed more, but Cy was on her in an instant and pulling her off of the half-strangled Mercy, forcing Lisa to unlock her fingers from around the woman's throat as he did.

"NO, Lisa!" Cy cried. He somehow managed to pry Mercy free of Lisa's grip and pull the angry young woman off of her. *"Calm down! Don't do it, you hear!!"*

"Let me go!" Lisa howled. *"I'm gonna kill that bitch for lying to us!! She's with Pandora, you hear?!! PANDORA!!!"*

Cy dragged the kicking and struggling young woman back to the weapons locker and forced her to sit down on the floor, his arms still gripped tightly around her. "No she *didn't*," he said, loudly but evenly. "She just didn't tell us the whole truth right away, but don't forget we didn't ask and we didn't have any reason to. Now she's doing it entirely on her own, and without us making her." His voice now dropped to a conversational tone, although it was still laced with emotion. "Don't blame Mercy for what her bosses did, Lisa. She's helped us and answered every question we've asked her so far. Remember that she's stuck in the same boat we are. She's just a link in a chain, and she and her people were left to die by that same bunch that was behind the death of your brother, my outfit, and everyone else in Metro City. Just because she really works for Pandora doesn't make her an evil person, okay? If it did, then I'm a baby killer for what the Army did to Vietnamese civilians back in 'Nam, and you're guilty for all the killing done among the white settlers and soliders by all of the American native peoples back in the Wild West. Neither one of us are killers, and neither is Mercy, so settle down. You're better than this. I know you are." With that he looked straight into her eyes. "Please?" he asked.

Cy's words had the desired effect. Lisa had stopped struggling to get free as she listened. At the same time, the still-gasping Mercy had struggled back to her seat, righted the chair, and sat back down in it, massaging her throat and taking deep breaths. As for Lisa, she was sitting still in Cy's arms by the time he finished. She looked back at him for the longest time, until he saw the anger melt from her face. It was replaced by a thoughtful expression. "This is all crazy, you know," she said in a very small and contrite voice.

"I know," Cy said. He let go of Lisa, then reached up and put two comforting hands on her shoulders. "Just remember. All of us have lost in this. Her too. We're all caught in this, and we're all stuck here together. That we have in common. What we've got to do now is work together for our common good so we can survive ... and we need her." He looked over at the recovering Mercy, and then back at Lisa. "I mean, where else are we going to get someone to play doctor for us if one of us gets hurt really bad?"

Lisa looked at Cy and he back, and then she let a smile begin to form on her face. "Okay," she said softly. "You're right. I just kind of got carried away, I guess. You know?"

"I know," Cy said with a smile. He gave her shoulder a small squeeze.

Lisa lifted a hand and put it on one of Cy's own. They looked at each other for several seconds, and then Lisa turned to Mercy. who had finally quit spluttering and had started to breathe normally again. "I'm sorry, Mercy."

"It's all right," Mercy said in a hoarse voice. "I understand. Had I been in your shoes, I might have done the same. I feel the same way about John. For what it's worth, you're forgiven." She stopped and coughed several times while a look of remorse began to fill Lisa's face. Mercy saw it, smiled and nodded, coughed again and cleared her throat, and then continued in a voice that was still touched with hoarseness. "Anyway, I know what I know because it was part of my job. You see, it was Pandora who was contracted by the U.S. military after the war to redevelop the U-virus for us, once they got their hands on it."

"But how did they do that?" Cy asked, as he guided Lisa back to her seat. "I mean, get the virus? You said yourself that the National Redoubt was destroyed during the war and all traces of it covered over afterwards."

"Well, they must have gotten their hands on it somehow in spite of that," Lisa noted.

"That's true," Mercy said. Again the sad smile returned to her face. "They got it *during* the war, before the Redoubt was destroyed, and in one of the most daring commando raids of the war. That too was part of the real history that got suppressed by the authorities, but I had to know it as part of my job. It's quite a story, really." She started to laugh, coughed instead, and then settled back down. "I won't tell you all of it because it would take too long, but I'll try to hit the high points. Back in 1943 an Allied deep undercover agent by the name of Anne Bradshaw, who was working as a communication technician at Luftwaffe headquarters in Berlin, began spotting some rather unusual message traffic regarding the National Redoubt. She began to monitor it under the cover of her job, and that's when she found out about Regenschirm. She let the Allies know at once, but they were skeptical at first and you can understand why."

"I'll bet," Cy said. Lisa simply nodded.

"They had a lot of freaky things going under the aegis of Regenschirm, but the two that concerned the Allies the most and us now involve what was being done with the U-virus. The first and most practical use the Nazis saw for it was to develop a weaponized form that they could use on the battlefield, and have the dead fight for them in the Nazi cause. *Anybody's* dead," she added, emphasizing the word *anybody*. "The second was using it in conjunction with applied eugenics and what little they knew of genetic engineering and cybernetics back then to create a race of super soldiers that they called *ubermensch*, stronger and faster and more powerful than any ordinary soldiers." Mercy gave a little laugh. "Actually the correct term is *supersoldaten*, but they used *ubermensch* because it was a racial term and they knew that would throw off Allied intelligence for a while, given the Nazi's own kooky racial doctrines and all. Put all of those new super soldiers together with an army of the undead for ready cannon fodder that could potentially number in the millions, and now you know why the Allies were so worried about Regenschirm."

"Good lord," Cy said. "That would have been like what MacArthur had to face in Korea back in 1950, when a big part of the Communist Chinese

Army came over the border to support North Korea and to keep him from beating them. The Allies would have been overwhelmed."

"Precisely," Mercy continued, "and when the Nazis had the Wehrmacht conduct a small-scale test of the U-virus on part of the Russian front earlier that year, they were able to punch a hole clean through it with the help of a local undead army of zombies they raised on the spot. The only thing that stopped them was that the Russians responded by calling in every tank, piece of artillery, and rocket truck into the area and hit them with everything they had. It was a close thing, but the Russians eventually succeeded."

"So what happened next?" Lisa asked.

The sad look returned to Mercy's face as she continued. "The Gestapo eventually figured out Ms. Bradshaw was a spy and she was arrested. It was too late for the Nazis, though. She had already supplied the Allies with enough intel on Regenschirm that they knew what they were facing, and they also had the hard data from that battle with the Russians to back it up. The icing on the cake was when they got the plans for the Redoubt itself, which was part of her last data drop to them before the Gestapo captured her. That's when the Allies put together a commando team to take out Regenschrim at its very heart: within the Redoubt itself."

"So what happened to Ms. Bradshaw?" Lisa asked.

"A lot," Mercy said, looking down. She swallowed hard, and then continued. "They tortured her just because they could, and for betraying what they were planning on doing to the Allies. She was eventually rescued, but she had been tortured pretty bad. Fortunately one of their own test subjects saved her life, and he took care of her until her brother came to rescue her."

"Her brother?"

"Yes. Major Jack Bradshaw. He was the leader of the commando team, and had been hand-picked for the mission because of her involvement in the whole thing. He was quite a guy, according to the official reports, and he had a really good team to help him rescue his sister and take out Regenschirm."

"We could use somebody like that right now," Cy commented.

Lisa managed a smile. "I thought we already had someone."

Cy caught her smile, then turned away with a sheepish grin. "Oh, I'm nobody. I'm just a soldier doing my job."

"You know, that's what he and all of the survivors from his team said after the war, when they finally got back from Switzerland after being interned there once their mission was done," Mercy said with a chuckle.

"*Switzerland?*" Lisa asked. Her face had taken on a strangely intent look that surprised both Cy and Mercy.

"Yes," Mercy said. "They had to flee over the border to Switzerland after the mission was over to escape getting captured themselves, since it was close at hand, and that's how they got interned there. Standard procedure for the Swiss, they being neutral and all that. That's where Major Bradshaw, his sister Anne, and the survivors of his commando team wound up spending the rest of the war. Why?"

"My grandfather on my mother's side of the family fought in the war," Lisa said, still with that strangely intent look on her face. "That's the white side, by the way, and why I'm only half-Cherokee. He was a Marine Raider who started out in the Pacific, but wound up in Europe helping out over there. The weird thing is that he only went on one mission after he got over there, but he wound up escaping to Switzerland too and getting interned there, just like these guys you're talking about. It was also in the same year: 1943."

Mercy's brow furrowed. "Maybe it's a coincidence. Maybe not. Tell me, what was the mission on which your grandfather got interned?"

"That's the thing," Lisa replied. "He never would talk about it. Both he and Grandma Zimmerman said it was classified."

"*Zimmerman?!*" Mercy exclaimed. She held her right hand up before Lisa, forefinger up, as if she were a schoolteacher about to make a point. "Tell me. Is your grandfather's name James Zimmerman, and did he hold the rank of first lieutenant during the war?"

"Yes to both," Lisa answered, "although everyone but us kids called him Jimmy. That's what he preferred. Why?"

Mercy looked excited. "Jimmy Zimmerman. Lt. James 'Jimmy' Zimmerman, United States Marine Corps. What are the odds? No. It's no coincidence. It's a miracle." Mercy suddenly stood upright and looked at Lisa. There was an almost surreal look to her face as she solemnly spoke her next words. "Your grandfather was the Marine Raider who went on that mission with Major Bradshaw to take out Project Regenschirm. That's why he got interned in Switzerland."

Lisa looked perplexed. "He was? How can you be so sure?"

"Because it's in the official records, and because of your immunity to the U-virus," Mercy said triumphantly. She now took in both Lisa and Cy with her gaze. "Listen to me. In his statement after the war to the Allied authorities, Lt. Zimmerman said that both he and Major Bradshaw were inoculated against the U-virus by an Italian scientist at the Redoubt who on her own decided to turn traitor and help them. She's the one who provided samples of everything to Major Bradshaw's team in a nicely packed case to take out with them, by the way. The U-virus, the vaccine, the antidote if infected, initial paperwork, the lot."

"So what happened to her?" Lisa asked. "That scientist?"

Mercy gave her a sad look. "The Nazis shot her after it was all over for being a traitor."

"Figures," Cy said disgustedly.

"Anyway, Lisa," Mercy continued, "that's why you're immune to the U-virus. You're immune because of your grandfather, who in turn passed his immunity on to your mother, who in turn passed hers on to you."

"Now wait a minute," Cy interjected. "I'm not doubting Lisa's immune. That's a fact none of us can argue with, and I guess that's as good as reason as any as to why she's remained clear through all of this. I've just never heard of immunities being passed on from mother to child and such. That's why they give you all of those inoculations when you're kids, right?"

"Wrong," Mercy replied. "A mother can pass on some of her own natural immunities to her unborn child while still in the womb. This helps the child out for the first few months after it's born, until its own immune system becomes strong enough to take up the load. You also have to consider the fact the U-virus isn't normal to begin with. It's in a class of man-made disease all by itself. Furthermore, it is possible for mothers to pass along conditions they have other than natural immunities to their children. Haven't you heard of crack babies, Corporal?"

"Yes, but that's with drugs, and this is different."

"Cy," Lisa said, cutting him off. He looked at her and she looked back. "Let it go. What Mercy is saying is right. We're dealing with something here that isn't normal and doesn't behave by the normal rules. Mercy knows far more about this than either one of us. Besides, according to her and if I heard her right, it's in my genes. I got this from my grandfather through my mother at conception, so you're barking up the wrong tree anyway. Let it go. Okay?"

Cy looked back at her for a moment or two, thinking of the irony of the situation. A few minutes ago, he had been the one trying to rein Lisa in. Now their roles were reversed. "Okay," Cy replied, emphasizing his response with a slight nod.

"Thanks," Mercy said to Lisa, and then continued to address them both. "Anyhow, the United States government, being the strongest power among the Allies, we got to claim that sample case as our own. After the war, it was turned over to what eventually became Pandora so they could further refine and develop the U-virus for our own use on the battlefield, if we ever needed it."

"Now that I can believe," Cy said disgustedly. "Makes me think of what happened with Agent Orange and the Vietnam War, or all of those LSD experiments they were conducting, or those little atomic 'accidents' and 'accidental' radiation exposure that's been happening all this time and which they've hushed up each and every time."

Mercy nodded. "You've got the picture. Both the government and Pandora have been experimenting with and further refining and developing the U-virus over the past forty years, just like they did with all of their other biological warfare stuff they weren't supposed to be developing and supposedly weren't. It's a lot tougher now, and it's available in both the original fast-acting and newer delayed-action forms."

"*Delayed action?*" Lisa asked.

"Right," Mercy replied. "It doesn't activate until a day or so after it's infected someone, and the infected take longer to turn. That way, any enemy soldier who got infected would take it back with them and infect his entire troop, or his whole base, or whatever before it would start working, and of course by then a few days would have passed and it would be too late."

"Damn," Cy said. "I can see how that would work in a war."

Mercy nodded. "It's the delayed action form that somehow got out of our lab complex north of town. That was what caused the Outbreak, and because of that nobody knew what was happening until it was too late." She smiled and chuckled. "And all this time, Mother Nature has been hard at work developing and refining her own solution to our little man-made nightmare. Furthermore, it's right here with us. I know I said this before but what are the odds of that happening? It's funny, the way she works sometimes. Well, not funny. Ironic would be more like it."

"So how exactly do I fit into this grand picture you're painting for us?" Lisa asked. One might have thought she was being sarcastic were it not for the look of complete honesty on her face.

Mercy pursed her lips. "My guess is that at some point," she said, "probably with your mother or you, most likely your mother, her body developed a specific genetic mutation tied to the X-chromosome that allowed her to synthesize the U-virus antidote on her own. To put it another way, that process became part of her genetic makeup, and only the high strangeness of all this made that possible. She then passed the genetic factor for that specific mutation on to you when you were born. Of course I'd need a proper research lab with the equipment to confirm it, but I'd be willing to bet money on it." She now directed her gaze at Lisa again. "If you ever have any kids, Lisa, they're probably going to be born immune. I'm also willing to bet that both your mother and brother are fully immune, just like you."

"That's something we'll never know, now that my brother's dead," Lisa said quietly, and neither Cy nor Mercy could miss the tones of bitterness and anger that touched her voice.

Mercy gulped, and then nodded. "I'm sorry, Lisa. I'm sorry I brought it up."

"I'm sorry too," Lisa replied. She let out a long sigh. "For all I know, Mom and Dad are both dead too. I haven't been able to get in touch with either one of them since all of this started."

"Oh, that's bad," Mercy replied. She then looked at Cy. "If that's true, then we've got to make sure Lisa escapes Metro City no matter what, and that she gets federal protection instead of winding up with my employers as soon as she can." She looked at Cy, who slowly nodded, and then continued. "You're the one-in-a-million wild card in all of this, Lisa, and it has everything to do with your inherited natural immunity. You're the living proof that Mother Nature can beat the U-virus, given enough time, and Pandora won't like that. They won't like that one bit, and you can make a good guess as to how they'll probably respond from there." She began to walk as she talked, pacing in a little loop in front of Lisa and Cy. "Natural immunity developing across generations. It's something we never considered. My specialty at Pandora was in researching and further developing both the U-virus antidote and immunizing agents that were originally developed by the Nazis for *current* victims, ones already infected. You have to give the immunizing agent to the subject before they get infected, because it's useless once they are. That's where the antidote comes into play, but even it has only a limited window of time before the victim is too far gone for it to work either." She stopped pacing and again looked at both of them. "I tell you all of that to tell you this: Pandora has never done any generational studies on the U-virus, the vaccine, or the antidote because there was no perceived need."

"Never?" Lisa asked.

Mercy nodded. "Never. With regards to the test subjects ... oh, how do I politely put this? They either died from their reactions to the test substance or were quietly, uhmm, *disposed of?* And of course, when you're working with people who are already sick or deathly ill, and have signed blanket waivers regarding their health - that's why Pandora had us at the hospital - you can test away without worrying about whether or not your subject is going to live through the test or anyone making waves provided you have both your story and all the paperwork straight. Furthermore, you'll get away with it because of those signed waivers."

"That's disgusting," Lisa said evenly.

"That's Pandora," Mercy replied, "and I admit both my own guilt and complicity in that." She gave them both a look of deep regret, and then resumed both her pacing and her talking. "I justified it on grounds of those signed waivers, and it being just part of my job, but still .... Oh, what's the use? I'm as guilty as hell and I know it. Oh, I never got my hands dirty with doing any of the actual *disposing*, but I knew about it, and that makes me guilty all the same." She looked at both of them earnestly. "I'd take it all back if I could, because what I did in the name of science is part of the reason why the three of us are in this mess right now. Maybe it's God's way of punishing me for my part in this." With that she fell silent and looked at the floor.

All was silent for a space, until Cy spoke. "Mercy, I forgive you. You'll have to answer for what you've done once we're out of here, but I'll let the proper authorities handle that. Right now survival is the most important thing on the table."

"Me too," Lisa chimed in. She gave a sad little laugh. "It's kind of funny, you know? Ten minutes ago I wanted to kill you, and here I am now willing to forgive you about knowing that others were being killed in the name of science as part of this mess." She gave another sardonic laugh, this one somewhat longer. "Oh, what a crazy, messed-up fix we're in here in what's left of Metro City!"

"Thanks," Mercy said, quietly but earnestly. "For both of you. And you're right, Cy. I will have to answer for what I've done once we're out of here. I know that, and I accept it." She took in a deep breath and let it back out again. "Anyway, back to the subject of your inherited immunity, Lisa. As I said, Pandora's never done generational studies because in their eyes they've never been warranted. You're the living proof that they should have. Like the Nazis before them, Pandora only needed the immunizing agent to protect its own and any federal government personnel involved in the research, and the antidote only for those occasions when things went wrong."

"Like with Metro City," Cy said gruffly, "only they wouldn't let you have more antidote."

Mercy pursed her lips. "I don't know what my superiors were thinking, but I know this. They let an entire city of seventy-five thousand people turn, and were going to let me and John and the rest of our people turn right along with them, just to save their own corporate asses." She now stopped pacing and looked straight at Lisa. "You know what'll happen if they ever get their hands on you."

Lisa nodded. "I'll disappear, or worse," she said grimly. "Like the Gestapo did to that Bradshaw woman during the war. Pandora will seize me and spirit me away out of sight and mind. They'll make sure I become just another victim of the Outbreak in public eyes. Once I'm out of the official record, they can then do with me whatever they want."

Cy's eyes widened. "The government would never let them do that," he exclaimed.

"Oh yes they would, if certain people in power who are hand-in-glove with Pandora got control of the situation," Mercy said evenly. "They'd make the both of us go away too, because we're witnesses to Lisa's existence. The SS had a term for it back during the war – *nacht und nebel.* By that they meant you would disappear into the night and fog and never be seen again. It would be as if you never existed. That's what's facing all three of us via Pandora for what we know, and the people who would do it don't give a damn about our constitutional rights or whatever. Understand?"

Cy started to say something and then stopped. He looked at Lisa. She had a worried look on her face. He next turned back to Mercy, and saw the same worried look in hers too, save that it was rooted in knowledge based on her own background and experiences with Pandora that neither he nor Lisa had. "All right," he conceded. "So how do we get out of this mess?"

"I think your original plan is still the best," Mercy replied. "Get in touch with your people beyond the barricade, and let them know we've survived. Don't mention what's special about Lisa until you can talk to your commanding officer."

"General Ryan's a good man, and he's not political," Cy responded quickly. "He's also well liked by President Reagan even though he's only a brigadier. He's even been invited to the White House a time or two on special occasions."

"There you have it," Mercy said. For the first time, Lisa and Cy heard the note of hope in her voice. "Try to get in touch with him by whatever secure means the Army uses. Once you do, then let him know about Lisa. After that, it'll be up to him. If he's as good a man as you say he is, then we should be all right."

"You don't mind if we don't go ahead and try to meet him halfway, do you?" Lisa said, leaning forward on her seat. "I'm talking about getting out of here, of course. I don't want to spend one more minute in what's left of Metro City than I have to."

"We won't," Cy said, getting back up to his feet. "Look, I've got everything split out and portioned for all three of us. We'll shuffle our weapons somewhat accordingly, but I'm ready to leave as soon as you two are. Before we do, though, we need to get to the hospital's radio transmitter so we can call the Army and let them know we're coming."

"We can't," Mercy responded flatly. "The zombies trashed the transmitter yesterday during their first mass attack on the hospital."

"Oh, great!" Lisa said with a groan, putting a hand to her forehead. "What, is the radio going to be smashed beforehand every time we get to one?"

"What about the phone?" Cy said. "You called us on the phone to get our attention, remember?"

"That's because Metro City Medical has its own private internal exchange," Mercy said. "All the outside lines have been dead since yesterday, once the Army imposed the quarantine."

"Okay, will have to save trying to communicate with my superiors for the police station, assuming we can still get there and its transmitter isn't wrecked either," Cy said, looking at both women. "Right now, we're going to get ready to saddle up and move out. Lisa, you get your AK-47, the MAC-11, and one of the new Walthers and ammo for all. I'll keep the China Lake and my M-16 and add to it the Ithaca, but I'll also keep my .45 and take all of what .45 ammo we've got left. I'll also keep your .45 in my rucksack for storage, Lisa. Mercy, you keep your pistol, but you're also going to get the other Walther and Lisa's M-16."

"Good call all around," Lisa said. She lowered her hand, got up, and went toward the rucksack and pile of gear with the AK by it. "Giving me both a pistol and machine pistol with shared ammo is a good idea."

"Why is that?" Mercy asked.

"Saves on the ammo load she has to carry," Cy responded quickly, before Lisa could answer. "I'm also betting she's a better shot than you, and can handle that MAC-11 better than you can," he added, giving Lisa a wink.

"One thing I should point out," Mercy said, picking up the unfamiliar weapon. "I've never handled an M-16 before."

"You're about to learn how," Cy said. He went to his own gear and began to put it on his person, motioning for Mercy to do the same with hers. "Once we're ready, Lisa, I want you to stay here and use these security monitors to find us the safest way out of here possible. Mercy, I want you to come with me. We're going to go out for a bit, and I'm going to give you a brief lesson on how to use an M-16. Just the basics, until you're comfortable with it. Lisa, I want you to have us an escape route planned by the time we're back."

"Got it," Lisa said, as she returned to her seat, set her AK and MAC-11 to one side but within easy reach, and then began to study the security monitors on both workstations.

"That's my girl," Cy said jokingly.

"You wish," Lisa shot back, but she did so with a smile.

"Hey, can you blame a guy for trying?" Cy responded with one eyebrow cocked.

Lisa turned in time to catch his gaze and held it for a few seconds. Her smile got even bigger as she responded. "Once we're out of here, Corporal Rappalo, I just might have to take you up on that."

"Is that an invitation to a date?"

Lisa regarded Cy for a few moments, then gave him a smile. "Maybe."

"Then I'm honored," Cy said, feeling a sudden flush come over his face.

"I'm sure you are," Lisa said. "You and Mercy better get that shooting lesson started, or we're going to be late getting out of here."

"Uh, yeah. Sure. Mercy?" With that, he escorted the ersatz nurse towards the security office door.

About twenty minutes had passed since Cy and Mercy had left Lisa alone in the security office. It was during this time that Cy gave Mercy the promised quick lesson in properly handling an M-16A1 assault rifle. After that, the two of them engaged in some brief informal zombie hunting among those that remained in the fifth floor south wing before making their way back to the security office again. They talked as they walked but kept their eyes peeled and weapons at the ready, just in case some zombies decided to pop out of a side door or some of the zombie bodies liberally scattered on the floor in the hallways were only playing possum.

"This isn't as bad as I thought it would be," Mercy said as she and Cy moved through the main hallway together. "Handling this thing, I mean, not the killing."

"I know what you mean," Cy replied.

"All the same, I can see now how people get sucked into that," Mercy went on.

"Into what?"

"The killing. Taking out whatever issues they have in dishing out death to anyone around them." She sighed. "I found it hard to pull the trigger at first, thinking of the human beings these things used to be, until I remembered what they did to John and the horrible way he died. After that it was easy." She gave Cy a knowing look. "I feel the same way about what happened to him as Lisa does about her brother."

'I know," Cy said. He forced a smile. "Just do us all a favor, okay? Don't let it get to you like Lisa did. We need to stick together if we're going to survive, and anyone getting obsessed over this thing will endanger us all."

"I know," Mercy said quietly, "and I think Lisa does too. We women just can't help it sometimes, you know? We're wired to be emotional. You guys are the ones wired to stay calm and cool and collected when the crap hits the fan."

"And sometimes we can get too cool and collected, and then you wind up with cold-blooded killers," Cy replied. "Personally, I don't think any of that normal psychological mumbo-jumbo applies in this situation. All of us have had our turn freaking out during the Outbreak. I did it when half a town full of zombies was chasing me down the street, you did it over the phone when you first got in touch with us, and Lisa did it a little while ago when she found out what you really are. Nobody's immune to the Outbreak, not even us guys. We've just got to take what punches we can and roll with the rest of it as we're able."

"Sound advice, Cy."

"Thank you, Mercy."

They were back at the security office by then. "Lisa, it's us," Cy called out. "We're alone." There was a buzz and the sound of the door unlocking. Cy opened the door and then ushered Mercy inside, closing the door behind them.

Lisa re-locked the door from the control board at the security station where she sat. "Welcome back," she said. "How did it go?"

"Very well, all things considered," Cy said with a smile. "Mercy did all right."

Mercy managed a laugh. "I'll never be able to handle this thing in full auto and keep it on target, but I'm all right on single shot."

"That's good," Lisa said encouragingly. "Now it's my turn. I've got good news and I've got bad news."

"Bad news first," Cy said, as he and Mercy came to stand by Lisa at the security station."

"I figured you'd want that," Lisa said. "The bad news is we're going to have to find another way out of here. Look," and with that she pointed to one of the security monitors on the second row above the control board. "That's my 'Cuda, and it's surrounded by the same sea of zombies that's currently filling the hospital parking lots and spilling out into both streets."

Cy's jaw dropped as he first looked at the monitor screen Lisa indicated and then what was showing on some of the other screens. "Good lord," he muttered. "Looks like there's thousands of them! There weren't that many when we were out there earlier."

"No, but as long as we've been in here, and that first batch knowing we were here, I'm guessing they called in a bunch of their friends," Lisa said grimly. "Or maybe the others homed in on the smell of fresh blood or something. I don't know. Anyway, I'm guessing every zombie on this side of town that's still mobile is down there, and they've filled the whole front of the hospital's lobby and central sections. We can't get back to my 'Cuda without a major fight, and there's too many of them for us to simply plow our way through them and out of here, Cy, like we did back at the Armory."

"It's like downtown all over again," Cy said softly. He looked at the newest member of their group. "Hey Mercy," he said, looking over at her, "what do you think?"

Mercy walked up to the monitors and studied their images for a few seconds, and then she spoke. "Pandora's main theory is along the same lines as the smell of blood concept Lisa mentioned. Zombies have altered senses due to their infection, and because of that they pick up on different things than we humans do."

"Like the smell of fresh blood, or perhaps they can sense where more humans, ummm, more *food* is located?" Cy said.

"Right," Mercy nodded. "They think it's a homing instinct of sorts. Not quite like a shark smelling blood, but more like ants responding to an imperative from their queen."

"Which begs the question," Lisa asked. "Where's the queen?"

"Pandora hasn't yet found an answer to that part," Mercy replied.

Cy looked thoughtful. "You know, we need to start taking this into account once we get out of here and get to our next stop. That is, assuming we get out of here."

"What's that?" Lisa asked.

"Giving the zombies enough time to gang back up on us," Cy said. "It's happened to us twice now, Lisa. The first time was at the Armory. This is the second time. We don't need a third, because we might not survive that one." He thought for a few seconds, and then added, "Now that I think about it, I'm guessing we have about twenty minutes at any given location, twenty-five tops, thirty at the most extreme. After that, we can expect to face what we're facing here right now. We've got to remember that next time."

"*If* there's a next time," Lisa added thoughtfully.

Cy nodded. "Yeah. *If.*"

Mercy had been studying the security monitor screens as Cy talked. She now spoke, looking at them both as she did. "Cy, there may be a way we could get to Lisa's car, save ammo, and even possibly fight our way to the streets and beyond," Mercy said. As the other two watched, she walked over to where the medicine cabinet was mounted on the back wall. She picked up the bottle of rubbing alcohol and brought it back with her, holding it up before them. "We can use these. The hospital is full of them, and we've got plenty of gauze to use for flaming wicks."

"Ahhh, Molotov cocktails," Cy said, and he couldn't help but grin.

"That's a good idea," Lisa said, allowing herself a smile, "but it still doesn't guarantee success. We'd have to carry an awful lot of them to both clear a way to my car and clear space around and in front of it so we could get out. I don't think we can lug enough down there along with our existing gear to do the job."

"What about flaming torches?" Cy asked. "Plenty of crutches around here, and other things that are long and straight around which we could wrap alcohol-soaked gauze or cloths."

"Another good idea," Lisa said. She thought a moment, and then continued. "We're still facing the same problem of being too encumbered with everything we'd have to carry. Also, once a torch goes out, those zombies will probably be on us before we have time to light another."

"Oh," Mercy said. She looked down at the floor. "Well, I tried."

"We can still use part of your idea," Lisa said encouragingly. "The Molotov cocktails, and even your torches, Cy. I think they're going to be essential to my own plan, and that's the good news."

"What's that?" Cy asked.

"I think I've figured out another way out of here, one that gets us past most of the zombies and gets all of us to the MCPD station on the other side of the block. It means we'll have to abandon my 'Cuda and leave it behind, much as I don't want to, but we can probably get more wheels at the station. That's where we wanted to go after this in the first place, remember?"

Cy looked at Mercy and she back, then both of them looked at Lisa. "Go ahead," Cy encouraged. "We're listening."

Lisa flipped a series of switches on the control panel before her, and a new set of images promptly flashed up on the screens of the top row of security monitors. She then picked up a piece of paper from in front of her that looked very much like an enlarged street map, and held it up before them. She pointed to it or to the appropriate monitor as she talked. "I found this on one of the desks over there. It shows the outside layout for not only the hospital, but the entire block. That includes Southwest Sporting Goods down the way and the MCPD substation on the other side. Two places where we need to go anyway, Cy. Now look here," and with that she pointed to the center of the map. "See this long alley? It runs the length of the block from the back of the hospital all the way to the back of the MCPD substation, and halfway down it also connects to the back of Southwest Sporting Goods. Those are the only three entrances or exits, if this map is right, and that makes this alley very convenient for us. Also, as you can see on these monitors, the emergency entrance at the back of the hospital is fairly free of zombies, and that's where we can get into the alley from our end. That's the entrance right there, off to the side of where the ambulances drive back out," she said, pointing to the next to last top monitor to the right. "That's how we can still get to both places, even though we'll be on foot now because of us not being able to use my car anymore."

"That's big enough to drive a truck down," Cy noted as he looked first at the map and then at the image of the alley entrance on one of the monitors.

"That's probably how the trucks got in to unload their freight at Southwest Sporting Goods," Lisa said. "See how this side drive from the front keeps any approaching vehicles clear of the hospital's emergency entrance looparound? I'll bet there's a matching one at the other end at the police station."

"Probably," Cy said. "Question. Why aren't there a lot of zombies back there? You'd think there would be, the way they're all over the front here."

"I can answer that," Mercy answered. "There's wrecks at both ends of the looparound. They're fairly sizeable, as both involve ambulances and trucks, with a few cars thrown in for good measure."

"I remember seeing one of those when we came in," Lisa observed.

Mercy nodded. "Those two pile-ups have got the whole back of the hospital pretty well sealed off from the outside. The only zombies that can get back there are ones that either find a way to crawl through or find a way through the hospital's first floor."

"And with the front fire doors pinned, plus that extra set we pinned on our way through there, then the back half of the first floor should still be fairly well clear," Cy added.

"It won't stay clear for long, once they realize we're down there," Mercy said.

"Agreed," Lisa said. "That's why we need to block the alley entrance behind us." She pointed to a catering truck that appeared to either be parked or stalled near the alley entrance. It was in perfect physical condition, although both of its cab doors were open and there were blood smears both on them and its front fenders. "We can use that truck as a barricade. It's in a perfect position, and we don't even have to start it. All we have to do is take it out of gear and push it in front of the alley entrance."

"You mean two of us push it while the third covers?" Cy suggested.

Lisa looked at him for a moment, and then nodded. "I stand corrected, and you're right. Once it's in place, we can crawl under it to the alley, and then set it on fire with our alcohol bottles once we're inside. That'll hold the zombies for a while."

"Sounds good," Cy said. He gave Mercy a look. "What do you think?"

"Me?" Mercy said. "I'm no fighter. You guys are the fighters. I'm just a medical researcher."

"A medical researcher turned zombie apocalypse survivor," Lisa said. When Mercy looked at her, Lisa gave her an encouraging smile. "You're part of the group now, Mercy, despite a past you honestly regret and what happened between you and me earlier, and I'm sorry for that last part.

Anyway, your opinion counts just as much as either of ours. So what do you think?"

Mercy looked at Lisa for a bit, and then at Cy. He gave her an encouraging look in reply. "Go ahead," he said.

"Okay," Mercy said. "I've no objections. Sounds good to me."

"Then let's saddle up and get out of here," Cy said. "We'll stop along the way and pick up as many alcohol bottles as we can comfortably carry, as well as crutch ends or anything similar we can use for torches, and plenty of gauze to wrap and burn on their ends, and after that it's the back stairwell and on our way."

"You might want these as well," Lisa said, as she both snagged her long guns and came to her feet in one fluid motion. She slung them over one shoulder, reached into one of her firesuit pockets, and then pulled out something, which she offered to both Cy and Mercy. In her hand were two cheap disposable cigarette lighters. "Found them in the desk along with that map," Lisa said, and then she gave Mercy a wink. "I've already got mine. I was thinking along the same lines you were with the Molotov cocktails, but you beat me to the punch in saying it. That's why I let you go ahead with it."

"Thanks," Mercy responded with a grin as she took the lighter, put it in her pocket, and then reached for a very large medical shoulder bag in which she had stowed all of her non-medical gear. That was in a smaller bag already slung over one shoulder. "At least all of us are on the same page,"

"And that's a good thing," Cy finished, brandishing his Ithaca as he did. He noted that Lisa hesitated, standing in front of the security workstation as she looked at a certain image on one of the screens of the second bank of security monitors. He moved up beside her to see for himself. The screen's image was a somewhat fuzzy and out-of-focus long shot view of Lisa's HemiCuda, still very much in one piece and still where she had parked it, but surrounded by a sea of zombies in constant motion around it. She became aware of his presence and turned to him. On her face was one of the saddest looks he had seen her give since he had first met her on their shared Outbreak adventure, aside from when she had talked about her late brother. "Sorry about your car," he said, his voice soft and introspective.

"I appreciate it," Lisa said. She bit her lower lip. "It's my decision, of course, and I know it's the right thing to do, given the fix we're in, but ... well ... I'm going to miss that car." She continued to stand there, looking at the monitor, fingering the set of car keys she was now holding in her hand. She managed a faint laugh, and then looked at him with sad eyes. "It's one of a kind, Cy. You know?"

"I know," Cy said, still keeping his voice low. He tried to put as much comfort and care in his own eyes as he could. "Maybe you can get another one once we get out of here."

"A Barracuda, maybe," Lisa replied, her voice also low, "but not a HemiCuda. They're too rare." She suddenly drew herself up, took in a deep breath, and then let it back out again. She shoved the car keys back into one of her firesuit pockets and then gripped her MAC-11 again. When she resumed speaking, her voice was calm and in its familiar normal tones. "Anyway, I've made my decision and I'm sticking to it." She again looked at Cy. "You know what else? I may have lost my brother, and my family, and along with them one of the rarest and best muscle cars in the world, but I've gained something just as important in return."

"What's that?"

Lisa looked him in the eye. "A new friend," she said quietly

Cy returned her look eye for eye. "Me too," he responded in a low tone.

They stood there for several seconds, simply looking at each other. Mercy remained respectfully quiet where she stood. After a few seconds, Cy cleared his throat. "Well, ummm, we better get going, you think?"

"I don't think, I know," Lisa said, as she suddenly grinned and brandished her new MAC-11. "Mercy?"

"Just waiting for you two to finish up making goggle eyes at each other," Mercy said, nodding as she held her own new M-16 at the ready.

Lisa blushed. Cy started to say something, stopped, then said something else instead. "Okay then," he stated, as he began to head towards the door. "Let's move out."

CHAPTER 5
SIDE QUEST

The three of them had made a sweep of the fifth floor for the ingredients each needed for torches and Molotov cocktails. Each now had the floor end of a normal crutch tucked into their gear harness or in Mercy's case, through the straps of one of her carry bags. Each had been removed from the rest of the crutch and wrapped with a fair amount of medical gauze that had been thoroughly soaked in rubbing alcohol. These would be lit and used as torches at the appropriate time. All three also carried several rolls of unsoaked gauze and as many alcohol bottles as they could comfortably handle in addition to the rest of their gear. As Lisa had correctly predicted, the amount they could carry would have only been sufficient to get them to her car, had that been their plan. Instead, what they had was more than sufficient for their new plan to escape the very real trap in which they now found themselves.

The three of them were in the process of moving down the back stairwell in the central section of Metro City Medical Center to its first floor. It was the quickest way to reach the emergency entrance. All three remained silent, the tension mounting as they came closer to the first floor, and yet the sound of the zombies remained muffled and somewhat distant. All three had their weapons up and at the ready. Cy was in the lead with his M-16, while Lisa was right behind him with her MAC-11 and Mercy brought up the rear with her M-16. Once they reached the bottom landing, they stopped and looked at each other. There were no moans or scratching sounds outside the stairwell door. Those still sounded as if they were coming from farther away.

"Sounds like they haven't breached the fire doors yet," Cy half-whispered, his head turned and cocked to one side.

Lisa's head was likewise cocked. "It's about time we got another lucky break in this adventure, you know," she said, also in a half-whisper.

Cy nodded, then addressed the two women. "I'm going to open the fire doors and then jump to one side. If you see anything moving, shoot first and ask questions later."

"Right," both women responded.

Cy positioned himself so he could reach the door's latch bar from one side. He looked at the women, nodded again, then pushed hard and pulled his arm back as quickly as he could. The door swung open to reveal a dark and empty hallway.

"Now," Cy urged, as he sprang from cover and bolted through the door, with both women hot on his heels.

The trio ran through a short hallway that ended in the waiting area for the emergency entrance. As with the front entrance, there were a number of half-eaten bodies here and the entire area was saturated with a very rank smell. The humans couldn't help but cough as they moved through it to the emergency entrance. It was shut, but the glass had been smashed out of both doors and one of the nearby floor-to-ceiling window panes. The three didn't bother with the door. With a run and a leap, they were through the broken-out window and outside the hospital. They ran for the alley entrance, but were brought up short when a pair of moans sounded from nearby. Both Lisa and Cy turned and opened fire automatically. The moans instantly changed into bloody gurgles as two zombies, one in the remains of a policeman's uniform and the other in that of a paramedic's, spun around and crashed to the ground.

"That's done it," Cy exclaimed. "The zombies now know where we are."

"Come on!" Lisa urged, as she again resumed running for the catering truck. "Let's get this done before they come in force!"

Even as she shouted the words, another zombie came around from the front of the truck and charged her. Lisa whipped up her MAC-11 but the sound of a short but controlled full auto burst from Cy's M-16 beat her to the punch. The zombie staggered back and was spun almost halfway around from the force of the hits, which wound up leaving a fair-sized bloody splatter pattern on its upper left side. A split second later there was another such short burst. Most hit its upper body and one found the right side of the head, popping it back and causing a geyser of blood to shoot up in the air. It stumbled back another step and then fell in a scream of agony to the pavement. At the same time there was the sound of single shot fire from Mercy's M-16, coming from farther behind them, but by that time Lisa had made it to the cab of the truck. No keys in the ignition, of course, but that had been expected. She hopped into the drivers seat, smashed down the clutch pedal with her left foot, and took it out of gear. "Cy!" she called. "It's ready!"

"Stay up there and steer!" Cy called. "Mercy! Go full auto! I gotta push the truck!"

"I can't aim on full auto!" Mercy called back, even as she hit and downed two more zombies with single shot fire.

By now Cy had ran to the back end of the truck. He turned and put his back to it, bracing himself against the truck so he could push while still holding and shooting his M-16. "Do the best you can!" he called, as he began to push with his legs. "Pull down when it does, and short bursts only!"

"Right!" Mercy called, even as she thumbed her selector switch to full auto and readied herself again.

The truck began to move. Lisa had hopped out of the cab and was pushing from up there, keeping one hand on the steering wheel to guide it and pushing with everything she had. Cy was doing the same – backpedaling, straining from the effort, and shooting as required. Slowly but surely the truck moved, rolling from where it had been parked and across the alley entrance. There was the rat-a-tat-tat of an M-16 on full auto from behind them. Mercy could barely control her rifle that way, even as she had said, but fortunately a stray ricochet managed to hit the zombie at which she was aiming. It promptly screeched and quickly wriggled back the way it came. There was another full auto burst from Cy's M-16, even as he fired and pushed at the same time. The truck was still moving, but the edge of the alley fence was coming up fast. Lisa waited until the last possible minute and then jumped out of the way, so she wouldn't be hit when the driver's side door of the cab hit the fence edge and slammed shut. "Cy!" she called. Cy also jumped clear, and two seconds later the front end of the truck hit the alley wall on the far side and crunched to a stop, the sound of smashed and broken front lights mixing with the gunfire and zombie wails. Cy rolled and came back up quickly, continuing to shoot at the zombies, even as there was another short full auto burst from Mercy and he saw Lisa pop up from under the middle of the truck's box back. It had been parked almost perpendicular to the alley proper, and in its new position it completely blocked off the alley. The only way to get to it was to crawl under the truck, just as Lisa had done. That was exactly what she had planned.

There was more gunfire, this time from both ends of the looparound. Mercy and Cy were positioned on each end, holding off the zombies that were continuing to crawl through the gaps in the wrecked vehicles. Lisa paid them no heed. She pulled a bottle of rubbing alcohol from her gear and began pouring it on the truck, moving up and down it until the bottle was empty. She repeated this with more of them, until all exterior parts of the truck she could reach it were thoroughly doused. She now had only one bottle left. She called out to the others. "Truck's ready!" she yelled.

"Head for the alley!" Cy called back, as he began to slowly backpedal away from the wreck on his side of the looparound and towards the alley entrance. "Mercy, you next! I'll be last! Lisa, get ready to light it as soon as I'm through!"

"Right!" Lisa called in reply. Quick as a flash the young racer again dove under the side of the box back end of the truck and crawled into the front part of the alley on the other side. It was a tight fit given the weapons and gear she was carrying, but she made it. She called out as soon as she was back on her feet again. "Mercy!"

"Coming!" Mercy called back. She fired off one more round from her M-16 at the zombies crawling through the wreck on her end of the looparound, then turned and ran for the alley entrance. Cy had backed up far enough to cover both ends of the looparound and was swinging his M-16 back and forth, redirecting his covering fire as necessary. It was not enough. Wounded zombies were clearing the wrecks on both ends. Mercy made it to the truck, squeezed under it with her gear, and then came out from under the other side. At the same time Lisa had pulled her makeshift torch and had already lit it. It burned brightly as she anxiously called to Cy. "She's through! Come on, Cy!"

Cy fired off two final full auto bursts, one at each end of the looparound, then turned and quickly slung his M-16 over one shoulder. He sprinted for the alley entrance and the truck blocking it, while at the same time almost a half-dozen wounded zombies came to their feet and started to half-shamble, half-stagger after him. He had too much of a lead, however, as he dived for the underside at the middle of the truck. A flurry of scrambling arms and legs later and he was through, with Mercy helping to pull him clear. As they did so, and while the zombies were closing on the truck blocking the alley entrance, Lisa threw her lit torch. The truck went up in flames instantly as soon as the torch hit it, and there was the sound of zombie wailing and screeching on the other side. On the alley side, the three humans were running down the alley and away from what they knew was about to happen. Approximately six seconds later, it did.

KA-WHOOOOOMMMMM!!!!!

The catering truck's gas tank exploded, taking the truck and some half-a-dozen zombies with it and sending flaming debris in all directions. An entire flock of crows which had been roosting on the nearby power and telephone lines immediately took to the air, flying as fast as they could and cawing madly. So too did a big black raven that had been roosting with them; however, its ascent was a silent one as it quickly rose and furiously flew away with them. As for Cy, Lisa, and Mercy, they as one dived behind the closest piece of cover, which happened to be a dumpster off to one side, and huddled behind it as metal shrapnel, burnt rubber, and pieces of ruined food went everywhere. It took about three seconds for the worst of the rain to end, but the trio waited a little longer before cautiously poking their collective heads around the edge of the dumpster to look back the way they came. Some distance away, the alley entrance was bathed in flames and they could still make out the ruin of the burning frame and body of the catering truck, along with what looked like the remains of a couple of bodies before and under it. Mercy shivered and turned away.

"That ought to hold 'em for a while," Lisa observed, as the flames and smoke continued to rise into the night sky.

"Until the fire dies down," Cy quipped, also looking at the flames, "but that won't be for a while yet. We still need to be long gone by then." He turned to say something to Mercy, stopped at what he saw beyond her farther down the alley, and then nudged Lisa gently. "Hey, look at that."

Lisa turned so she could also see down the alley. Less than a dozen yards away was the beginning of a large opening to its right side. It was blocked off by a chain link fence with triple strands of barbed wire on top. It also had a large double gate in its middle covering a gap in the fence large enough for two vehicles to pass each other. Mounted on the fence itself off to one side of the gate was a large sign with the following legend: SOUTHWEST SPORTING GOODS / BACK ENTRANCE. She allowed herself a little laugh. "Our next stop, folks."

Everyone stood up and turned to look down the alley at the gate before looking at each other. "Why are we going to stop there?" Mercy asked.

"To ammo up," Cy responded immediately. "You and I used up a fair amount of our ammo covering Lisa so all of us could get out of the hospital." With that he promptly reslung his M-16 and unslung his shotgun. A worried look from Lisa caught his eye. Cy made a point of giving her a grin. She gave him a look, then smiled back and said nothing. "Lisa also needs more ammo for her AK-47 assault rifle," Cy said, looking away from Lisa and at Mercy. "This is probably the only place we're going to be able to get it on our way out of town."

"What's that?"

"It's that big long gun she's been carrying but you have yet to see her use, because she's hardly got any ammo left for it."

"Why can't she use ammo for this?" Mercy asked, lifting up her M-16 in her hands to emphasize her point.

"Wrong size shell," Lisa responded gently. "AK shells are a lot bigger."

"Oh," Mercy said, and then her face formed into a wry smile. "Shows you how much I know about guns."

"But you're learning, Mercy," Lisa said, and gave her a friendly wink in reply. "You've come a long way in a short time."

"Speaking of long ways," Cy said, and with that both women turned to look at him, "ten minutes, Lisa, fifteen tops. That's all the time I want to spend in there."

"Or the zombies will gang up on us again," Lisa answered, "like they did back at the Armory and just now here. I understand."

"Any idea of where to look so we can speed things up?"

Lisa nodded. "The best two places are in the back storeroom and in the cabinets behind the sales counter in the gun section out on the sales floor. The back part will have a secured storage area for valuable merchandise, and all of the extra ammo will probably be locked in there." She gave an ironic chuckle. "Everything will probably be locked, of course."

"Of course," Cy said. "That means we'll need to find the keys for both, and that'll be time consuming."

"I could try picking the locks," Lisa said, "but no promises."

"That's even more time consuming," Cy observed.

"Why not do both?" Mercy suggested. "Let Lisa try while we search for the keys?"

"That means splitting up," Lisa noted, "and that might be dangerous."

"We might have to, given the fix we're in," Cy said. He thought for a moment, and then drew himself up. "Okay, here's the plan. We go in and check the back first. If we can't get what we need back there because of any lock, then you will stay and try to pick it," he continued, looking at Lisa, before his gaze turned to Mercy, "while you stay with her and watch her back. In the meantime, I'll go up front to the sales floor and see what I can find." He now looked again at Lisa. "Hopefully by the time I'm back you'll either have that lock picked and you guys will already be loading up on ammo, or I'll have the keys to either that or the cabinets up front and we can load up after unlocking them. Either way, we need to be done and heading out within ten minutes, fifteen tops, like I said earlier."

"Understood," Lisa said, nodding in agreement.

"Sounds like a plan," Mercy added, also nodding.

Cy now waved towards the gate in the fence on the side of the alley. "Okay, let's do this. The sooner we get done, the faster we can get to the police station."

The trio had no trouble getting into the back lot behind Southwest Sporting Goods. The double gates were closed but they were not secured. Instead of finding a chain and padlock as the humans had expected, they instead found nothing. There was only a drop pin on one gate and a simple chain link latch on the other holding both in place. With both women providing him cover, Cy lowered and let go of his weapon, so that it dangled in front of him from its shoulder sling, and then used both hands to open the gate. He then swung open the side with the drop pin. It was well oiled and moved silently inward, as Cy walked with it until he reached a old concrete slab set in the pavement that had a short piece of metal pipe sticking down in it. Cy stopped, lined up the the gate's drop pin with the metal pipe, and then lowered the drop pin in place so the gate would stay open. He then looked around. Nothing had moved inside the lot, and the only movement outside were some of the crows returning to their former roosts on the nearby power and phone lines. Cy looked back to the alley, gave a grin, and then waved at the others as he swung the other gate back and out of the way.

The back lot was empty, and they had no trouble gaining entrance to the back of the building. The back door beside the main loading door was wide open, and there was blood on the handle. They went in single file. Cy was first, then Mercy, and then Lisa bringing up the rear. They stopped as soon as they were inside the back storeroom, however, due to the sight that greeted their eyes. There was a wide aisle that ran down from their end of the back storeroom to the other end between numerous two-tier heavy-duty storage shelves full of boxes of various sizes. Despite the semi-darkness within, they could clearly see about half-a-dozen zombies clustered around something less than a dozen feet away from their end of that long aisle. It was a ruined body in the process of being eaten, and there was blood all over that part of the floor. Only a few feet away from one of its half-eaten hands was a crowbar, with blood and *something* covering its bent end. There were also the remains of two other bodies farther down the aisle, as well as the bodies of three more zombies with their heads bashed in. The way the bodies were arranged down the aisle suggested that the three had been tackled and taken down while running down the aisle from the other end, with the one with the crowbar putting up one hell of a fight before his end came. The zombies gathered around that final body, the one closest to the three humans, turned around or looked up as one to gaze at them, the intruders who dared to interrupt the gruesome feast they were enjoying. They snarled or moaned and began to come to their feet in preparation for a mass attack. Three shotgun blasts and a liberal peppering of machine pistol and assault rifle fire later, and whatever threat they might have posed was now permanently ended.

Cy walked up to the first body and the lifeless zombies now scattered around it. Mercy followed him, while Lisa hung back and began looking over that part of the back storeroom. "Looters," he said, pointing with his weapon to the crowbar. "Must have gotten surprised in the act by our undead friends here."

"Nothing down here," Lisa said, rejoining the group. She looked down the aisle. "I'm guessing that what we want is down there, given the way these bodies are arranged."

"That's what I'm thinking," Cy said, as he sidestepped both the bloody remains and the zombie bodies. He then began to walk down the center aisle towards the other end, shotgun raised and at the ready, with both women following him in likewise weapon-ready modes.

"What about that crowbar?" Mercy asked as they walked past it.

"Leave it," Cy advised. "We're loaded down enough already. We can always come back for it if we need it."

The three saw what the looters had been after as they approached the far end of the back storeroom. It was a section of smaller standard store-sized modular shelving separated from the larger warehouse type shelving by a heavy steel security cage, the size of a small room, which enclosed it completely. Within the cage and on the shelves inside were all kinds of valuable sporting goods merchandise, including boxed and cased weapons and multiple boxes of different kinds of ammo, and everything appeared to be undisturbed. The reason for this was clear. The door to the security cage was as stoutly built as the rest of it, with a reinforced metal frame and heavy gauge wire mesh securely welded to it, and with two diagonal reinforcing bars to prevent warping at the corners. It also had an embedded keyed lock and interior deadbolt combination. The door hinges were located inside the security cage and were thus unreachable from the outside. Numerous scratch and pry marks around all edges of the stoutly built door testified to the numerous and ultimately frustrated efforts of the looters to break inside before the zombies arrived and killed the lot of them.

The three stopped in front of the security cage door. Lisa chuckled as she looked at the markings on the door edges. "Wasted effort," she stated. "Those guys were never going to pry this door open with a crowbar, the way this cage is built."

"Can you pick the lock?" Cy asked.

Lisa knelt down and took a look at it. "That's a Master® lock," she said, noting the manufacturer's markings. "They're tough. It's a key lock, though, same as the Yale® I picked earlier. I can try, Cy, but it's probably going to take a while."

"Go ahead and get started then," Cy said. He looked at Mercy. "Per the plan, Mercy. You keep an eye on her."

"Where are you going?" Mercy asked.

"Up front, like we planned, to see if I can find a key or if there's any ammo still on the sales floor," Cy said. He pointed with his weapon at a nearby door beyond one of the large shelving units. "I'll bet that's the way up front. Be back as soon as I can."

Lisa had already released her MAC and let it hang on its sling, while she produced the bent heavy duty paperclip she had used to pick the padlock back at the hospital. She was now using it to work the lock. "Speaking of soon, time check," she said.

Cy looked at his watch. "Just under eight minutes."

Lisa stopped what she was doing and made a point of looking at Cy. "You be careful, you hear?" she said.

Words unspoken passed between them as they looked at each other. "I will, Lisa," Cy promised. He made a point of giving her a grin. Lisa did the same, and after a beat went back to work on the door lock. He again looked at Mercy. "I'll call out if I get in trouble, and I'll also call out once I'm done and back at the door. That way you won't shoot me."

"Good point," Mercy said, allowing herself a smile.

Cy looked again at Lisa, who was concentrating on working the lock, and then back at Mercy. "Don't let anything happen to her, okay?" he asked.

"I'll do my best," Mercy said, and then added with a smile, "After all, you two have that date once we're out of here, right? I wouldn't want either of you to miss it."

Lisa looked up at those words. She and Cy looked at each other, then back at Mercy with grins. Cy laughed softly, and then headed for the side door while Lisa went back to work on the lock.

Cy shouldered his shotgun and pulled out his .45 ACP as he moved into the back part of the sales floor. He held it in a classic double-handed walking carry as he moved down one of the main aisles. As he started his search, he inwardly allowed himself to be amazed at a woman's power of deduction. Lisa had guessed correctly that Cy was running low on M-16 ammo and had swapped weapons earlier for that reason. He also allowed himself a small smile. She was worried about him. That was a good sign, insofar as their newfound friendship was concerned.

All of the signs were there that the store had been thoroughly looted. Shelves and j-hooks were mostly bare, with only items of no significant use in the Outbreak left behind. One of the few things left that was on the modular section that held medical supplies for camping was a shrink wrapped three pack of Bactine® in its typical small aerosol cans. Cy looked at it for a moment. There was no reason it should have been left behind when the shelves around it had been emptied, unless the looters were too loaded down to take it with them. Strange. He looked around, then released his left hand from his walking carry. He used it to first open his rucksack and then pick up and somehow squeeze the three-pack in there, despite it already being fairly full. It was medical, and it was something Mercy might be able to use. He quickly checked his watch, then resumed his two-handed walking carry and moved on.

The area for gun and ammo sales was in the back corner opposite of where he had entered, on the same end of the building as the side entrance to the back storeroom. Cy saw right away that he wasn't going to find anything there. The area had been completely emptied of everything, with the glass to all of the front display counters for pistols smashed and emptied of all contents. All of the display cabinets in the back for long guns, as well as the low-profile secured storage cabinets beneath them, had either been pried open or their glass smashed and part of their inside wire mesh pried up and away for outside access. Cy gave everything a quick once-over, knowing he wasn't going to find anything they needed but looking all the same, just in case he was wrong. Nothing. The only thing he found of any significance were the barrel lock keys for the counters and cabinets, still on their ring and still hanging under one of the counters on a hook behind a display frame, where they would be out of sight from the customers. Cy shook his head, checked his watch again, and moved on.

Lisa continued to work the lock on the secured storage area while Mercy stood guard, occasionally looking up and down the long aisle of the back storeroom to make sure they didn't get surprised from either direction. She could hear the younger woman cursing under her breath. "What's wrong?" she asked, still searching the back storeroom with her eyes.

"It's this damn lock," Lisa said, almost spitting the words out. "It's not like the padlocks I'm used to picking. I can't get the tumblers to fall right." She leaned back on her heels for a moment and blew some loose strands of hair away from her face. "If this were a padlock, I'd probably have it open by now." She then brushed away the loose hairs that had fallen back down in her face, leaned forward once more, and resumed working the lock.

Mercy was looking rather thoughtful as she continued her visual sweeps. "A question, if I may."

"Go ahead."

"I've noticed you two have grenades."

"Yeah. What of it?"

"Why didn't you use them to help us get out to your car so we could get in it and escape?"

"Same problem with using those rubbing alcohol bottles as Molotov cocktails," Lisa said evenly, as her brow furrowed while she worked. "We didn't have enough of them. We could have also blown up my car with a misthrow or a thrown one bounced back at us by all of those zombies, and then we'd have been out there and exposed surrounded by that entire bunch with nowhere to go and probably not enough ammo to fight our way back in through all of them."

"But couldn't you have just plowed your way through them with your car, like they do on TV and in the movies?"

Lisa stopped working and looked up at Mercy, giving her a long and measured look. Mercy instinctively drew back, not understanding why Lisa was looking at her like that. When Lisa spoke her tone was even, and her words were carefully chosen. "Mercy, I'm guessing you don't know the first thing about situations like that, so let me explain. It's simple physics. If you're going to plow your way through a lot of massed bodies, you have to have a rather large mass moving at high speed to break into the clear on the other side. Otherwise their mass, as close together as they are and always piling up under and around you the farther you plow into them, will eventually stop you before you reach the other side. My HemiCuda didn't have enough mass and I didn't have enough room to even begin getting it up to speed to do that. We would have needed a big, heavy vehicle, like a panel truck or bus, or even a tractor-trailer rig, to plow our way through so many zombies."

"But they do it on TV all the time."

"They set those stunts up beforehand so it'll look like they're doing that, but it's all in the camera angles and how they set it up," Lisa explained. She turned and once again resumed working on the door lock, continuing to talk as she did. "You can't do that in real life. I know. All of us stuck on the track had to try that, once everybody began turning zombie. The others didn't make it out because they got stuck in the crowds about two-thirds of the way in, and do you want to know what happened to them?"

Mercy shuddered. "No, but go ahead and tell me."

"The zombies pulled them out of their stock cars through their open windows and ate them on the spot." She bit her lip as she made a peculiar half-jerk and half twist with her hand holding the wire in the lock, and then cursed. "Damn lock. Anyway, I got lucky and found in front of me a part of the crowd thin enough to force my way through. After that it was to my 'Cuda as quick as I could and out of there." She now began a series of half-twists and slight jerks with the wire in the lock. "That's why we didn't even try, Mercy. The odds were against us."

Mercy nodded. "Thanks for telling me. I'm sorry."

"It's okay," Lisa said. She gave a sigh and again leaned back. This time she let go of the wire and put both hands on her knees. "Nobody can know everything. Like me. I definitely do not know how to pick this damn lock." With that she reached up with her right hand, balled it into a fist, and gently hit the lock plate with its butt end. There was a clicking sound, and then the door swung silently inward, much to the surprise of both women. It swung almost all the way around to the shelving unit next to its hinges before it finally coasted to a stop. Lisa watched it swing, her eyes wide and her mouth slightly open. "I don't believe it," she muttered.

"Looks like you did it," Mercy said with a smile.

"Yeah," Lisa said. At once she was on her feet and inside the security cage. She ignored the boxed weapons and went straight to the ammo. After a bit, she took off both her side pouch and rucksack, then placed them on a table in the center of the security cage that seemed to be there specifically for that purpose. She picked out two groups of boxed ammo and began shoveling boxes of each, separated by size and box type, into either her side pouch or rucksack. Mercy continued to stand guard but occasionally glanced her way. "What'ch'a got?" she asked.

"Enough AK ammo to see us through the rest of this little adventure, I hope," Lisa said gleefully, as she continued to load up both of her bags. "They've also got extra of the other sizes we need. Mercy, give me your bag that doesn't have your medical stuff, and I'll load you up with 5.56 and .38."

"What about Cy?" Mercy said, as she unslung one of her shoulder bags, quickly handed it to Lisa inside the cage, and then resumed her watch.

"I'll get his ready. That way all he has to do is scoop it up once he gets back. Time check?"

Mercy looked at her wristwatch. "He's been gone about eight minutes."

"Then he'll be back anytime." Lisa had finished with her own bags, and now began to fill Mercy's. "Better listen for him, and make sure you don't shoot him, okay?"

"I won't." Mercy paused a beat, and then ventured a question. "Hey, Lisa?"

"What?"

"You like him, don't you?"

"I just met him today."

"But you like him, don't you?"

Lisa paused, looking thoughtful. "Well ... kinda ... yeah, I guess I do," she admitted, then quickly went back to work.

Mercy nodded and gave her a grin. "He's a lot like you, you know. Strong, forceful, determined, resolute."

"He's a soldier."

"And you're a stock car racer, a woman in a very competitive and usually male profession." Mercy's grin became even bigger. "As I said, you two are a lot alike."

Lisa allowed herself to smile as she worked. "Maybe we are, Mercy. Maybe we are."

It was then that they heard Cy's voice. "Mercy? I'm fixing to come back in now."

"Okay," Mercy called. Lisa straightened, and both she and Mercy turned to face the side door. Lisa gave her a sideways wink and Mercy returned it, but both remained silent as they waited.

Cy came in at a trot. He looked worried, almost jumpy, as he hurried over to them. "Oh, you got it open. That's good, because I never found the keys and everything up front has been smashed open and emptied."

Mercy let Cy slip past him and he entered the security cage. "Figures," Lisa said, as she pointed to the pile of ammo boxes on the table. "Here's yours."

"Thanks," Cy said. He quickly opened his rucksack, pulled out a shrink-wrapped three-pack of Bactine® and set it on the table, and then began to shovel ammo boxes inside in its place. "That's for Mercy. It's the only thing I found out there we could use."

"Why the rush?" Lisa asked, noting how fast Cy was stowing his new ammo. "We've still got a couple of minutes. Well, one now." She then handed off the sprays to Mercy through the door, who promptly stowed them in her own gear.

"Maybe, maybe not," Cy said as he worked. His voice was as anxious as the look on his face. "I risked going out front to see if I could find the vehicle the looters were using. I found it all right, but it was wrapped around a telephone pole and burned out. It also looks like all the ammo they had stolen exploded or went off once the fire got to it. That's not all," he added as he finished with his rucksack, quickly closed it, then looked at Lisa. "The zombies are on their way, coming up the street from the hospital where we left them."

"Then we've got to get out of here," Lisa said intently, as she followed Cy out of the security cage.

The three of them began to quickly walk down the long aisle to the other end of the storeroom, past the loading doors and to the open side doorway through which they had first entered. They stopped after taking only a half-dozen paces, however. Movement among the bodies farthest from them had caught their attention.

"Did you see anything earlier, Mercy?" Cy asked, his shotgun automatically raised and pointed down the aisle.

"No," Mercy replied, her assault rifle also raised and aimed. "No zombies came in here the whole time you were gone, Cy, I promise."

"Whatever it is, it isn't a zombie," Lisa added, her MAC-11 likewise raised and aimed. "It's too small. Must have slipped in by sticking to the shadows."

"Yeah," Cy said. He risked taking another step forward.

RRRREEEEEERRRRRRAAAAAARRRRRRWWWWW!!!

78

To everyone's surprise, a large and rather bedraggled looking alley cat suddenly popped up from behind one of the bodies on the floor in front of them down the aisle. It had bloody patches on its fur and an unearthly reddish hue in its eyes. It also had its jaws clamped down on the wrist of a severed hand missing its middle finger, with the others half-curled and frozen in rigor from its former owner's final death agonies. The alley cat stared down the three armed humans on the other end of the back storeroom, and then began to make the combination half-warbling and half-growling noise that cats sometimes make whenever they are jealously guarding their food.

Rawrl-rawlr-rawlr-rawlr-rawlr-rawlr-rawlr-rawlr ....

"Oh, crap!" Mercy exclaimed under her breath. "A zombie cat!"

"Be glad there's not a pack of them," Lisa half-whispered, her own voice just as excited. "I don't think we'd survive that."

"We can't let one zombie cat stop us," Cy said urgently, keeping his shotgun aimed at it while the cat continued its seemingly demonic growling. "Those zombies in the street are less than five minutes away."

"Somebody shoot it?" Mercy suggested with a trembling voice.

"I've got a better idea," Lisa said. "Trust me?"

"Go ahead," Cy answered. All the frightened Mercy could do was nod her head.

Lisa locked eyes with the zombie cat. It continued to glare at them, still gripping the hand in its jaws and making its jealous guarding noises. Suddenly Lisa raised her right foot and then stamped on the floor as hard and fast as she could. "*SCAT!*" she yelled. The cat took off at once, still gripping the severed hand in its mouth, as it bounded up and back and then raced through the open outside door.

Mercy breathed a visible sigh of relief, but Cy didn't waste any time. "Come on!" he urged, as he began to run for the back door himself. Lisa was hot on his heels, and Mercy followed a half-beat later.

The trio flew out of the back door of Southwest Sporting Goods as if they had been shot from a cannon. They ran all the way to the back gate and through it in a few seconds, despite their heavy individual loads of gear, weapons, and ammo. All three came to an abrupt stop once they were in the alley, however, as soon as they heard the new growling. It was coming from both ends of the alley. It came from the fire and smoke of the burning remains of the catering truck swirling around the entrance at the hospital end, and it came from the shadows that bathed the exit at the police station end. Suddenly a new set of growls joined the first, only these were coming from behind the humans. These new growls were not coming from zombie cats. They were too deep throated for any but the biggest of felines, and there were none of those in Metro City. Cy, Lisa, and Mercy immediately formed a defensive circle with their backs to each other and their weapons facing outward, with each one of them covering a different threat zone from where the growling was coming. A few seconds later, they saw with their own eyes what was making those sounds.

Three of them leapt through the spark-filled column of smoke above the flames of the catering truck to alight on the alley paving stones on that end of the alley and stood there, facing the three humans down at the center of the alley. Three more slowly emerged from the shadows darkening the police end, with slavering jaws and mouths agape. Four more appeared on either side of the back end of Southwest Sporting Goods, two on each side of the building, slowly but surely padding their way in stalking fashion into the back lot and towards its back gate, in which the humans were perfectly framed. All were growling, and all were glaring at the three humans with undead hungry eyes. They were not alone. Perched on the power and telephone lines above was the rest of the same flock of crows that had been forced away earlier by the exploding truck. All of them had returned to the alley, and with them had come the big black raven as before. It was sitting on top of a utility pole above the others and looking down on the proceedings below as if it were an English high court judge about to pronounce a sentence of doom. It made no sound, but many of the crows cawed and flexed their wings, as if in anticipation of the potential feast that was about to be spread on the paving stones below them.

Lisa ignored both the crows and the raven. Her attention was on the threat in front of her. "Zombie dogs. Just what we need," she half-whispered, tightly gripping her MAC-11. "German Shepherds. Probably infected K-9s from the police station kennels."

"Oh, crap!" was all a frightened Mercy could get out, her assault rifle visibly quaking in her trembling hands.

Cy took in a deep breath and then let it out quickly. "This is like a Western, you know?" he said, trying and failing to sound nonchalant. "We die quick, or we die slow."

"I'll die slow," Lisa said quickly.

"I don't want to die at all!" a visibly nervous Mercy said through clenched teeth.

"Then we've got to fight if we want to live," Cy stated. He drew a bead on the nearest infected K-9 coming down the alley, its claws clattering loudly on the paving stones, as it and the others began to lope and pick up speed.

"Right with you," Lisa said, as she prepared to quickly spray all four of the infected K-9s coming up the lot with her MAC-11, which were also beginning to lope as they moved quickly towards its gate.

"Me too," Mercy added, as she steadied her assault rifle by raising it to her shoulder and aiming it at the nearest infected K-9 on her end. By now it was halfway down the alley and leading the others in their charge, its claws ticking loudly as it ran.

"Eat this!" Cy declared, as he pulled the trigger and his shotgun roared.

CHAPTER 6
WELCOME TO THE MCPD

The next five minutes or so found Cy, Lisa, and Mercy in the fight of their lives inside the alley with the three separate packs of infected dogs attacking them. For each of them it was a virtual frenzy of shooting, dodging and twisting, short runs while reloading, and then more of the same. It also became clear, now that they were having to get up close and personal with their frenzied foes, that not all of them had come from the police station per Lisa's initial guess. Two of them were wearing the remains of seeing eye dog harnesses, and they had been among the group that had attacked from the direction of the hospital. Two of the ones that had charged Lisa across the back lot of Southwest Sporting Goods were wearing thick heavy collars to which were attached broken chains or leashes. In the end, it didn't matter from where any of them came. They were there, they were attacking en masse, and the three humans were barely holding their own against their faster and more agile foes.

What saved the trio was the arrival of the zombies. The first zombie staggered around one side of Southwest Sporting Goods straight into Lisa's line of fire. It promptly staggered and fell. When it did, the two infected dogs Lisa had been fighting on that side of the building promptly went after it. That left Lisa only two to deal with, and one of those was already badly wounded. It got a lucky break when a second zombie came lurching through the open side door of the back storage room in search of food. It became food instead for the wounded dog, while Lisa quickly killed the other and then went to help her friends with the remaining dogs. Cy had already killed two of the three attacking him, while Mercy had only managed to wound her foes. One of them had also taken a big piece out of the back tail of her lab coat during the fight, narrowly missing biting her in the process. All of the remaining dogs in the alley regrouped once Lisa joined the fray, and shortly thereafter they promptly abandoned it when more zombies entered the Southwest Sporting Goods back lot. The change in their course of action was easy enough to understand. The humans were shooting at them. The zombies were not. Therefore, the zombies were the easier kill, and thus the surviving dogs went after them with a vengeance.

"*Girls!*" Cy yelled to get their attention. He motioned with his shotgun towards the police station end of the alley. "*Run for it!*"

They ran. The trio's escape run promptly turned into a chase, as two of the surviving infected dogs, both K-9s and both still in fair shape despite their wounds, promptly broke away from the melee caused by the zombies and ran after them. It turned out to be a close thing. Lisa was the fastest despite the weight of her gear, and made it to the end well ahead of Mercy, who was a distant second. Cy made himself the rearguard, occasionally turning and firing at the two infected dogs as he ran. Lisa charged through the open gate at the end of the alley only to find herself having to deal with three zombie policemen who immediately lunged at her. She dived and twisted, successfully ducking away and coming back up with her MAC-11 doing her talking for her. Mercy came through the gate at the same time, stopping and swinging around so she could take it in hand and close it once Cy came through. It was almost identical in construction to the door to the security cage inside Southwest Sporting Goods, with a heavy-duty keyed lock that would engage once the gate was pushed shut. How it got open or how long ago that had been did not matter to Mercy, so long as the lock would work and hold the door once she closed it. It was now Cy's turn to come running through the gate, and Mercy slammed it shut as soon as he cleared it. The gate held as both dogs ran into it, yelping in agony as they hit hard and bounced back into the alley. One of the zombie policemen had gotten away from Lisa's counterattack at the same time this was happening and was now coming after Mercy, half-limping and half-lunging towards her on a badly wounded leg. Cy's shotgun roared as he blew its head off. Both infected German shepherds continued to snarl furiously and throw themselves helplessly at the closed gate, while Cy helped Lisa finish off her last two foes. A few seconds later more zombies began to stagger up the alley towards the gate. The infected dogs promptly turned and went after the food they could actually get, instead of the food that they could no longer reach. The sounds of fighting moved into the alley as both Lisa's MAC-11 and Cy's shotgun fell silent. It was over, and the three survivors had made it to their next goal.

The three humans now stood together again, in their ring as before and weapons at the ready, only this time they weren't fighting. They were catching their collective breaths. They were standing in the approximate center of the back parking lot of the Metro City Police Department (MCPD) substation on that side of town. There were two police cars parked there, a new one and an older one, as well as several regular automobiles and one small import pickup truck. A guard shack next to a gated entrance connecting the back lot to the one in front on that side of the building completed the picture. The gate was closed, but it did not appear to be locked. That gate, the one blocking access to the front, and the back doors of the police station were the only access points to the back parking lot other than the alley gate. Thankfully for the sake of the three survivors all were currently locked or blocked in some way, and this was what gave them their brief respite and allowed them to gather themselves once again.

"Oh God," Mercy said, still visibly shaking. "Let's not do that again anytime soon, you two. Okay?"

"Only if the zombies and other infected let us," Lisa replied. Her breathing was more even than Mercy's, but she too was catching her breath.

Mercy gave Lisa a sideways look but did not speak. As for Cy, he had already caught his breath and was looking around. "Well, we're here," he stated, "and we need to get moving as soon as you two are ready. I'm guessing we've got about the same amount of time here as we did back at the sporting goods store before the main horde of the zombies show up. That'll be ten to twelve minutes or so, given the distance involved."

"We need more," Mercy said, as she drew herself up and turned to look at Cy, her breathing almost back to normal.

"We're not going to get more," Lisa said, stating the obvious. She too had now turned and was looking at Cy.

The Army corporal took them both in with his gaze. "She's right, Mercy, so let's get cracking. Our plan is still as before. We'll call the Army on the station's transmitter and get some body armor while we're in there. We also need to get a new set of wheels, since we had to leave Lisa's back at the hospital."

"We can do that right now," Lisa said. She walked over to the older police car, stood by it, then let go of the suppressor of her MAC-11 and patted the car's fender. "This one will do nicely."

Mercy cocked an eyebrow. "So we steal a police car?"

"We're going to appropriate one for military use, given my presence and our current status," Cy said with a grin. "Or something like that. That's how General Ryan would do it."

Mercy still looked doubtful. "But why not the newer one?" she said as she pointed to it.

"Because it's a Ford Fairmont and it's a piece of junk," Lisa replied tartly. "The Ford Fairmont police car is one of the worst police cars ever made. Weak engine, poor performance, poor handling, and a cheap flimsy frame. There's a story going around that a crook broke out of one of them even while handcuffed by kicking the back door open. That's how bad they are. You're not going to do that with this baby," she said, patting the fender of her choice again. "Dodge Royal Monaco. Late Seventies police package, looks like. It's a classic. It has everything you'd ever want in terms of performance in a police car." She now gave her companions a grin. "Like Elwood Blues said in the movie, you know. *It's got a cop motor, a 440 cubic inch plant. It's got cop tires, cop suspension, cop shocks. It's a model made before catalytic converters, so it'll run good on regular gas.*"

Cy grinned. "*The Blues Brothers.* I get it."

Mercy too was smiling. "Good movie and good point."

Lisa grinned back at them. "All right. That's that. Now to buy us some much needed extra time ..." she said, letting her voice trail off as she looked around. Her eyes suddenly locked on something in one of the lot's darker corners. "There we go," she said, directing her MAC-11's barrel at her find. "That pallet of tires will do nicely, as well as anything else we can find that will burn."

"Burn?" Mercy asked, as she and Cy both followed Lisa towards the pallet.

"Burn," Lisa said as they reached it. She looked them over briefly and then nodded. "Oh, yes. Brand new. Excellent."

"What's a pallet of new tires doing in the back lot of a police station?" Mercy asked.

"They probably got delivered here to put on their police cars as they need them, or to be hauled to their preferred auto shop later," Lisa said. "Who knows? Who cares? Anyway, they're exactly what we need to get started."

"Are you thinking what I think you're thinking?" Cy said, still grinning.

"I sure am," Lisa said, grinning back at him. "We're going to spend the next ten minutes building a fire barrier in the street in front of this station, on the side down which we know the zombies are going to come, and we're going to ignite it before we go inside. We're going to use these tires for the base and stack on top of them everything we can find that's flammable, and we'll use the alcohol and torches you two have left from the hospital to ignite them. Tire fires burn for a very long time, and that'll give us the extra time we need to properly search the place, and find and do everything in there we have to."

"Sounds like a plan to me," Cy said, as he shouldered his shotgun on its sling and reached for one of the topmost tires on the pallet.

They had the fire barrier in place and ready by the time the first group of zombies turned the corner of the block some twelve minutes later. A full single row of tires had been laid across the street from one side to the other, with everything flammable the three could find within easy searching distance piled on top of them. Everything had been thoroughly soaked both with all of the bottles of alcohol Cy and Mercy still had and with a full five-gallon jerrican of gasoline Lisa had found sitting beside the guard shack. It was also during her search of the guard shack in order to find more flammables that she found the keys to the Dodge police car, hanging inside a keybox mounted on the wall. It had been locked, but the keybox key had been in the top drawer of the guard's desk. Lisa had immediately pocketed the Dodge keys but left the ones for the Ford Fairmont hanging on the hook before resuming the search for more flammables.

They waited until the first group of zombies had drawn up close to the fire barrier and two more had rounded the block and were on their way. Cy was positioned on the end across the street with his lit torch, while Mercy had hers on the station end. At a signal from Lisa the two stuck their torches into the barricade and ran for cover when it ignited. The fire chased down both ends of the barricade into the middle, completely surprising the zombies and setting on fire one that had gotten too close. It whirled about, screaming in agony as it burned and setting several other nearby zombies on fire as well, before collapsing to the pavement a half-minute or so later. The process continued to be repeated for the next few minutes, and soon all of the zombies that were not yet ablaze had turned and were half-running and half-stumbling back the way they came.

The three humans stood in the street in front of the MCPD substation, weapons in ready positions but not using them. They instead watched as the carnage unfolded before them.

"Man, oh man," Mercy said in awe. "Look at 'em burn."

"That was a great idea, Lisa," Cy said.

"Yeah," Lisa replied. She hefted her MAC-11. "Now let's get inside and get done, before it burns down and the zombies come back." She turned and began walking quickly towards the police station's smashed front doors, with Cy turning and walking with her almost immediately.

"But what's going to keep them from coming around the other side of the block?" Mercy asked, as she too turned and hurried after them.

"Nothing," Cy said. "Let's just hope they don't figure that out until we're done inside."

Mercy gulped but did not quit moving. She had caught up with the others by the time the trio approached the doors.

MCPD officer Joseph "Joe" Frisco sat on the floor of the substation's main lobby, with his back propped up against the front of the reception counter behind him. He was no longer in pain. He was no longer sure of the time of day, or of even what day of the week it was. He had been drifting in and out of consciousness for quite a while. Each time he drifted back, he had found more of his body had gone numb. It had started in his toes, then moved into his feet, then up his ankles and next his legs, and that was how the creeping paralysis eventually worked its way with him all the way up to his neck. To his surprise he found he could still breathe despite the paralysis in the rest of his body; however the motion was ragged, and he gasped in and wheezed out every time. He couldn't help it. He could also feel the numbness creeping up his neck. Both the back of his neck and his ears were tingling. It wouldn't be long now, he guessed. He was turning, and there was nothing he could do to stop it.

He had seen motion outside the front doors for some time, but his blurred eyes couldn't make it out. Probably more zombies. Then there was a brilliant flash off to the right, accompanied by the sound of zombies screaming and the acrid smell of a large tire fire. *Fire?* Who had started a fire, and why? No ... there shouldn't be anyone left to start a fire. Not long after that three shapes came into view, walking up the sidewalk toward the front doors. No, it couldn't be. Everyone was dead or turned ... and yet the shapes kept getting closer and louder. He had to reach them. He had to let them know he was still alive. He had to get their attention for Raul's sake. With an effort, Joe put all of his rapidly fading strength into calling out. He mouthed the words. No sound. He tried again, even harder, and at last the sounds came out. "Hel-lo? Any-one?" The sound of movement and voices ceased for several seconds. Whoever it was, they were very close now. Joe tried again. "Pleeeaaassseeee ... hurrrrrrryyy."

There was the sound of running feet. Seconds later the three shapes before his eyes became three people who quickly came through the ruins of the front doors. They sidestepped the wreck of the broken barricade in the lobby and came around to stop in front of Joe. The group consisted of one man and two women. The man was black and looked like someone from the Army or National Guard, given his uniform and accessories. The younger of the two women was wearing a black two-piece racing firesuit with red and white highlights, along with tall black racing boots. She looked like an Indian, with long dark hair and ruddy skin to complement it. She looked familiar, but right now he couldn't place her. The older was Asian in complexion, with short black hair and a haggard-looking face, wearing a torn labcoat over regular clothing. All three were heavily armed, and both the man and the younger woman had on military rucksacks, while the older woman wore both a large shoulder bag and what looked like an extra small one. Both the older man and younger woman stopped and gave Joe surprised looks, while the older woman in the labcoat rushed over and quickly knelt down beside him. She opened one of her medical bags, took something out, then began to examine him with whatever it was.

"Oh man," Cy said, looking at the badly wounded policeman before them, propped up against the lobby reception counter as if he were a stiff-jointed action figure. "How is he, Mercy?"

"Not good," Mercy said, as she looked him over. She took the time to take a brief look at his name badge. It read FRISCO, JOSEPH. As for Frisco, he remained silent while Mercy continued with her examination. He seemed to be concentrating on making himself breathe, with which he seemed to be having difficulty. After a few more seconds, Mercy put her gear away and looked back at Cy and Lisa. "It's no use. You can't do anything for them when they're this far gone. He could turn at any time."

Frisco's jaw worked, but there was no sound. Mercy started back at the motion. Cy and Lisa raised their guns and trained them on him. Again the policeman's mouth moved, but this time he managed to speak. "Raaaaulll ..." came the faint words from the poor man. "Help ... Raaauuuulllll ...."

"Raul?" Lisa asked. "Who's Raul?"

"Ill-leegh-ahlll ..." Frisco managed to get out. "Good guy ... just ... illegaaalll .... Holding for ... for INS ... until ... Outbreak hit ...." He stopped, drew in a ragged breath, and then continued. "Holding cell ... isolated ... not infected ...."

The three looked at each other, and then back at the dying policeman. Mercy looked skeptical. "I'll be the judge of that," she said evenly.

"Look," Cy said, before Mercy could continue. "We don't have a lot of time, and you don't either, given your condition. Here's the deal. We need to get to the station armory for body armor and other supplies, and we need to get to the station's radio transmitter so I can call out for help. Tell us where those are, and we'll go see if this Raul fellow can be saved. Okay?"

Frisco looked at the others for several seconds. The only sounds to be heard were his spasmodic breathing and the faint moans of zombies elsewhere in the building. Joe finally nodded. "Deal," he said firmly. He took in another shuddering breath, then continued. "Radio room ... second floor .... By ... chief's office .... Got ... to go there ... anyway. Keys ... to armory ... and holding cells ... in there." With that he paused, gave them a long look, then spoke again. "You ...," he said, swinging his head slowly around to face Lisa. "You're ... Lisa ... Stanridge."

"Yes," Lisa replied.

Frisco smiled, despite his pain. "First time ... I've seen you ... for real .... You're ... pretty ...." he said. Lisa forced a smile, listening as Frisco continued. "Hope ... you ... make it ... out ...." he struggled to say. "You ... and ... your friends."

Lisa nodded. "God knows we're gonna try," she answered, still doing her best to maintain her smile.

Frisco nodded back, then suddenly convulsed. The others hurriedly backed away. He looked up at them with eyes that had all but glazed over, and his fingers were frozen into stiff claws. "Gooooooooo ...." he snarled. "Tuuuuurrrrrrnnnniiinnng ..."

The others turned and ran past him towards the far hallway. As she ran, Lisa fought to keep her tears back. She knew MCPD officer Joe Frisco wouldn't be there waiting for them when they returned. There would be a mindless zombie in his place, and it would be just another one they would have to kill in order to survive.

The trio didn't stop moving until they had put and pegged into place a pair of stout fire doors between themselves and the front lobby. Once they were done, Cy turned to the two women and sighed sadly. "Damn," he said.

"Yeah," Lisa agreed.

"At least now we know where to go and what to do," Mercy pointed out. "His death won't be in vain."

"No it won't," Lisa said, as she again hefted her weapon. "What do you think, Cy? Stick together and maintain strength in numbers, or split up to cover more ground in less time?"

"I don't see why we have to," Mercy pointed out. "Like the police officer said, everything is where we can get to it along the way."

"Yes, but Cy's radio call to his superiors outside the quarantine line is going to take time," Lisa countered, "and we don't know how long our fire barricade outside is going to hold off all the zombies out there."

"Not to mention the ones in here with us," Cy finished, "and that now includes Officer Frisco. He'll have turned by the time we get back down to the lobby."

"Oh yeah," Mercy said, turning away and looking at the floor. "Poor man."

"Poor Randy," Lisa added softy, also looking sad, "and poor John," she continued, looking at Mercy. When Mercy raised an eyebrow, Lisa explained. "Randy was my brother's name."

The erstwhile nurse nodded in understanding. "Poor everyone," Mercy finished, and then both women fell silent.

The hallway remained quiet for several more seconds, until Cy spoke. "Here's the plan. We split up. We'll stay together until we get to the second floor and I can get to the radio room. If the transmitter is still good, then I'll stay there and make my call while you ladies get the keys we need from the chief's office. Head on downstairs after that, unlock the Armory, and see if this Raul guy Officer Frisco told us about is still human and can be saved. Hopefully I'll be finished with my radio call by then and I can head on down to join you. One last trip to the station's Armory for all of us and then we're out of here. Agreed?"

"Agreed," both women replied in unison.

"Then let's do it," Cy said, hefting his shotgun into the ready position. He led the way and the two women followed, heading down the hallway towards the building's main stairwell.

In the meantime, outside the MPCD substation, beyond the fiercely burning fire barricade in the street, those zombies who had not been consumed by the flames of either the barricade or their flaming fellows were milling about aimlessly. They were at a loss as to what to do next. They knew where the food was, only they couldn't reach it because of the fire. A few were beginning to wander outward, seeking easier prey, but the rest remained in the general area. They remembered enough from their former humanity to know that fires tend to burn down after a while unless they had more fuel upon which to feed. All they had to do was wait, so they waited. They spent their time either fussing with each other, or watching as lone members of their group would occasionally wander off to wherever, or watching the crows feed on the burned bodies of their former companions who had perished in the flames. They had flown in from the alley not long after the fire at the barricade had subsided somewhat, and then they had swooped down upon the fallen. The zombies watched as the crows used their powerful beaks to peck and tear at the charred flesh on each body, ripping out long and thick strips to swallow with an almost arrogant tossing back of their heads. They also watched as the big black raven that seemed to be their leader, and which had been both the first to emerge from the alley and the first to pick its dinner, fed on the best of the bodies that had fallen on their side of the fire barricade. None of the crows dared to challenge its choice of the corpses, and all of the zombies shrank away in fear from it. Even their infection-damaged senses could tell that there was something unusual about this particular raven, something unhealthy, something ... incredibly *evil* in the intelligence that seemed to shine from its unnatural sable-colored eyes. As did the zombies at the National Guard Armory earlier that day, the zombies here at the MCPD substation kept well back from the big raven and did not molest it in any way, lest they fall victim to whatever evil it truly represented.

Inside the front lobby of the police station, Joe Frisco's body continued to convulse. His eyes rolled up into his head, and a low but steady moan continually emanated from his twisted mouth. Suddenly he stopped moving and froze in an arch of agony as a loud and shrill cry sounded from outside. It was the cry of a raven; however, it was augmented and amplified to an incredible degree. Frisco's eyes opened wide in terror at a sight only he could see, and his mouth opened in a soundless scream as he was forced to endure that terrible cry. It seemed to be intended for him and him alone, for nothing else reacted to it either inside or out. Frisco's last conscious thoughts as a human were of feeling his life drain from him as quickly and impersonally as one might flush a toilet. The cry lasted only for several seconds, but Frisco's body collapsed to the floor as soon as it stopped. His eyes were wide open but they remained rolled up into his head. His mouth was open but no sound came out, nor did he breathe. Police officer Joe Frisco was as dead as a doornail, and now there was nothing left to keep the virus from finishing its claim on his lifeless body.

Outside in the street beyond the fire barricade, the big black raven was standing tall on top of its choice of the corpses, its head cocked and turned towards the MCPD substation door. Its beak was open but it cried no more. Its posture and bearing suggested that of a human which has just finished an excellent meal and needs to burp. It flapped its wings and let out a single, normal, raven-like *Awk!* Immediately all the crows around it feasting on their own corpses stopped whatever they were doing and cried their approval. *Caw! Caw! Caw! Awk! Awk!* cried the raven again, as if accepting it, and then it went back to feeding. So too did the crows. The nervous zombies in the background could but watch that mass of unearthly black avians peck and tear, peck, and tear, rip and swallow, and thoroughly and savagely enjoy their most gruesome of meals.

Back in the lobby of the MCPD substation, two zombies dressed in the remains of police uniforms lurched to their feet. They staggered and shuffled into view from the darkest of its shadows. They came up to and stopped beside the stilled corpse lying before the reception counter in the front lobby. It suddenly twitched, convulsed twice, then gathered itself and began to get up. It did so in a manner suggesting that of someone who has forgotten how to do something, and is figuring out how to do it again even as they try to perform the deed. Eventually the corpse which had once been MCPD officer Joe Frisco rose to its feet and stood before its fellows. It was a corpse no longer, but a fully reanimated zombie. No words were spoken, at least not in any form recognizable to humans, but it seemed as if the three held silent communion and agreed on something. They then turned as one and began a slow but steady, half-shuffling and half-staggering walk towards the hallway down which the three humans had fled some time before.

CHAPTER 7
EXPLORATIONS

The MCPD substation was smaller and more compact in design than the main station in downtown Metro City. That one had three floors, two basement levels, and a fairly good-sized underground parking garage that connected directly with the first basement level. The smaller substation had only two floors, one basement level, and large parking lots front and back instead of a parking garage. The one in front was for visitors and the one in back for police use only. That was why it was fenced, with the main entrance protected by a heavy duty gate with a guard shack by it. There were only two entrances to the building, front and back, both with double doors. The ones in the back were still intact; however, the front ones had their glass shattered and the remains of a barricade in front of them as stark testament to the earlier fury of the Outbreak in that part of town. The main or ground floor held within its walls reception lobbies both front and back, public restrooms, a storage room for various supplies and miscellaneous items, a custodial closet, various duty offices large and small, a ready room for on-duty officers, and a restricted access combination locker room and restroom/shower area for off-duty officers. The upper floor held the station chief's office, a couple of other private offices, the evidence storage room, the radio room, the conference room (which also doubled as a formal briefing room), and a general purpose storage room. The sole basement floor held the station's armory, firing range, detention cells, and K-9 kennels. Even though the Outbreak survivors had already been told where to go and what to do by the late Joe Frisco, large station maps intended for pubic viewing were posted both at the entrances to each lobby and near the doors to every level of the station's only stairwell. In addition there were directional signs at key locations throughout the building clearly pointing the way to various designated locations, as well as signs on or next to every door. The maps were redundant, but were there for the sake of the public. They could also prove useful references, in case the survivors lost their way.

There were also the zombies. This had been expected, of course, given that every other building they had visited so far had been infested with its share of zombies both male and female. Most of the ones here were of police officers mixed in with the occasional random civilian types, and of the former there were four basic types. There was the generic *police zombie*, typically dressed in the bloodied and sometimes torn and ragged remains of their uniforms. About half of these were wearing gunbelts but none of them had their guns. These had probably been dropped wherever they had turned zombie. Searching these upon killing them would always yield a fair amount of .380 ACP ammo for Lisa and Mercy's pistols, as well as Lisa's MAC-11. The second and less common was what they came to call the *tactical zombie*. This type was always dressed in bloodied SWAT-type fatigues but without any kind of armor vest or gear harness. It almost always had a military-style gunbelt with a strap-on leg holster that sometimes still had the pistol in it. These also yielded various amounts of loose .380 ACP ammo, along with a full clip and sometimes two for their pistols. None of these worked with any of their guns, but they took them anyway to empty and refill their own clips later util they could carry no more. Third was the *armored zombie*. This was like the tactical zombie save that it wore both a Kevlar armor vest and a body harness with fittings for shotgun shells. No shotgun, of course, and these were as hard to kill as had been the armor vest wearing security guard zombies back at the hospital. Cy would always scavenge what shells were still good from their bodies once the trio finally put one or more of these down. The last was the zombie of the station chief himself, but this author shall refrain from describing that one until the appropriate time. Cy, Lisa, and Mercy wound up having a tougher time than expected fighting their way back through the MCPD substation's first floor to its stairwell, then up the stairs and down the second floor's main hallway to where the radio room and chief's office were located. On the other hand, the ammo they gathered from the bodies almost but not quite made up for what they had to expend in this process.

Lisa had snorted once they had downed one of the armored zombies that still had its pistol, which had given her an opportunity to get a good look at it. "Star Model S," she had said disdainfully. "Spanish Colt .45 knockoff, but chambered for .380 ACP instead of .45 ACP. A good enough gun, but not for what they needed. Their gun supplier was probably making a profit by clearing out his back stocks when he got the contract for this, so he could stock up on new nine millimeters. That shows you how cheap the MCPD has been lately. Cheap cop cars and cheap guns." she finished, shaking her head as she did.

"What's the problem?" Mercy had asked, and then stopped herself. "I'm sorry, I'm forgetting you're an expert on guns."

Lisa gave her a smile even as she straightened up, leaving the pistol with the body. "Most police departments are switching to clip-fed nine millimeters, just like the Army's about to do." She had given Cy a wink with that last sentence, and he had grinned back at her. Lisa had then resumed addressing Mercy. "If the MCPD had done that, this gun would have been a Smith and Wesson Model 39, or a Beretta, or the like. Don't get me wrong. .380 ACP is a decent enough round for what it is, as you've seen, and it's very handy for us right now that they did it in terms of restocking our own supplies, but that wasn't the best choice for a new police handgun. That was the budget-cutting choice. Their old service revolvers were probably .38 Specials, same as your pistol, and those are better bullets than this gun uses. "

"What's the difference?" Mercy asked.

"More punch and longer range. That's why .38 Special was the standard police round for years, until they started the switch to nine millimeter." Lisa gave a short laugh. "Just so you'll know, .380 ACP is one of the favorite choices for concealed carry pistols. It's about the biggest round you can build a handgun around while keeping it as small as possible, and also keeping it fairly low on recoil when you shoot it. You'll notice the difference once you start using that new pistol you've got." She now gave a laugh. "Speaking of which, your new pistol also has a very famous celebrity endorsement on its side."

"Who's that?"

"James Bond. The Walther PPK was his handgun of choice."

"Oh. So why were the security guards at the hospital using those?"

Lisa was about to reply but Cy spoke up before she could. "Okay, that's enough with the small arms lesson," he gently prodded, shooting Lisa a grin as he did. "Remember, Lisa, our time in here is limited. Let's move on, ladies."

Lisa gave him a grin, and then nodded. After that the trio again resumed moving through the darkened hallways of the MCPD substation.

It took a while to clear the second floor main hallways of all zombies. Once they had finally downed the last zombie blocking their way, the trio stopped in front of the radio room door. Cy tried the door handle, and it was unlocked. He nodded at Lisa and Mercy, who were standing well clear, then suddenly jerked it open and came around with his shotgun at the ready. The radio room was empty of zombies, or of bodies for that matter. Best of all, even though it had the same scattered papers and various small objects strewn on the floor that they had seen in other locations within the building, the radio equipment itself appeared to be undamaged.

"Hot damn, but this is a stroke of luck!" Cy exclaimed, as he quickly went inside with both women hot on his heels. "Maybe the best one yet!"

"Is it still good?" Lisa asked, fingering her weapon while Cy quickly checked everything over.

"Looks like it," Cy said, as he picked up a headset with attached boom mike with his free hand, put it on his head, and flipped a big red switch on the console. The two women immediately heard a burst of static from a speaker somewhere in the room, accompanied right after that by indistinct chatter and the occasional soft frequency squeal. "We got power too." He looked back at them. "As long as nothing's wrong with the main antenna, then we're in business."

"Then we'd better get moving," Lisa said. She looked back at Mercy. "Are you ready?"

Mercy managed a weak smile. "As ready as I'll ever be."

"Lisa?" Cy asked.

Lisa turned back to look at him. To her surprise, Cy was offering her his free hand. "Good luck," was all he said.

Lisa looked at Cy's hand for a moment, then let go of her MAC-11's suppressor and took it. She clasped it firmly as she spoke. "You too."

The two remained clasping hands for a few seconds more, and then let go. Cy now looked at Mercy. "And don't let anything happen to you either," he said.

"Who, me?" Mercy shot back with a grin. "I'm just along for the ride."

Cy chuckled. "Get out of here, you two, and I'll see you downstairs."

"Roger on that," Lisa said, shooting Cy a wink. He winked back, and together she and Mercy left the radio room.

Many miles away and somewhat to the north, well beyond the quarantine line that now encircled the whole of Metro City and a good part of the surrounding countryside, U.S. Army Brigadier General William T. Ryan (the T was for Terence, but no one dared to bring that up in his presence) was in a meeting with his senior field and staff officers who were part of the Metro City operation. The loss of the rescue convoy had been a hard one to take, and General Ryan had both publicly taken responsibility and admitted to a ravenous press that both he and his staff had seriously underestimated the threat level that had faced them. Now that the reporters had been shooed away - or forcibly extracted back to their waiting areas, in a few isolated cases - this staff meeting could take place. It was being held inside the large furnished field tent that Ryan was using as his headquarters, and he was currently making plans with his senior officers as to what to do next. At that moment they had just finished listening to a brief being delivered by one Captain Bill Walters, who was in charge of the six OH-58 Kiowa helicopters being used for aerial observation within and above the quarantine zone. He had some interesting news for the general.

"So what you're saying is that there are survivors, and at least one of them is one of our own people?" Ryan said from his position at the head of the table.

"Yes, sir," Walters responded. He handed the general a set of color photographs. Ryan looked them over as Walters continued, then passed them down the table for the others to see. "We've positively identified two of them. The soldier who is with them is Corporal Cyrus Rappalo, sir, from the relief convoy. The tall dark-skinned woman with them is Lisa Stanridge, the semi-pro race car driver."

"Hooo-wee!" one of the other captains at the table exclaimed. "Lisa Stanridge! Corporal Rappalo is a lucky guy!"

Ryan smiled. "Let's stay focused, people." He again looked at Walters. "Any idea as to who that female nurse is, or doctor, or whatever?" he asked.

Walters shook his head. "No sir. We're still trying to get information regarding the current staffing at Metro City Medical Center."

Ryan pursed his lips. "Do you know where they're heading?"

"The MCPD station on the other side of the hospital," Walters said immediately. "They're probably going there for extra ammunition and supplies."

"Just what I would do," Ryan agreed, nodding his head. "Do you think they'll use the station transmitter to contact us?"

"If it's in working order, sir. Corporal Rappalo is a good soldier, per his record."

"I see." Ryan smiled. "Thank you, Walters."

"Yes, sir. You're welcome, sir."

Ryan furrowed his brow for a few moments, as if thinking hard, then spoke again. "Any chance of dropping the closest Kiowa to them to the deck, so we can pick them up and get them out of there?"

"No sir," Walters said, with a bit of a nervous edge to his voice. When Ryan looked hard at him, the Army captain explained. "Sir, every time our Kiowa in that area gets too close to the station, a big flock of crows flies up from the roof and starts to buzz them."

"Crows?" Ryan said incredulously. "*Buzzing* them?"

"Yes, sir." The nervousness in the voice of Walters was now more pronounced. "They keep swooping at them as if they're trying to attack the helicopter. I know it sounds crazy, sir, but it's true. Our people have to keep backing off for fear of sucking one of those crazy crows into the motor, or something equally bad. You know, kinda like a bird strike with a plane?"

"Only this time an Army helicopter in the middle of a zombie outbreak is involved," Ryan said evenly.

"And it's not just at the MCPD substation," Walters continued. "It's anywhere within the quarantine zone. Every time our Kiowas swoop in for a closer look, huge flocks of crows are there to drive them back. It's uncanny, sir."

Ryan again pursed his lips and furrowed his brow for a couple of seconds before speaking. "What's your opinion, Walters? Speak freely, son."

The captain gulped, and then set himself. "Sir, and I know this sounds insane, but I think those crows are deliberately preventing us from landing. It's almost as if they want Corporal Rappalo's group to get out of there on their own, without any assistance from us. Either that, or they're trying to claim the town for themselves, sir." He paused, looked the general in the eye, and then added, "There's an awful lot of carrion down there on which they can feed, sir."

Ryan cocked an eyebrow and gave Walters a look. "Oh, really?"

"Yes, sir." Walters looked down. "Sorry, sir. You asked my opinion."

Ryan nodded. "And so I did." He forced a smile. "Thank you again, Walters."

"Y-yes, sir." With that the captain stepped back from the table and assumed a position of parade rest.

Ryan reached up with one hand, closed his eyes, and began to massage the bridge of his nose. His aide, staff officers, and everyone else inside his headquarters tent watched but did not speak. After about a half-minute of this he stopped, lowered his hand, and looked up at them. "Well, I'm not about to let a flock of damn crows keep me from doing my job. Major Kendricks?"

One of the men seated further down the table came to attention. "Yes sir."

"Get on the horn with upstairs. Tell them I've got survivors confirmed on the ground inside the quarantine zone, but that the situation within the zone has devolved even more and that I need proper air support to get them out. Cobras or Hogs if they'll let me have them. If they have any questions, refer them to me directly. Also see how many more portable flamethrowers they can get to us here."

"Yes, sir." The major stood and saluted. Ryan remained seated but saluted back, and with that the major left.

Ryan now gave his people a smile. "I hope Corporal Rappalo and his two lady friends can hold out until we can get to them." There was nervous laughter and a few nods around the table in response.

At that moment a young female second lieutenant bustled her way in through the front entrance. "General Ryan, sir!" she said, rushing up to him and then coming to attention beside him to salute.

Ryan returned the salute. "What is it, Lieutenant?"

"We've made radio contact with the survivors, sir."

"Speak of the devil," said one of the other Army captains at the table.

Ryan ignored the comment. He stood up and everyone else at the table followed a half-beat later. "Who?" he asked the lieutenant.

"The caller identifies himself as Corporal Cyrus Rappalo, sir."

"Our missing man," Ryan announced. He looked at his staff, who looked back, and then back at the lieutenant. "I'm coming with you." He looked back at his staff again. "The rest of you to your duties. I'll let you know what I've decided once I've talked with the corporal and hear for myself his account of what's really happening in there."

"Yes, sir!" everyone responded, briefly coming to attention before most of them scrambled away to their various duties.

"Mind if I tag along?" came a voice from the far end of the tent. Ryan, his aide, and what few soldiers remained with him looked down to see a civilian in a rumpled dark suit with tie still sitting at the table. He was a rather bland-looking man save for the hint of a bemused smile on his face.

Ryan snorted. "I suppose, Mr. Dahl. I'm sure Pandora's just as interested in this news as we are."

"Thank you," the man said somewhat smugly. He stood up, neatly put his chair back into place, and then began to walk towards them. "I can assure you of Mr. Nye's approval on this."

"I'm sure you can, Mr Dahl," Ryan growled at him. He abruptly turned on his heel and left the tent before Ryan could reach him, the others quickly following after him. He did that so Dahl would be unable to hear Ryan contemptuously mutter under his breath the phrase *butt kisser*. Nevertheless, the bemused smile on the face of Carlton Dahl, Pandora's official on-site representative to General Ryan, grew even bigger as he picked up his pace and quickly followed after the general and his men.

Lisa and Mercy found the door to the station chief's office unlocked. At Lisa's signal, Mercy quickly yanked open the door from the side while Lisa covered the doorway with her MAC-11. Nothing leapt out to attack her from within. Instead, she was greeted by total silence and the sight of a semi-darkened room beyond the doorway, along with a now-familiar incredible odor. It was the same odor she had smelled in the back storage room of Southwest Sporting Goods, in the waiting area by the first floor nurse's station at Metro City Medical Center, and in the home of her aunt and uncle when she had found the savagely mutilated remains of both her younger brother Randy and his cousin. It was the smell of an open-air slaughterhouse on a hot summer's day. She walked slowly forward until she was standing in the doorway. She looked around inside for several seconds, the barrel of her weapon moving with her eyes. She then turned and looked back at Mercy, who by now had come around the door and was standing behind her, brandishing her assault rifle and her nose twitching at the smell. "Looks clear," Lisa said. "Let's go in."

Lisa had only taken three steps into the office when the lights suddenly came on. She almost jumped, then looked back at Mercy. One of the researcher's hands was on the light switch. "Sorry," Mercy said. "Force of habit."

"It's okay," Lisa replied with a nervous chuckle. "You startled me, that's all." She started to say more, but suddenly realized that Mercy was no longer looking at her. She was looking beyond her with an expression on her face that managed to combine both horror and utter revulsion. Lisa turned to see for herself what Mercy saw, and sucked in her breath involuntarily.

There was a body lying on the floor in the middle of the room, and also in the middle of a rather large irregular splotch of blood on the room's carpet. It was the remains of a portly man, probably in middle age, who had at one time been wearing a policeman's uniform. *Had been* was the operative phrase here. It was quite obvious that the zombies had been here long before the two still human women had arrived, judging from the state of the remains. Lisa felt her stomach begin to churn and had to steel herself against that horrific sight.

"You never really get used to it, you know," Lisa heard Mercy say quietly behind her. She turned to look at her, and saw that Mercy's face was set just as hard as her own must have been. "It's like what happens with soldiers during a war. They see so much of death and killing, and dead bodies everywhere, that they get numb to it. Even for them, though, they never really get used to it. That's part of the reason why many suffer from PTSD afterwards. Their minds have to shut it out at the time, but it comes back to haunt them later in their nightmares." She gave a low chuckle. "I know I haven't gotten used to it. I don't think I ever will."

Lisa nodded. "Let's just get what we need and get out of here," she said in a low and slightly shaky voice.

The pair quickly moved to the desk in the room and began to search it, Mercy the left side drawers and Lisa the center and right. It took just under a minute for Lisa to find two sets of keys on two key rings in the uppermost right side drawer. One was a normal key ring, and the other was a set of oversized and heavy keys, resembling large skeleton keys and of the kind used for cell doors. She held them up for Mercy to see. "It'll bet these are what we want."

"And the other?"

99

"Station keys, most likely. We'll take them too. We might need them for the Armory," Lisa said, as she pocketed both sets of keys.

Mercy started to say something in reply, but she was interrupted by another sound in the room, It was a rustling sound, very similar to the one Lisa had heard in the hospital parking lot some hours before, but this time it was mixed in with a peculiar slurching and slurping sound, very similar to what one might hear if a person were wading though jelly. The ruined body on the floor began to rise, much to the horror of both women. The motion was also accompanied by exaggerated raspy breathing and an almost animal-like guttural groan. They didn't wait to see what would happen next. Even as it came to its feet on its ruined legs and began to turn towards them, both women were already running for the door. They were out of there and running down the hall before the thing could even take its first step.

"And that's the situation, sir," Cy said into his microphone.

There was a crackle of static, and then Cy heard the response of General Ryan over the radio room speakers. *"Roger that. Sorry to tell you this, but we can't land a chopper at your location due to those damn crows."*

"Crows, sir?"

"Yeah. They go after our bird every time we get close. Damnedest thing my pilots have ever seen."

Cy grimaced, remembering their own sightings of both the crows and the evil-looking raven that had been leading them during their adventure. "Probably has something to do with the Outbreak, sir," he offered.

"Probably. Do you have any evac plans of your own?"

"We've already secured alternate transportation, sir," Cy responded. "It's an MCPD Dodge Royal Monaco squad car, unit number 12. I'll have Lisa turn on the lights just to make sure you find us. We'll be heading north on Highway 9 once we clear the beltway, sir, since that's the quickest way out of town to the quarantine line and you from our location."

There was a pause on the other end before the response. *"That's going to take you right past the Pandora complex, Corporal."*

"Yes, sir," Cy responded, "and we talked about that. Mercy, I mean Ms. Parks, believes that since that was the origin point of the Outbreak, then the virus may have already burned itself out in there. On top of which it's about the only option out of town we've got from where we're currently located, sir. The city beltway is too jammed up for us to reach any other way out of Metro City in a reasonable amount of time, and that'll give the zombies plenty of time to find us and gang up on us again, sir."

"Point well taken, Corporal. All right. We'll go ahead with your plan, and I've sent for some better air support to help us out. As soon as they get here, I'll send out one of those units to intercept you on the way and provide you air cover until you get within range of us. Once that happens, we'll come through the quarantine line and pick you up."

Cy paused as he heard a door bang open and then the sound of feet running down the hall. That was probably Lisa and Mercy, he guessed, and they must have found more in the chief's office than just the keys they needed. He decided it was time to wrap up his radio call. He kept one eye on the door to the radio room as he spoke again. "Sir, one more question, if I may?"

"Go ahead."

"What does the chopper you've got watching us say it's like out there?"

"Well aside from all those damn crows on the roof of your building and everywhere else, those zombies are bunching up again behind that fire barricade of yours. It's burned down quite a bit, and they'll probably try to breach it before long. Also, more are starting to come up around the other side of the block. I'd say you're going to have visitors fairly soon."

"Shit!" Cy exclaimed, then quickly added, "Sorry, sir."

"That's all right, son. I understand. Get what you guys need in there, rescue that other survivor, and get the hell out of there as fast as you can. We'll be waiting for you north of town, and I'll get you that air cover as soon as I can. Ryan, out."

"Yes, sir. Rappalo, out."

Cy set down the mike, and then put both hands on his shotgun. He hadn't heard anything else in the hallway since Lisa and Mercy had left, but he had the strangest feeling that something was out there. There was also the fact that he had never heard that distant door close, but that might have been due to the hydraulic hinges fitted on most of the doors in the building. He had no way to prove something was there, no way to see or sense it, and yet he knew it was there. He carefully got up from the radio console and then walked to the radio room door, holding his shotgun at the ready. The only sounds to be heard were the fall of his own feet on the carpeted floor and the loud beating of his own heart. He stopped in front of the door and listened, shotgun at the ready. Still nothing. Not a sound. He decided to risk it. Trading his shotgun for his .45 ACP, he held the heavy caliber pistol in his right hand while he opened the door with his left.

Framed in the open doorway before Cy was an irregular shape indicating the remains of a man. It had at one time been a somewhat heavyset police officer of middle age, but not anymore. Both the virus and the zombies had ravaged the body, and it was a miracle that what remained of it was even mobile and sentient. It locked its one remaining eye on the human before it, let out a guttural growling half-roar, and began to both raise its arms and lurch forward towards Cy. It suddenly arched and flew backwards as the roar of a .45 ACP filled the air, and what remained of its head was blown off and both splattered and smacked into the far wall. Cy didn't wait. He barreled his way into and past the headless body as it fell, racing down the hallway and towards the stairwell so he could rejoin his friends. Privately he hoped that they were all right, as he made the stairwell door, yanked it open, and darted inside.

The black limousine sat some distance away from the Army vehicles. It was parked in such a manner so that it could pull straight out and onto the highway for an easy departure. It had taken some trouble getting it parked that way, given the overwhelming Army presence behind the quarantine line, but allowances had been made in the end. After all, its chief passenger was a very important man, with insider connections high in both political and military circles. It would not be good for one's future career to inconvenience him too much.

That important person was currently seated in the back of the limo and engaging in a conversation with one of his subordinates on his car phone. These were the direct ancestors of modern cell phones. They were essentially the same thing, but big and bulky due to the limitations of 1980s-era analog and first-generation digital electronics. Car phones were also very expensive in this era, and were normally limited in ownership to those businesses that needed them and those individuals who could afford them. Brian Desmond Nye, the current chief executive officer and chairman of the board of directors for Pandora Corporation, was such a person. He was a thin but spry looking man in his early sixties, with a head that was still full of silver-grey hair. He also had the coldest cobalt blue eyes most folks had ever seen. They matched his normally cold demeanor and frigid personality. He also had a penchant for wearing white three-piece double-breasted suits with black shirts and matching white shoes, and he was wearing such today as he sat in his limo and talked on his car phone.

"So the Army has made contact with survivors of both the Outbreak and the rescue convoy?" Nye said, his voice as level and chilly as any given side of a block of freshly cut ice.

"*Yes sir,*" came the disembodied voice of Carlton Dahl over the car phone. "*One soldier and two civilians, including one of our own. Mercy Parks, one of our people from the hospital.*"

"Interesting," Nye replied. He looked at the man sitting with him in the back of the limo. "Mr. Voormand?"

Piter de Voormand was a Dutchman and a naturalized American citizen, who had used his considerable skills to work his way up the corporate ladder at Pandora and into the important position of being Mr. Nye's chief personal aide. *Corporate hatchetman* might have been a better term to describe how he had done that, and how he continued to prove both his talents and personal loyalty to Nye on a regular basis. Unlike Nye, he wore a two-piece suit that was a rich shade of sable, his shirt was white, and he had sandy blond hair touched with grey. He too had blue eyes, although his were of a more friendly shade and had green highlights around their corneas. "Mercy Parks," Voormand responded. "Excellent researcher. She was one of our top liason people at Metro City Medical Center. Engaged to be married to John Hartman, another of our top researchers there. She was also among those who contacted us requesting more counteragent when the Outbreak first became known, as she and her fellow staff had used what little they had to save themselves. We refused, of course. After that we lost contact with her, until now that is."

"I see," Nye said, nodding in agreement as he did.

"It will be interesting to hear what she has to share, provided the Army returns her to us," de Voormand continued.

"*That's going to be a problem, sir,*" Dahl said on the phone. "*She's appealed to them for protection. Says one of the people who's with them is naturally immune to the enhanced U-virus.*"

"Naturally immune?" One of Nye's eyebrows had gone up at the news. "Which one?"

"I believe you know her, sir," replied the disembodied voice. "Lisa Stanridge, the stock car racer."

Both of Nye's eyebrows went up at the same time as a look of surprise filled the face of Piter de Voormand. "She survived?" de Voormand said incredulously. "The woman who beat our own racing team for the Bellville Cup?! And she's *immune?!* How is that possible? Besides, word had it she had died with everyone else at the track outside of town."

"It seems she got away," Nye said calmly.

"Well," de Voormand mused, "her father is a full blood Cherokee Indian well versed in the old ways of his people, according to her published bio. She also has an uncle who's a Vietnam vet and is something of a survivalist." He was now looking rather thoughtful. "Perhaps she was trained by both of them."

"Perhaps." Nye's eyebrows had lowered, but there was an intensity to his expression that had not been there before. He spoke again into the car phone. "Who is her other companion?"

"Corporal Cyrus Rappalo, U.S. Army. He was from the convoy. They're currently trying to rescue a Mexican illegal by the name of Raul Esteban who's locked up inside the MCPD substation."

"What a waste of time," de Voormand muttered. "Damn illegals." He would have said more, but a cross glance from Nye silenced him.

"Go on," Nye said into the cell phone's handset.

"I've already done a check on Esteban, sir," Dahl said. *"He's an itinerant laborer who got picked up by the MCPD last week because of his immigration status. He was supposed to be turned over to the INS later this week, but then the Outbreak happened."*

"I see." Nye furrowed his eyebrows and put the hand with the car phone's receiver under his chin. His aide de Voormand remained quiet. He knew his superior well enough by now to know that assuming a classic Thinker pose was a habit of his whenever he was concentrating, so he held his tongue until he was done. As for Nye, he remained frozen in this position for several seconds, then lifted his head and returned the receiver to his ear. "So Ms. Parks says Ms. Stanridge is naturally immune, and is apparently trying to keep her away from us. That's not very nice of her. What a bad employee." He paused to lick his lips, then looked at de Voormand and added, "Do we still have communications with our facility north of town?"

"Computer modem access only, sir. No personnel have responded to our calls on our private lines from the first day of the Outbreak onward."

"Understandable," Nye said. "Modem access will be enough, I think.," He gave de Voormand a firm look. "Do we have any *ubermensch* at the Metro City facility?"

"Only one, sir," de Voormand responded immediately, "and it's one of our early modified prototypes. That's not our main *ubermensch* research facility, as you know, sir. It was there only for viral testing purposes and such."

"It will have to do," Nye said evenly. The coldness returned to both his face and his voice as he spoke again into the car phone. "That will be all. We will take care of it on our end. Thank you, Mr. Dahl. Keep me informed of any further developments."

"Yes, sir." There was a loud *klik!* as Dahl broke the connection on his end.

Nye reached forward and hung up the car phone, then leaned back and looked at his aide. "Is the necessary gear there for it to equip itself properly, if given orders to do so?"

"No, sir," de Voormand replied, "but I'm sure it can scrounge up whatever it needs or find appropriate substitutes from the resources at hand. This *ubermensch* is one of our own, even if it is an early one, and those are designed to both adapt to limiting circumstances and to make the most of them."

"Good," Nye said, nodding as he did. "You know what you need to do. Contact our computer center and have them issue the necessary orders via the modem line." He then handed his aide the car phone receiver.

"Yes, sir." de Voormand took the receiver from Nye, leaned over the phone proper, and began to dial.

Nye now reached up and rapped the polarized window that separated the back of the limo from the front with the knuckle of his right middle finger. The limo immediately started up, pulled out, and headed down the highway away from the quarantine line, and from what was left of Metro City. They had only been on the road for a minute or so when de Voormand finished his call. He hung the car phone's receiver up and then looked at Nye. "Your orders are being carried out, sir."

"Very good."

de Voormand hesitated, and then spoke again. "If I may ask, sir, where are we going?".

Nye allowed himself a thin smile. "To establish our alibi, of course."

"Yes, sir," de Voormand said. He too smiled. "And to prepare our story for the press, I presume."

"No story," Nye corrected. "The truth. That is, *our* truth. Not *their* truth. *Our* truth, just as we've been doing all along. The only truth they need to know, as it's the only truth worth telling and the only truth that the public ever needs to know."

de Voormand shook his head, although he was still smiling. "I'm afraid the press is having a difficult time buying our truth as we've been telling them, given all that has happened so far."

"They will eventually," Nye responded with conviction, "once we ensure that our truth is the only truth that can be obtained. After all, we can't have either the press or the public engaging in needless speculation, urban legends, and wild conspiracy theories. They need to be led to our truth in such a way that they will accept it no matter what, even if it means we have to have a hand in shaping events towards their reaching our truth. Do I make myself clear?"

"Absolutely, sir."

"Good."

With that, both men fell silent. The limo continued to move down the highway until it disappeared from sight.

CHAPTER 8
THE LAST SURVIVOR

The first thing Lisa and Mercy saw as they neared the stairwell landing for the first floor were three shapes moving up towards them. They had just reached the next-to-last landing to where they were now and were about to make the final turn towards the landing that the two women were now on. The zombie of Officer Joe Frisco was in the lead, and it was accompanied by two other police zombies. One was in the remains of a normal uniform, while the other was an armored type. It wore both a bloody and torn dark blue SWAT coverall and a bloodstained Kevlar body armor vest on top of that. The last thing two of the three zombies felt were a veritable fusillade of .380 ACP bullets and 5.56mm NATO standard assault rifle rounds tearing through their heads and upper bodies, as both Lisa and Mercy stood their ground and opened fire. Both the Frisco and normal police zombies went down immediately, letting out screeching wails as they did, but the armored zombie did not drop. Its armor vest had protected it from most of its hits, and the few that found parts of its body to hit only seemed to make it angry. It jerked around this way and that until the rain of incoming fire ended, then it let out an angry roar and began to run the rest of the way towards the two women. It was stopped cold in its tracks by the angry bark and bite of an AK-47 assault rifle on full auto. Lisa had swapped guns once she realized what was happening, and now directed a steady stream of fire at the armored zombie with a weapon that had just enough punch to pierce its body armor, given how short a range to target was involved. It stumbled back, lost its footing, and began to wail as it tumbled over the rail and then fell down the center of the stairwell shaft. Less than two seconds later there was a bone shattering *krak!* as it hit the bottom and broke both its back and its neck. It never moved again.

Lisa and Mercy did not wait to enjoy their victory. Their time was limited, so they quickly made their way around the first two zombie bodies as they hurried down to the station's basement level. They looked at the body of the third just long enough to make sure it was permanently out of commission, and then readied themselves for opening the basement level stairwell door. Lisa had swapped weapons again on the move in an effort to conserve her ammo for their group's best assault rifle, and now held her MAC-11 in her hands once again. At a nod from Lisa, Mercy yanked open the door and stepped aside, quickly pulling up her assault rifle in order to bring it to bear on any target that came through that door. It was a good thing she did, because an infected K-9 leapt through directly at Lisa. A burst from Mercy's M-16 knocked it aside as Lisa dodged downward and scrambled towards Mercy, and then her own MAC-11 was up and she too was firing at the infected K-9. It went down in a writhing pile of agonized yelping, which finally stopped when it quit moving and lay still in a pool of its own blood next to the body of the broken zombie in the center of the stairwell floor. Both women heard the ticking sound of claws across a concrete surface as soon as that kill was done. They were the same they had heard in the alley earlier, and that they knew to be the sound of an infected dog charging to the attack. This time both were in plain view of the open stairwell door and could see the darkened hallway beyond, so they set themselves and waited. About two seconds later a second infected K-9 rounded a corner at the far end of the hallway and commenced a dead run towards them. They dropped it less than a third of the way with their combined machine pistol and assault rifle fire. They remained where they were and listened, but all remained silent until they heard a strong voice cry out with a thick Spanish accent. "Hey! Anyone there? I want out! Me last human left! Please!!"

Lisa turned to Mercy. "That would be Raul, I think," she said.

Mercy nodded. "Let's go get him."

The pair edged their way down the hall. As they drew closer to its end, they could see that not only was there another open hallway to their left, but also two doors to their right. The first one was closed and a quick test proved it to be locked. A sign next to it read ARMORY. The second was an open doorway to their right directly across from the other hallway. Its sign read KENNELS, and the fact that the door was wide open explained much.

"Hello?" the not so distant voice pleaded again. "Anyone there? ¿Hola? ¿Hay alguien ahí?"

"Definitely Raul, I'd say," Mercy half-whispered to Lisa.

"Uh-huh," Lisa responded. She kept moving ahead, slowly and carefully, her MAC-11 raised and at the ready, and Mercy did likewise.

The hallway ended in a large barred-off area with a single barred sliding door, which was currently open. In a fair-sized cubby hole off to one side were a duty officer's desk, a large double-door metal storage cabinet, and a smaller three-drawer filing cabinet. The duty officer's desk had the expected clutter on it, in which there was nothing obviously useful. Of more interest to the pair was what lay beyond the metal bars. It was a cell bay with six average sized cells, enclosed on three sides by concrete-lined cinder block walls just like those used in the rest of the basement. The fourth or front side of each cell had the expected metal bar frames embedded in the walls and inset sliding barred metal doors, practically identical to those at the front of the bay. All of the cell doors were closed and locked so their occupants could not escape. Five of these held zombies, and they began to moan and howl and reach through the bars towards the two human women as soon as they were aware of their presence close by. The sixth cell held a human. It was the one at the far end and to the right from the cell bay's sliding door. He was practically plastered against the front bars of his own cell at the corner farthest away from the next adjoining cell, so its zombie couldn't reach him, and he looked towards the two women with pleading eyes and a fearful face. "Ah! *Señoritas!* Please let me out! I am not infected, and I want out of here!! *¡Me cago en la hostia!* Please!!!"

"All right, all right, settle down!" Lisa half-shouted at the man. "Give us a little bit, okay?"

"*Si,*" the man said, still looking fearful and clutching at the bars. He gave a sideways look at the zombie in the cell next to him, and then back at the women again. "Hurry!"

Lisa moved close to Mercy so she could hear her above the din of the incarcerated zombies. "To reach him, we've got to go straight past those other zombies. The only way to do that is to walk in the exact center of the hallway. Veer just a little bit to either side, and one of those other zombies will grab you."

"Tricky," Mercy said, looking down the cell bay and then back at Lisa.

"I'll do it," Lisa offered. "You stay here and get your gear ready, so you can test him once he gets out."

"Right," Mercy said, as she moved over to the desk and began to set up her medical gear. "I'll also check out this stuff here. Maybe I can find something useful."

"Right," Lisa said with a nod. She then turned back to the cell bay, took in a deep breath, let it out again, then she began to move down the exact center of the cell bay's hallway with her MAC-11 in a walking carry.

It was just like the ancient Greek myth of old. The zombies in the other cells were like the lions in one version she had read, straining at the most extreme to get her, arms fully extended and clawed fingers raking empty air mere centimeters away from her on either side. She could have shot them, of course, and that would have been that, but she didn't want to waste ammo like that when they were already locked up and there was another way. It was a nerve-wracking way to be sure, but it was a way, and it worked. It took Lisa less than half-a-minute to walk the gauntlet of the zombies, and then she was at the front back corner of the farthest cell on the right, and holding the hand of one very frightened Mexican illegal.

"*Gracias, señorita,*" the man exclaimed. "You've got some *cojones*!" He realized what he had said, and then his face broke into a nervous grin. "Oh, I am sorry. You know what I mean," he added quickly.

"I know," Lisa said, smiling back at him. The zombies in the other cells continued to whine and moan and reach through their bars in a vain effort to get at her, but she ignored them. She let go of the man's hand and then began to fish around in one of her pockets. "Raul, is it?"

"*Si.* Raul Esteban. I'm from Guadalajara." Raul's face suddenly broke into a big grin. "Hey, I know you! You the stock car racer, Lisa Stanridge! I watch you on TV. You good, and you pretty too."

Lisa couldn't help but laugh. "Why, thank you."

"How you know my name?"

"Officer Frisco told us," Lisa said, as she fished the cell keys out of her pocket and began to try each of them on Raul's cell door.

"Joe!" Raul exclaimed. "Where is he?"

"He's dead," Lisa said quickly. "Let's leave it at that." The next-to-last key on the ring proved to be the right one. The lock on Raul's cell door clicked, and then Lisa slid it open.

Raul emerged at once but stopped beside Lisa. He now looked sad. "Oh, I am sorry to hear that. Officer Frisco, he good man." He now looked down the cell bay hallway, currently full of waving and clawing zombie arms on either side and echoing with zombie cries, and gulped. "So how we get back out, *Señorita* Stanridge?"

"Just call me Lisa," Lisa said, "and we do it the same way I got down here. Stick to the center of the aisle and don't go to either side for anything, unless you want a permanent embrace from our undead friends there."

Raul shuddered. "Why not shoot them?"

"And waste ammo?" Lisa gave Raul an encouraging look. "You can do it, Raul. If a girl like me can do it, then a big guy like you surely can."

Raul laughed nervously. "Me, I not so big. You half-head taller than me, Lisa."

"But you're stocky, and I'll bet you're strong too," Lisa further encouraged. "What kind of work do you do?"

"Manual jobs," Raul said. "Road work, construction, buildings. When I can get them and when they don't check my papers. I got to work on skyscraper once, in Dallas. That was incredible, working so high up."

"Then think of this like that," Lisa said. "You're back on the job in Dallas, and you're having to walk one of those I-beams high up on that skyscraper. Know what I mean?"

Raul gave Lisa a look, then gulped and nodded. "*Si*. Okay. I do it. *Gracias*, Lisa."

"You're welcome."

Just under a half-minute later the two were out of the cell bay without even a scratch, and Mercy was giving Raul a quick once-over. She had already drawn a sample of Raul's blood and was testing it with her portable analyzer. "I have to test your blood to make sure you don't have the virus, just to be sure," she explained, "and then I'm going to give you something to make sure you never get it. I also have to make sure your blood and what I'm about to give you is compatible." She looked up at him. "You're very lucky, you know, being locked up and isolated like that."

Raul shook his head. "It no fun, I tell you. I also very hungry. I have plenty water, but I no eat anything for two days. Nobody left to bring me any."

"There's a candy bar in the side drawer of this desk," Mercy noted. "It'll have to do for now. Lisa, could you get it for Raul? He can eat it after I'm done."

"Sure," Lisa said, as she moved around the pair so she could get at the desk drawers.

"*Gracias, señorita ... señorita ...*"

"Parks," Mercy said. "Mercy Parks, but you can call me Mercy." She finished what she was doing with Raul's blood sample, and then looked up at him. "You're clear, Raul, as I hoped you'd be, and your blood checks out. There's just one more thing left to do, and that's to make sure you never get the virus."

"How you do that?"

"I'm going to give you some of Lisa's blood," Mercy said, as she pulled a vial out of her small medical bag with a handwritten label containing a rich red liquid.

"What?" Raul exclaimed.

"Don't worry," Mercy said, as she opened a package containing a hypodermic, stuck the needle in one end of the vial, then drew out a carefully measured amount of the liquid. "Your blood types are compatible. Not an exact match, but compatible. This is going to be like a PRP injection, only I'm doing it with Lisa's blood instead of yours. I know you don't know what that is, so I'll explain as I'm doing it. Put your right arm on the desk please. That's good. Ah, nice veins. Hold on ... stick." With that, she stuck the needle of the hypo into one of Raul's surface veins. She continued to talk as she slowly and carefully injected the sample of Lisa's blood into Raul's vein. "A PRP injection is when they take out some of your own blood, concentrate it, and put it back in to help out elsewhere in your body. In this case, Lisa's immune because her body makes better stuff than we use to immunize people against the virus. That's why I'm giving you some of her blood instead of mine. Hers is a lot better, and it's possible that your own body might learn how to make the stuff in her blood too. Not only will you be immune after that, but any kids you might have later will be too."

Raul laughed nervously. "I no plan that far ahead yet."

Mercy allowed herself to smile. "Understandable. I'd normally use an IV for this but I don't have one, so I've got to do it this way and I've got to do it very carefully. Just a little more ... there. All done. Coming out now ... there. Hold this please, while I wrap it." A few seconds later Mercy was packing up her gear, and Raul was looking at a medical wrap holding a sterile pad against the inner part of his right elbow.

"Here," Lisa said, handing Raul the candy bar.

"Ah! *Gracias*, Lisa!" Raul exclaimed, as he tore off the wrapper and all but inhaled the candy bar in just a few bites.

It was at that moment that they heard fast-moving footsteps approaching. Lisa already had her MAC-11 up and covering the hallway as Mercy reached for her M-16, which she had leaned up against the storage cabinet before setting up for Raul, who also looked around in alarm. To everyone's great relief they saw Cy make the turn and run down towards them. "Cy!" Lisa exclaimed, lowering her weapon.

"Lisa!" Cy called back as he came into the room and joined them. He stopped in front of Lisa, and looks passed between both of them. Then the moment was gone and Cy was addressing the other two people in the room. "Mercy. Oh, and you must be Raul." He took his hand from the stock of his shotgun and offered it to the stoutly built Mexican. "Welcome to our little survival party."

"*Si*," Raul replied, taking Cy's hand and shaking it firmly. "Glad to be part of it."

Cy then turned and positioned himself so he could address everyone. "Listen up, folks. I've been in touch with General Ryan outside the quarantine line. They know we're here and they've been trying to get to us, but they've not been successful." He now gave Lisa a grin. "Our winged friends out there go after their helicopters every time they try to fly in to pick us up."

"They're no friends of mine," Lisa said evenly. "Sounds to me like the Raven Mocker is having fun with us."

"Raven Mocker?" Raul said, and the fear returned to his face again. "Oh no! I hear about her from some of my Indian friends on the job. *!Ella es una mala hijo de puta!*"

Cy had to fight the urge to laugh, and could not stop a big grin from forming on his face. "Take it easy, Raul," he said. "We're only talking about flocks of infected crows here, not some Indian legend."

Mercy cocked an eyebrow. "You know Spanish?" she asked. "What'd he say?"

"A little," Cy responded. "You don't want to know."

"And the raven," Lisa added. "Don't forget the raven, the one that keeps following us."

"*¡Ai, yi, yi!*" Raul said, and now he looked worried. "Out of the frying pan into the fire, as you say!"

"Well the crows aren't after us," Cy said evenly. "They're only going after the Army helicopters, and that raven doesn't do anything but watch us. Me, I think it's just a bird that's taken a fancy to us, like strays sometimes do to people who are nice to them, and I'm going to treat it just like any old bird until I'm proven wrong. In the meantime, let's focus on the here and now, folks, and our present predicament. General Ryan says his spotters in the air tell him that the zombies are ganging back up outside beyond our fire barricade, which is burning low. He also says that more zombies are coming up from the other side of the block."

"Oh, God," Lisa replied. "We've got to get out of here before there's too many of them to break out."

"After we stop by the station Armory first and make a quick search for those armor vests we wanted," Cy reminded her. "You ladies did remember to pick up the keys, right?"

"Right," Lisa said, as she pulled the smaller of the two key rings out of one of her firesuit pockets and held it up before him.

"Good," Raul said, giving her a smile. Lisa smiled back and then put the keys back in her pocket as he continued. "Remember, getting those armor vests is part of the reason why we're here." He now looked to the others. "And while we're at it, we've got to get Raul here some weapons."

"*Si,*" Raul agreed.

Cy waved towards the hallway and then put his free hand back on the stock of his shotgun. "Then let's move, people. Time's a-wastin' and we don't have much of it left."

Their subsequent visit to the station's Armory was a short and hurried one. Unlike the weapons stores at the National Guard Armory and the Metro City Medical security office this one had been fairly well emptied. There were still items of value they could pick up and use despite that. There was a lone Star Model S pistol in the emptied small arms locker, there were still a couple of boxes left of .380 ACP ammo to go with it, and there was both a full box of 5.56mm NATO standard assault rifle rounds and enough loose shells lying about to almost fill half of a second box. There was also a police rucksack with MCPD markings similar to the ones Lisa and Cy wore. All of them agreed it should be Raul's, as he had none. Cy had in turn given all of the 5.56mm ammo they had found along with the two boxes of .380 ACP to Raul to fill it. He had then handed Raul the Star pistol, then unslung and handed the stout Mexican both his M-16A1 assault rifle and his bandolier, which by now was mostly full of empty clips. "These are just loaners, okay?" he said. "They're the Army's, not mine. You can fill the clips with those shells when we have time."

"*Si,*" Raul had said with gratitude as he accepted the weapon. "*Gracias.*"

"Have you ever used long guns before?"

"Only rifles and shotguns."

"Ever use a clip-fed rifle?"

"*Si.* My grandfather had old Army carbine from war. Good gun."

"Good enough. Just remember that this thing will go full auto on you if you've got it set for that and hold the trigger down too long. See this selector switch right where your thumb goes? Thumb it here for single shot and here for full auto. I'd give you some quick lessons like I did with Mercy earlier, but we don't have time."

"*Si.* I do my best."

"I'm sure you will, Raul."

It was the three Kevlar body armor vests which were still in the MCPD Armory that had proven to be their biggest prize. After a brief discussion with the others and looking them over, Cy gave the biggest to Raul while Lisa and Mercy got the two smaller ones. These didn't fit the two ladies very well, but the fact they were made from flexible Kevlar plus judicious use of their adjustment straps helped in this regard. The men guarded the door while the ladies donned and fitted their new body armor, then they swapped places so Cy could help Raul put on and adjust his own. Lisa had given Cy a wry smile as he had started helping Raul, but Cy had only grinned, patted his own old-style Army armor vest, and shrugged his shoulders in reply. Once they were done, they put back on the rest of their gear and left the MCPD Armory. All that remained now was to break out of the place and escape Metro City for good.

Between ten and fifteen minutes or so later, the sounds of the moans and groans coming from a couple of hundred or so zombies gathering on both sides of the MCPD substation and the cawing of the crows perched on both its roof and on the nearby buildings and power lines was interrupted by the starting of a Dodge 440 motor. It revved up to full power, while at the same time red and blue lights began to flash behind the building. Suddenly an older model police car sailed out of the back parking lot into the front lot through the open gate that connected the two and headed straight for the street. There was a young woman with red skin and long black hair wearing a black two-piece firesuit with red-and-white trim and a black MCPD Kevlar armor vest at the wheel, and she handled that police car as if she were a pro (which she was). A black Army soldier in full combat gear shouldering a China Lake grenade launcher was hanging out of the front passenger window. He opened fire down the street as soon as the police car whipped around northward into it. There was an explosion in front of and slightly off to one side of the moving police car and zombie bodies went everywhere. The police car kept moving, slowly but surely picking up speed, following the path that the the explosion had cleared through the zombies on the north end of the street. Once it was clear of the zombies the police car's tires squealed as it took off, racing down the street, top lights still flashing. Soon enough it disappeared into the darkness beyond.

The raven had never stirred from its perch. Instead, it had watched the proceedings with considerable interest, while the zombies scattered or were blown away and the crows flew off in all directions. It cocked its head sideways as only a bird can, looking northward up the street in the direction where the fast-moving police car had disappeared. It then returned its head to normal, flapped its wings twice, then settled back down and began to call. *Awk! Awk! Awk! Awk!* it cried as it sat on its perch. Had there been any humans left in the area to hear it, one might have sworn that the raven was laughing.

It took Lisa about fifteen minutes using the side streets and back alleys to bypass the traffic and wreck choked beltway, and to find an exit to Highway 9 North that was still open. After that it took another fifteen to twenty minutes to work her way around the abandoned and wrecked vehicles that all but clogged it on the north end of town. Once Lisa worked the MCPD squad car past the last of these, however, the number of wrecks and abandoned vehicles thinned out considerably. Lisa was able to pick up speed and drive at something close to normal, only slowing whenever these were encountered and had to be driven around. She also handled that Dodge Royal Monaco police car as adroitly as she had handled her own HemiCuda, Cy noted. He had never been a racing fan, but he could now well imagine how she must have been on the track, and how she had managed to win the much-coveted Bellville Cup despite her youth. It gave him something else to admire about her as they rode on. Whatever Lisa was thinking about him she kept to herself.

Mercy had asked that the regular radio be turned on, so she could hear the news. It was near the top of the hour, and Cy turned it on just in time to catch the tail end of an infomercial advertising investment opportunities in mobile telephone transmission towers. There was a pause, and then the top-of-the-hour network chimes sounded on the station to which they were listening.

BONG! Be-dah, ba-dah-ding!

"*This is the Mutual News Network,*" sounded a deep resonant voice, followed almost immediately by a sharper and somewhat higher pitched one. "*Mutual News. I'm Christopher DeWitt. The crisis in the American heartland at Metro City continues through the evening of its third day, with the entire population transformed into mindless zombies and the U.S. Army struggling to maintain its quarantine of the entire affected area. Earlier today the Reagan Administration confirmed reports that a military relief convoy which had been sent in on a mission to locate and rescue any survivors had been wiped out by the zombies. More on that in a moment.*

"*In a related story, Pandora Corporation spokesman Piter de Voormand assured the public that it was cooperating in every possible way with both the government and the Army in resolving this deadly situation. This includes a pending investigation into how the virus that caused the Outbreak leaked from its facilities north of Metro City in the first place. And now back to our top story.*

"*This just in. The Army has confirmed contact with four human survivors inside Metro City who are currently trying to escape the city to safety. According to their official press release, the survivors are identified as U.S. Army Corporal Cyrus Rappalo, Metro City Medical Center Senior Nurse Mercy Parks, Mexican immigrant laborer Raul Esteban, and the famed semi-pro stock car driver Lisa Stanridge, winner of last year's Bellville Cup race. Corporal Rappalo is currently the only known survivor of the Army relief convoy, and he encountered and joined forces with the other three during his own efforts to escape the doomed city. The Army has assured us that it will do everything it can to save these four from the tens of thousands of zombies that are currently stalking the Metro City quarantine zone, killing and eating everyone in their path.*

"*In other news, the new government in Iran condemned the United States ...*"

Lisa suddenly turned the radio off. "That's enough of that," she said somewhat acidly.

From the back of the police car, Mercy spoke. "At least the Army revealed we're alive. Publicity. That's the best thing they could have done for us right now, outside of rescuing us."

"*Si,*" came the muffled agreement from Raul, whose mouth was full of food as he sat beside Mercy in the back. They had found some more packaged snack food shortly before they had evacuated the MCPD substation, and the hungry Raul had wolfed all of it down. She now helped him reload the ammo clips for the M-16 that Cy had loaned him, while he finished chewing the last of his food.

"I agree," Cy said from beside Lisa. "Now that the public knows we're alive, Pandora can't just go and bump us off or something."

"I wouldn't put it past them," Mercy said. "They've got the people and resources to pull that kind of thing off, and I've heard rumors of them doing stuff like that during my time with them. Nothing you could ever prove, mind you, but still ...."

"Well I for one hope it all works out," Lisa said. She still had her eyes on the road, as she was the one driving. "Think positive, folks." She found an opportunity to give Cy a quick glance and a grin, and then she refocused on her driving. "I hope the Army picks up on us soon. Right now, we need all of the help we can get."

As if on cue there was a loud squawk from the police radio inside their car. *"MCPD squad car on Highway 9, this is U.S. Army Air Cavalry unit Zulu Tango Four. MCPD squad car on Highway 9, this is U.S. Army Air Cavalry unit Zulu Tango Four. Respond please."*

Cy grabbed the mike and keyed the switch. "Zulu Tango Four, this is Corporal Rappalo. Boy, are we glad to hear from you! Where are you, over?"

"Pop a window and look up, Corporal, over."

Cy immediately did so and stuck his head out of the window of the fast moving police car. When he brought it back in a few seconds later, he grinned at the others. "There's a Huey Hog heading our way. That's a gunship, and from what I can see it's packing quite a weapons load." He then keyed the mike again. "Roger that, Zulu Tango Four. Welcome to our little going-away party, over."

There was a laugh over the speaker. *"Glad to oblige, Corporal. We'll be your escort to the quarantine line, just in case the zombies get frisky. Say, what'd you do with all of those crows everybody else was reporting, over?"*

"Nothing," Cy responded. "Why, over?"

"We ain't seen one since we crossed the quarantine line, over."

"I haven't heard or seen one since we left town," Lisa observed, still keeping her eyes on the road and remaining focused on her driving.

"Yeah," Mercy said. "That's weird."

"Let's not knock our luck," Cy said, then keyed his mike. "I guess they decided to skip our farewell, Zulu Tango Four. Anyway, I see you're packing. What have you got, over?"

"We've got dual miniguns, side rocket pods, and a gunner in each door, over."

Cy grinned. "Man, you guys have got some Hotel Sierra there, over!"

There was another laugh. *"That's right, Corporal. Our orders from General Ryan are to make sure that all of you get out of there alive, especially the two ladies riding in there with you, over."*

"Thanks for riding shotgun for us, Zulu Tango Four, over."

"Not a problem. Glad to oblige, over."

By now the Huey Hog gunship had closed the range, swung around and was positioned above and just behind the rapidly moving police car on the highway, matching both its speed and direction. As it had done so, everyone inside had gotten a good look at it, and saw for themselves how heavily it was armed. Like most UH-1C/M Iroquois gunships ("Huey" was that particular chopper model's popular nickname) it sported dual side-mounted, six-barrel 7.62mm M134 miniguns keyed to the pilot's controls along with two standard 7.62mm M60 machine guns on waist-high pintle mounts in each side door, with both positions manned by live gunners. It also had two side-mounted cylindrical pods carrying a full battery each of 2.5-inch anti-personnel rockets. No one said it aloud, but everyone inside the patrol car felt a sense of relief wash over them once their gunship escort was in position and began its escort mission. They were still not yet out of Metro City, but now they had some of the best protection possible for getting out given the circumstances. It seemed as if nothing could go wrong, and that their eventual escape was all but assured. So it seemed at the time.

What was not known to the Metro City survivors were the events that had taken place earlier that evening some miles north of their current location, events that under normal circumstances might have seemed perfectly ordinary. This was the Outbreak, however, which made them extraordinary, and the dramatic conclusion which they came to would not have been ordinary even under normal circumstances.

Somewhere deep within the bowels of the now-abandoned Pandora Corporation Industrial Complex north of Metro City, whose main entrance was only a quarter-mile and to the east of Highway 9 North and connected to it via a surfaced two-lane road, somewhere in the heart of its lowest levels underground, a certain old style multi-line touch tone desk phone had begun to ring. It rang three times, one of its white line lights flashing in sync with each ring, and then that light went solid as the call was automatically answered. Over the speaker connected to that phone was heard the alternating high-pitched squeal and mid-tone warbling of two computer modems syncing up with each other, and then the tones merged into a single stream of steady but rapid pulses. One by one, several banks of period-proper mini-computers and data storage devices had activated in succession and then began to process the data being fed through that call. Readout lights flashed and old-style magnetic tape reels whirred as their contents were read and fed into an old fashioned and rather large hard drive storage system. The data thus collected on that hard drive was then fed into another bank of mini-computers in another location deep beneath the industrial complex. More lights began to flash and this time were joined by text and graphic readouts flickering away on CRT-equipped consoles that had none but the dead left to man them. Somewhere unseen, a 132-column printer came to life and began to chatter away, spewing out printout after printout on old-style sprocket fed wide carriage paper where nobody was left alive to read it. But that was not all.

Not far from where all of the computer activity was taking place was a very special lab. Inside that lab was a very special storage canister sealed within a heavy armored shell. None but the dead were left to see when the lights in that lab came back on as if by themselves. None but the dead were there to hear and see that armored shell crack apart and then get lifted away in two cleanly cut halves on huge hydraulic arms to reveal a very large vertical tank standing on end and completely full of a sickly colored liquid which hid its contents from view. None but the dead were there to witness when that interior tank was drained from the inside and from its base of the fluid which had previously filled it, thus allowing the contents of that canister to stand on its own two feet. None but the dead were there when the front half of that tank popped open as if by itself, and then swung back and out of the way as if moved by an invisible hand. None but the dead were there when the creature that had been stored inside that special storage canister reached up and yanked out the data feeds and life support lines that had been connected to various parts of its head and upper body, and then ripped away the oxygen mask that had covered the lower half of its face. That face was one of a demigod straight out of Nazi Aryan dreams, with blond hair and eyes that were an unreal brilliant shade of cobalt blue, but its skin was the color of a corpse and it was on the body of a completely naked muscled hulk that stood between nine and ten feet tall. The owner of that body was more careful with those lines connected to its lower midsection, ones designed to effectively remove body wastes, but those too were quickly and efficiently removed. With that its body was completely free of every connection that had kept it alive and sustained it while it was being stored inside that tank. The eyes opened, closed, and then reopened, the lungs breathed in deeply, and then the owner of both stepped out.

All of that had taken place about the same time as the Metro City survivors had been making ready for their dramatic escape from the MCPD substation. Even now, as the survivors raced northward under the supposed protection of the Huey Hog, another force had emerged on the scene and was preparing to stop them before they could escape. It was a threat more unlike and considerably more deadly than any they had faced so far ... and not even the raven that now flew northward in their wake knew what was going to happen once their new foe forced them into confrontation with itself.

CHAPTER 9
CONFRONTATION

The first sign of what was in store for the Metro City survivors came as they began to pass the outer edges of the sprawling Pandora industrial complex north of town. Just about the time they saw its double layered, barbed wire topped outer fence begin some distance off to their right through the trees, the police radio in their car came to life. *"Corporal Rappalo, this is Zulu Tango Four. Corporal Rappalo, this is Zulu Tango Four, over."*

Cy had the mike in hand and was ready to key it before the gunship pilot finished speaking. "This is Corporal Rappalo, over."

"Better tell your driver to slow down, Corporal. The highway is completely blocked ahead of you, over."

Cy felt the MCPD patrol car begin to slow. He looked over at Lisa. She nodded in acknowledgment but kept her eyes to the road. She looked worried. "Ask him how bad," she said.

Cy nodded back, then keyed his mike again. "Advice taken. Lisa wants to know just how bad, over?"

The response was immediate. *"There's no way around anywhere that we can see. Not on the highway, or on the shoulders, or on the median. And none of this was there when we flew over here earlier, Corporal, over."*

Lisa's eyebrows went up. Cy looked incredulous. "Come again, over?"

"Like we said, Corporal. The road was clear when we flew over earlier, over."

Even as the Hog pilot finished speaking, the still-slowing MCPD patrol car rounded the turn in the highway. Lisa's eyes opened wide at the sight now before them, and she quickly brought the car to a full stop. Beside her, Cy looked amazed. In the back, both Mercy and Raul looked shocked. The section of the highway before them, one which should have been straight and level for the next two miles, was completely blocked just as had been described. No, not just completely blocked. It was thoroughly blocked with an obvious deliberate effectiveness. One could see the long marks on the pavement, on the shoulder and median, and the road for the nearby side exit leading to the Pandora complex where something had dragged vehicles ranging in size from small economy cars to 35-ton tractor-trailer rigs, and then arranged them and stacked them fairly neatly across the full width of the highway and its shoulders from one side to the other. Both whole and once-whole automobiles had been stacked two high in order to maintain an even height with the tractor-trailer rigs across the full length of the barricade. There was also a fair amount of metal and glass debris around it, all of it from the vehicles and scattered up and down its full length. The whole thing was a sight both amazing and ominous.

Everybody got out of the patrol car, partly to stretch their legs but mostly to stare at the barricade. Everyone brought their weapons with them but they held them loosely, given the complete absence of any visible or obvious threat. None of them noticed as the raven which had been following them up the highway alighted in a nearby tree. It was quite alone, and it looked with interest down on the four small humans standing by their car not far away from the big and imposing barricade that blocked their way.

"Good God," Lisa finally managed to say.

"*Si*," Raul said. "Holy Mother, what could have done this?"

"I've got a good idea as to what, although I didn't think Pandora had any here," Mercy said. She turned to Cy, and there was an anxious edge in her voice as she spoke. "We've got to get out of here, right now."

"Why?" Cy said. He had automatically tightened his grip on his weapon as she spoke. "What is it?"

"An *ubermensch*, " Mercy said, "and it's probably still in the area."

"Jesus," Lisa exclaimed, immediately bringing up her AK-47. She had suddenly become tense as a bowstring. She held her weapon at the ready and was slowly sweeping it around, looking in every direction for their perceived foe.

"*No comprende*," Raul said. "What is *ubermensch?*"

Even as Raul asked his question, Cy had quickly moved back to their car. Mercy had turned and was talking to Raul while Cy reached in, grabbed the mike for the police radio with his left hand, pulled it out as far as he could so he could prop his shotgun's stock on his left forearm and keyed it. "Zulu Tango Four, this is Corporal Rappalo. We need immediate evac now, over."

"*What's up, Corporal, over?*"

"Given the evidence, Ms. Parks believes that there's an *ubermensch* loose in the area, over."

"*What's that, over?*" the pilot asked.

"The thing that piled up this roadblock so fast, over," Cy immediately shot back. He too was looking around uneasily. "Call General Ryan and tell him. He probably knows about them. Emphasize that we're in immediate danger and we need out of here now, over."

"*Will do, Corporal. Over and out.*"

Even as Cy finished with the radio call, Mercy had been speaking in low tones with Raul. His eyes opened wide as she finished. "You are serious, Mercy?!" he asked incredulously.

Mercy gave him a faint smile. "*Si,*" she answered softly. "Now you know everything we know about what's out there."

Raul shook his head. "*¡Lagartos saltano!*" he exclaimed, brandished his new long gun and looking around in the same manner as Lisa and Cy already were.

"What did he say?" Mercy asked. She too was brandishing her own M-16 and looking around.

"Oh, nothing," Cy responded, but shooting Raul a wink and a grin. Raul grinned back. Mercy frowned, but said nothing.

Just then the car's police radio squawked. "*Home Plate to Corporal Rappalo, this is General Ryan. Home Plate to Corporal Rappalo, this is General Ryan, over.*"

Cy let go of his shotgun's stock with his left hand, reached into the police car so he could grab the radio's mike, and pulled it out as far as its cord would allow, and cradled his shotgun on his left forearm while keeping his right hand on its pistol grip and trigger. "Home Plate, this is Corporal Rappalo. I read you, over."

"*Zulu Tango Four has filled me in on what's happened. I'm authorizing them to come in for an immediate touch-and-go pickup. It's against my better judgement, but I don't see that we have a choice. You haven't seen any of those blasted crows around, have you?*"

"No, sir."

"*Any zombies?*"

"No, sir. Strangely clear, but that might be our new friend's doing."

"*Zulu Tango Four, over?*"

"*No sir, not a sign of either one, over.*"

There was a pause, and then the radio came to life again. "*Okay. Corporal, as soon as Zulu Tango Four is down have your people in there as fast as they can so they can get up and out of there. Understand me, son?*"

"Yes, sir."

"*Ryan, over and out.*"

Raul looked at Cy. "What is touch-and-go, *señor*?"

"That's what the Air Cav does whenever they've got to do a pickup in a hot LZ, I mean landing zone," Cy answered immediately. "What happens, Raul, is that the chopper comes in at high speed and barely touches the ground, hovering just long enough for us to get on board, and then it takes off at high speed. That's why they call it touch-and-go." He now looked at everyone and spoke loudly, with a note of command in his voice. "Everyone stay together by the car! When the chopper comes in, run as fast as you can to it and grab something as you get on! It may take off while you're still climbing on board, and we don't want to drop anybody when it takes off."

"Understood," Lisa said, moving in close but still doing her visual sweeps.

"*Si!*" Raul said, coming up from Cy's other side.

"The quicker, the better," Mercy said, also moving in close.

The sound of the approaching Hog grew louder as it descended and came closer. Everyone could see it as it came in, its Army green paint scheme making it quite visible against the black clouds that were slowly rolling across the darkened sky. Both it and the whole area were lit by the light radiating from the Pandora complex. All of its outside lights were on, and the spillage was more than enough to light everything around it for some distance with an unnatural grey glow. There was a smell like ozone in the air, along with the whirring sound of the approaching Hog's rotors and the regular rumble from its motor. It was now close enough for the four on the ground to make out details of its chain guns, to see the Army gunners standing at the ready behind their machine guns on the door pintle mounts, constantly sweeping the ground below them and looking for their unseen foe. They had good reason for doing so. Within seconds the Hog would be down on the deck and at its most vulnerable. If the enemy both they and the Metro City survivors feared was still in the area, then that was the time when it was most likely to attack. That is, unless it chose to attack now.

Suddenly and without warning a utility pole rocketed skyward from a clump of trees just past the entrance to the Pandora complex. Only the crew of the Hog could see from where it came. All the survivors could see was that pole, which looked brand new and had probably been stacked by the road for impending utility work, suddenly take off into the air like a ballistic missile on full burn. It was heading directly for the descending Hog, on a course as straight and true as an arrow shot from a bow. The four survivors below could hear over the police car's radio as the pilot cursed, and see as he jinked his Hog hard to the right. He narrowly avoided that first pole, but not the second. It had shot up from the same clump of trees towards the Hog as soon as the first was halfway on its way, and whatever had hurled it had correctly anticipated the Hog pilot's dodging move. That second utility pole hit the Hog with such force that it was knocked upward, as the pole pierced its bottom and rammed its way up through its motor, stopping only when it hit the spinning main rotor. The main rotor stopped too, and the fatally wounded Hog immediately flipped over and started to go down, the anguished cries of its pilot and crew sounding on the police radio, but only briefly. Within a second of it being hit, the Huey Hog exploded, dropping a fierce rain of metal shrapnel and flaming debris below.

Cy's group immediately scurried to the nearby shelter of a tractor-trailer rig that had been turned on its side and placed as part of the barricade blocking the highway. They huddled up against its overturned trailer, watching as the main body of the Huey Hog, blazing fiercely and tumbling in its downward arc, fell squarely on the MCPD squad car. There was another explosion almost as fierce as the first one, and the four survivors could feel its fierce heat as they went to their knees and covered their faces with their arms. They could hear metal shards being driven by high speed peppering part of the barricade on either side of them, but fortunately none of the hits were close. After that it was over. All they could hear was the sound of fierce flames burning, and all they could smell was acrid smoke. They uncovered their faces and opened their eyes to find the MCPD squad car a fiercely blazing ruin, with the main body of what was left of the Huey Hog sitting on top of it. Part of the thrown utility pole that had downed it was still sticking up and out of it, its creosote-soaked wood burning fiercely. It looked for all the world like an oversized middle finger stuck up by some angry pagan god and held towards the four survivors to mock their escape attempt from Metro City.

The survivors weren't given time to recover from that terrible event. Even as they looked upon that horrifying scene, there was the sudden and immediate sound of a large mass in motion in the air. Cy was the first to react, looking around and up and immediately swapping his shotgun for his China Lake due to what he saw. Lisa was a split second behind him, her eyes locking on to this new incoming threat and her AK-47 accurately tracking it all the while. It was already sailing through the air on a downward arc when it cleared the barricade and landed halfway between them and the burning wrecks that had been their means of escape. It hit the pavement with a loud *WHUMP*, cracking it in the process, then in a split second whirled around and came upright as it faced them in a fighting crouch. Both Mercy and Raul now brought their own weapons to bear. Cy gritted his teeth and he heard Lisa growl. Mercy sucked in her breath rather loudly. Raul spoke for them all, although what he said was in Spanish. "*¡Chingada madre!*"

Both Lisa and Cy immediately opened fire. Both the loud ratcheting of an AK on full auto and the *th-woonk!* of a China Lake opening up filled the air. Both were excellent shots and should have hit their targets, but the *ubermensch* was too fast. Their fire found only empty air where it had been, as it quickly dodged to one side and toward the flaming wrecks of their rescue vehicles. There was a small-scale explosion as the grenade Cy had fired exploded harmlessly, while Mercy and Raul added their fire to that of Lisa and Cy's. By that time their foe had made it to the wreckage. It picked up a large piece of flaming metal, one of the sections of the downed Hog's tail boom, and promptly flung it back at them. The group was forced to scatter in order to save themselves. Lisa and Cy dove to one side and Mercy and Raul to the other, just as the burning boom piece slammed into the section of overturned tractor-trailer where they had been standing. This was what the *ubermensch* wanted, for its next swift sprint brought it within arm's reach of Lisa and Cy. It effortlessly backhanded Cy with such force that he was sent rolling and tumbling off to one side while it grabbed Lisa. It lifted her up in one hand by the neck and squeezed so hard that she was forced to drop her weapon. The two of them remained that way for a few seconds, the *ubermensch* holding the half-choked Lisa up in the air, she grasping and straining furtively at his iron grip and kicking it as hard as she could with both of her booted feet, but to no avail.

Mercy could do nothing but stand there, her assault rifle up and aimed at the *ubermensch* but unwilling to shoot for fear of hitting Lisa. Not so Raul. The stout Mexican laborer immediately slung his own assault rifle behind him and then charged the creature. It was a reckless yet brave thing to do, and it was like trying to tackle a tree. Raul hit its legs square and wrapped his own strong arms around him while his momentum carried him into and around the thing throwing him off of his own feet. It stumbled somewhat and swung about quickly, trying to see what had hit it so low. As it did, though, it lost its grip on Lisa. The speed at which the thing was turning when it let her go flung her away as if she had been thrown by a catapult. Less than a second later, the out-of-control Lisa smacked full length into the front end of the overturned tractor-trailer rig, hitting squarely where the lower windshield fared into its nose. There was the sound of shattering glass, accompanied by an anguished cry from Lisa and the sound of breaking bones. She hung there but for a moment, and then she fell unconscious to the pavement in a tumbled sprawl, her lower left leg twisted under her at an unnatural angle, a shard of broken glass sticking out of her left eye, and blood flowing freely from multiple cuts and wounds.

It was now Raul's turn to cry out as the *ubermensch* kicked him away as easily as if he had been a football. The short but burly man was sent sailing through the air back first and with his limbs trailing behind him, all the way from the burning vehicles over the edge of the pavement and into the tall grass of the shoulder beyond. All of the wind was knocked out of him when he finally hit the ground, and he rolled and tumbled for some ways, losing his assault rifle as he did, until he finally came to rest. The *ubermensch* now turned on the only human still standing within its immediate field of vision. Mercy was terrified but held her ground, keeping her own assault rifle aimed at the creature. Suddenly she had an idea and acted on it. "Don't you dare!" she shouted. "I'm with Pandora! Mercy Caroline Parks, medical center liaison team! Check your data!" The thing hesitated, Mercy's words apparently having their desired effect ... and that was when a grenade round launched from a China Lake came through the nearby flames and slammed into the creature.

KA-WHAAAAMMMMM!!!!

The creature staggered and twisted back, gripping at the stump of a right arm burned and blown off at the elbow and screaming in agony from its bloodied head. Another form staggered around the wrecks of the burning helicopter and police car, China Lake before him. It was Cy. He was bleeding from the mouth and his Army issue helmet was missing, but it was Cy. He cocked the China Lake and fired again. This time the *ubermensch* managed to dodge just in the nick of time, resulting in a near-miss, but it was definitely wounded and its response time down from the solid hit Cy had landed on it earlier. Even as Cy swapped his empty China Lake for his shotgun, the *ubermensch* turned and took off in a stumbling run southward down the highway, blood trailing from its head, the stump of its right arm, and shrapnel wounds in its left calf from the grenade near-miss. Mercy began shooting at it with her assault rifle but her aim was bad, and it managed to stay well ahead of her fire. It picked up speed somewhat as it made the turn in the highway, and then it was lost from sight.

"Cy!" Mercy called.

Cy held up a hand. "I'm all right," he shouted back, heading to the side of the road where Raul lay. "Just some broken teeth. Go help Lisa!"

Mercy nodded and took off towards the fallen Lisa at once. Cy ran towards Raul, wiping the blood from his mouth with one sleeve. He was already conscious again and struggling to get back to his feet. "*Ai, yi, yi*, but that thing's got a foot!" Cy heard him say, and then he both heard and saw the Army corporal approaching. "*Señor* Rappalo! How's Lisa?!"

"Mercy's taking care of her," Cy said, as he came close and helped the Mexican back on his feet. "How are you?"

"I feel like I come from the bad end of a bullfight, but I okay. How's Lisa?"

"Let's go see," Cy said, as he put an arm around Raul and helped him back up to the road. The burly laborer was limping despite his best efforts to hide his discomfort. "You need to have Mercy look at that leg as soon as you can."

"I will, once I know Lisa is all right," Raul said sadly. "Is my fault she got hurt."

"No it isn't," Cy assured him. "You probably saved her life. You didn't know that thing was going to let loose of her when it did, but I'm still glad you went after it. You were the only one who could, you know. Like I said, you probably saved her life."

"*Si*," Raul said, still looking sad, "but I still no feel better about it."

The pair snagged Raul's assault rifle on the way back. By the time they did, Raul was walking on his own although he was still limping. In the meantime, Mercy had broken out her medical supplies and had been working feverishly to treat Lisa's wounds. The glass shard had been removed from her ruined left eye and it had been bandaged. There were also a number of bandages covering other parts of Lisa's body, in particular her left arm, left side, and left knee. Mercy looked up as the two men approached. "Got anything for some splints?" she asked.

"No, but I'll go get something," Cy said immediately. "How long?"

"At least a foot for her arm and side, and two for her leg," Mercy said. "Lisa's left arm and left knee are both broken, and I also need to brace up her left side. She's got broken ribs where she hit the brace in the middle of that windshield."

"Holy Mother," Raul said, quickly crossing himself.

"All right," Cy said. "Raul, you stand guard until I get back. I think Mr. Super Nazi cleared the field of zombies before we got here for his own ends, but they might start coming back any time."

"*Si*," Raul said, hefting his assault rifle.

Cy was back within five minutes, with his .45 ACP in his gun hand and with an assortment of broken branches and long metal shards under his other arm. He set them down next to Mercy and the fallen Lisa. Mercy had removed the young woman's rucksack, side pouch, and armor vest, and had her lying as prone as the young woman's many injuries would allow. To himself Cy wondered how she had managed to do all of that by herself, and then decided it was best not to ask. The medical researcher had first handed Cy something to wipe the rest of the blood from his mouth, and then rummaged in her medical bag for a bit. She pulled out a pill bottle, shook out two pills, and handed them to him. "Acetaminophen," she said. "Your broken teeth are going to start hurting like hell once the shock wears off." Cy took them and tossed them straight down, even as Mercy quickly picked through what Cy had brought and separated out the ones she needed for each of Lisa's broken ribs and limbs. Cy then helped her with Lisa in order to set the splints, while Mercy fixed them in place with surgical wrap and Raul continued to stand guard. Mercy had already straightened out Lisa's broken arm and damaged leg as best she could Lisa's left leg was where they first started with the splints, and they were helped by the fact that Lisa was still unconscious.

"Is she all right?" Cy asked anxiously.

"No, but she's out of it for now, and that's a good thing," Mercy said as she first arranged the splints around her leg. "Hold these, please. Thank you." She then reached for a roll of surgical wrap and began to wind it around both the splints and Lisa's left leg, so her broken knee would be held in place. "If she weren't, she'd be screaming her head off from the pain, and I don't have anything strong enough to give her for it."

"I guess you're right," Cy said. He fell silent while Mercy finished wrapping Lisa's leg and promptly started on her broken arm. Again, as before, Cy held the splints in place while Mercy secured them with surgical wrap. A thought crossed his mind, and he decided to voice it. "You saw how that thing went straight for Lisa?" he asked.

"I saw," Mercy answered. There was a bitter edge to her voice. "That means Pandora knows about her." She sighed. "I'll bet they've got someone inserted at the quarantine line, maybe even with your General Ryan, and that's how they found out."

"Mercy, I don't think General Ryan would betray us like that."

"He probably didn't," Mercy interrupted, "if he's half the man you say he is. There are other ways of finding out. They could have somebody friendly to them on his staff, for example. Or they could have their man planted as a particularly nosy reporter. There's all kinds of ways they could have found out."

"Possibly," Cy conceded.

"Okay, I'm done here," Mercy said, abruptly changing the subject. "You'll have to help me with her side." She moved up somewhat and placed the makeshift splints at specific locations on Lisa's heavily bandaged side. Cy could not help but notice the amount of blood that had soaked through the bandages in places. "Don't worry," Mercy said, as if reading his mind. "It's congealed. I got her bandaged up just in time, but she lost a lot of blood before I did." She fixed the splints in place with surgical tape while Cy continued to hold them. "Lift her up a bit for me please, so I can get this wrap under her, but carefully. Work your hand under her upper back ... there you go. Okay, just enough so you can catch this as I slide it under to you ... there. Now again ... there. And again ... there." This went on until Mercy had firmly wrapped Lisa's side splints in place. "Okay you can let her down now. Gently ... gently ... there. Good. You would have made a good male nurse, Cy," Mercy finished, trying to smile as she did.

Cy gave Mercy a look. "How bad is she, Mercy? Honest truth."

Mercy bit her lip. "Honest truth. Bad, Cy. Really bad. Her left arm is broken and I had to reset her shoulder on that side before you got here. It was dislocated. Her left knee is more than broken. It's shattered. She'll never walk again without total knee replacement surgery at the least, and even then I'm not sure. She's got two broken ribs, maybe three, and that's why we had to be so careful in lifting her. She's also lost her left eye, as you saw earlier, and a lot of blood from all of those glass and metal cuts when that thing threw her into that truck. She would have had a lot more but for that armor vest. That's also what saved her from being killed outright. If she hadn't been wearing it, then her chest might have been crushed or she could have a broken back, or both. It absorbed and sluffed off the worst of the impact. She's also got indeterminate internal injuries, but I'm hoping they're not too serious. At least she's not coughing up blood. Not yet." Both her face and her voice lost all emotion with her next words. "Cy, she lost too much blood from her arm before I could get to her. She's going to die unless we can get her somewhere that's got the stuff I need to give her a proper transfusion. That also needs to be a place where I can properly care for her like she needs, and there's only one place within reach where I can do that." With that, she made a point of looking away from him and towards the side road that led to the Pandora complex.

Cy's eyes followed Mercy's, and he furrowed his brow once they too settled on the side road. "That thing wanted us to go in there, Mercy, otherwise it wouldn't have set up this barricade the way it did." He waved to the stacked and positioned vehicles behind them to emphasize his words. "That's its lair, you know? It probably knows that place like the back of its hand, and there wouldn't have been anywhere in there we could have hid from it."

"Maybe that's true, but whatever its plans were changed the minute you hit and wounded it," Mercy replied immediately. "Didn't you notice it didn't go back there?"

"I couldn't help but notice," Cy shot back. "It took off down the highway and made me miss my last shot, streaming blood from that stump of an arm and squealing like a ... like a ... oh my God."

"What?"

"I know where it's going," Cy said with alarm, as he scrambled for Lisa's pack.

"What are you doing?" Mercy asked.

"I need Lisa's grenades. I'm out," Cy answered, as he began to rummage through the pack.

"You're out? So if that thing had attacked again, then ..."

"Yeah." Cy was fishing the grenades out of Lisa's pack as quickly as he could find them. "And when it comes back, and you can bet it will, it ain't coming to socialize."

"So where'd it go?"

"Back to town. It's heading for what's left of my convoy. It wants the heavy weapons we had with us."

"Heavy weapons?!" Now Mercy's eyes went wide with alarm.

Raul, who was listening in even though he was standing guard, also looked shocked. "Is coming back? What kind of heavy weapons you bring with you, *señor*?!"

"Oh, the usual," Cy said, as he finished pulling out the last of Lisa's grenades from the pack. He immediately brought his China Lake around and began to reload it with the grenades as fast as he could. "Lots of grenades along with several single-shot grenade launchers, a lot of M-16s and a fair number of heavier M-60s, and a few M2 50-caliber heavy machine guns mounted on some of the APCs and Humvees." He finished loading the fourth and last grenade and quickly hung the other two on his gear harness. He also reached over and scooped up Lisa's AK-47 along with the side pouch in which she kept its preloaded ammo clips, and then put on the pouch while he gave Mercy a worried look. "If that thing comes back with any of that, our goose is going to be cooked." He immediately came to his feet. "Raul, stay here and guard them. I don't think either Mr. Super Nazi or the zombies will be back for a while, but I'd like to play it safe all the same."

Raul gave him a look. "Where do you go, *señor*?"

Cy made sure both his China Lake and shotgun stayed slung back over his shoulder, and then he pulled Lisa's AK up in front of him as he spoke. "I remember seeing some abandoned vehicles down the highway before we made that last turn and wound up here. I'm going down there to see if any of them still have the keys in them." He now looked at Mercy. "We need something to move Lisa into wherever we're headed inside the Pandora complex."

"The main research lab building," Mercy immediately answered. "Everything I need is in there." She gave Cy an anxious look. "What are you going to do if the *ubermensch* didn't head to town like you think it did?"

Cy shot her a grim look. "I'm gonna pray," he said. With that he turned on his heel and took off in a slow, loping combat run, the AK held before him in a combat carry as he headed southward down the highway towards the curve.

Raul watched the Army corporal go. "*¡Ay carumba!*" he said softly.

"Come again?" Mercy asked.

Raul turned to look at her. She was tending Lisa again, wiping the blood from what parts of her face weren't covered by bandages with a cloth. "Is like some nightmare version of *Dia de Muertos*, you know, only for real."

"What's that?"

Raul gave a nervous laugh. "Is what we call Day of the Dead. Is a holiday where we remember family and friends who have died. Our Halloween, if you like, but we celebrate it two days later. There is story that sometimes the dead rise on *Dia de Muertos* to revisit with everyone one last time. Only ..." and with that his voice faltered.

"Only what?" Mercy prompted.

Raul shivered. "Only I not know I would really meet the dead when I come over border this time. If I know, I stay back in Guadalajara with my mother and father and sister. If I ever escape and get back, I stay there this time."

Mercy gave a nervous laugh. "I don't blame you. I'd probably do the same too." She now leaned back on her haunches and looked at him. "So why did you come north, Raul?"

Raul shrugged his shoulders. "Oh, the usual. More money, better jobs, places to work where few questions are asked so long as you do good job. I work hard, send most money home to family, keep only enough to live here." He gave a little laugh. "Is a living, as you *gringos* say. Only this time I get caught."

"How?"

"INS came through on random sweep, checking papers. I no have any, so they pick me up. MCPD hold me until they make arrangements to deport me. That was when I met Joe. Nice guy for *gringo* cop." He shook his head. "So sad he die and turn zombie."

"Yeah," Mercy said quietly. "So sad."

"Is good thing Lisa no can turn if she die, right?"

Mercy's brow furrowed and she gave Raul a stare. "She's not going to die, Raul," she insisted. "Not if I can help it. Not if we get her to the Pandora lab in time."

"*Si.*" Raul nodded, and then turned to look back down the highway.

Mercy looked at Raul for a bit. "Hey," she said, "want me to take a look at that leg?"

Raul shook his head. "I okay for now. You look when *Señor* Rappalo get back."

"Sure."

There was another pause, and then Raul spoke again. "*Señor* Rappalo, he gone long time now."

"Yeah," Mercy said quietly. "He gone long time."

The Pandora medical researcher who could also play nurse again leaned over the prostrate and unconscious form of the young half-Cherokee female stock car racer before her. Lisa's breathing had become shallow, and what of her skin was visible given her many bandages had turned very pale. Mercy gently picked up Lisa's right hand and held it in both of her own. It was cold and clammy to the touch. "Hang in there, Lisa," she said quietly. "Don't die on us. I know you've got an incredible will to live, young lady. I've seen it. Give Cy the time he needs to get us some wheels so we can get you to that lab and some proper care. Hang in there, okay? Don't die, Lisa. Please. Don't die."

About a quarter-mile away, high in the branches of a tall pine tree on one side of the highway, the large raven that had followed the survivors from Metro City was roosting and surveying the scene below. It saw the short but burly Mexican standing guard over the Asian-looking female tending the fallen half-Indian woman, ready to take on anything and everything that might come their way. It turned its head the other way and saw quite a distance away and around the turn in the highway a black U.S. Army corporal, going from one abandoned vehicle to another, searching for any that were drivable and still had the keys in it. It turned its head back to the first scene, to the barricade across the highway by the Pandora complex side road, and its eyes were drawn to the young half-Indian woman lying prone on the pavement. She was a pretty thing, or had been before that man-made monster messed her up and left her on the verge of death. Such a sweet soul. Such a sweet, delicious soul ... and it was almost time. It wouldn't hurt to hasten things a bit, as it had done with the dying white man back in town. He had been merely filler, to round out the corners, but this was a sweet, juicy, tender soul, one that would make a meal all in itself. Yes, it wouldn't hurt to hurry things a bit. The raven flapped its wings once on its high perch, and then opened its beak to give the cry that would start the process of swallowing that sweet little soul.

Even as the raven's beak opened, there was an abrupt loud clap of thunder that boomed and rumbled across the sky. A wind out of nowhere shook the trees. The raven promptly closed its beak, fighting to keep its perch. Down on the ground, all three of the humans still on their feet looked up at the sky in amazement from their respective locations. They could not see the raven and that was a good thing, because saying its feathers were ruffled would have been putting it mildly. It flapped its wings again, as if gathering itself, and then opened its beak again to cry. Once again there was an immediate and loud clap of thunder and an invisible wind shook the trees. The raven almost fell off of its perch this time, as that wind from nowhere buffeted it and the echoes from the thunder continued to rumble for several seconds. This time the humans below looked amazed, but the raven no longer paid them any mind. It had found its footing and resumed its perch on the branch it had claimed for its roost. Its head was cocked slightly, as if listening to the rumbling above. There were words in those sounds only it could hear and understand. When it was done listening it snapped its head up in sudden defiance, and then slowly lowered it in an almost reverent bow, as if reluctantly acquiescing to some unheard command. It remained in that pose for a few seconds, and then with a whirring of wings its head popped back up and it took to the sky.

Cy had just found a beat-up old orange Datsun pickup with the keys still in it and gas in the tank when he heard a sudden flapping of bird wings. He turned his head in time to see a large raven suddenly shoot from the upper branches of a distant tall pine tree as if it were in some kind of hurry. He saw it sail up and into the murky sky above, and suddenly it was gone. He rubbed his eyes and looked again. Nothing was there save rolling black clouds. He took in a deep breath, let it out again, and then shook his head. "Just a bird," he muttered, as he got into the driver's seat of the Datsun and fired up the motor.

CHAPTER 10
A CHANGE OF PLANS

"*Bring him in here!*" General Ryan bellowed.

"Yes, sir!" said the soldier at the back of the tent, smartly saluting as he did. He then turned on his heel and quickly departed through the flaps of the field headquarters tent. When he returned a few minutes later, he came with two burly MPs who were escorting Carlton Dahl. The stern looks on their faces and the furious one of Ryan's was counterpointed by Dahl's own apparent benevolent calm. The Pandora representative was literally planted in place before the army general by the two MPs, who stood there glaring at him while he looked blandly back.

"What the *hell* just happened, Mr. Dahl?!" Ryan snarled.

"Looks like you lost a helicopter," Dahl replied quietly. He now gave the Army general a questioning look so obsequious that it bordered on the edge of being surly. "Didn't you know?"

"Of course I *know!*" Ryan roared. "*HOW* in the *HELL* did *THAT* happen?!"

"How should I know?" Dahl replied calmly. "This is your show, not mine. I'm here only to advise and to keep Pandora updated on the—"

"That was a Pandora *ubermensch* which took out my gunship and killed everyone aboard!" Ryan bellowed. "What was it doing in there, and how the hell did it escape confinement?! It was my understanding that your Metro City complex was for viral research and development *ONLY!!* That thing shouldn't have been there *AT ALL!!!*"

"So it was," Dahl said, forcing a thin smile. He had the look of a man who was patiently dealing with an unruly child. "General Ryan, I'm not responsible for what other branches of Pandora may be doing or might have done, nor can I know what they do unless they tell me. I'm a liaison man. I can but inform and advise, once I have the necessary facts."

"Then you had better start informing, mister, and damn pronto," Ryan barked. "You have all of the goddamn facts you need. Now start talking, because both you and Pandora are in enough hot water already."

Dahl's thin smile somehow managed to become even thinner. "Don't forget, General. If you choose to ignore common sense and inform the public about us and our research, you will also be informing them about the unlawful actions of your own superiors as well." He laughed softly. "Now you really don't want to spill the beans on them, as they might say, do you?"

"I don't give a fuck what I spill," Ryan barked, "so long as it isn't any more of my people's blood than necessary. What just happened shouldn't have happened at all, and wouldn't have unless Pandora is up to something on their own." He now leaned in close to the Pandora representative. "Well? Are they, Mr. Dahl?"

Dahl paused before responding. He maintained his thin smile as he did. "If they were, do you think they would tell me?"

Ryan paused at that. He looked at Dahl for a long time. Dahl matched his gaze eye for eye, and the two stood there staring at each other for almost a full minute. It was General Ryan who broke eye contact, as he turned to address one of the MPs beside Dahl. "Sergeant, this man is under arrest."

"On what charge?" Dahl asked blandly.

"Accessory in a conspiracy to commit murder, for starters," Ryan said. He now allowed himself the slightest of smiles. "I can think of plenty more."

Dahl's smile now became one of bemusement. "You can't do this. I have rights—"

"You've got nothing," Ryan shot back, angrily waving a hand. "Don't forget. This is a military quarantine zone under martial law. We are the law here, not the civilian government, and right now you and your people at Pandora are in a fine pickle as far as we're concerned." He again addressed the MP. "Now get him out of here."

"Yes, sir."

Dahl said nothing more as the MPs escorted him away and through the tent flap. He maintained the air of an innocent man to whom a great wrong has been done, even as he left General Ryan's presence. The general looked for a while at the tent flap after Dahl's departure, then added with a snort, "Little prick."

"Sir?" his aide asked. He had been standing quietly off to one side until now, while the exchange between Ryan and Dahl took place.

"Nothing," Ryan said. He took a deep breath, let it back out, then looked at his aide. "Get on the blower and call up the people who are bringing in that special equipment I requested. Tell them I need it here yesterday, given what's happened."

"Yes, sir," the aide replied, heading for the tent flap.

Another Army soldier popped in before the aide could leave. He was a fresh-faced young man wearing second lieutenant's bars, and he looked excited. "General Ryan, sir?"

"Yes?" The general turned to look at him.

"Radio telephone call, sir. It's the President."

"I'll be right there," Ryan replied briskly, joining both his aide and the lieutenant as the three of them left the field headquarters tent in a hurry.

At approximately the same time, in his personal office high atop a skyscraper in another city somewhere in the United States, Pandora CEO B. D. Nye sat at his desk pretending to read some routine reports from other of Pandora's many activities. They were the least of his concerns at that moment, and the look on his face betrayed him. It managed to combine both anger and frustration simultaneously. The call signal sounded on the intercom on his desk. Nye immediately dropped the papers on his desktop and pushed the respond button. "Yes?"

"Mr. de Voormand to see you, sir."

"Let him in," Nye said crossly.

The door was opened by Nye's secretary, who waved de Voormand in. He stepped through the door, not waiting as she closed it behind him, but instead walking directly to Nye's desk. Nye made a point of carefully arranging the reports he had just set down, and then he gave his top aide a very cold look. "What happened?" he asked crisply. "What went wrong?"

"I think you need to see this, sir," de Voormand said, pulling a Betamax® videotape out of one of his jacket pockets. "It's the video camera security footage from the closest fence camera we got of the *ubermensch* in action, right up to the point when we lost contact with it."

"Lost contact?" Nye asked, arching his eyebrows.

"Just a minute, sir," de Voormand said, as he went to a cabinet beside the front door, opened it and pulled out a rolling cart with both a large television and a Betamax VCR, then moved them to the nearest power outlet. "Once you see, you'll understand."

Nye waited while de Voormand finished setting up, turned on both the TV and the VCR, inserted the tape, and started it playing. Only the drumming of the fingers on his desk betrayed his impatience. That stopped as soon as the videotape began to play. The remote feed from the fence security camera at the Pandora facility which had captured the action was grainy and in black-and-white only, with no sound, but it was enough. Both Nye and de Voormand watched with considerable interest. For de Voormand it was his second time, for Nye the first. When they came to the point in the fight after the *ubermensch* had flung Lisa into the truck, kicked Raul away, and then been confronted by Mercy, de Voormand paused the tape.

"Interesting," Nye said, leaning forward in his chair and clasping his hands before him. "Do we know what she was saying?"

"No, sir," de Voormand admitted. "The camera was too far away. Whatever it was, it made the *ubermensch* hesitate as you saw. That's when this happened." And with that he restarted the tape.

Nye again watched with interest as the drama of the remainder of the fight unfolded before him. Once it was done, he nodded. "That's enough, I think."

de Voormand stopped the tape and turned off both the TV and the VCR. He then looked back at his superior. Nye was looking rather thoughtful, but said nothing. After several seconds of this, de Voormand decided to risk an intrusion. "Sir?"

Nye almost imperceptibly started. He looked up and over at de Voormand. "Yes?"

"I have a theory, sir, if you want to hear it."

Nye allowed himself to lean back in his chair. "Go ahead."

"Sir, I think Ms. Parks identified herself as a Pandora employee. She would know that we've conditioned all of our programmable products not to cause deliberate harm to anyone who works with Pandora. Well, the ones that don't defy or break their conditioning, that is. Once she did that, it would have hesitated in order to check its own memory and find our implanted ones confirming her story. Whether it was true or not is beside the point. She made it hesitate, and that's when that soldier, Corporal Rappalo, was able to shoot and wound it."

Nye smiled faintly. "I was thinking much along the same lines, Piter. Congratulations."

"Thank you, sir."

Nye slowly shook his head. "Bad girl, Ms. Parks. Very bad girl ... but we will deal with you in due time." He again looked up at de Voormand. "So why did it not return to the complex?"

"Sir, all *ubermensch* are conditioned to adapt to changing circumstances. It apparently planned to lure Ms. Stanridge and her friends into our complex so they would be on its own field of combat, so to speak, which it knew better than they and thus would have the advantage. The fact that it was badly wounded before it could fully execute that plan changed the situation, so it adapted accordingly. That's why it left, sir."

Nye let out a chuckle. "So it was logical for it to run away, eh?"

"Not run away, sir. It's going into Metro City. I'm willing to lay odds that it's after the heavy weapons left by that Army convoy when the zombies wiped it out earlier. Once it has its selection of those, then the odds will be in its favor again and it will return to finish the job."

"Assuming the Army doesn't get in there first," Nye said with a smile.

de Voormand shrugged his shoulders. "If they do, sir, they're going to get to experience the power of an *ubermensch* firsthand, instead of watching old films and reading reports. Plus, if we're really lucky, it'll find Ms. Stanridge first."

"If," Nye repeated. He let out a little laugh. "That's a mighty big word, Piter, as the saying goes."

"Yes, sir," de Voormand responded.

Nye thought some more before speaking again. "I presume it would be logical to assume that since the *ubermensch* is now longer be under our control due to the damage it sustained, then it may significantly deviate from its programmed orders."

de Voormand gulped. "I would say that's a safe presumption, sir."

"Safe?" Nye said, giving him a look. "Not for anyone in its path."

"No, sir," de Voormand said nervously.

"And that includes Ms. Stanridge."

de Voormand looked even more nervous. "Yes, sir," he said meekly.

Nye sighed. "Well, so much for that operation, and for being able to convincingly market our version of the truth."

de Voormand did not respond. Instead, he looked to the floor, while a single bead of sweat formed on his right temple and began to run down that side of his face.

Nye got up from his seat and walked over to look out the wide picture window at the back of his office. It offered a beautiful nighttime view of the nearby neighboring skyscrapers, and the lights of the city below stretching off into the distance. "I suppose I'd better leave the country while I still can," he said calmly.

"Yes, sir," de Voormand said, looking up at him. "I've already made the necessary arrangements, sir."

Nye's head turned just enough to see his chief assistant from out of the corner of one eye. "You have?"

"Yes, sir. That's part of my job, sir. Anticipating what you might need at any given moment in time."

Nye now turned to look at de Voormand face-to-face. The two stood there for a while like that, saying nothing, just looking at each other. Eventually Nye stirred, walked forward, and then offered his hand to de Voormand, who took it. Nye smiled at him. It was the warm smile Nye reserved for friends and trusted subordinates, and not the ice-cold smile he usually gave everyone else. "Thank you, Piter. It's too bad it came to this, and I would hate to lose you. You've been an excellent right-hand man. Do your best to deal with this while I'm away, and try to manage to come back to me on the other end if you can."

"Yes, sir. I'll do my best, sir."

"Good." With that the two shook hands. Once they were done, Nye let go and walked past de Voormand and headed for the office door. de

Voormand turned to watch him go. Nye stopped as he opened the door, and held up a hand with the forefinger raised. "One more thing."

"Yes sir?"

"I want you to investigate Ms. Stanridge's living relatives, as well as the family tree of anyone who went on that mission in World War II which retrieved the *untotenvirus*. We may need a fallback plan."

"Yes, sir."

Nye went through the door. de Voormand heard him talking to his secretary. "June, I'll be out for a while. Mr. de Voormand will take care of things while I'm gone." There was more, but by then the door had closed behind him. Back in the office, de Voormand breathed a sigh of relief.

"Yes, Mr. President," General Ryan said respectfully into the phone. "That's my plan, sir. If that thing's going to prevent them from getting out, then we've got to go in to get them."

"How are you going to avoid a repeat of what happened with the relief convoy yesterday?" asked a kindly older voice familiar to everyone from his many appearances in public and on media.

"We're going to be a lot better armed than they were, sir," Ryan replied. "The best they had were 50-caliber machine guns. I plan on going in with flamethrowers and flamethrowing vehicles, sir."

"And the ubermensch?"

"We'll have regular tanks along with both rocket-propelled grenades and shoulder fired missiles to deal with that, sir, and I'm also requisitioning more helicopter gunships. That thing screwed us over the first time because we didn't know it was there. It's not going to screw us over again, sir, now that we do."

"I see." There was a pause. *"General, I know you've probably been asked this before, but I'm going to ask again. Is there any hope for any of those other poor folks besides those four?"*

"No, sir," Ryan said firmly. "None at all. Once you've been infected beyond a certain point, and everybody in Metro City save those four are well beyond it now, then there's no saving them."

There was another pause on the line. *"Well, I can tell you're doing the best you can given the circumstances. You get those four out of there. Do whatever you have to do, General, but do your best to save them, no matter what it takes. Nancy and I will be praying for you and your men."*

"Yes, sir," Ryan respectfully replied.

"Good luck, General Ryan. Goodbye."

The line clicked, then began to buzz. Ryan handed the receiver back to the radio telephone operator, who hung it up. The general then looked around at his men. Those in the radio tent were looking back at him, a few more had their heads stuck through the flap, and even more were standing outside waiting for orders. "All right," he said confidently. "The President and the people are counting on us to pull this rescue off. Let's do it."

"Sir," Ryan's aide said.

"Yes?" Ryan said, looking at him.

The man was beaming. "Those special packages you ordered have just arrived."

Ryan grinned. "Well, all right then!" He waved to everyone. "To your posts, men! We've got some civvies to rescue!"

A chorus of *yes sirs*! sounded from both inside and out, after which both Ryan and his men immediately scurried to do their jobs.

One second Lisa felt incredible pain pass through her entire body. It was the worst in her left side, left arm, left knee and left eye as her body slammed into the windshield and upper part of the front end of the overturned rig tractor. The next second she felt no pain whatsoever. In fact, she felt nothing at all. Instead, she found herself adrift and weightless in an inky black void. She could see herself, and to her shock she discovered that all of her clothes were gone, but she didn't understand how this could have happened. She also didn't understand why she could see herself, given the total darkness surrounding her. Most people would have panicked given the situation in which she found herself, but not Lisa. She then realized that she was no longer in the world she knew. She was somewhere in the spirit realm. That meant ... oh, no. No, no, a thousand times *NO!* She had so much of life left to live. Surely it wasn't her time! Immediately Lisa closed her eyes, shutting out the void that was trying to claim her, and focused on calming herself. Once that was done, she began to will herself to live with every fiber of her existence. At once she felt her body begin to move upward. A light began to grow somewhere above her, which became bright enough that she could detect it even through her closed eyelids, but she remained focused on willing herself to live. She continued to rise faster and faster, the light becoming ever brighter around her, until it was so bright that she could almost feel it. Suddenly it was gone, and she found herself once again standing on her feet. She could also sense that she was wearing clothes once more, although they weren't the same she had been wearing before. Something had obviously changed, but for good or for ill she could not tell the way she was. She decided to risk it, and opened her eyes.

Lisa Stanridge found herself standing on a vast empty plain under a dark twilight sky. There was no sign of the others, of the highway and its vehicles, of the *ubermensch*, of the Pandora facility, of Metro City, or of the surrounding landscape that she knew. It was just her and that empty plain, with mountains both dark and ominous in the distance in all directions. She could also see that she was no longer nude, nor was she dressed in her racing firesuit and tall racing boots. She was attired instead in traditional pre-colonial Cherokee garb and matching moccasins for women. *My father's people*, she thought to herself. *Does this have something to do with him? But no, it can't. He's not here. He's ... I don't know*, she admitted to herself. *I don't know what's happened to him, or to Mom.* She looked around, taking in everything she could see, and another unpleasant thought flashed in her mind. *I didn't succeed. Maybe I'm dead after all.*

At that moment something flew past the right part of her upper body with such speed and force that it almost knocked Lisa off of her feet. She stumbled, then came back around in a street fighter's crouch even as the thing came into view in front of her. It was a giant raven, and it was on fire. It flew ahead and up, emitting an extremely loud and piercing cry that hurt Lisa's ears, and she had to fight the urge to clamp her hands over them. Despite her predicament, she at once recognized that particular flaming bird. "*Kalona Ayeliski!*" Lisa cried aloud.

The giant flaming raven slowed and wheeled about sharply at Lisa's cry. It hovered in mid-air for a moment before her, then came down and alighted but a few paces away. It cocked its head and looked at her strangely, and then there was a sudden flash of light and shifting of form. Before Lisa's eyes the burning bird morphed into the image of a young native American woman dressed the same as she was, in pre-colonial Cherokee clothing. There were significant differences, however. The newcomer's skin was not ruddy like Lisa's, but as pale as moonshine. Her clothing had shamanistic trappings, and she had a headdress made from raven feathers. Her lips were blood red, and so were her fingernails, which were at least two inches long and tapered to sharp points. Finally, the newcomer's eyes were not those of a human. They were those of the raven, and one could almost imagine black fire dancing within those jet black orbs. The newcomer stood there for a moment, eyeing Lisa up and down, and then spoke. When she did her voice had a husky tone, yet with just enough of an echo effect to suggest power scarcely veiled. "So ..." the figure said, "... you know my name. From your father, no doubt."

"Yes," Lisa said, drawing herself up before a member of one the most feared groups of Cherokee spirits: the ones they called the Raven Mockers, who preyed on the dying and ate the hearts of the dead. "My father schooled me well in the old ways of his people. I know who you are, witch."

"Then you know why you can see me, and hear both my words and my cry," the figure responded.

"Yes," Lisa said. "I know. My body hovers on the edge between life and death. That's why."

"And were I to strike," said the figure, lifting a hand as she did, "I could have your soul this instant." There was a splurting sound as the tips of the fingers of the woman's uplifted hand exploded in blood and shattered skin, and five very long razor sharp claws extended to their fullest length.

Lisa held her ground, although it took an effort. "Yes, you could," she admitted. A thought crossed her mind, and she voiced it. "Then why don't you?"

The figure laughed. "Because it is not your time, girl." The claws were suddenly retracted, and once again the figure's hand was whole. "If it were, I wouldn't waste time talking to you. I would swallow your soul and be done with it." She laughed again. "And yours is such a sweet and tasty soul too." She began to lean towards Lisa. Lisa in turn stepped back. There was a loud rumble of thunder in the sky, and the figure looked up. It was the only time Lisa ever saw the Raven Mocker with fear in her eyes. After the thunder ended, the figure leaned back and resumed her previous pose. "It is no matter," she said. "My sisters and I have been enjoying quite the feast in the ruins of the white man's town from where you came."

"You have?" Lisa said. It was more statement than question.

"Yes." The figure now gave a soft laugh. "It beats the regular routine. We've gotten tired of playing six-hand canasta with Apollo and Aphrodite and the others over at Odin's. The Rabbit and Loki always try to cheat." She laughed again. "No, this event you humans have caused, it is such a delight to our kind. Ahhh, to feast again as in the days of old!" With that she gave a satisfied sigh.

"Apollo and Aphrodite?" Lisa said. "Odin and Loki? Those are legends and myths."

The figure looked sternly at her. "Are you calling me a myth, girl?"

Lisa shook her head. "Not with you standing in front of me. I can't deny the reality of that."

The figure smiled thinly. "Then know this human. We gods and spirits are real. Very real. All of us."

"If so, then why did you leave?'

The figure laughed. It was an evil laugh that chilled to the bone. "Leave? We didn't leave your kind, girl. Your kind left us, long ago. Nevertheless we are still here, and we still occasionally intervene when the situation calls for it. Such as right now, for instance. That is why I am here with you, instead of feasting with my sisters and our familiars."

Lisa's eyes narrowed. "Why is that, witch?" she asked.

"Because for you I am serving as the messenger of Unhlahnauhi, he who the white men call the Great Spirit. I am to inform you that now is not your time. That path that your life is to follow does not lead to me. Not this path, anyway." With that the figure laughed again.

"I don't understand," Lisa said.

The figure stopped laughing and looked at her darkly. Her eyes seemed to glow with black fire as she spoke. "You will be returned to the land of the living, but your life will not be as you wanted it to be. That is inevitable, given what has happened to you. Even so, yours is a soul that Unhlahnauhi deems worthy of returning, for he sees great things ahead for you. That is, if you stay on the new path that is laid before your feet."

"And if I don't?"

The figure smiled. It was the most evil smile Lisa had ever seen in her life. "Then I will be waiting for you," she said, as she opened her mouth to reveal both an upper and lower row of bloody needle-like teeth.

Suddenly the mouth opened wide and the figure screamed with the cry of the giant burning raven. It rushed Lisa, and she had no time to flee. It enveloped her with its burning wings, clamped its flaming claws around her legs, and Lisa cried aloud in tremendous pain. She felt inhuman eyes looking at her, and an inhuman beak pressed against her head, as the frightening sound of Kalona Ayleiski's inhuman laughter filled her ears. She was lifted from the plain and carried away at great speed, her entire body alight with both pain and fire, rising from its surface and rapidly ascending into an eternal twilight that surrounded them both, enveloped them and swallowed   plain was empty once more, as were the twilight skies above, for both Lisa and her inhuman companion were gone.

Mercy had been sitting quietly by Lisa's bedside when she was startled by the wounded young woman abruptly coming to consciousness and gasping for breath. She quickly turned and put both hands firmly on her to prevent her from rising, being careful to avoid her injured left shoulder. "Hey, settle down!" she ordered in her most professional manner. "You're safe now, okay?! You're safe!!" Lisa struggled a few seconds more, trying to breathe while fighting the pain from her broken limbs, and then she finally settled down. Mercy did not let go of her until she was lying still on the bed. "There now," Mercy said. She forced a smile. "Isn't that better? You're in no condition for any kind of gymnastics, so you just lie there and take it easy. Okay?"

Lisa looked up at her with her unbandaged right eye. She was suddenly very tired. She knew she was only feeling a fraction of the pain she should have been feeling from what were obviously major injuries, but it hurt all the same. "How ... bad ...?" she asked slowly, and in a very weak voice. For some reason she was having great difficulty putting words together.

"Bad enough," Mercy finished for her, and then she forced a smile, "but you're alive. Be grateful for that." She reached over to a nearby tray table and picked up a hypodermic. "I'm going to give you something for the pain, okay?"

Lisa nodded. It was easier than trying to speak.

It took only a few minutes for the drug to take full hold on Lisa. She now felt numb, with not a trace of the pain that had accompanied her abrupt awakening. Even so, there were parts of her that were more numb than others. Her left knee, her upper left arm and side, and her left eye. She suddenly realized she couldn't see out of it, and that there were bandages both over it and on her head, covering a fair part of its left upper side. She breathed in and out several times, as deeply as her injured left side would let her, and then turned left to look with her one eye that remained uncovered. She saw she was in an examination room of some sort, and that she had been placed on a gurney along one wall, which was to her right. The left side rails were down, but it was for more than it being the side away from the wall. She had been stripped of all of her clothing, which was neatly stacked on a nearby counter with her boots at its feet, but her many dressings and a partially pulled-up blanket combined to cover her sufficiently. There was a long tube leading from a blood bag hanging from an IV stand to a nearby transfusion machine, and another tube led from it to a needle that had been inserted into and then taped to her lower left forearm. Mercy was seated in front of her on an examination stool on one side of the bed, with the wheeled cart beside her she had seen earlier full of medical implements. Cy and Raul were nowhere to be seen.

"Cy ..." Lisa managed to get out. "Raul ..."

"They're standing guard," Mercy said. "They're making sure that thing doesn't come back to finish the job it tried to do on you. Now just rest and take it easy, okay?" She again forced a smile for Lisa's sake.

Lisa saw through Mercy's facade. She slowly licked her lips, put all of her will into the effort, and finally managed to speak a complete sentence, although she did so slowly and softly. "How ... am ... I ... hon-est ... truth ... Mer-cy ...."

Mercy bit her lip, and then spoke. "You're in bad shape, Lisa." She paused for a moment, finding the exact words she wanted to say, then continued. "You've got a serious concussion, and there's probably brain trauma involved. That's why you can hardly talk. Your left shoulder was dislocated and your left upper arm broken in two places, both from being thrown into that truck. That's from where you lost a lot of blood, because one of those breaks tore into the main artery for your left arm. I managed to stop the bleeding and to get both your shoulder and your arm bones reset, but you won't be using either for quite a while. You've also got two ribs on your left side that are definitely broken and possibly a third. Not sure there due to the swelling. You've got major swelling and bruising on your midsection from where your body hit the center support brace for that truck's windshield. I'm guessing severe internal bruising there at the least, but hopefully that's all. You haven't coughed up any blood, and that's a good sign. That and your ribs could have been a lot worse but for that armor vest you were wearing, so be thankful for that. Going on, your left wrist is sprained and you've also got major lacerations up and down your left side from all those metal shards and broken glass from that truck." She fixed her gaze on Lisa with the most serious look Lisa had ever seen on her face. "Also, your left knee is shattered. It's completely toast. That doesn't mean you won't be able to walk again, provided you don't have serious nerve damage, but you'll either have to wear a leg brace from now on or opt for total knee replacement surgery. I've heard lots of good things about it, so there's hope there. First things first, though." She now forced a smile. "Can you feel your legs at all?"

Lisa was silent for several seconds. Her face twitched, as if she were concentrating. After a second or two both legs moved and Lisa groaned in pain. "Left ... hurts ...."

Mercy laid a reassuring hand on the injured young woman. "That's a good thing, believe it or not. That means you'll walk again, given enough time and the right treatment. Now I want you to try something else. Know what a kegel is?"

Lisa nodded. "Yes ...." she said softly.

"All right. See if you can do one."

Lisa's face contorted in pain almost immediately and she groaned. "Aaaaaaahhhhh!"

"Again, that's a good sign," Mercy said. "You've still got feeling down there. Maybe your plumbing isn't too badly messed up."

Lisa smiled faintly at the old joke concerning the female anatomy. "No ... ba-bies ... soon ..." she managed to get out.

Mercy smiled back, although her smile was tinged with sadness. "At least not until you've been thoroughly checked out and gone through some serious therapy. Again, you better be thankful you had on that armor vest. It could have been a lot worse."

The pair fell silent for a while, Lisa doing nothing but breathing, until she had gathered enough of her strength to speak again. "Left ... eye ... Mercy ..." she said, looking directly at her with her one good eye. "Left ... that ... out ...."

Mercy looked away. She didn't want to say what she was going to have to say, and yet she didn't have a choice. "When you were thrown into the front of that truck," she said evenly, fighting to control her own emotions, "the impact broke the windshield. That's part of the reason why you're all cut up on your left side." She now turned and looked directly at Lisa. "One of those glass shards went into your left eye. That's why you don't have a left eye anymore."

Again the room fell silent. Mercy was looking down now, still fighting to control her emotions. Lisa looked at her for a while with the one eye she had left, and then she spoke. "I ... see ...." She let out a single low laugh, although her face grimaced in pain as she did. "No ... I ... don't ...."

"Oh, Lisa," Mercy said, laying her hand on the battered young woman once again.

Lisa let out another painful short single laugh. "Is ... all ... right ..." she said slowly. Her voice now firmed up with as much conviction as she could put into it, given her weakened condition. "Am ... go-ing ... to ... live ...."

Mercy looked again at Lisa and smiled. "Well, it's nice to see you've got your confidence back."

Lisa slowly shook her head. "More ... than ... that ...." She stopped and lay quietly for a moment, again gathering her strength. Mercy was watching her intently but said nothing. Once Lisa was ready, she began forcing the words out again. "Had .... spir-it ... vision ... while ... un-der ...." Again she paused and gathered herself. Mercy remained quiet. Once Lisa was ready, she spoke again. "Heard ... and ... met ... the ... Ra-ven ... Mo-cker .... Said ... it ... was-n't ... my ... time ...." With that Lisa let out a long sigh, then looked up quietly at Mercy. "Did ... I ... die ...?" she asked.

Mercy looked surprised. "Yes you did," she admitted. "It happened right after we got you here. You life force had sunk so low that you flatlined shortly after we got you into this room. You were clinically dead for twenty-three seconds until I could revive you."

Lisa nodded. "That ... ex-plains ... it ...."

"Lisa," Mercy began, "people think they see all sorts of things when they're on the brink of death, or are clinically dead as in your case—"

"*No*," Lisa said loudly, grimacing at the pain from the effort. Mercy stopped speaking and gave her a look of alarm. Lisa took several deep breaths, then spoke again. "Real ... *real* ...."

"I'm sure it was for you, Lisa," Mercy responded softly, trying not to sound condescending.

Lisa gave her a look, but it was several seconds before she spoke again. "One ... thing ... bo-thers ... me .... a-bout ... vi-sion ...."

"What's that?" Mercy asked.

Again Lisa looked Mercy in the eye. "Ra-ven ... Mo-cker ... said ... no-thing ... a-bout ... Cy ... or ... Raul ... or ... you ...."

The badly injured woman stopped speaking after that. Her eye remained locked with Mercy's, however, until Mercy broke away. She instead looked at the nearby wall, with a rather pensive expression on her face.

CHAPTER 11
REFLECTION AND PREPARATION

Lisa watched as Mercy finished unhooking her from the transfusion machine. "That's enough of that," she said confidently. "I think your own body can take it from here." She gave Lisa one more check-over before tucking her under her bed sheets again. "Got to get you decent for a visit from Cy," she said sweetly as she worked. "I told him I'd let him know when I thought you were strong enough to see him."

"Thanks," Lisa said weakly.

"You're welcome," Mercy said as she finished. She stood up and gave Lisa a look. "Now you just lie there and look like the pretty young woman you are, and I'll go get him for you."

"Yes ... ma'am," Lisa said, managing a faint smile as she did.

Lisa heard the examination room door open and close, and the sounds of another set of doors doing the same somewhere beyond the room. She looked around while she waited, and at one point her eyes fell up her biker boots sitting beside the nearby counter. She remembered seeing them before, and a quick glance up revealed her clothes, washed and neatly folded, her firesuit on bottom and her underwear on top, sitting on top of the counter with her armor vest and the former contents of her pockets neatly arranged beside them. Lisa blushed. She had forgotten that Mercy had undressed her in order to better treat her multiple injuries. She was pretty well covered by her bandages and the bedsheet, but even so! By then she heard the sounds of the outer doors opening and closing again, only this time there was the definite additional sound of booted feet coming down the hall. The door to the examination room opened, and Lisa looked over to see Mercy escorting Cy in. He grinned at her and she weakly smiled back, while Mercy closed the door behind them.

"Hi," Lisa said. She hoped she wasn't still blushing.

"Girl, but are you a sight for these tired eyes," Cy said, grinning from ear to ear as Mercy escorted him up to Lisa's gurney. He pretended not to see her neatly folded clothing sitting on top of and her biker boots standing in front of one of the nearby counters. To Lisa, Cy looked genuinely glad to see her, and she was definitely glad to see him.

Lisa's brow now furrowed as she gathered the words she wanted to say. Cy looked concerned and started to say something, but Mercy placed a hand on him to stop him. They both waited until Lisa spoke. "Raul?" she finally managed to get out.

"Standing guard outside," Cy immediately responded. "We've been taking turns at that, one watching and the other sleeping, while we wait for that thing to come back."

Lisa nodded. "Yeah ..." she said slowly. "Back ...."

Mercy now interposed herself between the pair and addressed them both. "Cy, you can see how bad a shape Lisa is in, so keep it short, simple, and brief. Try not to make her speak too much, okay?" She now left them and headed for the door, picking up her assault rifle along the way. "I'm going to go keep Raul company for a while," she announced, as she reached the door and stopped to face them. "Just in case our expected guest decides to show up early for the party."

Cy had by now moved up close to Lisa's side. "I'll come get you when we're done," he said.

"All right," Mercy said. "Until then." She opened the door and left, with it closing by itself behind her on its hydraulic hinge.

Cy felt a set of weak fingers playing about one of his hands. He turned toward the gurney, going down on one knee as he did, and firmly but gently gripped Lisa's right hand. It was the one that had been trying to get his attention. She sighed pleasantly as he did. "You ... o-kay?" she asked, still in the same weak voice.

"Well, my broken teeth are starting to hurt," Cy admitted, "but that stuff Mercy gave me is dulling the worst of the pain, I'm guessing. Aceto, ahsepto, something-or-other."

Lisa managed another weak smile. "Ty-le-nol® ..." she said. "You ... need ... what ... she ... gave ... me ...." She had to stop and catch her breath, and with that Cy looked concerned, but Lisa was still smiling. After she had gathered herself, she continued. "Could ... floor ... a ... bull ... Cy ...."

"You probably need it," Cy offered.

Lisa nodded. Her thumb began to weakly play across the back of Cy's hand. Cy pretended not to notice as she gathered herself and spoke again. "Had ... spi-rit ...vision ... Cy ... saw ... the ... Ra-ven ... Mock-er ...."

One of Cy's eyebrows went up. "I'll take your word for it," he said carefully. "What'd she have to say?"

Again the weak smile played across Lisa's bandaged face. "Not ... my ... time ... Cy ... I'm ... going ... to ... live ...." Again she stopped to catch her breath and gather herself.

"Well, that's a relief," Cy said, and he showed it. "I mean, if the Raven Mocker said it then it's got to be so, right?"

Lisa now looked sad. "Cy ... she ... said ... noth-ing ... a-bout ... rest ... of ... you ..." Lisa's remaining eye was beginning to tear up. "Oh ... Cy ... I ... want ... you ... live ... want ... that ... date ... when ... we ... we ..."

Even as tears filled Lisa's remaining eye, Cy had already reached over with his free hand and picked up a small towel from Mercy's medical cart. He used the towel to gently dab at her eye. "Hey now, none of that, Lisa," Cy said reassuringly. "Let me tell you something. I intend to survive, Raven Mocker's promise or not, and you wanna know why?" He leaned in close. "Because I've just confirmed me a date with the most wonderful woman in all of Metro City, that's why, and I ain't gonna break that date for nothing. And I'm gonna do my best to make sure Mercy and Raul make it too. I mean, we're the only four humans left in Metro City. That's gotta count for something, you know?"

Lisa let out a little half-sob, half-laugh. "Yeah ..." she said, her voice filled with emotion. "Hey ... Cy ...?"

"What?"

"Kiss ... me ...." she said faintly. "Now ... just ... in ... case ... please ...?"

Cy looked at her for a moment. She looked back expectantly. He began to lean his head down toward her forehead. Even as he did, he felt her weak right arm try to pull him lower.

"Down ... here ..." Lisa's voice was even weaker than before.

He went with the pull, and in a few seconds their lips met. It probably didn't look very romantic as kisses went, since he couldn't put his arms around her like he wanted due to her injuries, but both of them put everything they had into it. When it was over, and Cy finally pulled back, Lisa was wearing the most pleasant look he had ever seen on her face. She slowly nodded, as if reading his mind. "Thanks ... Cy ...." she said in a very weak voice.

"You're welcome."

Lisa now managed a faint laugh, although he could tell the effort made her injured side hurt. "We ... have ... that ... now ... just ... in ... case ..."

Cy realized he was still holding Lisa's right hand. He now held it to him and patted it with the other one. "Just in case," he agreed in a half-whisper.

"In ... case ..." Lisa said softly, and with that she pulled her hand back towards her. Cy let go, and she laid it by her side. She smiled again at him. "Go ... get ... 'em ... sol-dier ..."

Cy lingered in his pose over Lisa for a little longer, and then he straightened up. He put the towel back on the cart and unslung Lisa's AK from his back. "Yes, ma'am," he replied. "I need to hand you back over to Mercy anyway." He paused, and then held up the AK for Lisa to see. "You don't mind if I keep using this, do you?"

Lisa slowly shook her head. "No .. go ... a-head ... Cy ..."

"Thanks."

Cy nodded, turned, and headed for the door. He was about to open it and go through when he heard Lisa speak again. Her voice was still faint. "You ... live ... Cy ... hear ...?"

Cy shot Lisa a confident look. "Yes, ma'am," he said assuredly. He then opened the door and left.

Mercy was standing behind cover not far from the doors to the main lab building when she heard them open. Mercy looked over at them, assault rifle automatically tracking with her hands as she did, just in case it wasn't who she thought it was. It was, and she sighed in relief as she lowered her weapon and stepped out from behind cover. "Hey, Cy," she said in greeting.

"Hey," Cy said, coming quickly to her, Lisa's AK held before him in a casual combat carry. He stopped once he reached her side. "Where's Raul?"

"Right there in the bushes where you left him, only now he's sound asleep," Mercy said, motioning with the front end of her M-16 to the spot. Cy looked and then nodded. "Poor fella," Mercy continued. "I didn't try to wake him up. He looked dog tired."

"He was," Cy replied. "He offered to let me sleep first. When I tried to refuse, he just looked at me and said," and with this he effected a Spanish accent, "'*Señorita* Stanridge will be most upset if you not there when Mercy finish with her and she wake up, *si*?"

"*Si*," Mercy agreed with a gentle laugh. "That look on her face when she saw you, well, I think you were the best medicine I could have possibly given her." She now gave Cy a grin. "And she for you."

"You got that right," Cy agreed heartily, giving his own pleasant chuckle as he did. Both her laughter and his chuckle quickly faded away, to be replaced by somber faces and the unnatural stillness of the night in that place. "So how's she doing?" Cy asked quietly.

"About as well as might be expected," Mercy said flatly. "You know the extent of her injuries. I've got her stabilized, but that's about all I can do. I don't have the medical knowledge to do more. She needs major surgery, especially with her smashed left knee and the possibility of internal injuries, and I'm not trained for that." She gave Cy a look that was almost pleading. "Has the Army—?"

"They know we're here," Cy responded quickly. "Raul says he saw an observation helicopter fly over while I was asleep, and then come back for a second pass. He waved at them and they waggled the 'chopper to let him know they had seen him, and then zipped away. After that, nothing."

"Why didn't they land and pick us up?" a surprised Mercy asked.

"They probably had orders not to, given what happened last time," Cy said. "Remember, General Ryan was bending his own orders on pickups when he ordered that Hog down to the deck to get us."

"And that's when the *ubermensch* knocked it out of the sky and killed everyone on board," Mercy stated evenly.

"Right," Cy said. "You think he's gonna risk that happening again, given the current situation? No, he's not. He's probably guessed what we found out ourselves once we got here. That thing smashed the radio transmitter while it was getting ready for us, so we've got no way to get in touch with him other than visual sighting. He also has every reason to believe that the *ubermensch* may be hiding somewhere, just itching to take out another of his helicopters like last time. He's not going to come after us until he has forces sufficient and strong enough to deal with that thing once and for all. I'm guessing he's putting together an armored column even now, this time with tanks and other heavy-duty weaponry instead of just heavy machine guns, and that column is going to come straight down that highway out there, guns blazing to make sure we get rescued."

"But you don't know that."

"No, but it gives me hope," Cy insisted. "Don't deny me my hope right now, okay? It's one of the few things that's keeping me going."

Mercy nodded. She then cracked a smile as she added. "That, and knowing Lisa's still alive."

Cy paused for a moment, then returned her smile with one of his own. "Yeah. That too."

The former Pandora medical researcher now looked thoughtful. "Question," Mercy said, "and I want an honest answer."

Cy looked at her. "Okay," he answered.

"Did she tell you about her spirit vision thing?"

Cy paused a beat, and then nodded. "Yes, she did."

"Not that I believe it, but still ...." Mercy let the words trail off, and didn't finish them, looking away and across the building's front parking lot instead.

"Yeah," Cy said. "I'll be honest, Mercy. I'd be having a hard time swallowing it if it wasn't for all of the freaky shit that's happened to us already on this little shared Outbreak lark of ours. I also saw some strange things happen when I was young and living back in Tennessee, things neither I nor anyone else could explain by normal means." He gave a chuckle. "Let's just say that while I'm a skeptic, I'm one who keeps an open mind."

"I still tend to think she had an NDE hallucination," Mercy said flatly, trying to sound authoritative but not doing a very good job of it. "I mean, the way that supposed message from the Raven Mocker focused on her as being safe, or saved, or whatever and the rest of us—"

"Oh, so that's the part bothering, you," Cy said. Mercy's head snapped around to see him regarding her in a very Spock-like fashion, with one eyebrow raised. "You're worried because you don't have a guarantee to live, like she supposedly does now."

"Nothing of the sort," Mercy snapped. "It's very delusional, and just the sort of thing I'd expect when ...." She stopped speaking when Cy's expression changed from Spock-like to a definite frown. After that she looked contrite. "I'm sorry, Cy. I'm tired, so tired. Maybe all of this is finally getting on my nerves, and the fact that there's a wounded *ubermensch* out there getting ready to do its best to kill all of us, Raven Mocker delusions notwithstanding, isn't helping."

Cy stepped up to her. Much to Mercy's surprise, he lifted a hand and put it on her shoulder in a show of friendship and support. "Hey, it's okay. We're all on edge right now, and you know what? I'll bet you've had the least sleep of any of us." Mercy blushed and looked away as Cy continued. "Why don't you go back in there with Lisa and take a catnap if you can, in the time we got left? You look like you could use it."

"But what if the *ubermensch* comes back?"

"Oh, I'm sure there'll be gunfire aplenty to wake you up," Cy joked. "Now get going. I think we've left Lisa alone long enough." He gave her a wicked grin. "Hey, maybe there's a zombie inside somewhere that thing missed while it was setting its trap for us, and it thinks Lisa would make a nice appetizer."

"That's not funny," Mercy said, suddenly lifting a knuckle and biting on it. She lowered it and looked at Cy. "I'll go all the same, though. Thanks, and thank you for the talk."

"Not at all," Cy said, as he removed his hand and put it back on his weapon. "Sleep well, Mercy."

"Sleep?! After what you just said?!" Mercy pretended to exclaim, but there was a tired twinkle in her eyes. She turned, and then trotted up the building stairs.

Cy watched her go. He waited until she was gone, and then he chuckled. He then looked up to the top of the building and spoke. "You get all of that, Raven Mocker?"

The big black raven perched on the top edge of the building, on the part that was directly above the building entrance, cocked its head from one side to the other and then back again as it stared down at the human male below addressing it. It did nothing else. It was an ordinary action for any bird, and yet there was something sinister about it when it was performed by this particular bird, this oddly unusual raven which seemed to be strangely fixated on the Metro City Outbreak survivors. Cy had noticed it was there as soon as he came back outside, but he had said nothing about it for Mercy's sake. Now he stared at the raven and the raven stared back. They stood that way in a good old fashioned staredown, until Cy eventually broke eye contact and turned away, laughing as he did. "Fine," he muttered. "You win. Have it your way." He heard a rustling of feathers and brief flapping of wings behind him as he walked to where Raul was sleeping, but he pretended to ignore it.

Cy settled himself down behind the hedge close enough to Raul to where he could wake him up in an instant, and yet still be able to see the front gate of the Pandora complex. Of course there was no guarantee that the *ubermensch* would return that way, but it was the only entrance accessible from the highway. Given what he had seen and experienced of the creature's capabilities so far, he guessed it would favor the direct approach to its prey. The front gate was not the straight line approach from Metro City, but it was the easiest without having to cut through lots of backwoods and hilly terrain without even a gravel road of any appreciable length in the general direction to follow. Besides, the creature had set its original trap to force their group in the direction of the front gate and into the complex itself. It had wanted them inside the complex all along. Well, here they were. All that was left was for the creature itself to finish whatever it was doing and then get there. Probably fixing up its injuries and loading up on usable Army weapons, ammo, and armor from the ruins of his convoy, Cy firmly believed. He looked at his watch, and then both nodded and grunted.

"Eh?" Cy heard a sleepy voice beside him say. "What you say, *señor*?"

"Nothing," Cy replied quietly. "Go back to sleep, Raul. We've still got time."

"But how you know?"

"I just know. Trust me."

"*Si*." There was a pause, and then. "Miss Lisa?"

"She'll live, thank God, but she's messed up pretty bad. That's why we gotta make sure we stay alive long enough for the Army to come rescue us. Now go back to sleep, okay?"

"*Si, señor.*"

Before long, Cy heard the sound of soft snoring. He turned his head to look up at the raven perched on top of the main lab building. "You'll let me know when it's time, Raven Mocker?" he asked softly.

The raven cocked its head at the human, first one way and then the other. It then righted it and stared straight at him for several seconds, while he continued to watch. This time, it was the one that first broke eye contact, as it raised one wing and stuck its head under it in a pose of sleep.

Cy laughed softly. "As I guessed. We still have time. Thanks."

Back outside the city quarantine barriers, General Ryan watched as a small convoy of twelve Army flatbed tractor-trailer rigs pulled into the main staging area for the armored column he was getting ready to deploy into Metro City. Six of them carried vehicles that looked a lot like vintage M48 Patton tanks, the Korean War era precursor to the M60 Pattons with which his forces were currently equipped. Each one was conspicuously marked MARINES, and each came with a crew of U.S. Marines in full battle dress with field kits to assist, but the Army personnel pretended like this was perfectly normal procedure while on deployed duty. The other six flatbed rigs carried what were unmistakably M113 Armadillo armored personnel carriers (APCs) all marked U.S. ARMY, but each had an extra unusual-looking weapon mounted on its back which vaguely resembled a scale-down tank turret. Ryan, his aide, and a new person in the form of a senior Marine colonel watched and chatted as their men went through the process of starting up both the old tanks and modified APCs, then driving them off the flatbed trailers. "God, but those tanks are dusty, sir," Ryan's aide remarked with a smile.

"Those are among the last of the old Marine M67 Zippo tanks," General Ryan replied with a smile. "Right, Bob?"

"Right," replied Colonel Robert "Bob" McKeegan, USMC, from his position beside General Ryan. "Been in storage ever since the war. You guys still have some of your Zippo APCs in service, but I heard you got rid of your own Zippo tanks and most of your Zippo APCs before we did. Anyway, they did very well at the Battle of Hue, as I saw with my own eyes," he ended, giving a smile only a seasoned combat soldier could give.

"You got that right," Ryan responded. "The higher-ups have been getting rid of both kinds whenever they could ever since the war ended, keeping only the minimum they deem necessary. Politics and diplomacy and all that." He gave a short laugh. "Didn't think we'd need them any more."

"Shows you what they know."

"Yeah. Lucky for us I remembered we still had this batch of Zippo APCs assigned to a unit over at Whitefield, and you were kind enough to point us to the last six old tank Zippos you guys still had, Bob."

"My pleasure," McKeegan replied. "One last workout before they get cut up into sardine cans. Going out with a bang, or maybe a big flame in this case."

"Do they still work, sir?" Ryan's aide asked.

"The motors are still good, son," McKeegan said, "otherwise we couldn't have got them onto the flatbeds. The true test is about to begin, though. Watch."

A large area had been cleared in front of and to each side of the lead Zippo APC. Its driver swung it around so the man mounting the weapon in the back would have a clear line of fire through the cleared area. Both looked to the officer in charge, and then he to General Ryan and Colonel McKeegan. McKeegan grinned and waved towards the APC, and then Ryan barked a command to its crew.

"FIRE!"

The gunner hit the firing switch on the weapon. A rod of fire shot from the weapon on top of the APC. It sailed a good 200 yards or so almost all the way down the cleared area, leaving both flame and oily black smoke in its wake. It stopped as soon as the gunner released the firing switch. Everyone was grinning, including both Ryan and McKeegan. "Good!" Ryan shouted to them. He turned to look at his Marine friend. "Your turn, Bob," he said.

McKeegan didn't waste any time. "Bring up the first tank!" he ordered loudly.

The same procedure was repeated, but this time with one of the old Marine Zippo tanks. Its Marine driver trundled it into position, and its Maine gunner rotated the turret until it was also aiming down the cleared test strip. McKeegan looked at Ryan, who grinned and nodded, and then it was McKeegan's turn to snap the order.

"FIRE!"

The same thing happened as before. A long and hot rod of flame shot from the turret's barrel and down almost the full length of the cleared area. It stopped as soon as the Zippo tank's gunner released the firing switch inside the turret.

"Not quite the range of the APCs, sir," Ryan's aide observed. "A good ten yards less or so, I'd say."

"Close enough, for what we've got to do," McKeegan replied. "They can't help it if they're older. They'll still do the job all the same, just like they did at Hue." He looked at Ryan. "Satisfied, Bill?"

"You betcha," Ryan grinned back. He now turned to address the officer-in-charge. "Okay, I'm satisfied. Pass the word to get everybody formed up. We're gonna saddle up and move out as soon as we can, once everyone's ready."

"Yes, *sir!*" the officer replied. He spun about on his heel and then scurried away, barking orders left and right as the two senior officers watched.

Somewhere over the Atlantic, flying across international waters in a private corporate jet whose ownership, registration, and crew were fortunately not American, Pandora CEO B. D. Nye accepted with thanks the drink that had just been offered him by a rather good-looking stewardess. If he had been a much younger man, he might have allowed himself both the luxury and pleasure of admiring her aft view as she moved up the aisle in order to reach the cockpit and offer service to the cockpit crew. Instead, he again settled back into his seat, took a long and slow sip from his drink, then set it in a drink holder within easy reach of his seat. After that, he let his head sink back and closed his eyes. He wasn't trying to sleep, however, and remained fully conscious. What he was doing was remembering. He thought no more of Piter and June, of the rest of Pandora, or of events in the now-distant Metro City. He was instead remembering last year's Bellville Cup, and the come-from-behind last-minute win that had been brilliantly executed by a beautiful half-breed Cherokee female stock car racer taking part in her first major semi-professional race on the NASCAR Sportsman Circuit. Had he but known back then. Had he but pressed his case more strongly. That had been his fault, he decided. He had underestimated her and her importance in the grand scheme of things, given his lack of pertinent information at the time, and now his mistake had come back to bite him. Had he but known, then maybe. Nye opened his eyes, picked up his drink and took another long and slow sip, then again put it back in its holder. This time he did not close his eyes, but looked out the window at the sunlight dancing above the tops of the clouds. They seemed to invite him to come away with them, back to a time and place that were now no more, so he could revisit those past events once again ... and again revisit where he had first gone wrong with Lisa Stanridge.

The 1982 Bellville Cup Race was over at the Metro City Motor Speedway, which was located a short distance outside of town. The awards ceremony had just finished, Lisa had stepped down from the winners' stand after posing for several pictures with the second and third place winners, and had just handed off her first-place trophy to Rob Vesper, who was now standing beside her with his wife Cathy. He was the owner of Vesper's Auto Service, and he had given Lisa a stock car racing sponsorship when no one else would, her being a virtual unknown along with the unspoken issues of both her gender and her Indian heritage. Lisa had been fortunate in hooking up with Rob, because he believed in people having the chance to prove themselves. As a result of his faith in her, his business fortunes had sailed up along with her subsequent successful racing career. The three of them - Lisa, Rob, and Cathy - were now walking to one of the exits on the side of the track when they found a large party of suited men approaching them, escorting two other suited men in their midst.

"Uh oh," Rob said, leaning over to Lisa and half-whispering to her. "That's Mr. Nye and his chief hack from Pandora. I'll bet he's pissed off that you beat both his handpicked racing team and that car he had specially built for them."

"I'll be careful," Lisa said, as she locked eyes with Nye. They remained locked as Nye's group approached, the ring of outer bodyguards parting to accommodate Lisa and the Vespers within their circle and then closing again. Once the group had stopped moving, Lisa and Nye were less then two feet apart with eyes still locked. The Vespers looked worried. The face of Piter de Voormand, Nye's chief hack as Rob Vesper had called him, remained completely bland and emotionless. On the other hand, there were powerful emotions working behind the eyes of one B.D. Nye, although he was doing his best to conceal it.

Lisa decided she would be the one to break the ice. "Hello, Mr. Nye," she said calmly. "This is an honor."

Nye's face suddenly cleared as he forced a smile. It was as cold as his cobalt blue eyes. "No, Ms. Stanridge. The honor is mine, and I commend you on your driving skills today."

"Thank you, sir," Lisa replied evenly, maintaining eye contact all the while.

Nye paused and looked slightly to one side, as if searching for the right words, then locked eyes with Lisa again and resumed speaking. "It is because of those driving skills and your obvious determination to win that has caused me to approach you." He now smiled again. "How would you like to drive for me?"

Lisa looked surprised. "For you?"

"Yes, Ms. Stanridge," Nye said. "I'll cut to the chase, because I'm a direct man. I don't believe in employing losers. That's why those who drove for and worked on the Pandora team today have already been served their walking papers. I believe in only winners, and you proved today that you are a winner, and that you have both the drive and skill to keep winning. That's the kind of people I want working for me. That's why I'm offering you the chance to be the driver around which I will build my new racing team."

"What do I get?" Lisa asked.

"The best support and the best vehicle that money can buy," Piter de Voormand said, stepping forward. "This is a once in a lifetime chance, Ms. Stanridge. You would do well to take it."

It was obvious that the pair was expecting an immediate answer. Instead, Lisa turned and looked at Rob and Cathy. They smiled for her sake, although she could see that they both were trying to hide their worry. She then looked back at the two Pandora men, set herself, and answered them. "I'll cut to the chase too, Mr. Nye, since I also believe in being direct. No thanks." Both of Nye' eyebrows went up and de Voormand couldn't hide his own surprise as Lisa quickly continued. "You see, I value friendship over money, and I couldn't ask for better friends than Rob and Cathy. They supported me when no one else would. They've also gone out of their way to help me with everything I and their mechanics needed to put together a car that beat that one all your money bought you. Like I said, Mr. Nye. No thanks. Not now, not ever. Rob? Cathy?" With that she made a point of linking arms with them, Rob to her right and Cathy to her left, and together the three of them walked away from the two Pandora men. The ring of bodyguards parted soundlessly at their passing, and then closed again behind them just as silently.

"You're making a big mistake!" de Voormand called after them. "No one turns down B.D. Nye!"

"I just *did!*" Lisa called back with a laugh, not even looking back. She grinned at the Vespers and they back, and together the three of them walked away, leaving a dumbfounded de Voormand and a very quiet Nye behind as they watched the trio depart.

The sound of the plane's engines gradually drifted back into his consciousness as B. D. Nye's mind returned to the present. Of course all that had been a year ago. He had let her go as insignificant, a good-looking girl with more beauty than brains, who didn't have the common sense to take the best deal she might ever get in her insignificant little life, and had moved on to more pressing concerns. He had been so wrong in his initial assessment of her, he admitted to himself. That half-breed Cherokee stock car driver who was obviously a lot smarter than she looked was now front and center in the grand drama that was being played out in the dying Metro City ... and it could be proven that Pandora was directly responsible for her being in her current sad shape, provided the poor girl somehow survived her injuries, somehow survived the death warrant that the now out-of-control *ubermensch* was still trying to serve on her, and somehow lived. Even if she didn't, the word would spread and the virtual presence of Lisa Standridge would figure large in subsequent press coverage, as well as the official government investigation that was sure to come. Nye harrumphed softly at that last thought. Oh, but the fed would be doing its best to play CYA on this too while maintaining at least the semblance of public service. Both their ass and Pandora's were in the same sling, but they controlled the process and would find a way to extricate themselves in the long run. Pandora, a private military contractor with no public service obligations whatsoever, would be sacrificed for the sake of public expediency. Translation: so more than a few congressmen and bureaucrats whose hands were as bloodstained as his in this mess could escape and retain their positions of power, while his head and the that of the rest of Pandora corporate were lined up on the public chopping block.

Oh, but how the worm turned sometimes! Only this time, those poor politicians weren't going to get to carry B. D. Nye's head through the halls of Congress in triumph for all the world to see while they got off scot free. That was why Nye had consented to being spirited out of the country as fast as possible by de Voormand. Nye knew where this was heading. He had seen it happen too many times before to others in his youth, but it wasn't going to happen to him. He would even the score, even if he had to do it from abroad. de Voormand had made sure of that. de Voormand had made that possible. He was a good man, the Dutchman. Nye hoped he didn't lose him because of this mess.

"Sir?"

Nye was interrupted in his train of thought by the pleasant voice of the stewardess. So intent had he been in his reflections that he had not noticed when she had left the cockpit and come back down the aisle, a tray full of empty used paper cups and odd used food wrappings balanced in one hand, and then stop by his seat. He looked up at her and forced a smile. "Yes?"

The stewardess smiled down at him. "The captain wants you to know that we'll be reaching the coast of Europe soon. After that, we'll be touching down for a brief refueling stop before continuing on our way."

Nye continued to smile. "Thank you."

"You're welcome, sir. Can I get you anything else, sir?"

Nye reached over, picked up his glass from his holder, and held it up for her to see that it was still mostly full. "No thanks, miss. I'm doing just fine here, thank you."

"Yes, sir." With that, the stewardess continued on her way to the back.

All was quiet inside the Pandora complex north of Metro City. In fact it was too quiet. There were no sounds of night animals, or even of night insects. It was just ... quiet. The only sound that could be heard was Raul's soft snoring from the bushes not far from where Cy stood watch, keeping an eye on the main gate. There had been not a sign, not a peep, not even a hint of either the *ubermensch* or the Army relief column he believed, no he *knew* General Ryan was putting together. It should have been on its way by now. What was holding it up? Cy thought about it for a while, snorted, and then checked his watch. He smiled, and then walked over and began to shake Raul gently. "Hey Raul, get up," he said quietly. "It's four-o'-clock." Instantly Raul scrambled to his feet, assault rifle in hand. He was up so quickly that he almost knocked Cy over in the process. "Easy, easy!" Cy exclaimed. "It's me, buddy, not Big and Ugly."

Raul looked at Cy for a few moments, as his head cleared and his eyes adjusted to being fully awake again, and then he grinned. "Sorry, *señor*. I was having bad dream." He now looked around. "Any sign of that thing?"

"Not a peep since I wounded it and it ran away," Cy said.

"Oh, good," Raul said. "Maybe it no come back?"

"Oh, it's coming back, believe me," Cy said. "It's got to finish the job. That's the way those things work, Raul, like a trained dog or shark. Besides, if I were in its shoes, that's what I'd be planning and eventually doing. It'll be back before sunrise. I'd bet money on it."

Raul gave a grunt. "So why you think it take so long?"

Cy spoke evenly. "I've been thinking about that all night. I got a good solid hit on it with one of my grenades, so maybe it wanted to treat its own wounds before arming up. I wouldn't put it past the intelligence of those things, if what Mercy told us about them earlier is true."

Raul laughed. "Strong. And smart. And tall too. I wish I were like that."

Cy eyed him for a moment, and then gave a chuckle. "At least you've got the strong and smart parts. Also, don't forget you being short is one of the reasons why the *ubermensch* didn't notice you until you tried to tackle it."

"*Si*," Raul replied with his own chuckle, but returned to his pensive look all too quickly. "Anything else?"

This time Cy let his worry show. "Personally, I think why it's taking so long to return is that it might have made itself some kind of suit of body armor from the stuff my fellows were wearing, before the massed hordes of the zombies took them out yesterday."

"*¡Ai, yi, yi!*" Raul exclaimed in a low voice. "You really think so?"

"Wouldn't put it past it," Cy replied. "You saw for yourself how smart it is when it attacked. Who did it zero in on?"

"Lisa," Raul promptly responded.

"That's right," Cy said. "The most important member of our group insofar as surviving the Outbreak is concerned, and I'll bet its masters at Pandora gave it that information before sending it after us. It also cleared out this area of zombies and other threats, wrecked the radio transmitter in here, and set up the roadblock before we arrived as part of its attack. It's smart, Raul. It's smart and it's cunning, like a fox, and it knows how to use every resource at its disposal to do its job. That's why I'd be willing to bet money it'll be coming back wearing some form of body armor. It's not going to let me hit it with a grenade ever again."

Raul's face fell. "But if that thing protect itself, then what do we do, *señor*?"

In response, Cy lifted up one hand and clasped Raul on the shoulder. "The best that we can," he answered, "and we do it as long as we can, until the cavalry comes over the hill."

"*Si*," Raul said, clasping Cy's hand in return. They stood like that for a moment, and then both let go.

"What was that dream, if you don't mind my asking?" Cy said, as the two of them settled down in kneeling positions behind the hedges and bushes, with the both of them facing the front gate.

"Oh, it was bad," Raul said. "I was being chased by this big black bird. As big as an eagle, and mean as all out. No matter where I go or how fast I run, it stay right on me."

"So what happened?"

"I wake up by you shaking me."

Cy chuckled. "Sorry."

"Is okay. I no like bad dreams."

Cy looked at something behind Raul, then at him again. "Don't look now, Raul," he announced, "but there's a big black raven behind you perched on top of the lab building."

Raul abruptly turned and looked to where Cy had indicated. His eyes opened wide, and he almost jumped out of his skin at what he saw. "*¡Mierda!*" he exclaimed. "The bird from my dream!"

"That's no dream," Cy said. "That's our new friend."

"Friend?" Raul said, his disbelief clear to hear.

"Yeah," Cy said. "I've been thinking about it. I'm willing to bet this is the same raven we saw back at the police station, and the three of us before that at the hospital, and Lisa and me at the Armory before that. I saw it the very first time as I was being chased down the street by all those zombies that overpowered my convoy." He now leaned toward Raul, speaking in a low tone but in a quite deliberate manner. "I'm also willing to bet it's either a Raven Mocker or a familiar of one, like Lisa's talked about."

"A Raven Mocker?!" Raul exclaimed. He looked at the bird again, which still perched in its sleeping pose, then back at Cy. "No wonder I have that bad dream. Oh man, this is almost as bad as that *ubermensch* thing!" He now looked serious. "So which of us you think is after, *señor*?"

"Not Lisa, oddly enough," Cy said thoughtfully. "She says she had this spirit vision thing while she was out, during that brief time she was clinically dead, and that it told her it in that vision that it isn't her time. Says the Great Spirit won't let the Raven Mocker take her, because she still has a great future ahead of her." Cy laughed softly. "I'm not saying I believe it, but I hope for her sake she's right."

"But if she is, then what's it still doing here?" Raul asked nervously. He was trying to look at it, while trying to look like he wasn't trying to look at it. As for the raven, it never reacted to Raul's antics, remaining apparently frozen in its pose of unperturbed sleep.

"Two reasons, I'm guessing," Cy said, and this time he looked rather pensive. "One, to make sure she lives. Orders of the Great Spirit, and all that. Guarding her from one monster by making another serve as her personal bodyguard, perhaps."

"Man," Raul said with obvious awe. "To have a Raven Mocker as bodyguard. *Esto es loco.* That is how you say, it blows the mind?"

"Yeah," Cy replied. "There's also reason number two."

"What is that, señor?"

"It's after one of us."

Raul's face blanched. "One of *us*?!"

"Yeah." Cy looked as serious as he had ever been in the short time Raul had been part of the group. "Since the Great Spirit isn't going to let that thing have Lisa, it's probably going to want another victim, and the rest of us are conveniently available. Lisa was upset when she learned that Great Spirit's order to the Raven Mocker didn't cover me or you or Mercy, and she made a point of telling that to both of us." He paused, gave a grunt, and then continued. "Since it's not going to be allowed to feast on Lisa's soul, Raul, it's going pick one of us instead for dinner once it's good and ready. The question is, which one of us will it choose?" he finished, looking straight at Raul.

Raul gulped. He looked at Cy, then back at the presumably sleeping raven high above, then back at Cy again. "*Desgraciado.* That's too much, man. I wish you no tell me that."

"You shouldn't have asked," Cy said.

"I wish I hadn't," Raul said. He again looked back at the raven for a bit, then back at Cy. "I mean, is like having Grim Reaper back there, waiting to swing that big blade, you know?"

"I know, but you've also got to figure on Big and Ugly having to watch out for that same blade too." Cy shook his head. "That's the only good thing about this, Raul, as far as I can tell. Lisa's probably got the best protection in this world right now, or maybe the other world, or whatever. I don't know, but for you and me and Mercy, it's like walking a tightrope over a fire pit with both ends of the rope being set on fire while you're still only halfway across."

"*Si*," Raul agreed. He again looked at the raven and then back at Cy. "So what do we do?"

Cy made a point of resetting himself in his position. "I don't know about you, Raul, but I'm tired of having to deal with all of this existential shit, and on top of all of the Outbreak stuff too. All I'm gonna do from now on is focus on my job, and that's to make sure you and Mercy stay alive and Lisa doesn't get any more banged up than she already is, until the Army can get in here and rescue us. That at least I can do, so I'm doing it. And as for our unexpected company back there, well, there's nothing I can do about it, so I'm not going to worry about it anymore. I'm only going to worry about those things I can do something about, understand?"

"Not really, but I think I do like you." Raul now better positioned himself behind his own cover as well. "*Si*. I help you make sure that thing no hurt Miss Lisa no more."

"That's reason enough," Cy said. The U.S. Army corporal smiled at Raul, the stout Mexican illegal grinned back at Cy, and together the two of them kept watch on the Pandora complex main gate.

Mercy awoke with a start. She glanced quickly at a nearby wall-mounted clock. It read 4:06 AM. She came to her feet from the chair in which she had been sleeping and looked down at the gurney where her patient lay. Lisa was still there, heavily swathed in bandages and slumbering peacefully. There was no sign she had been disturbed in any way. Mercy looked around the room. Nothing had changed. Everything was where she had left it. She got up, grabbing her assault rifle as she did, walked to the nearest window, and peeked between two of the slats in the closed window blinds. Both Cy and Raul were still guarding the entrance to the main lab building, and they appeared to be talking to each other. Only then did Mercy allow herself to relax. She went back to her seat, propped the assault rifle back up where she had it before, and then took in and let out a deep breath. The long nap had done her a lot of good. she decided, as she flexed her arms and fingers. Even so, she wanted to be wide awake and ready when the *ubermensch* returned. Unless things changed, and until the Army was able to come up with a new way to get to them, one Mercy Parks was currently the last line of defense for poor Lisa Stanridge. She had done everything within her power to save the poor young woman's life after the first attack by the *ubermensch*. She would do her part to make sure that thing didn't get a second chance.

Mercy let her eyes wander to the neatly folded pile of Lisa's clothes sitting on the nearby counter. She had been forced to remove all of them when prepping Lisa for treatment, given the number and extent of Lisa's many injuries, and she had taken the trouble to clean them as best she could as a means of passing the time. She eyed Lisa's black racing firesuit, now showing damage on its left side both top and bottom, and felt a twinge of jealousy go through her. There had been a time when she could have worn something like that without shame, only she had been too uptight and straitlaced to even dare. For her, the best years of her life as a young woman had been spent first at college and then at medical school, always studying and prepping, rarely socializing save with that small clique of fellow students who were in the same boat as she, and never taking the time to dress herself in a way that would deliberately catch a man's eye. Unlike most of her friends, she fortunately hadn't become stuck that way. She had met John not long after she had been hired by Pandora, and the two had become close as the years rolled, their careers advanced, and their friendship grew into more than just that. She was also glad that they shared their love both in public and in private before the Outbreak happened, because now she was never going to get to do that again. John was dead, and he was never coming back. Never.

Mercy stifled a sob, and forced the thought of John out of her mind. She couldn't do anything about that. It was done and long over. She couldn't save John, but she could save Lisa. If it were humanly possible, she swore to herself, she was going to save Lisa. By saving her she could save others, and perhaps even the whole world, from the catastrophe that had swallowed Metro City. That thought made it worth it. Yes, she would save Lisa, even if she had to put her own life on the line to do it.

At the same time that General Ryan's forces were finishing their preparations, and Lisa's group of survivors was making ready to be rescued by them, a singular humanoid figure of abnormally large size and wearing a mishmash of scavenged body armor and various weapons raced back up Highway 9 on foot from downtown Metro City. The *ubermensch* was bloodied and showed numerous wounds on those parts of its body which its new makeshift body armor did not cover. The stump of its right arm had been crudely dressed, and yet the wound on the side of its right head remained open and was particularly hideous, with a large patch of skull bone showing and tendrils of torn flesh and hair trailing away. It ignored the constant pain from its head just like it ignored the constant pain from its amputated arm and the lesser pains up and down its right side and lower left calf. Its simple mind disregarded such trivial matters. It had been honed and developed to receive and obey orders without question and to adapt to changing circumstances in the most direct and efficient manner possible. It had no way of knowing that its now-damaged mind had re-interpreted what it could still understand of its orders regarding the four Metro City Outbreak survivors. As it currently interpreted them now, its duty was to terminate Lisa Stanridge and all companions with extreme prejudice by any and all means necessary, and that it was expendable itself in this regard. Period. That was why, once it had recovered sufficiently from its wounds to restore a fair portion of its combat effectiveness, it had realized that it would need more and better resources for its task than what was available at the local Pandora facility.

The *ubermensch's* original data feed had included information on the earlier Army convoy that had previously tried and failed to rescue any Metro City survivors before being taken out by the zombie hordes. It knew that the convoy personnel had been equipped with both body armor and heavy weapons. That was why it had acted on this information. Now it was returning to its primary mission, with enough armor and weaponry scavenged from the wreck of the Army convoy and adapted to its unique physique to do its job. Now suitably equipped with defenses and weaponry superior to what its targets had available to them, it would do everything in its power to terminate them with the most extreme of prejudices. Furthermore, if the Army tried to interfere again, as it had tried to do with the downed Huey Hog gunship, then it would deal with them too. Its feet thundered as they pounded the road, its high-speed run intended to return it to the location of its intended prey despite the heavy burden of its new gear. It would let nothing stop it this time. For the *ubermensch*, either Lisa Stanridge and her friends would die or it would die. It was that simple.

CHAPTER 12
SHOWDOWN

A large crowd of zombies had gathered behind the barricade across the northern end of Highway 9 that ran out of the quarantine zone from Metro City. Somehow, someway, by what means unknown, they had found out that the human guards had been drawn back from there, and now several hundred of them had massed at that currently unprotected point to attempt a breakout. They moaned and wailed, pounded and pushed, massing their might as they attempted to break down the barricade by sheer strength and moving mass alone. It was stoutly built and held despite their efforts, but it creaked and groaned down the entire section where they were massed, visibly shaking and even twisting a bit with their efforts. There would eventually come a time when the torque of that massed force would be too great for the barricade to bear, but not yet. It was still holding, and only needed to hold for a little longer.

The zombies lessened their efforts as the steadily growing sound of multiple vehicle motors caught their attention. Soon they stopped altogether as the front end of a long column of U.S. Army and Marine vehicles rounded the far turn beyond the barricade and began to move down the highway towards them. In the lead were two tanks with Marine markings that had oddly flattened barrels, escorted by two U.S. Army tanks and a number of soldiers on foot bearing both automatic weapons and portable flamethrowers. Behind the tanks came three Army APCs and three Army cargo carriers fitted with large storage tanks, and behind those came more tanks, more APCs, more cargo carriers, a large assortment of both trucks and other Army and Marine vehicles, and even more soldiers on foot. Overhead and moving with them were two attack helicopters, longer and narrower than the one which had been downed earlier, and even more deadly looking than it had been. The zombies snarled and growled, and began to push and beat on the barricade again, sensing that a fight was coming and ready to make it happen. The barricade still held.

The armored column came right up to the barricade and stopped once they were about a hundred yards from it. The soldiers on foot held their weapons at the ready but did not fire. The men manning the heavy machine guns on most of the vehicles turned them to face the barricade and pulled their breeches to chamber their first shells, but they too held their fire. All of the tanks and all of the APCS that had what looked like little gun turrets on them traversed them and locked onto the zombie horde at the barricade, but they too held their fire. The zombies attempting to break down the barricade grew even more frenzied. Some of them clambered up on it as high as its razor wire fitted top would allow and began to pull back and forth. Those sections of the barricade began to twist and groan. More zombies followed suit. In mere minutes, perhaps even seconds, the strain on the barricade would be too great and its connecting sections would snap from metal fatigue. The barricade would fall, and then the zombies could devour their second military convoy.

"*FIRE!!!*" came General Ryan's shouted order.

Ryan's voice sounded through loudspeakers mounted on several of the vehicles. Both of the lead Marine tanks, which were M67 Zippo flame tanks, immediately opened fire on the barricade. Instead of spewing shells at them from their main guns, however, they fired two long and very hot burning rods of flame that hit the zombie horde dead center. The tank crews then began traversing their turrets back and forth in order to cover the entire horde with burning fuel, and creating a giant fireball at the center of the barricade. An intense wave of heat and the charnel stench of crisping flesh quickly filled the air as most of the zombies were incinerated where they stood. Some still lived even though they were on fire and tried to run away, but they did not get very far. They would attempt a staggering run away from the now burning horde for a half-dozen or so steps, then fall and move no more as their own flaming flesh was quickly consumed. The affair lasted perhaps twelve seconds at most, and it was no contest. By the time both of the Marine Zippo tanks quit firing their M7-6 flame guns, every single zombie that had been massed at the barricade was a burning corpse, and the barricade itself had twisted and bent from the intense heat.

"*CLEAR THE BARRICADE!!!*" came Ryan's next command.

The armored column parted, both of the Marine Zippo tanks spun around on their treads, and then they quickly moved back to the front of either side of the parted column. Up the middle came three regular Army M60A2 Patton tanks, save that the fronts of all three were fitted with M9 Combat Dozer Blades. Their turrets had been traversed around fully in order to prevent damage to their main guns, and now all three deployed side to side and as close as they could get across the highway. They charged the fire-damaged barricade and the burning bodies beyond at full speed, with the former collapsing immediately as they hit it and many of the burning bodies flying aside. A fair number of these began to pile up in front of them but they quickly stopped and reversed themselves, making them fall off their blades as they trundled backwards. One burning body fell over the blade of one of these tanks and was carried back with it as it continued to back beyond the hole in the barricade. Several soldiers equipped with firefighting gear wearing backpack tanks of spray foam quickly ran up and doused the body before pulling it off the tank and flinging it back towards the barricade. The charge by the three blade-fitted tanks was repeated three more times, until a sufficiently large hole had been cleared through the broken barricade and burned zombie bodies for the armored column to pass. By now most of the fires had died down and what few remained were being put out by those soldiers equipped to do so and Army firefighting trucks that had driven up through the parted column, although the stink of burned flesh still filled the air. The officer-in-charge of the clearing operation took one final look, then keyed his radio and relayed a report to General Ryan farther back in the column. He only had to wait a second after he was done before Ryan's third command sounded over the armored column's loudspeakers.

"FORM UP AND MOVE OUT!"

The Army firefighters and firefighting vehicles quickly cleared away to both sides of the highway, even as Ryan's armored column reformed. Once it had, it began to pass through the large hole in the broken highway barricade, maintaining a slow but steady speed as it moved farther down the highway. Marine Zippo tanks, Army Zippo APCs, Zippo support vehicles, regular Army tanks, transports and jeeps and other various military vehicles, General Ryan and Colonel McKeegan along with their aides riding in an Army Ford MUTT, and along with them the hundreds of armed soldiers on foot. The entire column cleared the barricade, with General Ryan leaving behind only a sufficient contingent with enough support to both mop up behind them and guard the hole they had made, and then they were on their way southward down Highway 9.

Colonel McKeegan gave General Ryan a grim grin as the column continued to move. "Now that's a sight I haven't seen since the war," he said.

"Let's hope this action is the only time we have to use these on American soil," Ryan replied.

McKeegan nodded. "Agreed." He now looked ahead. "How far away are those survivors?"

"Just under three miles as the crow flies, three-point-six by the highway."

"Damn," McKeegan muttered. "As slow as we're moving, that's gonna give that thing plenty of time to get there before we do."

"If it isn't there already," Ryan conceded. "We might find nothing but bodies and that thing waiting for us."

"And yet you're doing this anyway."

Ryan nodded. "I have my orders direct from the President himself. Besides," and with this he forced a smile, "I'm hoping they're still alive, especially that Stanridge girl. You know the saying. Hope springs eternal." He looked again at the road. "I just hope nothing else goes wrong with this op."

"Me too," McKeegan said with a nod, and then also looked at the road.

The two senior officers fell silent, saying no more as the armored column and its overhead attack helicopter escort continued moving southward down Highway 9.

It was the raven that alerted both Cy and Raul to the return of the *ubermensch* to the Pandora industrial complex. It *awked* loudly, then flew up from its perch and towards the main gate. Cy and Raul followed its movements just in time to see a very large high-speed blur running down the road from the highway entrance. Both immediately opened fire on it, Cy with his AK-47 and Raul with his M-16. The blur immediately swerved and dodged behind a large stone sign set near the main gate announcing the identity of the complex in big carved letters facing the highway for all passers-by to see. Cy stopped shooting and motioned for Raul to do so as well, and that was when the *ubermensch* popped back up from behind its cover, swung up a Browning M2 50-caliber machine gun, propped it on the stone sign, and opened fire.

Cy managed to get a good look at their foe before its return fire forced both him and Raul to scramble for cover themselves. Its appearance had changed dramatically since he had seen it stagger away down Highway 9, naked and missing the lower half of its right arm, with ugly wounds and burns on the right side of its head, right shoulder, right upper side, and right upper arm. Those had come from the single grenade he had managed to land on it. The creature now wore a crude smock woven together with rope and cargo netting from multiple Army armor vests and flak jackets, all of which had come from the ruin of Cy's rescue convoy in downtown Metro City. An Army helmet with the liner stripped out for a better fit was on its oversized head, although it did not completely hide the nasty wound and burns on the right side. Cy would later swear he had even seen a bare patch of skull surrounded by bloody and burnt skin in that head wound, during the few times he was able to get a look at it in the ensuing fight. The stump of its right arm now sported both a crude bandage and a tightly attached Army backpack for ammo storage. It had even more ammo in the crudely fashioned large pouch on its back that looked as if it had been made from a Humvee top cover, as well as multiple weapons. The creature was holding the back of the heavy machine gun with its one remaining hand, which was enough to work its double-handle trigger. Cy and Raul immediately scrambled to either side of the hedge as fast as they could, once they had seen the *ubermensch* bring up that big-ass weapon, so all that got chewed up where they had been were the ground and the shrubs that had once decorated that spot. A second later, seeing that it had missed its intended targets, the *ubermensch* redirected its fire at the Pandora main lab building. Its front windows shattered as multiple belt-fed .50 caliber shells tore into it, flying through the shattered windows and ripping through the front walls and into the rooms and hallways beyond. Within seconds, a young woman's anguished screaming could be heard above the din.

"*LISA!!!*" Cy yelled, a look of horror on his face as he hid behind the orange Datsun pickup their group had used earlier to get there. From his own position behind a nearby retaining wall, Raul shook his head and crossed himself.

The screaming stopped even as the *ubermensch* immediately redirected its fire at Cy. The Army corporal had to scramble for new cover as fast as he could, while the Datsun was shot to pieces. A spark from struck metal ignited the fuel in its gas tank and it promptly exploded. Cy was flung into another decorative set of shrubbery from the blast just as the Browning's breech clicked empty on a spent ammo belt. The creature tossed the now-useless gun aside and bounded towards Cy, reaching his position in two giant leaps and pulling an M60 from its back pouch as it did. Raul had popped up from behind the retaining wall and opened fire, trying to hit it on the move, but it reached into its right arm stump pack, grabbed something on its first landing, and then flung a grenade with the pin pulled at Raul while it flew through the air towards its second. Raul was forced to quit shooting and break cover. He ran madly to get behind a parked Pandora delivery truck across the way, and then the grenade exploded. By that time the *ubermensch* had landed less than a dozen feet away from Cy, who was still tangled in the shrubbery and fighting to break free. His struggling stopped as he looked up at the nearby *ubermensch*, towering above him despite the distance, as it whipped its M60 around and leveled it at him. It then brought up the stump of its right arm and used it to hold up the M60's ammo belt so it would feed properly, and then gave the poor human a devilishly wicked grin. Cy gulped, knowing there was nothing either he or Raul could do, that Lisa was probably dead and Mercy either also dead or badly wounded, and that his own impending death was less than a second away. He looked straight into the eyes of the *ubermensch* and mentally resigned himself to his fate.

Suddenly the head of the creature snapped around. Two new sounds now impressed themselves on Cy's consciousness. The first had been there before, starting low but steadily growing in volume, but the sudden ferociousness of the *ubermensch*'s attack coupled with its devastating results had helped to hide it. Now that first sound could clearly be heard. It was the rumble of multiple approaching diesel motors. The second was the sound of a 105mm main tank gun being fired from less than a thousand yards away. The *ubermensch* immediately took a great leap to one side, and a 105mm tank shell tore through the air where it had just been a split second later. It howled past Cy's position and sailed on down the Pandora complex parking area before slamming into one of the side buildings next to the main lab building. There was a tremendous explosion as the roof and part of the upper walls of the side building were blown apart and the pieces flung in all directions. Cy snapped his head around to the main gate. There was a U.S. Army M60A2 Patton main battle tank sitting there, its main gun still smoking and its turret traversing as it tried to track the still-moving *ubermensch*. Cy could see other tanks behind the first one, and both tanks and APCs with both Army and Marine markings moving up to the high security fence on either side, apparently intending to knock it down and plow on through. He now heard the whirring of helicopter rotors as two AH-1 Air Cobras came in flying fast and low, chain guns blazing at the *ubermensch*. It broke off its attack and immediately bounded away, twisting and dodging the rain of shells being directed at it. Cy looked at the back end of the road, and he could just make out other military vehicles of various shapes and sizes heading down it towards the complex. Inwardly, the Army corporal breathed a big sigh of relief.

Cy sensed rather than saw Raul break cover and run back to him. He felt tugging on his trapped arms and legs, and within a few seconds he was free of the shrubbery. He came back to his feet just as Raul was scooping up his fallen AK-47, and then the stout Mexican handed it back to him. Cy took it and together the both of them ran for the nearest decent piece of cover.

"Thanks, man!" Cy said as they ran.

"*Si!*" Raul exclaimed as he ran beside him. "Look like your cavalry, it come over the hill, eh *señor*?"

"*Si!*" Cy agreed wholeheartedly.

The pair found their new cover behind yet another retaining wall in front of another set of shrubbery behind the Pandora factory complex's administrative building. They dashed behind it and then crouched there, watching as General Ryan's armored column and air cover took on the *ubermensch*. Raul hunkered down and kept his assault rifle at the ready, quietly cursing in Spanish as he did. As for Cy, he gritted his teeth and wished his fellow soldiers the best of luck. They had to succeed, for Lisa's sake, if nothing else. They simply had to succeed.

As for the raven, it had somehow found its way back to the top of the lab building despite the battle now raging within the Pandora lab complex. It resumed its perch as if nothing unusual were going on, then watched with interest the proceedings below. Such a sweet feast of souls was about to be laid before it ... including one in particular it intended to claim in place of the one it had been denied.

Lisa was not dead, as Cy feared. She was still very much alive. Once the *ubermensch* had reappeared and the shooting began, Mercy had quickly left her seat and ran over to the wounded young woman. Earlier she had left the side of the gurney down so as not to impede her treatment of Lisa's many wounds, and now that stood her in good stead for what she did next. As soon as Mercy reached Lisa, she grabbed her under her arms and yanked her off the gurney, backpedaling as she did. This caused the both of them to fall on the floor, with Lisa on top of Mercy, and not a moment too soon. The air was now full of shattered plaster and flying lead as a series of high-velocity 50-caliber slugs tore through the examination room from the wall closest to the front of the lab building. Lisa screamed in agony from her body being made to twist and turn in ways that its wounded state could no longer accept, even as the hail of lead passed overhead mere inches from her. It tore through the upper part of the gurney where she had been lying but seconds before, it tore through storage lockers and cabinets, shattering glass everywhere and sending the shards flying along with a number of ricocheting slugs. Miraculously, neither Mercy nor Lisa were hit. She screamed again as Mercy jinked around and managed to get out from under her without lifting her up, causing her to drop to the floor. Mercy could do nothing for Lisa except keep an arm around her until the hail of shells stopped, and Lisa's screaming with it. Mercy looked at the anguished young woman with tears in her own eyes. "I'm sorry," she whispered loudly.

"I ... know ..." Lisa managed to gasp, her remaining eye streaming tears and her breath ragged. She spoke in a pain-filled hoarse whisper. "You ... saved ... me ... Mercy ... thanks ..."

"It'll try again unless it knows you're dead," Mercy said flatly, "and it doesn't look like Cy or Raul can hold it off this time." She looked around the room, trying to find her own assault rifle, and finally spotted its twisted ruin lying not far from the door. A 50-caliber slug had hit it dead center and almost bent it in two. She grunted, and that was when her eyes happened to fall on the counter where she had previously set Lisa's clothes and gear. Miraculously, neither they nor the that end of the counter had been hit. Her MAC-11 was there, still loaded and ready to go, along with her pistol and spare ammo. So were her racing boots and her damaged firesuit, still bearing a few bloodstains even though Mercy had done her best to clean them off. Seeing those gave Mercy an idea, and she now looked back at Lisa and smiled. "I think I know a way to make it go away." With that, she let go of Lisa and began to crawl as low as she could towards the counter.

"What ... what are ... what ..." Lisa struggled to say, still fighting her pain and doing her best to keep her voice down.

By now Mercy had reached the counter. The horizontal storm of heavy-caliber shells flying through the room had stopped, but the two could still hear automatic weapons fire from the front of the lab building. Mercy reached up and quickly pulled down first Lisa's MAC-11 and then her spare ammo from the counter top before grinning at her. "Catch," she said, as she drew her arm back and then flung them one at a time at the prone Lisa. The gun slid across the floor and smacked solidly into Lisa's thigh. The ammo pouch bumped up and stopped against her shin. Lisa grimaced and groaned softly both times as they hit her, but no more. With a painful effort she managed to reach around and grab the MAC-11 with her right hand, then pull it to her.

"Got it ..." she said in a hoarse whisper, then fell back to the floor, still clutching the MAC-11. She grimaced and groaned again as her back hit the floor, then turned her head and looked at Mercy. "What ... now ...?"

"You and I are almost the same size in clothes," Mercy said, as she now grabbed both the boots and the firesuit and began crawling towards the door as fast as she could. "I found that out when I was treating you. That's why I'm going to try tricking Big and Ugly into thinking I'm you."

"Mercy ...!" Lisa rasped painfully. She was unable to move her body, so she set the MAC-11 on her stomach before holding up a badly shaking right hand towards her. "Don't ...!" she pleaded, while the muffled sound of multiple diesel motors could now be heard faintly somewhere in the distance.

Mercy reached the door and then turned to look at Lisa. "You need to live," she said. "You know that." She looked around, and then risked lifting up high enough to open the door. She dropped back down after that as fast as she and crawled partway through. Mercy then stopped, looked back at Lisa, and gave her the saddest smile Lisa had ever seen. It was the smile of one who knew they were about to die, and was facing that death willingly as part of a cause greater than themselves. "I'm glad I met you, Lisa. Goodbye." With that, she hurriedly snaked the rest of the way through the doorway and let the door shut behind her on its hydraulic hinge.

"Mercy ..." Lisa wept, as her tears flowed freely from her one remaining eye.

The *ubermensch* was having a field day with General Ryan's armored column. In the space of a mere quarter of an hour, it had taken out the first tank at the Pandora complex main gate that had challenged it, another that was immediately behind it and couldn't bring its main gun to bear fast enough, a nearby Marine Zippo tank that had tried to hit it with its flame gun and missed, and one of the Army Zippo APCs that had been unfortunate enough to be in its way as it finished with its initial counterattack. In that short space of time it had also managed to down one of the Air Cobra attack helicopters with a very large boulder flung into its cockpit, and forced the other to leave the fray trailing acrid black smoke from an engine damaged by heavy machine gun fire. By then, almost a full company of Ryan's men with mixed weapons had hurriedly disembarked from their transports and ran up to join the fray, but none of them were able to stop it. It was too agile and moved too fast for them, regardless of the weapon they were using, whether it be M-16 assault rifle, M79 or M203 grenade launcher, portable flamethrower, or even a shoulder-fired Stinger missile at one point. Most of their weapons fire missed, and it simply ignored what few wounds it was receiving from the combined assault rifle fire. None of the gunners manning the vehicle-mounted weapons were having any better luck. They tried their 105mm main tank guns, their M7-6 flame guns, their vehicle-mounted 50 caliber and 7.62mm heavy machine guns, their tripod-mounted TOW missile launchers, but all to no avail. None of them could land a solid hit on the thing. It was simply too fast, and they couldn't pin it long enough to catch it in a crossfire. On the other hand, the *ubermensch* was single-handedly decimating Ryan's forces, grinding them down with its own weapons and grenades flung out of its stump arm pouch as if they weren't any threat whatsoever, picking up and sometimes even ripping away new weapons from them and their vehicles as it needed them, or even grabbing the occasional small vehicle or decorative boulder and using those appropriately. This was what it had been designed to do, Ryan belatedly reminded himself as he and Colonel McKeegan huddled down behind the wreckage of his Ford MUTT command vehicle. He looked down at the body of his aide, who lay dead beside him, and wondered how much longer his forces could hold out against that thing.

Awk! Awk! Awk!

The clear cry of a raven cut across the battlefield, getting everyone's attention. It also got the attention of the *ubermensch*. All eyes turned to see not a raven roosting on the top edge of the roof of the Pandora complex's main lab building, but a figure in a black racing suit and black boots running down the stairs, having just come out of the front doors and heading in a straight line for the building across the way.

"NO!!!" Cy cried. He knew it couldn't be Lisa. He knew who it was, what she was doing, and why she was doing it. It was Mercy in Lisa's racing firesuit, pretending to be Lisa. Raul's eyes opened wide and Cy's mouth opened even as he tried to make a second warning cry, but it never sounded. By then it was too late. With a triumphant cry the *ubermensch* jumped away from the Army APC whose flame gun turret it had just pulverized, crossing the distance in a single bound and landing only twenty yards away from the running Mercy, set itself and whipped its M60 heavy machine gun around into position, then opened fire. Mercy's body jerked this way and that, her run turned into a crazy lurching death dance as she moved. She stumbled, tripped, and then tumbled to the ground as multiple M60 rounds slammed into her from shins to sternum. She wound up rolling to a stop less than six feet away from the bottom stair to the building she had been trying to reach, her body surrounded by an ever-growing pool of blood.

Even as Mercy fell and the *ubermensch* laughed triumphantly, her diversion had given one of the regular Army M60 Patton tanks just enough time to finish traversing its turret, lock onto the *ubermensch*, and then open fire with its main gun. The *ubermensch's* reverie was abruptly cut short when it was hit squarely with the 105mm tank round that the Patton had fired. It was flung into the air, its M60 smashed to smithereens by shrapnel, and various of its body parts flying everywhere. Somehow its head remained connected to its now-limbless torso. This hit the ground hard some distance away and the creature bellowed in agony. It had also just happened to land directly in front of a Marine Zippo tank and less than fifty yards away. The creature didn't even have time to roll over and see its new threat, as the Marine Zippo tank's crew immediately locked on target and fired a long and very hot rod of flame at it. The *ubermensch* was immediately doused from its battered head to the bloody stumps of its legs in fiercely burning fuel. Its anguished bellow immediately turned into a screeching death wail and it thrashed about, trying to get out of the path of the flames with limbs that were no longer there, knowing full well that it was being flash-roasted alive. The air filled with the combined smells of burning flame gun fuel and copious amounts of overcooked flesh, just as an Army Zippo APC trundled into range and added its own rod of flame to that of the Marine Zippo tank. What was left of the *ubermensch* let out one more pitiful wail, then its scorched and almost skinless head fell down and moved no more. What remained of its body was already being consumed by the flames.

176

Cy saw none of this, although he could smell and hear it. As soon as the *ubermensch* had been taken out by the first tank he had popped out of cover and commenced a low combat run towards the fallen Mercy, Lisa's AK-47 held in a combat carry as he ran. Raul was right on his heels, although he ran like a civilian, and both Army and Marine soldiers came running up as well from several other directions. By the time Cy had made it to Mercy and was cradling her head in his lap, both General Ryan and Colonel McKeegan had raced up along with a team of three Army field medics. The regular soldiers immediately brandished their weapons and deployed in a protective ring around the group. Blood was freely flowing from all of Mercy's wounds, but she still managed to speak as Cy looked down at her and the others closed in. "Lisa," she gasped, "Lisa ... lab building ... help ... her ... careful ... armed ..."

"Go!" Ryan ordered two of the medics. They took off at once, one hand on their medical bags and a pistol in the other, as they ran for the lab building.

Mercy had started coughing up blood in the meantime. The remaining medic quickly examined her, then looked at the other three. He shook his head, and Raul choked back a sob. The stout Mexican let go of the stock of his assault rifle with his left hand, crossed himself, and began to pray in Spanish.

"Why, Mercy?!" Cy exclaimed, tears beginning to fill his own eyes as he continued to cradle her head. "Why?"

Mercy turned her head so she could look at him, and spoke with her bloodied lips. "For ... Lisa ... " she got out. "I ... was ... part of ... problem ..." She stopped and took a breath before continuing. "Now ... part of ... solution ..."

"Oh, Mercy," Cy said, gently stroking her hair. The tears were flowing fiercely from Raul's while he continued to pray. He didn't see a priest anywhere so he tried his best to administer some form of last rites. It was all he could do for her. Beside the pair, Ryan and McKeegan and the remaining Army medic remained respectfully silent.

The dying Mercy looked up at the sky. Her face had assumed a strangely anxious look. It wasn't one of fear; rather, it was one of a known threat that has been faced, that of a victim willingly accepting its fate. "Do ... do you ... hear it?" she asked.

"Hear what?" Cy said.

"That cry ... you know ..." Mercy said. She now looked over at Cy. "It's time, Cy ... goodbye ..."

"No ..." Cy said, sorrow now filling his voice.

Behind the group, perched in the middle of the top edge of the lab building roof, a certain raven that had gone unnoticed ever since it had alerted everyone to Mercy's presence had its wings partially spread and its head held high. Its beak was wide open as it cried, although no sound audible to human ears could be heard on this level of existence. Only Mercy and the other fallen on that battlefield could hear it; for its cry was for them alone, and only they could respond to its fateful summons. Mercy stiffened, and then her entire body began to quiver and shake. The same was happening with the other fallen soldiers scattered elsewhere around the Pandora complex. Mercy's eyes were open wide but she could no longer see. Her mouth was open wide, as if crying aloud, but she made no sound. General Ryan, Colonel McKeegan, Cy, and the medic looked at each other in wonder while Mercy's body continued to convulse and Raul continued to pray. Suddenly it was over. Mercy's body arched one final time and then fell lifeless to the ground. Her head lolled over in Cy's lap, her eyes and mouth still wide open. To Cy, as he looked at her, her body now looked more like a waxwork dummy than that of a formerly living being, despite the blood that still flowed from it and the warmth it still had. The same was true for the others who had clustered around the now-lifeless bodies of those soldiers who had fallen trying to fight the *ubermensch*. Cy abruptly snapped his head up and around just in time to see the raven on the roof edge close its beak, give him what might be described as a supremely satisfied look, then take to the air and fly off. General Ryan and Colonel McKeegan quickly followed Cy's gaze, as did many of the soldiers on foot, the tank crews, vehicle drivers, and other assorted military personnel. Even as all of them watched, the raven ascended higher and grew fainter against the dark, cloud-filled sky. Suddenly it burst into brilliant flame, gave a final and long *aaawwwwwwkkk!* in the voice of a normal raven, then rocketed away into the sky and disappeared.

"What ... the ... hell ...?" a slack-jawed Colonel McKeegan muttered.

"It was the Raven Mocker, sir," Cy said evenly. McKeegan turned to look at him. Both Ryan and the medic were already looking but not saying anything. "It wasn't allowed to take Lisa's soul so it took Mercy's instead, along with all of the other souls it could claim." He gave General Ryan a faint grin. "Long story, sir. I'll be happy to explain it at the debriefing."

"Yeah ..." Ryan said slowly. He was still having trouble believing what he had just seen.

Just then there was a faint call from the front of the lab building. "Cy ...?!" It was Lisa. She had been picked up and transferred to another gurney, and the two Army medics were carefully working it down the stairs to ground level.

"Lisa!" Cy exclaimed. He looked at both Ryan and McKeegan. "Pardon me, sirs!" he said quickly, and then ran over to her.

By that time the medics had gotten the gurney down the stairs, and Cy ran up as they were wheeling it down the parking lot. Lisa was in obvious pain, there was new blood that had soaked through her dressings, and she was crying, but the tears she was shedding weren't from the pain alone.

"Cy ..." Lisa sobbed, as she weakly held up her right hand. Cy immediately clasped it and walked beside her with the gurney, while the medics wheeled it towards the two senior military officers. "Oh, Cy," she cried. "Mercy ... she ..."

"I know," Cy said. "Just remember, Lisa. She did it for you. She did it so you could live, and save everyone else. She died so that all of us could have the promise of life that you hold within you, Lisa. Remember, she did it for you."

"Cy ..." Lisa said, and with that she began to weep.

By this time an Army ambulance had pulled up, and General Ryan directed the two medics to wheel Lisa's gurney to it. The third medic joined them as they lifted Lisa's body inside. At the same time a pair of regular soldiers came up almost unnoticed with what looked like a set of rolled tarps under one arm. They promptly set them down, unrolled one, and then worked Mercy's remains into a body bag. They then zipped it up and went on to do the same with the other bodies of the fallen, while other pairs of soldiers did the same in other places. As this was going on and the medics were finishing securing Lisa's gurney inside the ambulance, Cy turned to General Ryan. "May I, sir?" he asked.

General Ryan nodded with a smile. "Go ahead, corporal. We'll meet up later. If anyone gives you trouble, just refer them to me."

"Thank you, sir," Cy said gratefully. The three medics also nodded in acknowledgement, then one of them held the back doors of the ambulance open as Cy got inside with Lisa. Another joined them in there, while the two outside closed the doors. One of these got in front with the driver, and the other left to help his fellows treat the other wounded on the battlefield. The ambulance then drove away with both Cy and Lisa inside.

"Uhhh, *señor*? I mean, sir?"

Both Ryan and McKeegan turned to look at Raul Esteban. He looked nervous and could not look directly at them. He was holding out both his rifle and pistol, and he was looking down at the ground. "I, uh, maybe I no longer should have these, now that you here and me supposed to be in jail."

"That's right," McKeegan said. "You're that illegal they picked up during their escape." He looked over at Ryan. "Well, Bill?"

A regular Army soldier came trotting up before Ryan could answer. "Sir?" he asked Ryan politely.

McKeegan looked to Ryan, who nodded. "Yes, soldier?" he said.

"We're recovered everything that both ladies had in the lab building, sir. We also found these along with some of Ms. Stanridge's things on one of the counters. I'm bringing them to you. sir, as you ordered provided we were ever laid hands on them." He then handed General Ryan a set of car keys.

Ryan's eyebrow went up as he studied the HemiCuda logo and symbol on the attached tab, and then he looked at Raul. "For Ms. Stanridge's car," he said. "The one she had to abandon when her group had to evacuate the hospital, right before they went to the police station and rescued you."

"*Si*," Raul said, still looking down and offering his weapons to him.

Ryan looked at the soldier. "Take this man's weapons, soldier. Also take his ammo too. He doesn't need them anymore."

"Yes, sir," the soldier said. Raul handed both rifle and pistol to the soldier, then took off his ammo-filled MCPD rucksack and handed it over as well. When it was done, the soldier turned back to face Ryan. "What shall I do with these, sir?"

"Put them with our own stores for now. I'll decide what to do with them later."

"Yes, sir." With that the soldier left.

Ryan again looked at Lisa's car keys, and then at Raul. The Mexican illegal was looking back at him, his face half full of expectation and half full of fear. Ryan chuckled. "You know, as the senior military officer in charge of the quarantine, I should be taking you in so we can turn you back over to INS."

"*Si*," Raul replied with a gulp.

"However," Ryan continued, "I'm not going to do that just yet. You were a big help to your fellow survivors, and you can be a big help to me now. We're about to saddle up and move back out so we can go clear out the town. If my information is correct, then I need you to come along with us for a special job for which almost all the rest of my people and Colonel McKeegan's here are going to be too busy to do. I need them more for this op than for this little special job." He now offered the car keys to Ryan. "I want you to retrieve Ms. Stanridge's car for me. Can you drive?"

A surprised Raul looked at the keys, then up at Ryan. "*Si, señor!*" he exclaimed with a grin.

Ryan looked pleased. "Then that'll be your job, if it's still in any shape to be retrieved given the time that's passed. If it's not drivable but is still in good shape, let my people know and I'll arrange for a flatbed and crane to come get it. I want you to keep an eye on it from the time we get to it and you get it out of there until either we're done with this op and can come back to help you, or other federal authorities show up to take over in your place. Take it to my field headquarters outside the quarantine zone, and then park both it and you there until either of those happen. My people can show you the way." He now gave a chuckle and a grin. "That'll keep you out of the hands of the INS for a while longer. I owe you that much for doing your best to help Corporal Rappalo protect Ms. Stanridge against that thing. Can you do that for me, Mr. Esteban?"

Raul face now filled with pride. "*Si*, General sir!" he exclaimed.

"And no hot-rodding," Ryan added, still grinning as he handed over the keys.

"*Si!*"

It took General Ryan's forces about two weeks to clean out almost all forms of the undead, both human and animal, from Metro City and all of the surrounding countryside within the quarantine zone. By the time they were done, the decision had already been made by authorities much higher in the chain of command that Metro City would have to be destroyed as well. That took much longer, but eventually the entire city along with every human construction within the quarantine zone was decontaminated and razed to the ground in the months that followed. What few undead remained hiding in the city's abandoned buildings were destroyed at this time, and eventually what few remained in the surrounding countryside were hunted down and also destroyed by the end of the year. As for the former site of Metro City, even U.S. Highway 9 and other major federal and state roads which had previously run through the city were rerouted around its former site, and forests planted or in some cases transplanted to the appropriate places so that it could not be seen from the rerouted thoroughfares. At the end of this process, what few remaining bits of rubble and detria indicating that Metro City had ever existed save one were knocked down and bulldozed over, so that when all was done almost nothing was left on the site, resulting in an open plain covering about a hundred and twenty square miles.

The site where Metro City had once stood was claimed by the federal government as a protected reservation, with no opposition from state or local authorities on the matter. It was subsequently fenced off from pubic access and no visitors were allowed under any conditions, save for the occasional survey team to check up on the site every few months. Only one thing remained to remind people of what had once been there, aside from the security fence and warning signs against trespassing that were posted at regular intervals around its full circuit. Along the slowly deteriorating remains of the paved multi-lane road that had once been the southern end of U.S. Highway 9 going out of Metro City, one of the old city limits signs had been left in place. It was the only thing remaining of Metro City, and it had been left there as a memorial of sorts to the memories of both the city itself and those who had lived and died there. It could be seen at a distance from the gate in the security fence on that end of the former site of Metro City, if one cared to go there and bring a pair of binoculars with them, and its legend could still be read for years to come: WELCOME TO / METRO CITY / POPULATION 76,379. Rather, that is what it read before the Outbreak happened. One could still see the faded red spray paint that someone had used at the time to spray out the population number, then add a single word in red in the bottom right corner of the sign so that it would read POPULATION UNDEAD.

There came a day just over a month after her dramatic rescue from Metro City, when Lisa Stanridge was sitting propped up on the adjustable bed in her room at nearby Kramerville Memorial Hospital, and visiting with both Cy and her mother Nancy Stanridge. Lisa still had hard casts on her upper left arm, around her chest, and around her left leg at the knee, for her broken bones and her ribs were still healing. Initial surgery had been performed on her left knee to clean out pieces of broken bone and to prepare it for her total knee replacement surgery, but that was still in the not-too-distant future. There had also been other operations to properly set her broken ribs and reset her broken arm, so Lisa had spent most of the past month either unconscious or heavily sedated. The cast would be coming off her broken arm in about three more weeks. It would be two more months, give or take a week or two, before her reset broken ribs would heal completely. Also, both her regular doctor and the surgeon who was to replace her knee had informed Lisa that it would probably be four to six months after that surgery before she could even try to walk normally again. Finally, Lisa had a black eye patch over her left eye socket. She had lost that eye permanently due to what had happened, and she would be stuck with only one eye for the rest of her life, provided nothing else happened to her. "I'm just glad to be alive," she had told Cy and her mother as they visited. "It's going to take a while for me to get back up on my feet, but rest assured I will."

"I don't doubt it," her mother said with a smile. "You're like your dad in that. Both of you were always so stubborn." She then looked sad and fell silent.

Lisa reached out with her right hand towards her mother. Nancy took her hand and clasped it in both of her own. "Tell me, if you don't mind," Lisa said quietly. "How did Dad die?"

"He died protecting me," Nancy said, her face filling with a sorrowful look. "When we figured out what was going on, your father immediately put me into the storm cellar and had me bar the door from the inside. After that, he stayed up there, knowing that the zombies were coming and determined to make sure they couldn't ever get me." She made a sound somewhere between a sad laugh and a choked-back half-sob. "He gave them hell."

"I'll bet he did," Lisa said reassuringly, playing her thumb across one of her mother's clasped hands.

Nancy now managed a laugh despite her sorrow. "You know, when the Army finally showed up and rescued me, there were literally piles of zombie bodies around the farm and in front of the storm cellar's outer door. He gave them everything he had with everything he had available." She now looked sad again. "All they found were parts of him. The zombies ... they must have torn him apart at the end." It was all she could do to keep from crying. "I'll miss him ... and Randy too."

"Oh, Mom," Lisa said, squeezing her mother's clasped hands with her own.

"Sounds like your Dad was one helluva man," Cy said quietly from his spot beside Nancy. "I can see where you got your own determination and courage, Lisa."

"I was just doing like you, Cy," Lisa replied. "I was doing what I had to do in order to survive." She now gave a soft laugh. "I never knew I was going to hook up with you ..." and with this she gave him a heartfelt look, "... but I'm glad I did."

"Same here, Lisa," Cy replied tenderly.

Nancy looked at Cy, then at her daughter, then back at Cy again. She let go of Lisa's right hand with one of her own, and used the other to lift up Lisa's hand towards Cy. "Maybe you should be holding this instead of me," she said, as a smile returned to her face.

"No, you're her mother," Cy insisted. "I'll wait my turn, ma'am."

Everyone laughed at that. When they were done, Lisa pulled her hand back and gave Cy a look. "As long as we're speaking of turns, have you had any fun with those CDC people like I've been having? I swear, if they draw one more blood sample from me, then I'm going to shrivel up and blow away."

"No, not as much, but I've had my share of time with them too," Cy admitted. "So has Raul."

"Raul?!" Lisa exclaimed. "I was wondering what happened to him. I've been thinking that the INS got him once he got out of there and promptly hauled his ass back to Mexico, given that nobody's talked about him until now."

"Well, he's still here," Cy said, "although he's in detention. Not with the INS, though," he continued, as Lisa cocked an eyebrow and Nancy listened. "General Ryan got him when he came back out of Metro City, and he's kept him under the Army's care up until now. Says he's a hero for helping me to save you despite his illegal status, and so does the press. There's a lot of negotiating going on about him at higher levels right now, or so I understand, but for now he's not going to be deported." He chuckled. "They're keeping him over at Fort Bowden until they make up their minds. I got to visit him last week. He says it's the most comfortable jail he's ever been in. He also says he hasn't made up his mind on what he's going to do once the higher-ups finally make a decision on him, but he assured me that he's going to have one heck of a story to share with his family back in Guadalajara whenever he gets a chance to go back and visit with them."

"Well, I hope they'll let him stay," Lisa said, "or even make him a citizen. He didn't have to help us, or do his best to save me after I was attacked, and yet he did. They owe him for that. I know I do."

"That's exactly what General Ryan said," Cy agreed. "That's part of the reason why he kept him in the Army's custody, and wouldn't let INS have him."

"That's good," Lisa said. She fell silent, looking at her mother, then did a double-take and looked at Cy again. "Part of the reason?"

"Well you see ..." Cy began, but he never finished due to a knock at the door.

"May I come in?" a male voice announced.

"Certainly, Dr. Phillips," Lisa called out. "Come on in!" She gave Cy a quick look. "We'll talk about this more later," she said quietly.

"Uh-oh," Nancy said with a knowing grin, right before the door opened and Dr. Phillips entered the room. "You're in trouble now, Cy," she added in a low voice. Cy merely grinned back in reply.

Dr. Harold Phillips was a handsome man of late middle age, with a head full of pepper-colored hair and penetrating brown eyes set behind a pair of thin round wire frame glasses. He wore the traditional doctor's long lab coat over his dress shirt and slacks, with dress shoes to match; however, he wore a plaid bowtie instead of a regular tie. "Hello, folks," he said cheerfully as he approached, "and hello to my most attractive patient today."

"Thank you, Dr. Phillips," Lisa replied pleasantly. "Flattery will get you everywhere."

"Yes, I know," Dr. Phillips replied confidently. "Now let's get your checkup over with, and then I can visit just like your mom and boyfriend are doing."

"Doctor!' Lisa exclaimed, but her eyes twinkled as she did. Cy looked embarrassed. Nancy smiled knowingly but said nothing.

The examination was a routine one and was over in about ten minutes. The first thing the good doctor did was check her pulse. He then pulled a ophthalamoscope from one lab coat pocket and used it to check her right eye. When that was done he put it back and pulled an otoscope from his other lab coat pocket and used it to check both of her ears. Once that was done he put it back, set up the stethescope he had been wearing around his neck in traditional fashion, and then helped her to sit up fully before he used it to both listen to Lisa's heart and to check her breathing as much as the cast around her side would permit. After that he motioned for her to relax and resume her semi-reclined position on her propped-up bed while he made some notes on the chart on the clipboard at its foot. He talked as he wrote, hanging it up once he was done and then returning to her side beside Nancy, opposite of Cy. "Excellent, excellent. Your recovery is proceeding normally. In fact, if it weren't for procedure and all that, I'd turn you over to Dr. Watkins for your replacement knee surgery today, but you know how it goes."

Lisa nodded. "Everything in its right time, doctor. I've waited this long. I can wait some more."

Dr. Phillips nodded back. "That's the spirit." He now frowned, but pleasantly. "I still wish you'd change your mind about reconstructive surgery for that left eye socket of yours."

"Thanks but no thanks, doctor," Lisa said firmly. "We've already discussed this. No reconstructive surgery. As I said at the time, this ..." and with that she motioned with her right hand towards her new eye patch, "... is now part of me. It defines who I am and what I've become. Not a victim, not someone to run around and hold an eternal pity party, but a survivor. It's a symbol of what happened to me, and a reminder to others that it could still happen again, despite what they found in my blood to help prevent it, unless we act to keep it from happening again. You know what I'm saying?"

Nancy Stanridge looked on her daughter with pride. Cy was doing the same. Lisa now held out her hand to him, and it was his turn to clasp it firmly and smile at her, and she at him. After a few seconds of this, Dr. Phillips spoke. "Okay. I won't bring up the subject again. I don't agree with your decision, but I understand from where you're coming and I'll respect it."

"Thank you, doctor," Lisa said, looking at him as she did.

Dr. Phillips now smiled mischievously at her. "By the way, you've got more visitors outside, and those folks from the CDC are back again."

"Oh, God," Lisa said, rolling her eye in mock horror. "Doctor, please."

"Fortunately they're not here for more blood samples this time," Dr. Phillips said with a chuckle. "They just want to go over the story of your Outbreak adventure again with you, to talk about you and the special capabilities in your blood, and how that's going to affect you and your surviving family, as well as discuss any possible future plans involving you, and all of that."

"Can I see the other visitors first?" Lisa asked. "Please?"

"I haven't even told you who they are," Dr. Phillips said with a smile.

"I'd rather not deal with the CDC people again today, thank you very much," Lisa said crossly, pretending to be irritated. "If that's why they're here, then I want them to come back when I'm in the right frame of mind to give them a good piece of my mind." She now changed tone and spoke politely. "I'll take the mystery guests behind Door Number 2. Could you show the others in please, doctor, and tell that CDC bunch to come back another time?"

"That I will," Dr. Phillips said. He waved at Lisa. "Until next time, young lady."

"Until then," Lisa said. She, Cy, and her mother watched as Dr. Phillips turned, went to the door, and let himself out.

"I wonder who those other people are who want to see me," Lisa said. "I know the government's been shooing away the press, thank God, and they wouldn't have let anybody else in here unless it was official business or ..." Her voice trailed off as she looked at her mother. "Do you know?"

Nancy Stanridge grinned at her daughter. "It's a surprise," she said.

Lisa was about to respond when another knock came at the door. "Come on in," Nancy called, before Lisa could say anything.

The door opened and three people came into Lisa's hospital room. There was one man and two women, all of whom were in their sixties, judging from their apparent age. The man was still physically imposing despite his age and full head of off-white hair, and he was a full head taller than the small but still attractive older woman with close-cropped auburn hair shot through with grey who remained close to him. A little apart from them both was another older woman with medium length red hair done up in a small bun and likewise shot through with grey. She was still attractive for her age, although her face was marred by a mid-length scar that ran from the left side of her eye ridge down her left temple. She wore a short-sleeved dress, and Lisa could see that her arms were scarred as well. All of this she took in at a glance, because her face lit up as she recognized the older man and his petite companion. "Grandma and Grandpa Zimmerman!" she exclaimed happily.

"Howya doin', kid?" Jimmy Zimmerman said as he and his wife Clarissa took a place on the opposite side of Lisa's bed from Nancy and Cy, along with the older woman who had come in with them.

"I've been better," Lisa admitted.

"I hear you've had quite the adventure in Metro City," Clarissa Zimmerman said.

"Not as much as the one Grandpa had during the war," Lisa said, and with that she turned to him. There was a look on her face that was hard to describe as she spoke. "I now know what you did back then, Grandpa. Mercy told me about it before she was killed. I had no idea. You're a hero, you know? A real hero, and you never said a word."

"I couldn't," Jimmy admitted. "I was sworn to secrecy and all that. Had the world known what we went through, and what almost happened, well ..." He let his voice trail off as he took a long look at the still-recovering Lisa. "You're a hero too, you know."

"Oh, I'm nobody," Lisa said quietly. "I'm just a former stock car racer who got caught in a zombie apocalypse and had to do whatever it took to survive."

"You're somebody, Lisa," Clarissa Zimmerman quickly said. Lisa turned to look at her as she continued. "Never forget that. It's because of you, and the gift that your grandpa here gave your mother through his blood, and she then to you, that you're going to help save the world from that kind of thing from now on."

"We hope," Lisa added.

Jimmy nodded. "Yes. We hope. Speaking of hope," and with that he motioned for the other woman to come forward, "your grandma and I have someone we'd like you to meet." He waved at her as he spoke. "Lisa, this is Anne Willoughby, a longtime friend of our family. You've probably heard of her under her maiden name, Anne Bradshaw. Anne, meet our granddaughter, Lisa Stanridge."

Lisa looked at the older woman standing before her, her mouth partway open and unable to speak. It was some time before she could find the words to say. "Mrs. Willoughby ... I'm ... I'm honored."

"I'm just as honored as you, Lisa," Anne said. "We're birds of a feather, you know. Pebbles in the pond, at two different points in time, but each having its effect on people and events around them. That's what my late brother would have said."

The two said no more but merely looked at each other, their eyes saying what their mouths could not. Cy cleared his throat after a while, and then spoke to the others. "Uh, folks, maybe we'd better clear out, and let these two visit for a while."

"Sounds like a good idea," Nancy agreed.

"Let's go to the lounge just down the hall," Jimmy suggested. "I could use a good cup of coffee right about now."

"Hospital coffee is never good," Clarissa said, "but it sounds like a plan." She looked at him and he back, then she looked lovingly at her granddaughter, next at Anne, and then spoke to them both. "Just call the nurse's station when you two are done, and we'll come back."

"Thank you," Lisa said, still looking at Anne.

"Don't drink too much, Jimmy," Anne said with a smile, then looked at Nancy. "We'll call when we're done."

Nancy nodded, and she joined the group heading for the door. Cy was the last to leave, and he shot Lisa a smile before he left. Lisa returned it, the door closed, and then both she and Anne were left alone together to visit and share their unique experiences with each other: Anne and her ordeal with regards to Projekt Regenschirm four decades before, and Lisa and her Outbreak adventure in the here and now.

In a small country somewhere in that part of the world known as the Eastern Mediterranean, one that was fiercely independent and highly insular, and one that did not have and did not want any extradition treaty of any kind with the United States or any other democratically-minded country, Pandora chief executive officer B. D. Nye sat in a chair in one of the gate lounges of its main international airport along with his entourage, three persons of varying nationalities, and some half-dozen armed bodyguards. He watched through the wide windows of the lounge as the latest passenger airplane to have landed there taxi up to the gate where he was located. It was an older model Antonov An-24, a popular twin-engined Russian turboprop design that had been flying ever since the 1960s. The markings on it were in Cyrillic, although it was not a Russian-owned aircraft. It was in fact owned and operated by one of the state airlines of a neighboring country. It had been the last change of flights for one particular man who was now on board that plane, and who was about to disembark and meet with Nye. Only the occasional rapid glance of Nye's cobalt eyes betrayed his impatience as the Antonov came to a complete stop and shut down its engines. The final landing checks were performed once they had stopped moving, the front door to the Antonov was opened and a boarding ladder put in place, and then a pleasant female voice which was not speaking English bade the passengers farewell and hearty thanks for using their particular air service. Nye now stood up, and so did both his entourage and the three other individuals with him. They watched as the plane's passengers began to file out of the airplane and towards the airport, passing through a side door that connected directly with the gate lounge where they were standing. The man they were waiting for did not appear until fully two-thirds of the plane's passengers had disembarked before him. He wore a rumpled dark suit with red tie and contrasting shirt, and he was carrying an oversized attaché case.

Nye immediately walked up to the man and held out his hand. "Piter," he said, in a tone that was almost warm and friendly. "You made it."

Piter de Voormand took Nye's offered hand and shook it firmly. "I almost didn't," he said. "Interpol had a warrant out for my arrest on behalf of the fed, and I had to jump flights at the last minute to avoid them. That's how I ended up on that old rattletrap," he finished, thumbing out the window at the Antonov. He then gave Nye a knowing smile. "It never ceases to amaze me what a big wad of cash presented to the right person at the right time and place can buy you."

"As I found out long ago," Nye said, cracking the smallest of smiles at de Voormand's words. The two let go, turned, and walked back to where Nye's entourage and his three guests were waiting for them.

"Oh, I have something for you and Pandora," de Voormand said. He held up his oversized attaché case a bit so Nye would take notice of it, then lowered it again. "Samples of Lisa's Stanridge's blood."

"How ever did you get them?" Nye asked, and he could not hide the amazement in his voice.

"It wasn't easy," de Voormand admitted, as they finished their walk to the others. They stopped within the ring of bodyguards, and stood beside Nye's three guests as the Dutchman continued. "The fed had already moved in and foiled our efforts in getting access to the other Alpenfestung raid survivors and their descendants. However, one of my people checking out the hospital where they were keeping Ms. Stanridge discovered that one of the CDC people assigned to her case had a not-so-small gambling problem. After that, things went as you might expect and I was able to obtain these samples for you."

"And the CDC staffer?"

de Voormand looked at his watch, then back at Nye. "He died in a fatal road accident about fourteen hours ago. He happened to be passing through an intersection when a tractor-trailer rig with bad brakes ran the red light on its side and clobbered the poor fellow in his dinky little rice rocket." de Voormand grinned. "I'm betting they're still scraping what's left of him and his car off the front of that truck."

"And there's no way it can be traced to us?"

"Absolutely none, sir. We took advantage of a local trucker known to us who had a bad habit of skipping inspections and not keeping his rig in top condition. He was already in trouble with the authorities about that before this happened. Neither he nor they will ever detect the extra encouragement one of our people gave to his already failing brakes while he was sleeping, and he'll get manslaughter at the least once they try him."

Nye nodded. "Nice and neat. I like that. Good work, Piter."

de Voormand bowed his head in respect, then brought it back up again. "Thank you, sir."

"And what about Carlton Dahl?"

The Dutchman shook his head. "No go there, sir. General Ryan arrested him as soon as that business with the *ubermensch* went south. I hear the fed is going to throw the book at him, since he's the most senior Pandora executive they've been able to grab."

Nye sighed. "A necessary sacrifice, and he knew what he was going into when I sent him. We'll see to it that his family is well cared for until he gets out."

de Voormand nodded. "I wasn't able to see him myself, you understand, but I've been told from our contacts that he's taking the whole thing rather well, all things considered."

"Of course," Nye said. He now waved to the three men. "I'm glad you were able to secure those blood samples, Piter. That way our efforts can continue, and I've been having the most interesting discussion about our work with these three gentlemen." He nodded to each in turn, waving a hand in their direction as he did so, and they nodded back as he continued talking. "Piter, this is Colonel Dimitri Nevitch of the Soviet KGB. This is Colonel Sung Nook Tai of the People's Liberation Army of China, and this gentleman here with the turban is His Excellency Mohammed al-Ashid, representing the Ayatollah's government in Iran. All three of their countries have expressed considerable interest in what we might have to offer them with regards to our refined *untotenvirus* and *ubermensch* products and development programs, and what you have just brought with you is only going to sweeten our impending discussions even more." He again allowed himself a smile. "His Excellency al-Ashid is also authorized to negotiate on behalf of certain, ahh, third party organizations who would be willing to put our products to immediate use in the field, provided we can come to terms and such."

"Of course," de Voormand said smoothly. He smiled at the three men and again dipped his head in a slight bow, and they likewise did so in kind.

"Well, let's not keep them waiting, shall we?" Nye said. He waved toward the front of the building. "Our rides await. Piter, you're with me. Gentlemen, if you will take the second limo, then I will treat all of us out to eat at a most excellent and discreet local restaurant, and we can proceed from there."

With that, the entire group turned almost as one and left the gate lobby.

EPILOGUE

The time came soon enough when Lisa Stanridge underwent her total knee replacement surgery. This was the only one of her major injuries left to treat, for her broken arm and ribs were already well on the mend. It was a long and delicate operation, but it had already been done time and again with previous patients since the technique had first been successfully tried in 1974. The prognosis for Lisa was very promising, according to both her attending physician Dr. Phillps and knee surgery specialist Dr. Watkins. She remembered being wheeled into the operating room, conversing with the nurses and other hospital staffers who were to assist Dr. Watkins with the operation, even as the anesthesiologist was getting ready to put her under. A filter and feeder mask was put over her face, she indicated that she was all right when asked, and the next thing she knew she was coming back to consciousness in an outpatient room with her mother and Cy by her bedside, and finding out that the clock had rolled over into the next day while she was under and getting her surgery. As with everything she had undergone up until now she rolled with it, and almost immediately began to plan for and make arrangements for the day when she would be able to begin her physical therapy, and someday walk again.

A memorial service was held in Kramerville at the Easterbrook Cemetery just outside of town approximately a week-and-a-half after Lisa's knee surgery, in order to pay tribute to all of the victims of the Metro City Outbreak. A special salute was also scheduled as part of the event in order to honor the handful of Outbreak survivors who somehow escaped that calamity. Only forty-two men, women, and children all told were known to have escaped infection and survived the Outbreak itself. Of these, all but three came from the five-mile zone surrounding the city proper, and they had been discovered by General Ryan's forces after they had moved in to clean out the area of all infected. Lisa's mother Nancy had been one of these. Only three had come from inside Metro City itself: Raul Esteban, Cy Rappalo, and Lisa Stanridge. This memorial service was Lisa's first public appearance after her dramatic rescue and subsequent hospitalization for her many injuries. She came in a wheelchair with her immobilized left leg propped up, escorted by federal agents as bodyguards, but nevertheless she came. She had been told that the late Mercy Parks was going to be honored with a Presidential citation at the service for her part in both finding and saving Lisa, whose blood had proven to be the key in saving the world from the threat from

Pandora's refined *untotenvirus* strain. "Mercy would have done the same for me, had I been the one to die and not she," Lisa had said to Dr. Phillips when he tried to dissuade her from going, and that was that. She was now famous because of what Mercy had discovered and the federal government had subsequently revealed about her, so it was no wonder that an eager crowd of reporters was ready to mob Lisa as soon as the van bringing her to the service pulled up, and the side door was opened so that her wheelchair could be lowered on a powered lift. Fortunately, her new protectors kept all members of the press at bay, and they were not allowed to even get close to her. For her part Lisa waved and smiled as the press took its pictures from an enforced distance, but that was it. She politely ignored all of their shouted questions, paid her respects at the service, was invited to and agreed to say a few words on Mercy's behalf citing her courage and determination in trying to right the great wrong that Pandora's experiments had brought down on Metro City, and then she was escorted back to the van so she could be taken away to spend the rest of the day visiting with family and friends at an undisclosed location within the holdings of the Cherokee Nation, where she had been staying for her recovery. She left dealing with the press for a later time and place, when she would better feel up to that particular challenge.

It was the Cherokee, both her people and her late father's, who did the most for her aside from her medical caregivers during her subsequent recovery. For their part they had insisted on her staying with them, almost begging at one point, for she was now one of the heroes of the Cherokee Nation and they held her in great honor and respect. She had talked it over with Cy, her mother, and both sets of her grandparents, and in the end had agreed to stay with the Cherokee as they had requested. It worked out quite well, for they put both her and her mother up in the best hotel suite in the best casino that they had, and they made sure she had everything she needed to make her recovery as comfortable and as speedy as possible. They even paid her medical bills, and provided volunteers to assist her caregivers with the physical therapy she had to undergo in order to be able to walk again with her artificial knee, and for that she was genuinely grateful. The press never bothered her during her time with them, because the Cherokee wouldn't let them. Cy Rappalo was as frequent a visitor as his military duties permitted, and he made Lisa's recovery time even more enjoyable than it already was. In addition, between post-operation therapy, various other related treatments, and long periods of time with Cy, she found the opportunity to visit with and have several long discussions with Running Elk, the senior Cherokee medicine man in the area where she was staying.

During one such discussion, as they sat on an upper balcony of the casino while its customers came and went below them, many of them completely ignorant of the fact that the famed Lisa Stanridge was a resident guest there, Running Elk had again brought up the subject of Lisa's spirit vision. "It is most unusual," he ruminated, leaning on his medicine stick despite the fact that he was sitting down. "It is unheard of. No tales tell of Kalona Ayeliski giving up on her chosen prey, all the way back to the old times. Yours is the first."

"She didn't give up, honored one," Lisa said. "The Great Spirit wouldn't let her have mine. She told me that herself." She looked away and across the nearby highway to the tall forest on the other side. "I think that's why she took Mercy's soul instead. She wasn't going to be allowed to take mine, so she decided to claim that of one of the other three who were with me. She struck close, since she couldn't strike home. Getting the rest of the souls of those soldiers was just icing on the cake, and maybe helped make up on her end for the fact that she was denied mine."

The aged medicine man nodded thoughtfully. "And you say she told you that Unhlahnauhi had decreed that great things were in store for you, and that was why you were being spared?"

"So long as I kept my feet on the right path, whatever that is," Lisa replied, "only I haven't a clue. The Raven Mocker also said that she would be there waiting for me if I didn't follow that path, whatever it is." She looked at Running Elk. "What do you think, honored one?"

The medicine man said nothing in reply at first. He continued to look thoughtful, and he would occasionally tap the floor of the balcony with his medicine stick as he pondered the question. Lisa waited patiently, knowing better to disturb him until he was ready to speak. Eventually he drew in a deep breath, let it out again, then turned to Lisa and spoke. "Child, I do not know what Unhlahnauhi has in mind for the future path that your life must now follow. Only you can know that. There will be signs, and you mush watch for them. I cannot tell you what they are, or what they will be, for I do not know them either. They will be unique to you. Some may have already happened. Some may have yet to happen. Rest assured that there will be enough of them for you to know what is his desire for you, once you see them and realize them for what they are. Once you know what it is, then do it. Do it with all of your heart, your mind, and your soul, and that way Kalona Ayeliski need never visit you again."

The balcony fell silent. Running Elk's face was now serene, while Lisa's was the thoughtful one. She started to say something, stopped, started again, and stopped herself again. All the while the aged medicine man watched her, saying nothing. Lisa finally looked at him and spoke. "I'll do my best, honored one, even though I don't know what I'm doing."

Running Elk smiled kindly. "That is the way it always is, child. Sometimes I think we were meant to stumble towards the light, instead of having a clear beacon by which to see."

Lisa gave a gentle laugh. "That I cannot dispute, sir."

The two fell silent again, saying nothing as they quietly watched the activity in the casino courtyard below.

There was one thing that Lisa was never going to be able to do again, and that was to race stock cars professionally. That previously chosen life path was now permanently closed to her. The loss of her left eye mandated it, given the strict vision requirements NASCAR had in place both for its regular professional drivers and the semi-pro racers on the Sportsman Circuit, to which Lisa had formerly belonged. Nevertheless, she had earned a special place in the history of NASCAR despite the one and only year she had been part of the Sportsman Circuit, and there was also the added celebrity status bequeathed on her by both the Metro City Outbreak and her unusual connection to it. While Lisa would never race stock cars again, she was delighted when a special display about her, her brief racing career, and why it came to its sudden end was installed in the industry's main racing museum. There was also the satisfaction, however smaller in stature, of her still being able to re-earn her driver's license once her knee had healed sufficiently for her to walk on her own to take the test, albeit with a cane and a stiff leg brace. The vision requirements for earning her state driver's license were not as stringent as those for NASCAR racing, and she was by no means the first one-eyed person in her state to successfully past the test and get her license. Her final score was lower than she would have liked because of that. She still passed the test, and Lisa proudly sat with a smile on her face at the Kramerville DMV office while one of its clerks took her picture for her new driver's license. Cy had accompanied her to the DMV, and after that he treated her out to lunch. Both had a good meal and a good time together. "I'll bet this is one of those signs your medicine chief told you about in those long talks you two had," Cy said as they finished their meal.

"What's that?" Lisa said, feigning ignorance.

"You getting your driver's license back," Cy said, pretending to be authoritative. Only two things had changed about Cy since Lisa had first met him. Those was the extra chevron on his upper uniform sleeve and the extra colored bar on the ribbon rack he wore in front. He had been promoted to sergeant and given a medal by the Army for the part he played during the Outbreak, among other honors he had received. He hadn't let any of it get to him, and he remained the same old Cy that Lisa had grow to love. He now spoke to her in a mock deep-voiced Amerind manner. "Cherokee girl driving again is good medicine." He grinned and then added in the same tone, "May need to drive down future life path to come."

"Oh, Cy!" Lisa said in mock exasperation, playfully trying to punch him in the arm. He caught her fist and held it. They looked at each other, and then he drew her close. She did not resist, and with that the two of them kissed.

Their lunch was done but their day together was not yet over. There was one more place they had to go, and that was to a local vehicle storage facility on the outskirts of Kramerville. That was where General Ryan had deposited her recovered 1971 Plymouth HemiCuda on the Army's behalf, paying them well to keep it and maintain it in good shape for the day when she would recover, and come to reclaim it as her own.

The stern-faced man in the light blue flannel suit stood at the main gate to the Kramerville AutoPlex along with Del Cutter, the owner and manager of the facility. The two had hardly spoken a word save on business since the stern-faced man had arrived. Del didn't like him and the stern-faced man didn't care. He was there on official business. Del was there because he had to be there as part of that business, and he was determined to get this government creep out of his establishment as soon as possible. His unwelcome guest checked his watch, and then looked back at the highway. Less than a quarter-minute later, a late model Ford LTD Crown Victoria painted in drab olive green, and with U.S. Army identification stenciled on its front doors, came into view from the city end of the highway. It drove up to the main drive, turned onto it, pulled up to the main gate, and stopped.

The front driver's door of the car opened along with both of its back doors, and three people got out. One was the driver, an Army private in working dress as bland as nondescript as any other, and he quickly went around to the left back and helped the passenger there get out. She was a beautiful young woman with long black hair and distinct American Indian features, dressed in black racing leathers and with the boots to match. She was wearing a leg brace around her left knee and had to use a cane to walk, which she did with a noticeable stiff-legged limp, and she also had a black eyepatch over her left eye. The other passenger, who had been sitting beside her in the back and got out to the right, was a tall black man also wearing Army working dress, but bearing the triple chevrons of a sergeant on each shoulder. He too quickly came around the car, thanked the private, and then took over for him in trying to assist the young woman. There was a brief exchange between the two as the driver returned to the car, and after that the young woman walked on her own towards the two men at the gate. The sergeant walked right beside her, grinning at the young woman the whole time. She was smiling back but said nothing. Del allowed himself to smile. So *this* was the famous Lisa Stanridge, and he was about to both meet her in person and do her one very big favor. That other guy must be the Army boyfriend she had picked up during the Outbreak. Cy Rappalo. Yeah, that was his name. *Man, oh man,* Del mused. *What a shame to single men everywhere,* Del thought to himself. However he was married, and all he could do was wistfully window shop. His wife would have clobbered him had she ever found out what he was thinking during this piece of business. At least this special visit by Ms. Stanridge herself was going to help keep his mind off the federal whack job standing next to him.

Both Lisa and Cy stopped in front of the two men, while their driver backed up the Army sedan and then parked it off to one side of the main gate's drive. The stern-faced man came forward to greet them, but Del was ahead of him and already offering his hand. "Ms. Standrige? It's an honor, a real honor. I'm Del Cutter, the owner here."

"My pleasure," Lisa responded politely, in a voice as smooth as silk. She took his offered hand, Del could have sworn he felt a charge when she did, and he fancied hearing her voice tickling his ears while the words went into them. "I understand you've been taking care of my car for me after the Army retrieved it from Metro City. Thank you."

"You're welcome!" Del said proudly. He shook her hand, and then let go. He didn't want to, but he didn't want to be a total goofball either. "And me and my people have been keeping it in top shape too! Why we've—"

"That will be all, Mr. Cutter," the stern-faced man cut in. His voice was a smooth monotone, yet it grated on Del's ears like frozen asparagus. "I will let you know once we need you again. Thank you."

Del gave the man a stare. Lisa and Cy gave each other an amused look, but said nothing. After a bit, Del bit his lip. "Yes, sir," he said huffily. A bit of his smile returned as he looked at Lisa again, and she back at him. "Well, I'll go get the paperwork ready. I'll see you later."

"I'm looking forward to it," Lisa responded kindly. "Until then, Mr. Cutter."

That wonderful look that Lisa gave Dell with those words made him tingle all over. He didn't want to leave. He would have stayed if he could, but that government freak was making him leave. "Until then" he said back, with a grin on his face and a bit out of breath. He took one more look at Lisa, nodded at Cy, who nodded back, gave the stern-faced man another cool-eyed stare, and then turned and headed for a small side gate beside the main gate. The building that housed both his office and the autoplex's service garages sat beyond that on the other side of the fence surrounding the place.

The stern-faced man waited until Del was well out of earshot, then turned and addressed Lisa and Cy. "Sergeant Rappalo? Ms. Stanridge? I'm glad you could make it today."

"So are we," Lisa said in reply. She too had assumed a formal air, in contrast to how she had treated Del, and the tone of her voice was all professional. "I'm very grateful to General Ryan and the government for retrieving my car and keeping it for me until I was well enough to claim it back."

A smile now passed over the visage of the stern-faced man. On him it had a bit of a ghoulish air to it, but it was a smile nonetheless. "We were glad to be of service, Ms. Stanridge. You've done our country a most important service. The least we could do was perform a favor in kind."

Lisa eyed him for a bit before responding. "You don't approve of what General Ryan did, do you?"

The stern-faced man's expression went bland again. "It is not my place to approve or disapprove the actions of one who is outside both my service and my chain of command. I will say that what he did for you was not normal procedure in similar past cases. However, he has made his reasons clear for doing so and my superiors have approved his actions. It is not for me to judge."

"I see." Lisa was not fooled for one minute, but she decided to let the matter drop. "I understand you have my keys too."

"Ah, yes." With that, the stern-faced man reached into his pocket and pulled out a familiar looking set of car keys. He held them up and then handed them to Lisa, who took them. "I am sure you are aware that all of the other vehicles which were present in Metro City when it was cleared out were eventually disposed of, save for yours."

"And we're glad General Ryan made sure that didn't happen," Cy quickly said, before Lisa could respond. "Her car's kinda rare, you know."

"Indeed," the stern-faced man said. "The last of the old-style American muscle cars." He now smiled again with that same slightly ghoulish smile. "It would have been a shame to crush it up."

Lisa was beginning to feel about the man before her the same way that Del Cutter had obviously felt. She decided to cut to the chase. "Well, they didn't and it's here, and now I've got the keys. Can we go take a look at it, and then I'll sign the papers and get both it and us out of your hair?"

The stern-faced man nodded. "You may." He waved the both of them toward the side gate. "This way."

The group had first stopped by Del's office, since it was on the way. The stern-faced man had brusquely informed Del that he was to come with them, and to bring both the key for unlocking the storage bay that housed Lisa's car and the necessary paperwork she needed to sign in order to reclaim it. Del complied, and seconds later he was walking with them on the far side of the stern-faced man with a large jangling ring of keys clipped to his belt and a clipboard with a pen and clamped-on paperwork under one arm. The only time he looked happy was whenever he would sneak a look at Lisa. She caught him doing this once and smiled at him. Del smiled back, and after that his dark mood dissipated somewhat, although it never went away completely. It would not until the stern-faced man was long gone from his premises.

Lisa and Cy talked as they made their way across the autoplex, with the other two remaining silent. "I like that new outfit of yours," he said while they walked.

"You do?" Lisa answered.

"Yeah," Cy said. His eyes twinkled as he continued. "You want to know something?"

"What?" Lisa said.

"The way you look right now, with that outfit and eyepatch, leg brace, and cane, you look like a really sexy female version of a cross between Mad Max and Snake Plisken."

Lisa gave him a look as they walked, and then chuckled. "I see what you mean." She reached up and fingered the Cherokee talisman she wore around her neck. It had been her father's, and it had been found amid the zombie bodies he had left at the family farm once the search began for his remains. "Sometimes I feel like them too, you know. Like I've been run over, that the truck that did it backed up over me, and then ran over me again for good measure."

"But you survived, and that's the important part," Cy said reassuringly. "It's one of the things I like about you, Lisa. You're a survivor. You don't give up no matter what."

"Just like you," Lisa said. They looked at each other and their eyes locked. "Maybe that's why we go together so well."

"I'm not going to argue with that," Cy said.

It was at that moment that the stern-faced man cleared his throat. "Pardon me, Ms. Stanridge and Sergeant Rappalo, but we are almost there."

"Oh yeah. Right," Lisa said, turning away from Cy in an effort to hide her blush. Cy now had his own face locked with its eyes front. Del was grinning, and the stern-faced man simply looked stern as they finished their walk.

Lisa's car was located inside the fifth storage bay of a set of twelve inside a long building that was but one of three of similar construction. Del led them to the bay and unlocked it, then stood aside and waved his hand at Lisa and Cy. He made a point of not even looking at the stern-faced man as he spoke. "Would you like to the have the honor?" he said cordially.

"Cy?" Lisa said, looking up at him. "My left arm is still a bit weak."

"Of course," Cy said. He stepped forward, leaned down, grasped the handle of the cantilever door, and pulled upward. Daylight now filled what had been a dark automobile storage bay. With that, Lisa laid eyes on her prized 1971 Plymouth HemiCuda for the first time since she had been forced to abandon it during the Outbreak.

The car was in immaculate condition. Its body had a showroom shine to it, despite the fact that only sunlight was hitting it. It looked like the way it had been when the Outbreak had started, for all of the blood and other things from hitting zombies at various times had been cleaned away. Even so, Lisa noticed that there had been some slight changes. One of the headlights had been replaced. She remembered that one being broken during the Outbreak, when she had been forced to play road tag with one particular overeager zombie. The tires had also been replaced. They weren't the brand she normally used, although they were close and they had also been matched to her custom rims, with wider and larger tires in the back and narrower normal-sized tires in the front. She looked at Del, who had seen her notice the tires, and he grinned. "Uhhh, your tires were in bad shape, ma'am, so the Army replaced them. Yours are in the trunk and they've been cleaned just like your car, although they're pretty beat up."

Lisa gave a low but pleasant laugh. She gave Cy a knowing look and then looked back at Del. "I can imagine, the way I had to abuse them during the Outbreak."

Del smiled back. "Well, you'll find the rest of the car in tiptop shape, Ms. Stanridge. The Army paid us to give it full service and a full tune-up to boot, and to keep it that way until you came to get it. You can drive it out of here right now if you want, and I'm guessing you *want*."

"Oh, most definitely," Lisa said cheerfully. "Let me sign those papers for you, and then I'll be on my way." She again looked at Cy and gave him a playful grin. "Do you want to ride with me, or do you want to ride back in your car?"

"What do you think?" Cy said, with a grin even bigger than Lisa's.

Lisa laughed, and this time it was a full laugh. Cy also laughed, and Del laughed with them. Only the stern-faced man did not laugh. He simply looked at them, politely remaining quiet.

It was over in a matter of minutes. Cy spoke waited until Del was on his way back to his office, and then spoke. "I'll go tell the Army driver to take the car back to the base. I won't be gone long."

Lisa drew in close and gave him a quick kiss on the cheek. "I'll miss you anyway," she said lovingly. "Hurry back, you hear?"

"Yes, *ma'am*!" Cy said. He flipped her a salute, gave a quick glance at the stern-faced man, and then trotted off towards the gate.

The stern-faced man waited until Cy was gone until he spoke. "I understand that you will not be allowed to race stock cars again."

"Nope," Lisa said, as she softly caressed one of the front fenders of her 'Cuda. "Vision thing. You can't be a professional race car driver with only one eye."

"And yet you took the trouble of re-earning your driver's license despite that restriction."

"Yes, I did," Lisa said, still looking at her 'Cuda and playing one hand over it. "I'm a very determined girl."

"Which brings me to my point. Would you consider future employment with us, now that you can no longer stay in your past profession of choice?"

Lisa stopped what she was doing and looked at the stern-faced man. It took a few seconds before she found the words to answer him. "Me? Work for you guys? A federal agent, and all that?"

"Not quite," the stern-faced man said. "The administration is in the process of putting together a new organization to deal with the threat that Regenschirm technology poses not only this country, but to the world. Your blood may have held the key to saving the present, but there is always the future to consider. The government did not take that into account after the war, and it had to pay in the lives of its own citizens four decades later for that fatal oversight. The current administration does not want to make that same mistake; hence the new organization. We need people for it with your kind of experience and background, Ms. Stanridge, and it is also a definite benefit that you would be bringing with you many of the skills we would need in such people. We need you, Ms. Stanridge. Not just your blood and the things we can make from it. We need *you*, so you can help us in preventing another Metro City from ever happening again. Will you join us?"

The service bay fell silent. Lisa looked thoughtful, and stared into nowhere while the stern-faced man waited patiently. She finally looked at him and spoke. "What about Cy?"

"We intend for him to be part of this too, if he will join us," the stern-faced man said. "I wanted to ask you first. As the situation between the both of you currently stands, his acceptance will depend on your own."

A wry look passed over Lisa's face. "True," she said, and then her thoughtful expression returned. She again fell silent, saying nothing.

The stern-faced man waited for a few seconds, and then spoke again. "You do know that the man most responsible for the Metro City Outbreak, Pandora CEO Brian Nye, escaped custody along with most of his senior executive staff."

"Yeah," Lisa said, and this time anger could be heard in her voice. "It really pissed me off when I heard about it too, but I guess crooks in his class and at his level can pull off stuff like that. From what I understand, and what I've heard in the news about how they got away, that bunch are some pretty cool customers."

"And they have access to everything they need to set up shop somewhere else, some country friendly to their designs, and restart their work once more," the stern-faced man continued. "Pandora is an international company, and we have not been successful in seizing their assets abroad. A number of those are located in those aforementioned countries. Pandora may have already restarted its work for all we know. If that is true, then it is only a matter of time before the next Metro City falls victim to Pandora."

"Not if I can help it," Lisa growled. She snapped her head around to look at him just as Cy re-entered the service bay. "Okay, you convinced me. I'll do it, provided Cy does it too."

"Do what?" Cy asked, raising an eyebrow as he did.

"I'll tell you later," Lisa said quickly, then addressed the stern-faced man again. "We'll be in touch."

"Excellent," the stern-faced man said. "Then I shall leave you and Sergeant Rappalo to your own affairs." He reached into an inner jacket pocket and pulled out a business card, which he handed to Lisa. She took it without saying a word. "Until then, Miss Stanridge." Lisa nodded, and then the stern-faced man turned and left.

Cy walked up to Lisa, giving her a questioning look as he did. "What was that about?" he asked. "What did you just do?"

"Made arrangements for possible future employment," Lisa said, showing him the business card. Both of Cy's eyebrows shot up once he saw what was printed on it. He again gave Lisa a look. "You can't be serious," he said.

"Oh, but I am, Cy, and I want you do to it with me," Lisa said firmly.

"But—" Cy began.

"*Please*," Lisa said earnestly, although her voice remained firm. "Somehow I get the feeling this is what I'm supposed to do now."

Cy looked at her for a bit before he spoke. "You're talking about that spirit vision thing again, aren't you?"

Lisa nodded. "Running Elk said I would know the signs of what I was supposed to do with my life after the Outbreak when they happened, and that they would be unique to me alone. Once I saw them and knew them for what they were, then I needed to go in the direction they were pointing me." She moved close to him and slipped an arm around him, and he in turn slipped an arm around her. Her voice softened as she continued. "Consider this, Cy. I can't race anymore but I can still drive. In just a few weeks I'll be able to walk again without this brace and crutch, and it won't be long before I can run too. I even got my 'Cuda back, and that was nothing short of a near miracle. I'm now a celebrity, although it's not for what I had hoped it would be for. It's for the Outbreak, and for what's in my blood. Furthermore, there's *you*, and how you're now a part of my life that I don't ever want to give up. I can't go back to what I was and I don't want to either. All of this and more is pointing me to a new life I need to live, just like the Great Spirit wants for me, and that new life needs to be doing something to make sure that what happened to me, you, Raul, Mercy, Mom, Dad, Randy, and all those other poor people in Metro City never happens again if I can help it." She now gave a gentle laugh. "Joining up with that new government outfit that Mr. Creepy represents is the way to go. I know it." She now looked lovingly at him. "I hope you'll join up too. You're a survivor, just like me, and ... and I need you with me. Understand? I *need* you with me."

Cy bowed his head down until he and Lisa were touching foreheads. He looked lovingly into her beautiful brown eyes. "If that's what you really want, Lisa," he said softly, "if that's what you really think you need to do, then who am I to say no?"

"Then you'll do it?"

"I'll do it."

"Oh, Cy!" With that she raised her head up enough to kiss him.

It was about five minutes later when Del Cutter opened the main gate to the Kramerville Autoplex, and let out a green-and-black 1971 Plymouth HemiCuda with two occupants. The female driver of the vehicle waved at him, and he waved back with a big grin on his face. The driver then gunned its 426 Hemi engine, the tires squealed, and then it literally took off. It almost went on two wheels as it snapped around the corner from the autoplex's main drive to the highway, and then it barreled down the end of the highway leading out of Kramerville, its engine racing and the 'Cuda picking up speed all the while. It sailed down the highway until it went over a small rise far away, and then it was lost to sight. Del grinned, and let out a big sigh. He had done the famous Lisa Stanridge a big favor, both she and her Army boyfriend were happy, and that freaky government guy was gone, gone, *gone*. He looked again at the end of the highway, let out a short laugh, and then turned and headed back to his office. That bunch had been his last customers for the day. It was time to go home.

THE END

AFTERWORD

This story, like its predecessor *Projekt Regenschirm*, started out as a *Resident Evil* fanfic. In fact, it's the only one I ever completed in novel form. Its name is *Resident Evil: Exodus - The Tale of Elza Walker*, and you can read its final form on the Wattpad® free e-book service on the Internet. I wrote *Exodus* to demonstrate to Capcom that both the character of Elza Walker and the basic plot of the cancelled game known today as *Resident Evil 1.5* could not only be revised, updated, and made to work with the rest of the *Resident Evil* franchise, but that this could be done in such a way as to be just as enjoyable and exciting an adventure as any regular *Resident Evil* title released to retail. To make a long story short they politely declined to do anything with it, although they said it was very good and they praised my creativity. They also told me something else at the time which I've never forgotten. They said I was such a creative person that I needed to be writing my own original stories with my own original characters, instead of basing my work on theirs. That of course was when I rebooted *Regenschirm*, which then stood at 75% completion, from being my second *Resident Evil* fanfic novel into my first independent and non-derivative work, with all of their material removed and my own original material inserted in its place. To my great surprise it was immediately accepted for publication, and thus I now had my own original survival horror universe in which I could be creative without having to worry about infringing on somebody else's work. Capcom's advice had been sound, and I'm glad I listened.

There still remained the problem of what to do with *Exodus*. It was a finished work, not an unfinished one. Initially I released it as a free fanfic novel without charge of any kind, and Capcom did not object to that. I also gave Capcom written permission to data-mine it for whatever they wanted for their own projects, and again there was no objection. However, when I formally requested legal permission to have *Exodus* commercially published, and I did so *twice*, I was greeted with silence on both occasions. That was as good as saying *no*. They get to do that. After all, the *Resident Evil* franchise is their intellectual property, not mine. That's when I decided there would be no third attempt. Instead, I would do with *Exodus* what I had already done with *Regenschirm*. I would take it and strip it down to its core essentials. I would retain all of those ideas, concepts, characters, and plot points that were uniquely my own, discard all of the derivative Capcom material and replace it with my own, and completely rewrite it as an original work. Fortunately, I already had *Regenschirm* at hand to provide the necessary replacement backstory, so I adapted my efforts accordingly. I also realized that this reboot would free me of having to worry about the story hitting certain points at certain times and with certain characters, as it had to when it was still a *Resident Evil* fanfic novel. I could have my characters do whatever they needed to do whenever they needed to do it and in whatever location my revamped plot was leading them, instead of having to always line up their actions with this particular scene from that game or this other scene from that other game, and so on. Finally, I could not only keep those characters that were original to me, but I could take the best ideas and concepts I had for my revamped versions of Capcom's own characters in the story and use those as the basis for building up more of my own original characters to replace them. That is why although *Escape* has the same general framework as *Exodus*, the two are very different when it comes to the particulars of their content.

I think the most drastic change I made with regards to the characters that appear in *Escape* was with Lisa Stanridge, the story's main heroine. She still has the same fiery personality, independent streak, drive and determination, playful sexiness, and sense of caring with which I imbued my reinterpretation of Elza Walker for *Exodus*. It is there where the similarities end, however. I made Lisa a Cherokee Indian (well, half-Cherokee) because Amerind women playing significant roles in American horror stories are a very rare breed. That fact alone would set *Escape* apart from the pack. I could find only one other such example on a casual Internet search, and that is the character of Martha from the 1999 motion picture *Ravenous*. Doing so also allowed me to tap into Cherokee mythology and inject some true horror into my rebooted tale in the form of the Raven Mocker. *Escape* is not the first time that the Raven Mocker has appeared in Western media, but hopefully the way I present her is unique. Finally, Lisa's Cherokee heritage also allowed me to briefly touch upon the supernatural in other ways, and how it has and still may be affecting our lives even today -- and I get to do so in a way that hopefully pays proper respect to the Cherokee people and their long cultural heritage. None of those elements are present in *Exodus*. They are unique to *Escape*.

Escape was not the sequel to *Regenschirm* that I first intended to write. I had other ideas for sequels and spin-off stories. It is the sequel that I wound up writing because of the way things went with *Exodus*, that earlier completed work. Even so, I'm glad I finally decided to take up the challenge of rebooting that work into this form. As with *Regenschirm*, I would like to think that I wound up with a better and more entertaining story in the process. That's also not to mention one that's only half the size, given how my writing skills have improved since I wrote *Exodus*. Of course, only you the reader can be the judge, so I will leave it up to you. As for me, I have other books to write. Thankfully, not all of them are horror stories.

Take care everyone.

Richard Evan Mandel
1 May 2020

Suggested Soundtrack

"All Along the Watchtower" (The Jimi Hendrix Experience) - main titles
"Silent Running" (Mike and the Mechanics)
"Sober" (Tool)
"One of the Few" (Pink Floyd)
"Black Hole Sun" (Soundgarden)
"What If" (Creed)
"I Put a Spell on You" (Creedence Clearwater Revival)
"Woke Up This Morning" aka *The Sopranos* Theme (Alabama 3)
"Demon Speeding" (Rob Zombie)
"Prayer for the Dying" (Seal)
"Prologue" (Lorena McKennitt)
"The Bomb Run" from *Dr. Strangelove* (Prague Philharmonic)
"Land of Confusion" (Genesis) - final battle music
"Sirius" (The Alan Parsons Project)
"Ghost Dance" (Cusco) - end credits

About the Author

"Richard Mandel" is the pen name of author Sam Pettus. He is a writer of fact and fiction who choses not to limit himself to any particular genre or choice of material. His published works prior to this one include two video game histories (*Service Games: The Rise and Fall of Sega* and *The Hunt for Resident Evil 1.5*), an original World War II era survival horror novel (*Projekt Regenschirm*), an original pulp fantasy novel (*Passage to Portos*), and an age-spanning romance (Autumn Spring). He has written fan fiction for both the *Resident Evil* and Tolkien communities, he has written fan timelnes for both the TV series *Hogan's Heroes* and for the works of Japanese author Leiji Matsumoto, and he is a noted contributor to the world of classic *Star Trek* fan tech references. His published works are available through your nearest brick-and-mortar bookstore or online e-book seller, and his various fandom efforts can still be found on the Internet and downloaded for free at your leisure.

Mr. Pettus is a graduate of Arkansas Tech University, where he earned a bachelor's degree in mathematics, and he also served a brief stint with the U.S. Navy. After that he went into the civilian sector and worked a wide variety of jobs in various industries. He has worked in the retail industry, the manufacturing industry, the nuclear power industry, the information technology (IT) industry, and with various private firms. He jokes that at one time or another he has held almost every kind of job "from custodian to corporate vice-president and a lot in between." He also spent part of this time exercising his growing writer's skills as a records clerk, a procedure writer, and a developer of training materials for certain of his employers. After losing a well-paying IT job due to the nationwide wave of layoffs from the Bush recession of the 1990s, Mr. Pettus eventually found new and long-term employment as a mail processing clerk with the US Postal Service. He has been with them ever since, and it is this job that he uses to both finance his writing and his other creative endeavors. Mr. Pettus currently lives in Fort Smith, Arkansas.

CHECK OUT OTHER GREAT ZOMBIE NOVELS

Z BURBIA
by Jake Bible

Whispering Pines is a classic, quiet, private American subdivision on the edge of Asheville, NC, set in the pristine Blue Ridge Mountains. Which is good since the zombie apocalypse has come to Western North Carolina and really put suburban living to the test!

Surrounded by a sea of the undead, the residents of Whispering Pines have adapted their bucolic life of block parties to scavenging parties, common area groundskeeping to immediate area warfare, neighborhood beautification to neighborhood fortification.

But, even in the best of times, suburban living has its ups and downs what with nosy neighbors, a strict Home Owners' Association, and a property management company that believes the words "strict interpretation" are holy words when applied to the HOA covenants. Now with the zombie apocalypse upon them even those innocuous, daily irritations quickly become dramatic struggles for personal identity, family security, and straight up survival.

ZOMBIE RULES
by David Achord

Zach Gunderson's life sucked and then the zombie apocalypse began.

Rick, an aging Vietnam veteran, alcoholic, and prepper, convinces Zach that the apocalypse is on the horizon. The two of them take refuge at a remote farm. As the zombie plague rages, they face a terrifying fight for survival.

They soon learn however that the walking dead are not the only monsters.

CHECK OUT OTHER GREAT ZOMBIE NOVELS

CHECK OUT OTHER GREAT ZOMBIE NOVELS

900 MILES
by S. Johnathan Davis

John is a killer, but that wasn't his day job before the Apocalypse.

In a harrowing 900 mile race against time to get to his wife just as the dead begin to rise, John, a business man trapped in New York, soon learns that the zombies are the least of his worries, as he sees first-hand the horror of what man is capable of with no rules, no consequences and death at every turn.

Teaming up with an ex-army pilot named Kyle, they escape New York only to stumble across a man who says that he has the key to a rumored underground stronghold called Avalon..... Will they find safety? Will they make it to Johns wife before it's too late?

Get ready to follow John and Kyle in this fast paced thriller that mixes zombie horror with gladiator style arena action!

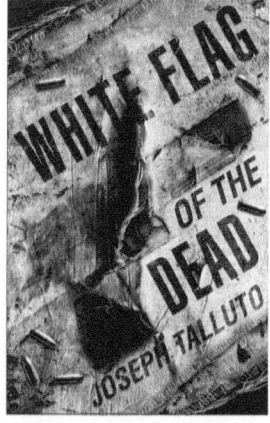

WHITE FLAG OF THE DEAD
by Joseph Talluto

Millions died when the Enillo Virus swept the earth. Millions more were lost when the victims of the plague refused to stay dead, instead rising to slaughter and feed on those left alive. For survivors like John Talon and his son Jake, they are faced with a choice: Do they submit to the dead, raising the white flag of surrender? Or do they find the will to fight, to try and hang on to the last shreds or humanity?

www.ingramcontent.com/pod-product-compliance
Lightning Source LLC
Chambersburg PA
CBHW031955170626
46807CB00006B/2499